C. L. Warrington

# Edge of the Blade

## Book One: Retribution

iUniverse, Inc.
Bloomington

iUniverse books may be ordered through booksellers or by contacting:

iUniverse
1663 Liberty Drive
Bloomington, IN 47403
www.iuniverse.com
1-800-Authors (1-800-288-4677)

ISBN: 978-1-4502-6282-8 (sc)
ISBN: 978-1-4502-6283-5 (ebook)

Printed in the United States of America

iUniverse rev. date: 11/30/2010

While there is an old saying that it takes a village to raise a child, it also takes a lifetime's worth of friends and family to write a book. The how's and why's of how this book came into being are far too numerous and personal to tell, but I can say with complete certainty that all of the people I've encountered during my life have inspired the heroes and villains within to some degree.

To my heroes who have inspired me: thank you for providing such rich, character-building experiences in both the literal and figurative sense. To those who are the opposite end of the coin: your words and actions of the past have now served a higher purpose in the present; the future does indeed look bright.

This work is dedicated to both the heroes and villains in my life, because without one you cannot have the other.

*Post tenebras lux*—after darkness, light.

# Preface

Creating this book has been rewarding as well as therapeutic, because it allowed me to take all the negative aspects of my life—much like Katrina did with the four daggers—and turn them into instruments of comfort and salvation. The subject matter may seem an odd fit for such ends, but anyone who knows me well enough should not be all that surprised.

There are many who have accompanied me throughout this journey of self-discovery that I would like to personally thank for their love and support, because without them this book would not have been possible. To my mom and dad, thank you for....everything. It might not be the best or most original expression of gratitude, but you know me well enough to see how grateful I am on a daily basis. Thank you for accepting me as I am—quirks and all—and for stepping back as I pursued my dreams.

To Uncle Cesar, Aunt Juanita, and cousins Ale and Didi, thank you for being there for my parents and I when we needed you most and for being a constant in an otherwise turbulent time in our lives.

To my family in Tennessee and Georgia, though we may be separated by many miles, you are always there in my heart.

To all my teachers, advisors, and mentors, thank you for not allowing me to accept mediocrity as my limit and for pushing me to do better than what I thought I was capable of.

To those who were not mentioned specifically, thanks for being a part of my life thus far; I am pleased to say that there are far too many of you to name individually.

# Chapter 1

The sounds of the city echo all around me as I pick my way over the scarred and pitted sidewalk near the heart of downtown San Antonio. I had come to the great state of Texas only six months before, but I could already sense that this city was going to be one of my more extended places of residence. I had occupied nearly every state on the eastern seaboard since coming to the United States at the turn of the century, and the time I spent at each location depended upon two things and two things only: were there others of my kind in the immediate area, and if so, how much danger did they pose to the human population?

With very few exceptions I invariably stumbled upon them in the great cities of the world. The groups varied from grand assemblages replete with hierarchies to loose conglomerations that were nothing more than street gangs, but regardless of their size or organization, they all preyed upon the city's human inhabitants to sustain their own lives. In every instance the groups were comprised of a Font and their progeny, human companions that had been transformed through a transfer of blood and who were now recipients of the Font's eternal legacy.

Fonts alone possessed the power to pass on their longevity to others, and the sheer magnitude of the lives that they had consumed over the centuries transformed them into beings of considerable power that the rest of us feared and respected.

While there was an undeniable bond between Fonts and progeny due to the blood transference, occasional displays of endearment did little to mask the real truth behind their relationship. When a Font created a progeny—when they shared their blood with a human—they shared a part of their life force with them. Their lives were now directly tied to one another and each progeny embodied a fraction of a Font's overall strength. When progeny fed upon the life force of their human victims, their Font garnered the lion's share of the feeding. If a progeny were to be killed, then their Font would suffer the loss of their lives, and if enough of them were to be killed, then the Font risked dying as a result. Fonts were therefore dependent upon their progeny and would stop at nothing to protect them.

That is, until the bond had dissipated between them.

On the surface it may appear that nurturing progeny is actually detrimental to a Font's existence, but in essence they serve a dual purpose. For one thing, they provide their Font with sustenance via the bond they share, and secondly, they are a show of status. The ability to create others of our kind resides exclusively within Fonts, and to have a number of these progeny at one's disposal is indication to others of our kind that they have survived for centuries and are formidable adversaries. Fonts were not born, but rather made into what they are by their own actions; each life that they consumed brought them one step closer to achieving this apex of our species, and in essence took them one step away from the bond that they had once shared with their maker. They had once started out as progeny, and only with the passage of centuries and innumerable victims did the bond between them waver and disappear. When they had accrued strength that surpassed that of their maker, the former-progeny were now powerful enough to assume the status of Fonts themselves, and the whole bloody cycle began anew.

Regardless of where I traveled throughout the world or what era I passed through, every Font that I had encountered was cruel, sadistic, and had an affinity for slaughter and carnage. No matter their upbringing during their human lifetime or the circumstances that led to their transformation, this behavior was inevitable. Countless innocents had died so that they could continue to live, had died so that their progeny could live and in essence keep them alive, and I despised them for it. My family and I had been on the receiving end of such treatment centuries ago and I knew what their victims had gone through. I knew the terror and the horror that had been their final moments of life, and I refused to stand idly by while others suffered a similar fate. No, if I had the knowledge, the means, *and* the fortitude to prevent such atrocities, then I would do so until every last one of them was destroyed.

I had long-since recognized the significance of the relationship between a Font and their progeny, and for the past three-hundred and twenty-eight years I exploited it to my advantage. The Fonts and their progeny—while formidable and protected—were not invincible. Like all things in this world they had weaknesses, and regardless of any allusions to immortality, they were not difficult to kill.

In order to destroy the Fonts and thereby end the whole accursed cycle of death and destruction once and for all, it was simply a matter of killing their progeny off one by one so that they could be dealt with.

Weak and disillusioned after the deaths of their progeny, the Fonts tried to escape to neighboring towns or cities that weren't quite large enough to hide them and their hunting activities. Desperate to replenish their strength in order to stay alive, they often killed whomever they could get their hands on and seldom concealed the bodies, thereby making it easy for me to track them down. When I caught up with them I was merciless in my treatment, and when they drew their last breath I was that much closer to honoring the oath I had sworn upon my family's memory centuries before. It was an oath that I had vowed to uphold until the end of the world, and each time that I destroyed one of them—a creature that I considered no different than the ones that had destroyed my family and forever altered my destiny—I was that much closer to regaining what I had lost.

This strategy set the precedent for how I lived my life, and I moved around constantly in this fashion for centuries while slowly driving their ranks to the brink of extinction. The advent of transatlantic travel made it possible for my kind to propagate elsewhere in the world, and I pursued them accordingly. In the century or so since my arrival in the United States, I had primarily occupied the eastern coast. It was only when I was satisfied that this area was relatively clean that I set my sights on the southern states.

I only knew Texas from the brochures and books that I had acquired, but I eventually chose San Antonio as my most recent base of operations. The color photos of the famed River walk and Spanish missions were oddly appealing to me and the cultural and geographical makeup of the area—the gateway to the American Southwest—was wholly different from anything I had ever encountered during my considerable travels.

The city of San Antonio has the distinction of being the second largest in the state of Texas, as well as being the seventh largest in the United States. The current population stands at nearly a million and half souls—a million and a half potential victims if my kind were to take up residence there. Something else drew me to the city other than the promise of a change in scenery or a challenging hunt, something I couldn't quite put my finger on, but I had learned to trust my instincts over the years.

My exodus to San Antonio is still relatively fresh in my mind, as if it were just yesterday that I was gazing out at the vaguely surreal landscape from the smeared and grimy windows of the plane. As I pulled out of the airport parking lot in my rented vehicle and headed out into the streets, I found myself growing more and more at ease. There was something intensely thrilling about the city as I took the downtown exit and felt the ambiance of my new home wrap itself around me. The massive steel and glass structures that extended skyward were nestled snuggly amongst the remnants of the city's illustrious past. The Alamo—the unequivocal symbol of pride and nostalgia to the natives—and the beautiful and grand hotels that spoke of bygone eras were comfortably at home alongside one another. The styles did not clash but seemed to compliment one another, creating a skyline that was both imposing in its modernity yet timeless in its features.

The neighborhoods themselves were a virtual amalgam of humanity that mirrored the unique architectural style of the city. Driving down one street, you would find yourself gaping open-mouthed at the majestic Victorian facades of the historic King William District. Turn down another street, and you could actually trace the progression from one socio-economic status to another. Corner markets run by independent proprietors with heavy bars over the windows, car washes, family-owned Mexican and Vietnamese restaurants, and the inevitable and predictable liquor store dotted the landscape. The houses here were shadows of their former selves and of their more upscale counterparts. Paint peeled away from the graying walls in heavy strips, the porches sagged under the weight of the top floors, and the ornate columns designed to support the whole structure were now held in place by large wooden braces that were deteriorating as well.

I was overcome by the passage of nearly four centuries while gazing up at these dilapidated homes. I was keenly aware that even in a city that was growing in leaps and bounds like San Antonio was that time goes on and that change is inevitable. Eventually everything will be swallowed up in the vast and immeasurable depths of time, and the vestiges of yesteryear ultimately mean nothing to the youth of today.

I sighed and turned the collar of my nondescript brown coat up to block the chill that suddenly swept down the nape of my neck. I turned and headed down the street away from the sagging remains of the house that I had been admiring while lost in my own reverie. It was in these moments of silent contemplation that I felt the loneliest, the most vulnerable. I hated feeling vulnerable and I hated the memories that accompanied such a reaction even more. I had resigned myself to a life of solitude and had accepted my fate centuries ago, however much I longed to change it. I knew that there was no value in trying to change the past. It was over, done with, finished. All that mattered was the here and now, the city before me, and the oath that I had sworn to my family to uphold until the world itself came to an end. I had come to this city, to these very streets to serve justice where it had previously been denied and to protect the innocent. This was no time for self-pity or reflection. This was a time to hunt, and I spotted my prey across the street a few yards up ahead.

I placed his age at about twenty, no more. He was gangly, medium-build, with a shock of greasy black hair falling over one side of his face. He was following a man who was obviously drunk down a sidewalk that terminated by a corner market that had closed for the night. To the casual observer he looked like he was just another young man out for an evening stroll, but I recognized the telltale signs of a predator when I saw them. The intensity that he stared at the other man with was anything but casual: it was calculating, deliberate, and analytical. He was sizing the other man up, looking for just the right moment to close the distance between them to strike. I was as sure of this as anything else in my life, and I tracked him discreetly from my vantage point across the street. I had encountered and systematically dispatched four individuals like him during my time here, and it seemed that he was going to become number five.

I knew that the presence of so many in such a concentrated area as the one that I was in meant that a Font had taken up residence here. Progeny don't live apart from their creator, and the fact that I had encountered five such individuals within the same general vicinity meant that the Font was nearby and had chosen to occupy this particular area. It was the perfect place where people could disappear unnoticed, or the discovery of their body would only signify a jump in statistics. No mobs with stakes and torches would come charging out of the mist in search of the creature behind the killings—at the very least the police would have a little more paperwork to file because of them.

The drunk weaved and shuffled his way down the sidewalk completely oblivious to the danger that lurked only a few yards behind him. I pressed my body up against the rickety metal fence that enclosed the weed-choked lawn of the house behind me, and allowed the night to swallow me up.

I watched as the drunk sat down heavily on a low stone fence, his body slouched with the effort. His head hung heavily on his chest as he swayed from side to side muttering incoherently to himself, his hands reaching in and out of the pockets of his trench coat in a compulsive manner. The man behind him paused in mid-step as the drunk sat down and glanced around the surrounding area for witnesses. His eyes flicked across the street to where I stood pressed up against the fence.

I froze.

I breathed shallowly through my mouth and concentrated on remaining absolutely still. His gaze passed right over me and he turned back to the man who was now humming softly and stamping his feet to some tune that was audible only to him.

I frowned.

Even in pitch blackness he should have been able to spot me. The auras of our kind burn brighter and more intensely than humans, yet he hadn't seen me at all. I kept my gaze fixed on him as he moved closer to the drunk in order to make sure that I hadn't been mistaken about what he was.

His aura flared out around him in a hazy nimbus of muted red and gold as I continued to track his progress. He was definitely one of us, but the dimness of his aura suggested that he was weak and hadn't been properly nurtured by his Font. This realization both puzzled and troubled me. Fonts typically choose their progeny with great care and train and nurture them for years before allowing them to undergo the transference. Numerous infusions of the Font's blood over time allow their progeny to be able to detect the auras of not only humans—potential victims—but others of their kind who may or may not pose any threat to them. By virtue of their extensive age and power, Fonts would not risk creating progeny that were weak or who were otherwise incapable of defending themselves. Progeny were a reflection of the strength and character of their creator, and the Font who had made this one had been careless—very careless.

Before I could consider the motives of the Font in question, the man moved closer and began to close the distance between him and the drunk. I had to act fast.

I moved away from the fence and looked both ways for oncoming traffic. I put my head down and tried to appear lost and nervous, then proceeded to cross the street directly behind the two men. I dug awkwardly in the pockets of my coat for my car keys and kept glancing anxiously around me. The man turned at the sound of my approach and his aura flared once more, obviously excited by the change in the night's entertainment. I made sure to catch his eyes for only the briefest of seconds before looking away, and then I veered sharply to the left towards the darkened alleyway.

In the space of that single glance I saw in his eyes that he had plans for me, and that he was going to enjoy acting them out. They were hollow, soulless eyes—the eyes of a killer.

I turned at the sound of his footsteps echoing sharply behind me and I let the fear show in my face. It was a convincing act, but an act no less.

He chuckled as I quickened my pace and attempted to outdistance him, and when I broke into a dead run he laughed gleefully and pursued me. All around me the remains of once-grand mansions loomed out of the darkness like menacing ghosts, and there were no street lamps to illuminate our progress. The moon peaked out from the soaring clouds above us, and the broken glass and scattered refuse littering the alley floor winked and glittered in the dim light. Glass crunched under my boots as I made a desperate attempt to reach a fabricated safety, and I could still hear my pursuer behind me taunting me with his laughter.

All at once a sign with the words Dead End came into view, and I couldn't help the smile that crept onto my face. The words were fitting for more than a few reasons, as my would-be assailant was soon going to learn.

I whirled around and saw him a few yards behind me grinning with undisguised malice. His teeth were a white slash in the dark, and the smile would have been beautiful except for the intent behind it. He took a step towards me, then another, his eyes roaming over my face and body in apparent appraisal.

I was going to enjoy wiping that look off his face. He was about to learn the hard way that appearances can be deceiving.

He paused and I saw the empty, soulless look come into his eyes. "You look lost; maybe I can help you." He took another series of steps toward me and I visibly cowered.

"Don't come any closer!" I made myself appear as small and helpless as possible, and I got the desired response.

The grin widened as his lips stretched almost painfully over his teeth, and I was reminded of the way a Great White looks moments before it swallows its hapless prey whole. He strode forward until he was only a few feet in front of me. "You didn't say please."

He launched himself at me in a blur of movement and knocked me into the overgrown lawn of a rambling red-brick Victorian, his arms gripping me in a steel-like vice as he attempted to hold me down. I shoved upwards with every ounce of strength that I could muster and we went flying backwards with the force of the momentum, striking the wall of the house with enough force to shatter bone in a normal human being.

Bricks cracked and crumbled under the ferocity of the impact as we continued to grapple for dominance, our hands locked tightly around each other's forearms to keep as much distance between us as possible. I whirled him around until his back was pressed firmly against the wall and I head butted him viciously. He yelped and his hands flew up instinctively to protect his face, and I used the momentary distraction to unsheathe one of the knives I had hidden under my coat.

He recovered from my attack quicker than I anticipated, and with a ferocious growl, his hands shot away from his face and gripped mine in mid-strike. He held my arms away from his body and I strained to gain an inch, my teeth gritted in concentration. I could see the tension singing along his arms as he struggled to hold me at bay, and for just the briefest of moments I saw doubt flicker in his dark eyes.

I planted my feet firmly on the ground and shoved forward to loosen some of the tension, and I managed to extend my right hand towards his cheek. The blade slid along the skin and sliced into it effortlessly. Blood welled upwards in a thick, red line and dribbled downwards along his jaw. He snarled in pain and then batted at the knife clumsily with his left elbow. I laughed at his feeble attempts, and he retaliated by lashing out and backhanded me brutally.

The blow sent me sprawling to the ground. My knife flew from my grip and skittered off into the darkness, which was just fine by me. I had a spare—three actually—but he didn't know that.

I lay on my side pretending to be hurt, and moved as little as possible. He knelt down beside me and his hands closed around a fistful of my hair. I was forcibly hauled to my feet, but I made no attempt to fight him. I was careful to keep my hands loose at my sides and away from the sheaths concealed under my coat. If he realized what I had planned for him I would quickly lose the upper hand.

"Not so tough now, are we?"

He flung me back against the wall and pinned me there with his weight, our bodies pressed so close together that barely a whisper could pass between us. He still had me by the hair and he brought it up to his nose, inhaling the scent.

I made a mental note to cut it short before the night was over.

"You smell so good; let's see how you taste."

I didn't like the sound of that, but I resisted the urge to go for my second knife. The fool was so busy enjoying himself that he had neglected to restrain my arms. It was both stupid and careless, and would soon prove fatal.

He leaned closer and his tongue flicked out, wet and eager. He began to trace the contours of my lips as if his tongue was memorizing every curve, and I turned my face away from him in disgust. He laughed and pulled me closer, obviously enjoying my reaction.

By now I had managed to undo the sheath holding the knife nearest my right hand and I was slowly working it free. His fingers bit into my cheeks and chin as his hands clamped onto my face and he kissed me, rough and sloppy. His teeth grazed my lower lip and drew blood, and I squirmed despite myself. He threw his head back and moaned in pleasure as he ran his tongue across his teeth, tasting me. Our kind could never resist the taste of blood—however unnecessary to our survival it was—and I was fairly certain that he would not be satisfied with so small a taste.

Long fingernails stroked the sides of my neck and I forced myself to remain still. I knew that he was capable of ripping my throat out with a flick of his wrist, and the last thing I wanted to do was make any sudden moves.

"I'm going to enjoy this," he whispered.

The nails raked harder, drawing blood in lines. The knife slid free from the sheath and I gripped it tightly in my hand, bracing for the kill.

I breathed along his mouth, "So am I."

Confusion chased away the cocky grin on his face and was soon replaced by anger. He was used to his victims begging and pleading for their lives, and I had spoiled the fun for him. Victims were not supposed to be cooperative or compliant, but I wasn't a victim. I had been one centuries ago, and once was enough.

The momentary pause was all the time I needed, and I brought the knife around in a slashing arc. The blade sank into the side of his neck with a satisfying, meaty *thunk* and he reared back screaming, hands instinctively flying to his throat. His weight shifted off of me and as his face twisted up in a mixture of rage and agony, I kneed him in the groin with everything I had. His eyes widened in surprise and he fell to his knees with a muffled grunt.

He stared up at me, and I saw the realization that he had bitten off more than he could chew cross his features. His aura flared brilliantly around him, charged and blazing with his heightened emotional state, and the myriad shades of red and gold danced chaotically within the swirling nimbus. My own body reacted strongly and violently to the energy crackling around him, and I felt the hunger rise within me. It screamed and raged in eagerness, demanding that it be sated.

I allowed myself to succumb to the primal urges sweeping throughout my nerve endings and embraced the thing that I was: vampire. To deny this would be tantamount to denying my very existence, and while the hunger may be a part of me, it was not the part that ruled my head or heart.

I longed to take the energy surging around and within him and make it mine, to take it into myself and make it a part of me forever. The hunger demanded it, the revenge burning in my heart demanded it, and ultimately *I* demanded it. I would settle for nothing less.

He saw the way that I was looking at him, and he knew, knew with absolute certainty that he was going to die and that *I* was going to be the one who killed him. I saw him then not as a being who had been thrown headlong into extraordinary circumstances—whether by his own actions or by the actions of others—but as a means to an end.

He saw these thoughts reflected in the iciness of my stare and he began to babble, saying nonsensical things as he sought to save the pale reflection of existence that had become his life of late.

His pleas fell on deaf ears and I flung myself at him and straddled his back, wrapping my arms and legs around his torso as hard as I could. He shrieked and bellowed, pitching and lurching violently from side to side in an effort to throw me off, but it was useless. I was older and more powerful and he was no match for me.

I brought the knife back around in a killing blow and twisted it into his neck until flesh met the hilt and his cries were forever silenced. Blood flowed over my fingers, and I raised them to my lips and licked them clean, savoring the salty and faintly-metallic flavor shamelessly. My body responded to the blood like it had countless times before, and my own aura flared around me, enlivened by the life force that imbued it. As the blood flowed down my throat and into my body, I felt the bond form between us as his life force opened up to me and responded to the thing that both animated and sustained me.

His aura flickered and shifted in and out of focus as the blood loss ravaged his body, and the intensity of my own aura increased in response. I had no words for how the process ultimately worked, but I had come to the understanding that it was reciprocal in that the life force of my prey ebbed and was eventually extinguished as my own aura drew the energy from them. My understanding may have been rudimentary, but the only thing I had to be certain of was that they died and that I lived.

I could already feel my own slight injuries beginning to heal from the influx of his life force, but I would not get the full effect until he ceased to live—then I would feed.

A strangled groan escaped his lips and he pitched forward as my weight rode him down to the alley floor. Blood began to pool underneath him and I watched it with a sense of bitter triumph. In that instant as his body began to convulse and his breath came in hitching gasps, the blood became something more than vindication for the violence that he had attempted against me. It was now blood paid back in full for the lives of my family who were slain centuries before. The body beneath me—for that is what it would soon be—may not have struck the fatal blow that had taken them away from me, but it was the principle of the thing that mattered. It was the driving force which compelled me to hunt down those who preyed upon the weak and to exact revenge when their victims could not.

The heart fluttered and the lungs struggled to draw breath, and I knew that death was close. I rolled off of him and twisted his head around so that his eyes stared into mine. I wanted to be the last thing that he saw before the light faded from them and was replaced by darkness.

He looked at me with undisguised hatred during his last moments, and then his eyes rolled back and his face contorted with the final agony. He was dead.

I stood up and immediately felt the bond grow and expand in intensity as his life force was expelled into the surrounding air. It swirled and coalesced around me, drawn to the blood that still coated my lips, seeking to reunite with the force of the bond that we now shared. I stood there with my head tilted heavenward, and my eyes squeezed shut in concentration. The energy danced and cajoled about me, prickling the tiny hairs on my arms. I inhaled deeply and immediately felt the energy plunge downward into the very marrow of my bones, healing and restoring me until I was whole and alive. The very cells of my body were infused with this renewed power, and I was filled to bursting. I flexed the fingers on my right hand and then my left, savoring the feel of his strength—his life—flowing through me. I fell into the swoon that always accompanied such a repast, and I allowed myself to drift weightlessly upon the waves of exhilarating bliss coursing through me.

I had lived to fight another day. I had vanquished yet another scourge to humanity and I was all the stronger because of it.

Within moments however, the intensity of the feeding began to taper off, the effects sizzling away like a dying flame.

I opened my eyes.

The body lay at my feet completely devoid of life. I looked down at it and whispered, *"Nemo malus felix."* No peace for the wicked.

I walked off into the darkness and retrieved my knife from where it lay yards away in the debris-strewn lawn. The bone handle gleamed like pearl in the moonlight and was worn to a smooth sheen from constant use. I ran my fingertip against the initials carved near the hilt—not mine, but the person whom the bone had once belonged to.

I shook my head. *Person* was too generous a term for the monster that the bone had come from, but they were long-dead and it didn't matter anymore. What mattered was getting out of here with the body, undetected.

I had hunted here often enough to know that it would only be a matter of time before a patrol car came cruising by looking for the drug dealers and gang bangers who frequented the area. The body had to be disposed of quickly, and it wasn't going to move itself. I bent down and pulled the second knife from the neck, wiped it clean, and tucked it back into the sheath around my waist. I reached my arms under the small of the back, slung the body effortlessly over one shoulder like so much meat, and then headed towards my car. I had parked it out of sight down a little side street that ran opposite the alley, which was concealed from the prying eyes of the public.

I popped open the trunk and dumped the body unceremoniously inside and then began wrapping it in the black plastic bags that I had already lain out in readiness for it. A steady rain had begun to fall by the time I finished wiping the blood off of my palms, and as I climbed into the driver's seat I gave silent thanks. The rain would take care of any traces of my kill and would wash away any physical evidence I might have left behind. The modern age had forced me to become almost obsessively-compulsive about such things, but I wasn't worried. The back alleyways of large cities almost always have blood stains in them, and no one seems to notice or care where they came from.

The engine roared to life and I pulled out slowly to avoid drawing any unnecessary suspicion. I didn't linger around the scenes of my killings longer than I had to.

I drove silently through the streets which were never completely empty despite the late hour. This made dumping the body within the city limits particularly difficult, so I was forced to find an alternative. I got on Highway 90 East until I reached the outskirts of the city and headed out into the sprawling countryside. Far removed from the lights and landmarks of San Antonio, the scattered farmhouses and ranches with their stone and wrought-iron gates were pure Texas. Most of the residents earned a living through agriculture or through cattle. Their distinctly bovine profiles dotted the landscape as they bedded down for the night in their little herds, and occasionally I spotted a windmill standing like a lone sentinel in the darkness. It was an idyllic setting and it brought back memories of my youth when times had been simpler, when I had been someone else entirely who would never in her wildest dreams have imagined the person that I would be today.

As soon as I passed the city limits I felt the tension ease out of my shoulders. A cop on patrol was a rare sight out here at this time, which is why I preferred to take care of business during the evening rather than the daylight hours. Most of my kind chose to capitalize on the myths and legends promulgated by Victorian-era authors and Hollywood studios that had cropped up over the centuries, because this created the perfect camouflage. If the vast majority conceived of the vampire as a creature that burst into flames in the light of day, drained its victims with a lethal bite to the neck, or which cowered at the sign of the cross—none of which applied to my kind—then we could walk as wolves amongst the sheep, undetected.

I chuckled bitterly. As if such a thing as camouflage were necessary here in America. The myths of the vampire originated in the Old World and were rampant in the Central Europe that I had once called home. No one took stock in myths and superstitious tales of blood-sucking corpses that could be warded off with garlic or holy objects, here in the states. If it were that easy to get rid of my kind, I would have capitalized on the idea years ago. As it was, I had to rely on my extensive experience and skills honed over the centuries to get the job done—that, and the four trusty knives nestled snuggly in the sheath around my waist.

It occurred to me again that the myths and superstitions pertaining to the "undead" that I had grown up on were largely misinformed, and had I known what to *really* look out for, I would have recognized the danger the moment it landed on my family's doorstep. If I had only known that these creatures looked just as human as the rest of us, I would have barred the door and turned the three people away to seek shelter elsewhere. If I had trusted my instincts and done this, my mother and father would have lived to a ripe old age and died safe and happy in their beds. If I had not ignored the warning in my head which shrieked of danger, Amelie would have grown into a beautiful woman who would marry and bear many children. If I had handled the events of my past with the clarity I had now in the present, I could have looked back on my life with a smile, rather than regret.

*If, if, if. . . .*

I turned on the radio to drown out my own thoughts.

To my right the road sloped downward and I steered the car effortlessly down the narrow dirt path that led to my own personal dumping grounds. I had begun renting the property because a large sinkhole that defied all attempts to measure its depths was located in the extreme northwest section of the land. The real estate ad on the Internet had listed it as a novelty—undoubtedly to attract attention from would-be-buyers—but I had been drawn to it for an entirely different reason. It seemed that there was seemingly no end to the wonders that the modern-age could throw our way, and the Internet was no exception. There was literally something for everyone there.

I reached up and pressed the small button on the remote clipped to my visor. The electric gate swung inwards and creaked slowly closed behind me, ensuring absolute privacy. A lone car passed by as I pulled in and continued on its way down the darkened highway.

I drove for another mile and then the road gradually gave way to a weed-choked rut that continued on into the darkness. As I got out and shut the door behind me, a cool breeze ruffled my hair around my face. The air had that indescribable earthy smell to it after a steady rainfall, but the rain had moved on elsewhere. The moon was obscured behind a mass of fleecy clouds, and no light illuminated my path as I made my way through the waist-high grass with the body slung over my shoulder. My feet led the way of their own accord as insects chirred and leapt around me, and the sounds of the night filled my ears. The knuckles dangled behind my back and made a raspy, rustling sound in the grass that sounded almost like footsteps, but I knew that I was alone.

When I finally reached my destination, I dropped to one knee and let the body slide to the ground. My fingers searched amongst the roots and rocks looking for the edge of the false door that covered the hole. To the casual passerby the ground looked uniform and undisturbed, but the entrance to the sinkhole had been concealed by a diorama of grass, dirt, roots, and rocks which had been mounted on a five-by-seven foot section of plywood. The surrounding dense vegetation hid the edges of the door quite nicely.

I dragged the body to the edge of the hole and kicked it in where it tumbled into the abyss. The plastic bags wrapped around it made a faint whistling noise that was soon swallowed up in the depths. I stood there for some minutes listening for the sound of it meeting solid ground, but it never came. Perhaps there was no end to the hole and it just went on forever and ever like I did.

I shut the door and made my way back to my car as quickly as I could. While hunting may be messy and dirty work, it was a necessary evil in my world.

# Chapter 2

I stared at my reflection in the bathroom mirror. My face looked ethereal and painfully young and innocent in the foggy glass, and I angrily wiped it away. I was neither young nor innocent, and illusion or not it still bothered me. I ran my hands through my damp hair and resisted the urge to twine the ends of my non-existent locks around my fingers. My hair had been cropped just below my earlobes, and although it seemed like such a drastic change for me, I decided that it was long overdue. It had never occurred to me to do this before, but then again I had never been picked up by my hair before tonight.

Apparently there was a first and last time for everything.

I cinched my robe tighter at the waist and padded softly into the living room. A stack of newspapers, maps, and assorted tabloids lay scattered on the table beside the worn armchair, and I flopped into it with a weary sigh. Several papers lay draped over the edge of the table, and as I reached out to right them I caught a glimpse of the topmost page. It was an independent pulp tabloid called *Elysium* that featured local and national stories on cults, Bigfoot, and alien abductions on a weekly basis. Every now and then they would do a cover story about government conspiracies and cover-ups, but it did little to improve their sales. The stories tended to lean towards the fanatic and overly-zealous, but occasionally there was a grain of truth hidden between the lines. It had been my experience that those who were deemed out of touch with reality were actually the most attuned to its myriad nuances, because they saw connections where others were convinced there weren't any.

Whenever I entered a new area to hunt for my kind, I began stockpiling issues of the local paper and any other publications within the immediate area. I would scan each of these, checking for anything in the news that would alert me to any unusual or unsolved murders in the area. This helped me gain a sense of where to start looking, or for that matter, to confirm my suspicions that the city was inhabited by a Font and their progeny. I always found plenty of coverage concerning gruesome and unsolved murders, but I had sadly reached the conclusion that they were the work of very human monsters rather than my own kind. I also took a more proactive approach and patrolled the back alleyways of the city on a nightly basis, looking for the slightest proof that my kind were residing here. Generally I followed a grid pattern in which I divided the city into quadrants and patrolled each one for weeks at a time. When I was confident that the area was free of any threat, I moved on to the next.

I patrolled the streets night after night when I first came to San Antonio, yet I found no trace of my kind. I grew increasingly frustrated, albeit relieved that the city had not yet become a hunting ground where the inhabitants were the prey. Soon enough however my suspicions were confirmed, and any relief I might have felt was abruptly extinguished. About a month and a half after my arrival, I was making my way through the crush of weekend tourist traffic in and around the Alamo Mission area when the familiar red-gold aura of my kind flashed out from the sea of very-human auras around me. There were two of them—young males just like my latest kill—and they were weaving their way casually through the throngs of tourists. I followed them through the streets for about a block or so before

I lost track of them in a crowded and very public section of town. Needless to say, multiple witnesses prevented me from dispatching them right then and there.

It was nearly six weeks later before I spotted another one and was able to deal with them in private. The rest had followed in relatively quick succession and I was beginning to wonder when the Font would come looking for me, demanding to know who was challenging their hold on the city. There could be no conceivable way that they would *not* know that I was here—the fact that five of their progeny were missing and presumed dead was clue enough, so why haven't they come looking for me?

I rubbed at my temples more out of habit rather than trying to ease a headache that didn't exist, and I got up from my chair to stare out the window. From my vantage point I could see the city spread out before me in all its wonderful and terrible detail. I could see the people coming and going as they went about their respective lives, and the fact that I was effectively an outsider looking in wasn't lost on me. I was the unofficial protector of the city and its inhabitants, yet I could never be of their world. There was no place in their reality for a being such as myself.

I felt the weight of the last three-hundred and forty-seven years bearing down on me, yet the knowledge that I had a purpose in my life came as a great comfort to me. If I had been an outsider haunting the periphery of society for centuries without a purpose to sustain me, I would have long since chosen death over obscurity. I had an obligation to the citizens of this great city and I would do my duty until the danger had passed. I would not waver in my convictions no matter how unbearable the loneliness would become.

The early morning traffic was beginning to clog up the streets, and the almost musical cacophony of blaring horns and shouted curses filling the air drowned out my reverie. Somewhere out there in the city a Font was greeting the new day minus another progeny, one less to complete their ranks. They should have been furious, vengeful, on the warpath as it were, yet here I stood unmolested within the safety of my own home.

Why?

I sighed and turned back towards the shabby and modest room behind me. I never truly settled in a place once I arrived and I seldom unpacked my things, ready to depart at a moment's notice should danger present itself. The sheath with my four knives lay on the unused kitchen counter still crusted with dried blood. I removed the knives one by one and set them down by the sink. Four blades that were identical in appearance save for slight variations in the sheen and color of the bone handles; four blades that were hundreds of years old and had seen so much violence and bloodshed; four blades that took everything I ever cherished away from me while in the hands of my tormentors— four blades that now had the power to preserve life in mine.

I polished each one methodically with a soft cloth while praying for the souls of my family, and then I placed each of them back into the sheath and slipped it around my waist. I shut the blinds and the sight of the awakening city vanished into the semi-gloom.

I pulled back the worn coverlet on the bed and allowed my body to conform to the lumpy mattress beneath me, ignoring the springs that shrieked in protest. I was tired, but not in body. I was tired in spirit.

The sheath lay securely around my waist and was a comforting and familiar weight as I closed my eyelids. I cleared my mind of any memories of what had recently transpired, and I shut myself off from those of the past as well. I said another prayer for the strength to persevere and asked for absolution of past sins committed.

Centuries ago I had committed the cardinal sin of *non facias malum ut inde fiat bonum*—you should not make evil in order that good may be made from it. I had spent the last few hundred years convincing myself that the sacrifices of a few would and had benefited the many. Every time I take one of the monsters out I am that much more convinced that the choices I made over three-hundred years ago were the right ones. Never mind that the options presented to those individuals were impossible, but I did what I could to ease their suffering. It's a shame that I have been unable to alleviate my own, but I have all the time in the world to come up with a permanent solution.

# Chapter 3

The man trembled slightly as he stood flanked by the two
bodyguards outside the drawing room door. They were big
brutes—tall, corded with muscle, undoubtedly strong—but
they were entirely unnecessary. There was no conceivable force
on this earth that could possibly harm what lay beyond the door,
so he figured that the show of force was merrily an indulgence
rather than a necessity.

His mind raced with what he had recently witnessed and he
longed to tell his mistress what he had seen. Part of him feared
her wrath over the loss of one of her children, but another part
knew that she would be pleased with the information that he
had gathered. His hands fidgeted anxiously as he envisioned her
seated on her brocade divan, her quick, obsidian eyes locked
on his face, her attention rapt as she listened intently to every
word he had to say. He saw her beautiful face break into a wide,
sunny grin—if sunny was an apt description for a creature that
thrived in darkness—and then he saw her beckoning to him
with a crooked, slender finger. He imagined the way that his
knees would shake as he knelt before her and took the offered
wrist, imagined the way that her blood would leave a scalding
trail down his throat as he drank.

*Her blood.*

He shivered and attempted to compose himself before going
in. His mistress made it a point to select only the strongest and

most loyal of her acolytes to stand by her side for all eternity. He hoped that the information that he had would ensure his place among them, and he didn't want to ruin the occasion with a clumsy display of manners.

The door opened just the tiniest fraction and a slash of blackness peeked out at him.

The bodyguards surged forward and he followed, every ounce of will directed at placing one foot before the other. The door swung inwards and the darkness poured out like a tide. At the center of it sat the ornate, brocade divan just as he had envisioned. His mistress reclined on it languidly, her feet resting lightly on the soft cushions with her head cradled in the palm of her left hand. Three men stood behind her just out of reach of the pale reddish light being thrown off by the twin candelabra burning on either side of the divan. He knew just by their profiles that they were her three dearest and most trusted progeny, and he also knew that they were scrutinizing his every move intensely, even though he couldn't see their faces.

The bodyguards bowed deeply and the man hurriedly followed suit. The woman regarded them coolly and as he tentatively raised his eyes to peer out at her through the tangle of his hair, she nodded slightly. They rose in tandem and the bodyguard on his right spoke first.

"Darnell has some information for you." The guards stood still with their arms clasped respectfully behind their backs as they waited for her to respond.

Finally she spoke. "Leave us."

The bodyguards withdrew quickly and silently as shadows, and closed the door securely behind them.

The woman sat up in one fluid motion and motioned for him to approach. His legs felt rubbery as he closed the distance between them, his mind racing with innumerable fantasies of what awaited him in her arms.

"Look at me."

He raised his head until their eyes met. Hers were like twin pools of darkness swimming in her lovely face and were fringed by a delicate sweep of thick lashes. It was impossible to read the intent behind those eyes and her face betrayed nothing.

"Tell me everything that happened."

She settled back against the plush upholstery and he began to speak, slow and unsure at first, but gradually the details of the night's events began to reveal themselves. He began by explaining that he had accompanied Reggie to his favorite spot to hunt, just as she had asked him to. He explained that Reggie had been stalking a victim for some time—a drunken man by the looks of things—but the sudden appearance of a woman crossing the street behind him had distracted him. The woman's actions were not intentional—at least that is what he had thought at the time—and as she proceeded to turn down the alleyway to their left, Reggie pursued her instead.

That was when everything had changed for the worse.

The woman, who had seemed so defenseless only moments before, had turned a knife on Reggie and had killed him within a matter of moments. Not only that, she had fed off of him like his mistress and the rest of her children fed off of humans.

Her fingers stopped toying with the hem of her dress and her shoulders visibly straightened. A strange smile curved its way around her face and her eyes glittered triumphantly. He finished the narrative by informing her that he had watched the woman dump Reggie's body into the trunk of her car, and that he had then followed her past the city limits out into the countryside. He had seen her pass through an electric gate onto private property and had then parked out of sight and waited patiently for her to emerge. He hung carefully behind her while he followed her back into the city and had then tracked her to an apartment complex in a low-income neighborhood. He had spied on the location for hours afterward to see what she would do next, and when she finally settled into bed for the day, he knew that he had struck pay dirt.

She turned towards him and the smile broadened. His heart swelled with happiness, and for just a moment he forgot to breathe.

She slid gracefully over to one end of the divan and patted the empty seat beside her with her hand. "Sit with me."

Somehow he managed to fulfill her request without tripping and let his weight settle onto the plush upholstery. She turned the line of her body ever so slightly until they were facing one another. He watched wordlessly as she raised her left arm and pierced the skin of her wrist with the tip of her right index finger. The blood welled up bright and thick, and as she extended her arm towards him she whispered, "You have served me well and shall be rewarded."

His mouth closed eagerly but gently around the lip of the wound and he sucked heartily, relishing the richness and vibrancy of the flavor. He sighed and shut his eyes tightly as he allowed himself to become lost in the overwhelming and invigorating sensations that coursed throughout his nerve endings. All the myriad tiny aches and pains in his body began to vanish, and he felt as if the blood were gradually washing away the ravages of time and the elements. He felt lighter, younger, more alive and powerful than he had in years.

The sense of her wrist being withdrawn from his mouth pierced through the red fog clouding his brain, and his soul cried out in negation. The brief infusion wasn't near enough to bring on the transference, but he was confident that it was only a matter of time before she brought him over completely. He wanted to experience this unparalleled ecstasy forever, and as the swoon overtook him and he rested his head against the swell of her bosom, he found himself repeating the pledge of loyalty silently to himself. He would continue to serve her as long as he could have this, this perfect peace and harmony.

She caressed his face as tenderly as a lover and murmured soothing words to him that he couldn't make out. She then called to each of the three men standing behind the divan by name. They had remained standing for the duration of the feeding, never saying a word, not a whisper of movement passing between them. They came out from behind the divan and stood patiently at her side awaiting further instructions.

Her hands encircled his face and she lifted his chin up until he was staring blearily at her. She smiled once again and spoke softly to him. "My sons and I have much to discuss regarding this woman you informed me about. We must deal with her soon before she causes any more damage. Would be so kind as to give us some privacy?"

She motioned towards the door and he found himself nodding his head sluggishly. The door was unlocked from the outside just as he reached it, almost as if the bodyguards behind it had been aware of his approach. He was ushered outside without a word and told to wait while his mistress came up with new orders for him. He nodded again and sat down heavily on one of the ornately carved armchairs that decorated the lavish foyer. He would cheerfully wait here for as long as she wished.

"We have a very serious problem."

The three men nodded simultaneously in agreement as the woman paced around the room, her hands sketching the air as she seemed to be considering her options. For months she had been trying desperately to understand who or what was killing her children, and for months she had tried desperately to understand the killer's motive.

Now she knew, of sorts.

Reggie's death earlier in the evening had been immediately apparent to her the moment it occurred, and while the accompanying weakness and momentary disorientation was not as intense compared to her other children whom she had nurtured for years, she was ignorant as to the exact circumstances. Darnell's observations had answered these questions for her quite nicely, and now that she had a sense of whom and *what* her adversary was, she was confident that they would be dealt with soon. She may be significantly weakened after the death of five of her children, but she was far from being dead. Unparalleled tenacity and the sheer will to live kept the weakness at bay, but she knew that if any more of her children were to be killed that it would be an entirely different story. She was still no closer to discovering why the woman did what she did, but she did have a clearer picture of how she operated. As far as she was concerned, it was a step in the right direction.

The three men stood like silent sentinels as they waited for her to continue. She opened her left hand and began to tick off imaginary points. "From what little we do know about our previously-unknown assailant, is that *they* are a *she*—most curious." Her index finger bent down towards her palm as she moved on to the next point. "We also know from Darnell's observations that this woman seems to have a soft spot for the weak and helpless, and she is willing to serve as a decoy if it means distracting their would-be assailant from killing them. Again, curious." The ring finger quivered slightly as it awaited its turn. "Lastly, she has killed five of my children and has forced me to take drastic measures to prevent further loss of life, yet my remaining children continue to cower in the shadows afraid for their very lives—this is simply unacceptable and I will not tolerate it any longer. I will not stand idly by while some brigand slowly dismantles everything that I have worked so hard for, what I have sacrificed so much for." She turned to gaze at the three men with pure adoration.

They approached her silently and their arms encircled her waist so that she stood entwined in their embrace. She kissed each one on the top of their head and whispered, "My sons, whom I cherish above all else on this earth, you should be made to feel safe within the confines of your own kingdom. I will make it so for you if I accomplish nothing else during my lifetime." She then slowly disentangled herself from their arms and sat demurely on the divan, her eyes glittering dangerously in the semi-gloom.

"I think that I have found a weak link that we can reasonably exploit, but I have to be sure that the woman's intentions are geared towards the preservation of the innocents." She said this with a sneer like it was something distasteful. After a moment's reflection, she chuckled softly to herself and the sound was like the tinkling of glass. "Yes, it seems I have found a way to draw her out into the open, and once she reveals herself..." Her fingers dug into the upholstery and it shredded under the onslaught. Bits of foam and expensive silk fell to the floor in a snowy drift around her bare feet.

The three men nodded knowingly and left the room. As the door closed behind them she continued to sit on the ruined divan, a strange smile playing once more on her beautiful face. She held up a handful of ruined silk until it was eyelevel. "This woman, like all things that are amongst the weak, is destined to be destroyed." She blew the material until it fluttered out of her hand and landed in a small clump on the floor.

# Chapter 4

The blinds on the fourth-floor apartment opened at a quarter till ten in the morning, and it was then that his quarry passed into view.

He smiled. *His quarry*—the term his mistress had used to describe the task she had given him was practically antiquated, but the underhandedness of it all thrilled him shamelessly. His grin widened as he watched the woman standing motionless by the window gazing out at the traffic that flowed by. With the sun shining fully on her flawless face, she was pretty in a way that made her stand out in a crowd. She sure as hell didn't look dangerous, but he knew better. He had seen her in action and she was positively lethal, a stone-cold killer that rivaled any that he knew of, which included himself.

He shook his head. Pretty or not, she had to go. She had effectively sealed her own fate the day she had walked into town and started something that she was incapable of finishing, something that his mistress was being forced to deal with.

He supposed in a way that he should be thanking the woman for all the trouble she was starting. After all, if it weren't for her, his life would have never been touched by his mistress and her fiery blood. If asked if creatures such as she existed— vampires for lack of a better term—he would have busted a gut laughing and said that you were crazy for even entertaining such an idea.

Now he knew better.

Now that he knew that such things were possible and were depending on him—*him*—to do their dirty work, he wasn't going to let the chance slip from his hands. So many other opportunities had passed him by in a similar fashion, but they were inconsequential in the face of what awaited him in his mistress' embrace.

The woman turned away from the window and disappeared into the confines of her apartment. He had no idea what her schedule was like, or for that matter if she even had one. Either way he was going to stake out her apartment for as long as it took, because his mistress needed to know what compelled her to protect the innocents of the city.

The idea that a creature like her could go against her nature and kill her own kind was as inconceivable as it was impossible, yet here she was in the flesh. But not for long.

He would find out everything he could about her and report back to his mistress. *She* would take care of her. She would take care of everything, and then…. He shivered as he remembered the way that her blood had made him feel: powerful, alive, and *wanted*. He had never had that before, but his mistress had changed all that.

He settled against the front seat of the car and began to carry out his orders.

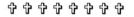

"Relax, Andy."

Dr. Bruce Ackerman chuckled good-naturedly as his old college roommate visibly squirmed on the examining table. Andrew Crossman cautiously cracked one eye open, but his muscles remained visibly tensed.

Dr. Ackerman sighed and crossed his arms over his chest. "In the nine years or so since we've known each other, have I ever once endangered your life—spur-of-the-moment keg parties excluded?" He stood there with the needle in one hand while the nurse practitioner did her best to hide the smirk behind her gloved hand.

Andrew opened both eyes and stared sullenly at the floor. "No," he mumbled and began to feel himself relaxing in slow degrees.

Dr. Ackerman smiled and approached him, needle in hand. "You'll feel a slight sting. If you feel anything more, you're free to sue me for negligence."

"Comforting." The needle pierced the skin of his forearm and Andrew winced slightly. The tiny pain vanished almost as soon as his brain registered it, and he averted his eyes as Dr. Ackerman began to fill several vials of blood. The nurse practitioner carefully labeled each one with his name as they were each placed into the plastic carousel.

When he was finished, Dr. Ackerman straightened and carefully removed the needle. He placed a cotton ball on the tiny wound and instructed Andrew to apply pressure. While he unwound a length of gauze from the roll on the counter, he paused and grinned mischievously.

"Hmm. Would you prefer a Band-Aid instead? I have Spiderman and Barbie ones—your pick."

Andrew casually flipped him off and continued to apply pressure while he considered that as much as he detested needles and anything to do with doctors and lab work, having your best friend as your physician definitely had its advantages. Most doctors were either too uptight or full of themselves to treat their patients as anything but lab rats, much less as human beings. Dr. Ackerman—Bruce—and he got along swimmingly, and it was a rare day that they didn't grab a beer or two after a long day pounding the metaphorical pavement.

Nine years ago—a virtual lifetime ago—they had been roommates while attending college. Bruce's outgoing personality and penchant for drunken mayhem made him the virtual poster boy for extracurricular excess. Andrew's quiet, introverted nature—which seemed to put him at odds with practically everything—was the polar opposite of Bruce's excess.

They immediately hit it off.

Andrew had been Bruce's wingman during more than a few dicey situations, and Bruce had effectively gotten Andrew out from behind his desk and out of his shell. Bruce claimed that if it weren't for him, the only memories Andrew would have had of their time at school was the inside of his textbooks. The memories that had followed were a tad hazy and the details slightly fuzzy, but they were memories nonetheless. Good memories.

After graduation they had each gone their separate ways, but had always stayed in close contact. There were more memories that followed during the years, but they were decidedly less cheerful. Bruce had pursued his career in medicine—how he managed to make the grade after nights of relentless partying was still a mystery to Andrew—and had gone on to residency while Andrew pursued his life-long dream of entering the field of professional journalism. Years later, the fruits of their respective labors couldn't be more different. Bruce had a Jaguar and a sweet little pad that he called home filled with antiques and contemporary works of art. Andrew had a rusty-green Geo that had seen better days, and an apartment that leaned more towards the term "flop house" than anything else. He worked full-time at an independent publication called *Elysium* that was known only to the local nut jobs, crackpots, and the hopelessly delusional.

Andrew supposed that he was being just a tad harsh and judgmental towards the publication's loyal readers, because if it weren't for them he and the rest of the staff would be out of work. Bob Garrett, the founder and self-professed ruler of all he saw, didn't seem to think much of Andrew's passion for truth and journalistic integrity, and he told him as much every chance he got.

More than once Andrew had found himself on the brink of storming into Bob's office and telling him in so many words exactly what he and the rest of the staff thought of him. Generally when these feelings overtook him he put his head down, counted to ten, and then got back to work on whatever features had been placed on his desk. Needless to say, a distinct lack of finances invariably steered him away from these thoughts and brought reality into sharp relief. As much as Andrew fantasized about telling Bob what a colossal asshole he was, it wasn't fair to drag his co-workers into the mix—no matter how much they agreed with him on that point.

Well, almost all of them.

Gary Simms, Bob's golden boy and self-styled God's gift to women, was the only exception to that rule. Gary had been working at *Elysium* for nearly five years now and had been there right at the start. Andrew still had no idea where Gary had gone to school or who had implanted the seeds of journalism in his brain, but the man couldn't even write a grocery list without throwing in a heavy dose of bullshit and sensationalism. He had innumerable sources—some reliable and more than a few questionable ones—scattered throughout the city in varying professional and independent capacities, and was the only one at the office who received regular amounts of "fan mail." These were generally manifestos scrawled in cheap journals, or in one instance, a homemade plaque that had a photograph of Gary clipped from one of his articles surrounded by bones, chicken feathers, and something dark that looked suspiciously like blood. The note attached to it explained that it was "for protection against the forces of evil that he"—meaning Gary— "so bravely sought out to expose to the world."

Andrew had liked to gag and so did the rest of the staff. Gary's ego had immediately expanded to epic proportions and he had hung the plague above his desk right over his computer. It sat between a framed copy of his first cover story and a certificate that Bob had presented to him and two other senior staff for their "loyalty and years of hard work." This little celebration had been topped off with the receptionist's homemade wedding punch and a sheet cake for twenty purchased at the local grocery store.

Yeah, the job definitely had its perks.

Andrew scoffed and swung his feet restlessly from his perch on the examining table. The whole thing—his boss, the publication and the feature stories—were one big cosmic joke. Bruce had managed to not only pursue his dreams, but had made them reality. Andrew suspected that as long as he continued to work at *Elysium* that he would always be running in place, and would effectively stay at square one indefinitely. He was twenty-six years old and had absolutely nothing to show for all his years of schooling, nothing to refer to at social events or his upcoming ten-year reunion to wow his old schoolmates. The most he had was a heap of a car and less than five-thousand in the bank, unless you counted an inextinguishable passion for the truth or an adherence to journalistic ethics. That had to count for something, although in Andrew's experience it hadn't counted for much at all.

He ran his hands up through his hair with his free hand while Dr. Ackerman finished wrapping his arm with the gauze. He patted the ends to make sure that they stuck together and then he stepped back with a grin.

"All done. That wasn't so bad, now was it?"

This was the third time in just over a month since he had visited his friend at his office, not for a social call, but as an actual patient. The strange and sometimes debilitating symptoms had begun months before—almost a year to be exact—but he had ignored them thinking that they were an unwelcome side effect of his job or the stress of daily life.

Matters had come to a head when the aches and pains had started up in his joints and his appetite had dwindled down to virtually nothing. His mother had expressed horror at his willowy build when he had come down for Thanksgiving, and had insisted on sending him home-cooked meals until he had managed to calm her down. He convinced her that it was the stress of his job that was getting to him, and both she and his father had expressed their disapproval of the kind of schedule Bob Garrett insisted on.

Months later he still wasn't feeling any better, and while his boss was still a pain in the ass, he couldn't be entirely blamed for Andrew's declining health. A series of infections had flared up since then and he had had a hard time shaking them. Bruce had prescribed a two-week long regiment of powerful antibiotics on his initial visit, but he extended the prescription for one more week when Andrew showed no signs of improvement. The results were exactly the same and Bruce had set up an appointment for him right away. He had even bumped several clients from his already-booked schedule to make room for him as soon as possible.

Andrew appreciated the gesture, but he was still convinced that it was nothing serious and that Bruce shouldn't have gone to all the trouble. Bruce had shaken his head and waved the issue away, saying that friends and their health took top priority over his other patients. He had then performed a routine physical and had discovered several swollen lymph nodes that seemed to be linked to the infections he was suffering from, and a series of blood tests to rule out the underlying cause were then ordered.

Andrew had immediately paled at the mention of needles, and Bruce had chided him with his usual brand of playfulness and professionalism that made him so popular with his staff and patients. The actual drawing of blood wasn't near as bad as he had expected, but the anxiety and uncertainty he felt at what could be causing his symptoms was making him feel a little sick.

Bruce seemed to pick up on his friend's discomfort. "Andy, you're a healthy twenty-six year old who's never been sick a day in his life. I'm sure that there's nothing wrong with you that I can't handle."

"Think highly of yourself, don't you?"

Bruce flashed him a knowing smile. "Yes I do, and that's what makes me so popular with the ladies." He winked at the nurse practitioner who blushed behind her mask. It was common knowledge around the office that Bruce and Jenna—Nurse Fowler to anyone not in the know—had been dating for almost two years. Things had progressed beyond serious, and the staff was actively taking bets on when the good doctor would pop the question.

Andrew raised his eyebrows and seemed surprised. "Is that true?"

She laughed and went along with it. "You're staring at living, breathing proof right here." She did a little twirl as if modeling her nurse's scrubs and Bruce whistled appreciatively.

"I love it when you do that."

"I know you do."

The look they shared was full of heat, and Andrew cleared his throat to offset the awkward silence that followed this little exchange. They both turned to look at him and then they both burst out laughing, obviously sharing some inside joke that he didn't get.

Bruce gently shooed her outside so he could talk to "his patient" in private, and she walked out of the room with an exaggerated sway of her hips. Bruce's eyes tracked her progress, and as the door shut behind her, he fanned himself dramatically with Andrew's chart.

"Man, I love my job."

"Yeah."

Andrew's half-hearted response wasn't missed by his friend who seemed to come back to himself. Until recently, Andrew had been in a relatively serious relationship with a woman named Rachel who was a receptionist for a high-end real estate business. For awhile it looked like she and Andrew were headed down the aisle, but his sudden illness and the mood swings that were brought on by his symptoms put a strain on their relationship—or at least that is how *she* made it sound. Everyone who knew her knew that Rachel liked to frequent the trendier clubs and had an affinity for the high life. She and Andrew couldn't have been more different, and at times it seemed like they were from different planets, but Andrew was deeply in love with her. He was so blinded by love that he couldn't see her glaring personality faults when they were staring him right in the face. The first time that Andrew had introduced her to Bruce, she had sneered that if Andrew would just get the idea of being a professional journalist out of his head and would just apply himself, then *he* could have been a doctor as well. The subtext of that little statement was more than apparent: if Andrew had just gotten the idea of being a journalist out of his head and had pursued a degree in medicine instead, then *she* would be living the life of a doctor's girlfriend, fringe benefits and all.

Bruce had immediately disliked her.

Andrew had just started working at *Elysium* and was convinced that despite the publication's rough exterior, that it had some redeeming qualities. He had been young and eager, but the passage of three years had changed his opinion considerably.

The modest paycheck that he brought home wasn't nearly enough to provide the kind of lifestyle that Rachel enjoyed, and when the mysterious symptoms began cropping up, he just couldn't keep pace with her relentless socializing. He had come home to an empty apartment and had found a note pinned to the fridge telling him in so many words that it was over.

Bruce had been there as much as he was able to, but the damage seemed far from being repaired. Rachel was Andrew's first serious relationship, and being burned that bad by someone you loved that much was bound to have consequences. Andrew was already on edge about his health, and then to be dumped when the chips were down? It was like adding insult to injury. Bruce had often wondered how someone as self-centered as Rachel could have ever attracted someone like Andrew, but he had come up short every time. Perhaps it was one of those great, cosmic mysteries that Andrew and his co-workers frequently wrote about. Perhaps it was a question that had no satisfactory answer. Rachel's faults had been many, but Andrew's only shortcoming was that he loved the wrong people for what he felt were the right reasons. The wreckage of his recent breakup was testament to this.

He felt a twinge of guilt at the flagrant PDA and tried to make amends. "Sorry about that," he motioned towards the closed door, "but you know how I turn to mush around smart, beautiful women. I'm sure that you have a few questions for me, right?"

Andrew nodded. "A few."

"Fire away then." Bruce set the chart down on the counter and took a seat on the little stool that sat on the floor against the cabinets. He clasped his hands in his lap and waited patiently.

Andrew latched onto the first and most obvious one. "What's all the lab work for?" He raised his bandaged arm for emphasis.

The question struck Bruce like a physical blow, even though any doctor worth his salt—whether novice or seasoned professional—should have seen it coming. As he had finished examining Andrew and scribbled the last of his notes on his chart, he had calmly turned his back so that his friend wouldn't see the look of terror on his face. There was little doubt that Andrew was suffering from something other than acute stress—the physical examination had more than confirmed that. He had then reached into one of the drawers that ran the length of the countertop, and explained that while everything looked good, he would still like to run some blood work just to be on the safe side. His hands trembled slightly as he stripped off the sterile wrapping from the needle, and he was keenly aware that Andrew was watching him. The mantle of professionalism somehow managed to stay in place despite the anxiety building up inside of him over his friend's deteriorating health.

*Christ, don't let him suspect that I'm keeping anything from him.* He took the tourniquet in one hand and casually rolled the sleeve of Andrew's shirt up with the other. *I know that it's wrong and that it goes against everything I stand for as a doctor, but goddamn it, I can't look him in the eye and tell him that I think he may have something seriously wrong with him—not until I have all the facts. I'll call Miriam and ask her opinion, and then we'll go from there. I promise.* He had no idea who he was making the promise to, but it felt suspiciously like he was justifying his own actions for his own peace of mind.

Looking at Andrew's anxious face, Bruce decided to tell him only what he needed to know, and *only* that until he knew with absolute certainty. He spoke as calmly as he could. "The lab work I ordered is primarily a CBC or Complete Blood Count. Once we have the results of that in...oh, say a week or so, I'll be able to eliminate some of the underlying causes for your symptoms. The fact that I found several swollen lymph nodes does seem to indicate that you have an infection somewhere in your body. The other tests I ordered are going to give me more details on what kind of infection we're dealing with, and hopefully a course of action." That was more or less the truth, but even Bruce was smart enough to know that deliberately withholding information from a patient—much less a good friend like Andrew—was still tantamount to lying.

Andrew nodded slowly at Bruce's explanation. He appreciated the fact that he didn't feel the need to infuse the conversation with medical terminology and jargon that would leave his head spinning, but he also knew that he was holding something back. Call it a hunch or just careful observation, but the set of his shoulders and the way that his eyes flicked restlessly around the room were raising alarm bells in his mind. Bruce sat there staring at everything but his face with polite, calm professionalism.

Andrew wasn't buying it.

"Bruce, level with me. It's bad isn't it? There's something wrong with me that is more serious than an infection, and you being the professional that you are, don't want to send me into a panic."

Bruce flinched slightly, but he quickly regained his composure. He knew that the longer the silence stretched out the deeper Andrew's suspicion would grow.

"Okay," he shifted his weight so that he was leaning forward almost conspiratorially. "I'll level with you because you're my friend and you had my back during more than a few drunken brawls during my younger years, but I don't want you to get worked up over something that may turn out to be nothing. Yes, the swollen lymph nodes coupled with all your other symptoms are a bit...concerning." He said each syllable carefully as if he wanted to make sure that Andrew didn't misinterpret what he was getting at. "The majority of the blood work is just for my own peace of mind, *and* yours," he said pointedly when Andrew pulled out the lining of his pockets to show how empty they were. "The best I can tell you is that it may turn out to be something either really bad, something that can be treated with prescription drugs, or it may be nothing at all. Until I have the report in my hands, I can't—I *won't*—cause you unnecessary anxiety, alright?"

The last word held a note of pleading to it, but Andrew wasn't about to press his luck or his friend's ethics just for his own benefit. It was enough that he was being completely honest and candid with him. He nodded and then slid down from the examining table. "So we'll catch a few beers after work?"

"Wouldn't miss it." And then on the heels of that: "Thanks, Andy."

A moment of silent understanding passed between them and then Andrew headed out into the receptionist's area to settle his bill.

Bruce bade Andrew goodbye with a final reassurance that everything was fine and that there was no reason to worry. His voice, expression, and mannerisms were entirely convincing, but his conscience wasn't buying it. He knew enough about chronic and life-threatening ailments to recognize the symptoms when he saw them, and Andrew was exhibiting one too many of them for comfort. The results of the physical and the noticeable wasting away all pointed towards bad news, and the lab work would reveal exactly how bad it was. Bruce didn't have enough extensive training to know exactly what to test for, but his colleague, Dr. Miriam Torres—one of the eminent oncologists in the city—would be more than capable of filling in the blanks.

As soon as he and Andrew parted ways, he hurried to his office and shut the door behind him. He dialed her cell number from memory and listened as the phone rang twice before being picked up.

"I should have known that on my *one* day off, that someone would buzz me to shoot the shit."

Bruce grinned. "My, aren't we chipper this morning?" He knew that the comment never failed to put a smile on her face, and for the first time in years, he missed not being there to see it. Years ago they had completed their residency together and had spent many long hours keeping the other awake—and sane— while making their rounds. The comment had quickly become the standard greeting between them each day when bleary-eyed and bone-tired, they managed to drag themselves towards the resident's sleeping quarters. No matter what the previous day had thrown their way, the one thing that they could look forward to was a brief moment of levity each morning. For residents, camaraderie and lightheartedness were almost as important as the critical training they received, and he and Miriam had hit it off with their extroverted personalities. They both appreciated the innate power of humor in serious situations, and firmly believed that laughter was the best medicine—for patients as well as physicians. They had dated briefly during this time, but they had both come to the conclusion that while they did share mutual interests—in this case the health and well being of others—that their dominant personalities tended to get in the way of things. They were both strong willed, confident, intelligent, and fiercely competitive. Their relationship had inevitably boiled down to simple science. Given that two dominant forces were bound to repel each other at some point, one could relent and thus terminate the opposition, or they could both refuse to budge and risk destroying one another. The decision to break up had been mutual, but their professional relationship had managed to survive intact. They were still on friendly terms and he frequently consulted her when he felt he had a patient that could benefit from her expertise.

She scoffed and he could almost envision her rolling her eyes. "Cut the crap, Bruce. I've been on my feet for seven weeks straight and I have some serious sleeping to catch up on." A massive yawn erupted on the other end of the phone. "Besides," she continued once the yawning had subsided, "shouldn't you be visiting with your patients? You know, dispensing meds and dispelling doubts, that kind of thing?"

"Actually, that's why I'm calling. I need some advice on a patient."

He heard movement on the other end and her voice sounded alert and awake. "Tell me everything—every symptom, every observation, no matter how minute." It was remarkable how quickly the calm professionalism could rise to the occasion, and he was convinced—not for the first or the hundredth time—why she was one of the city's best.

She listened in silence as Bruce described Andrew's symptoms and the results of the initial physical. He wracked his brain for every available detail. God forbid he over look something that could potentially jeopardize his friend's health.

After a space of heartbeats her voice came slow and measured over the phone. "I can see why you called me, and I'm glad that you did. If anything can be said about you Bruce—other than you're nearly as good as I am in the sarcasm department—is that your instincts are never wrong."

Bruce knew that the attempt at humor was for his own benefit, but he suddenly didn't feel like laughing. The situation had gotten progressively serious and he steeled himself for what he knew was coming next.

"I can tell by how quiet you are that you know what I'm about to say, and as much as I hate to be the bearer of bad news, it kind of goes with my job."

"That makes two of us."

Miriam nodded silently on the other end. Based on the symptoms that Bruce had described, the patient in question wasn't suffering from stress or any of its side effects, but from something far more serious. She could provide him with a list of possible suspects as well as a criterion of tests to perform, and she could even provide him with a rough estimate of how long this patient had to live depending on their results, but providing comfort was the one thing that was beyond her. Without the lab results, or for that matter, a second opinion, it was still too early to make any definite determination, but being prepared seemed like a good idea in any situation.

It was obvious from his tone and uncharacteristic silence on the subject that the case in question hit close to home. For all she knew it could be a friend or family member, but seeing as how he wasn't scrambling to volunteer the information, she wasn't going to push him for it.

She quickly dictated an extensive list of tests to run, and just for good measure even threw in a worst-case-scenario timeline. The patient could be suffering from leukemia based on the symptoms, and she gave him an annotated rundown of the stages, treatment options, and prognoses.

The only sound to punctuate the sound of her voice was the quick scratching of his pen on the other end of the phone. She heard him sigh wearily.

"Thanks, Miriam. I owe you one. You get back to your rest now."

"And I'll take two aspirin and call you in the morning." This was an old joke that the two of them shared, but today it felt strangely inappropriate.

He chuckled slightly. "Take care."

"You too," she said as the phone was abruptly hung up. She gently set the phone back on the nightstand and let her hands rest limply on the bedspread. She was bone-tired, but there was no way she was going to be able to get back to sleep. She didn't need to have a lab report in her hands to know that Bruce's patient was truly sick. The symptoms alone spoke volumes, and try as she might, she couldn't shake the feeling of trepidation away. She had never met this person, but for Bruce to contact her on her private line during his office hours meant that the case was personal in nature. There was a chance—a slim chance—that perhaps the symptoms being displayed were mimicking something less serious or life-threatening. She knew enough from experience however to not put all her hopes on this possibility. Life was seldom that forgiving or merciful, because if it were she would effectively be out of a job. She hated to have to tell someone in so many words that things didn't look good for their friends or loved ones, especially when it was so early in the morning.

She glanced at the bedside clock. Not quite 10:00 a.m. At this rate there was no telling what the rest of her day would turn out to be like.

She swung her feet out of bed and padded silently down the hall towards the bathroom. She pushed the nagging feeling of guilt away as she turned on the faucets and began running a hot bath. Bruce was her friend and he deserved to know the truth, no matter how much it may hurt. Sugar-coating was never one of her strong suits, and she preferred honesty and candidness to half-truths and wishful thinking.

*Better to prepare for the worst and hope for the best*, she'd always said, and while she wasn't sure if Bruce's friend would appreciate the logic or not, she hoped that everything worked itself out for the best.

"I'm going to run these down to the lab. Hold all my calls."

The receptionist glanced up from her computer screen. Dr. Ackerman hardly ever delivered specimens to the lab himself, and there was just the faintest bit of strain around his eyes as he spoke. His friend Andrew had just left the office minutes before, and she wondered if this latest visit was the cause of the good doctor's anxiety. She glanced at the plastic carousel filled with blood samples and then remembered that the crook of Andrew's left arm had been bandaged when he left. Her mind put two and two together, but she kept her expression polite and professional. "Yes, doctor."

Dr. Ackerman passed through the large set of double doors that separated the examining rooms from the diagnostic and imaging facilities. Several of his colleagues waved in greeting as he passed. He waved back, the gesture automatic and wooden, and then he pushed open the door to the lab. The sterile atmosphere hit him full force and he felt the knot in his stomach grow in intensity. More than a few times he had hand-delivered specimens that required immediate attention, and as Miriam had so accurately pointed out, his instincts were never wrong. He knew subconsciously that the favor he was about to ask was a blatant abuse of his medical authority, but his conscience didn't give a damn. This was his friend, and friends took precedence over everything else.

The lab technician looked up from the slides that he had been examining and smiled in greeting. "Dr. Ackerman! Feel like hanging out with us grunts today, huh?"

It was an old joke around the facility that "grunts" denoted all the technicians who ran the labs and reported the results back to the physicians, who then garnered all the glory.

Dr. Ackerman set the plastic carousel down on the counter. The technician eyed it speculatively and then glanced up at him.

"Frank, I need a favor." Dr. Ackerman fidgeted slightly as if he didn't quite know how to proceed.

Frank knew what he was asking him to do even if Dr. Ackerman didn't know how to say it himself. He held up his hand for silence. "Consider it done. What do you want me to check for specifically?"

Dr. Ackerman heaved a sigh of relief and smiled at him gratefully. Good friends and reliable colleagues were a rare thing these days, but to have a reliable colleague who was a good friend who didn't ask too many questions? Now *there* was something you couldn't put a price on.

"I have my suspicions about what is troubling this particular patient," he motioned towards the vials on the counter, "and I think that it would be a good idea to look at the thrombocytes and white blood cell count as well as a few other things."

Frank grabbed an old take-out menu that lay under a pile of printouts and began to scribble down the lengthy list that Dr. Ackerman dictated to him. He laid his pen down when he finished speaking. "You think that this patient may have leukemia?"

"The symptoms and the results of the physical I just conducted seem to point in that direction, but I'd rather be 100% sure before I tell him to start making arrangements."

Frank nodded. "I'll get started on it right away. With any luck I should have the results in a week, ten days tops."

Dr. Ackerman thanked him and attempted to make some small talk before leaving. It just didn't seem right to waltz in with such a tall order and then not even give the technician the time of day. The conversation was awkward and lacked the characteristic humor that Dr. Ackerman usually brought to it, and before long he announced that he had to get back to his office and the room full of patients that awaited him.

Frank turned back to the slide that he had been examining, jotted down a few more notes, and then pushed his chair back from the table. He pulled the first vial out of the carousel and began prepping it for analysis. Dr. Ackerman was rarely off the mark when it came to such diagnoses, but he sincerely hoped that this time the good doctor was wrong.

# Chapter 5

The days passed quickly, each one blending seamlessly into the next. I stepped up my nightly patrols in the alleyways in and around where my latest kill had taken place, but there was no activity, no sign that anything was amiss in the city. The only sound I heard in the darkened spaces were my own footfalls echoing around me, and the only vampire that I encountered stared out at me from my own reflection. I kept up my patrols religiously despite the relative lack of activity, convinced that the uncanny silence that followed the latest death was merely a prelude to a much bigger confrontation, the proverbial calm before the storm. So I waited and watched, watched and waited....

He liked to watch her, liked to see her emerge from her apartment night after night looking so human, so normal. She may have been able to fool the rest of the people she encountered, but not him—he had seen what she could do and knew her for what she was. His mistress had entrusted him to spy on her because of this knowledge, and was counting on him to learn more about her.

So far, the fruits of his labors had been productive.

Every night around 8:30 p.m. she left the confines of her fourth-story apartment and walked across the parking lot towards her car. After conspicuously readjusting the sheath containing the knives around her waist, she glanced around her to make sure that the coast was clear and then got behind the wheel.

After slowly pulling out and entering the street that ran parallel to the complex, she gradually picked up speed and then headed out towards the neighborhood close to where his mistress resided. Slowly, carefully so as not to arouse suspicion, she pulled the car over onto a street running beside the alleyway and turned off the ignition. She would sit there for a brief moment—whether to collect her thoughts or otherwise—before stepping out into the street. She would stand there with her back to the car scanning the area around her before heading off in the opposite direction. She walked casually, humanlike, as if she didn't have a care in the world. Nothing about her appearance or behavior gave any indication as to her motives for being there, but he knew better.

The grin widened as he realized that he was stalking her much like she stalked his mistress and her children. She was no more aware of his presence than the other inhabitants of the city, and it sent a ripple of excitement through his body. For nearly a week the pattern had held steady and he felt confident in taking the next step. He would enter her residence tomorrow when she left for the evening to see if there was anything else to be learned from her. So far, she had been entirely predictable. While he doubted that she could throw any more surprises his way, there was always hope.

# Chapter 6

Darnell was so anxious to tell his mistress everything that he had learned about the mysterious woman that he felt as if he were going to fly out of his own skin. The two bodyguards led him into the room once again, only this time there was a distinct absence of fear or anxiety. The divan that had been there on previous occasions was gone, and she stood in solitary splendor in the center of the room. The three men stood at a respectful distance behind her, neither of them saying a word.

She took a step forward and gestured towards him. "I trust you have news for me."

The way she pitched her voice made it seem more of a statement than a question. He hurriedly dropped to one knee.

The words tumbled out as he revealed to her in breathless detail everything that he had witnessed that week. Every night at precisely the same time, the woman would leave her apartment and drive to an area very close to where they now stood. She would then patrol up and down the streets and back alleyways looking for others of her kind. This pattern never deviated, and he felt confident in taking a more proactive approach to his task. He explained that on the seventh day of his vigil, the woman left to make her scheduled evening patrol around the city, and he knew that he had a few hours to enter her home and look around. The moment she exited the building he scaled the fire escape up to her fourth-story apartment, entered through the window which she had carelessly left open and wondered about leisurely, scanning the tiny room for anything that might be of use. On the battered coffee table lay six month's worth of back issues of the local paper, as well as a few independent publications. Several articles on gruesome, unsolved murders and missing persons had been highlighted or clipped out entirely, and were categorized in neatly-labeled manila folders. Many of the folders had hand-written notes on the covers, most of it speculation as to whom or *what* was behind the killings or abductions. A detailed map of the city was tacked to the wall nearest the window and had several pins marking locations on it. The pins were centered in the exact same neighborhood where they now stood, and each one was labeled neatly with a date. The most recent date was from the night that Reggie had met his untimely end, and the location matched where he had died.

He glanced up cautiously as he said this, and she smiled a slow, secretive smile. His heart filled with a level of hope that it had never dared experience before. His mistress had shown more kindness to him than anyone else in his life, but more importantly, she accepted and trusted him. She had trusted him with the knowledge of what she and her other children were, and she had trusted him to go about his business without any fear of what he would do with that knowledge. More than that, she had entrusted him with such an important task, and he had gone above and beyond to repay the favor. Not once in the few weeks since he had come to know her did she ever patronize him. Not once did she ever ignore him or make him feel that he was worthless or a burden. That was more than he could say for his old man, and she wasn't even human! Logic dictated that such a being wouldn't feel the need to bother with such volatile human emotions, but not her. She was something extraordinary that had come into his life, and he almost felt sorry for others like him who weren't fortunate enough to have known her.

When he was through speaking, she nodded her head and then took her three most trusted progeny aside and whispered in their ears. He looked on slightly confused and apprehensive. Did this mean that she was pleased with him and was going to reward him soon? He received his answer when she sent them away and knelt beside him on the floor.

For a moment he was too stunned to even realize what was happening, because the fact that she knelt before *him* was somewhat startling.

She took his face in her hands and gazed into his eyes. For the first time since he had met her he gazed back at her levelly. They stood frozen in that position for what could have been hours but what must have only been a few moments at most.

She smiled knowingly. "Yes," she whispered, and her breath ghosted lightly over his skin, "you *are* a worthy companion."

He watched wordlessly as she drew her right index finger above the swell of her left breast and the blood welled out in a dark flood. Her hands stayed frozen around his face as if she were waiting for him to make his choice.

He hesitated only a second before his head descended in a predatory swipe. As his lips latched around the gaping wound, she cried out in a mixture of pain and triumph. She cradled him against her as he drank until he was full to bursting, but still he hungered for her, hungered for the undeniable pull of her life force that saturated every drop. He could feel her pulse hammering through the wound as his tongue probed the edges, and she gasped and pulled him closer, crushing him against her. The perfume of her skin and the softness of her limbs were maddening, and he allowed himself to drown in her essence. He pulled on the wound harder and harder until her nails raked down the small of his back as she shuddered, and then she lay limp and pliant in his arms.

All at once the world seemed to tilt and the colors of the room swam before his eyes in dizzying, frightening streaks.

He found himself twisting away from her in a panic, and he screamed helplessly as his body began to contort and writhe of its own volition. It felt as if his bones were attempting to realign themselves beneath the flesh, and he clawed at himself in a frenzy. Small, helpless sounds punctuated the eerie silence of the room, and he was dimly aware that they were coming from him. He lay on the dusty floor with his back arched at an impossible angle as yet another wave of agony washed over him. The pain ebbed suddenly without warning, and his head lolled to the side as he collapsed in a heap. A mixture of relief and exhaustion washed over him like he had never experienced before, and as his eyes began to slowly focus on the room, he saw that she was still kneeling beside him.

She was surrounded by a strange, hazy film that alternated between shades of red and gold. Her expression was almost beatific in its sereneness, but there was just the slightest hint of pain around the eyes. Her hands hovered above the still-bleeding wound as if they were reluctant to stop the flow. He wanted to comfort and hold her, this lovely, mysterious creature who had shared something of hers more intimate than sex. He tentatively raised his right arm in a supplicating gesture, and as his own arm came into focus, he saw that it was surrounded by the same red-gold film. The twin films seemed to meld into one another and rippled and shimmered in sync with their breathing. As his vision swam with the colors that radiated out from them, the film began to shrink until it was cleaved to the outlines of their bodies. All at once it began to dwindle away to a single crimson strand that stretched between them like an umbilical cord. His mistress shuddered and clutched at the strand, stroking it lovingly. Every hair on his body stood up at attention as the sensation coursed down the length of the strand and caressed his skin. It felt as if millions of tiny fingertips were running up and down every inch of his body, and he tilted his head to the side and moaned in pleasure.

A slow, devious smile spread across her face and she opened her eyes and gazed at him possessively. He felt as if everything that had ever been denied to him in life was right there for the taking, but before he could rejoice in this realization, a wail ripped its way out of his body as the pain returned with violent, agonizing force. His vision went red and then he was spiraling down into crushing darkness, to a place mercifully devoid of all sensation. A high, keening laughter followed him down as consciousness eluded him and then he knew no more.

He awoke suddenly in a strange bed in a room that he had never been in before. The pain was gone and he was curiously aware of how still everything was around him, of how *silent* his body was. He took a tentative breath and then let it out.

The pain was completely gone.

The memory of what had recently transpired prompted him to look at his hands, and when he held them up in front of his face, all trace of the bizarre film was gone. He sat up and laid his palm on his chest. His heart still beat, but it was slower and more rhythmic. His skin felt relatively warm and as far as he could tell, his appearance hadn't significantly changed. The momentary disappointment he felt over this vanished as soon as he flexed his fingers around the cast-iron frame of the bed he was on. The metal groaned under his touch and when he pulled his hand back, there was a slight indentation in the railing.

The three men who always accompanied his mistress entered the room at that moment and said that there was work that had to be done. He could experiment with his new strength later.

He followed them obediently and joined the small assemblage of others like him, her chosen companions. They were silent as they followed the three men out of the house and into a battered gray van parked along the curb. They drove down the streets that led to the heart of downtown in complete silence, stopping only when they came to a relatively secluded street. They walked for a long time before the three men signaled for them to stop. A young couple was coming down the sidewalk towards them, their voices ringing unnaturally loud in the empty street.

The three men turned and smiled in unison, and for the first time their features were plainly evident in the dim light reflected from the streetlamps: they were identical, triplets.

Darnell saw then what had previously been hidden from him before in the confines of the drawing room, and he suddenly understood the seemingly odd and undeniable connection the three seemed to share.

The one on the right informed them that they were under strict orders to abduct two people and bring them back to their mistress. The woman who had been hunting her children—he made a sweeping motion towards the group and a few snarled in fury—seemed to have a soft spot for the innocent, and made it a habit of dispatching those who threatened their livelihood. The most important tool in her arsenal against such activities seemed to be the media, or more specifically the local papers, which she frequently scanned for signs of activity.

Darnell felt himself puff up with pride as the fruits of his labors were revealed to the group.

Their mistress had devised a plan to draw out this woman by committing a murder so brutal and so heinous that it would be splashed on the front page of every major and independent publication. This way the woman would be sure to notice it, and she would begin her search for the culprits on or near the location where the bodies had been discovered. To ensure that she followed this line of thinking, the bodies would be dumped in and around where Reggie had met his apparent end. The connection between the two events would therefore be undeniable.

The man smiled, revealing straight, perfect teeth that gleamed in the darkness. When that happened, he promised darkly, *they* would be waiting for her.

Darnell was dully impressed with the logic behind this little adventure. It was only afterwards that a few of the others admitted that they had some reservations about what they had done and what it would mean if the woman *did* find them. Would their mistress fight to protect them as she did the rest of her children? Perhaps the most burning question of all was why any of them had been brought over in the first place. From what little they did know about their mistress, she was at least a century or older and was powerful enough to have garnered control of the city. It stood to reason that because of this power, she could choose whomever she wanted to stand by her side throughout eternity, so why choose them? What could they possibly offer someone like her in return for such a gift? Neither of them had an answer to this, and suspicion and speculation ran rampant throughout.

Darnell felt confused. Surely their mistress had brought them over because she felt that they were worthy companions, not because she had some dark, ulterior motive. She was beyond such petty human emotions, and as far as he could see, she had no reason to screw any of them over. She had given them eternity—they should be grateful for that.

They shook their heads and pressed closer together, insisting that there was more going on than he was aware of. To convince him of this, they brought up an interesting point: if their mistress considered them equals with her other children, why then did they never leave her sight? These children didn't hunt the city as he and the newest ones did, and they never set foot outside the house. It just seemed like a massive coincidence that they were all brought into the fold just as the woman began hunting them down. They were mere pawns they insisted, expendable muscle that would be destroyed once the danger had passed and there was no longer any use for them. The fact that they were the ones charged with finding the woman proved it.

Darnell found himself considering these observations but stopped himself. No, his mistress would never allow harm to come to any of them. She had chosen them to be her companions, had chosen *him*. He just couldn't believe that what they had shared earlier in the evening had been a lie. She had approached him and welcomed him into the fold with open arms, had opened a vein and fed him the blood of eternal life—*her* blood. He was as much her child as the rest of them were, and no amount of speculation would convince him otherwise. He may be young and relatively inexperienced, but he *was* useful. No one had ever treated him as anything but a lost cause, but his mistress *believed* in him.

And for him that was enough.

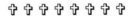

Her eyes glittered triumphantly as she watched the group disappear down the street from the house. Darnell seemed to be taking to his new nature and the task that she had given him just fine, and the energy that she had invested in his creation was dully justified.

Just then her vision swam out of focus and she gripped the ancient windowsill for balance. Her heart thudded painfully in her chest and the still-bleeding wound throbbed in unison. She closed her eyes and took a few calming breaths, but the sensation of falling did not subside. She barely managed to sink down into the ornately carved chair before her legs collapsed out from under her, and when she tried to sit up but her head lolled awkwardly on her shoulders. Despite the pain and disorientation, she knew that the debilitating weakness would eventually subside. Her sons and the newest progeny would have to feed soon, and she would be able to siphon energy from them as they did this. Being a Font definitely had an upside, but as she also knew, being a Font had a downside as well.

Some part of her knew that it had been foolish to create another progeny so soon after the death of five of her children. Darnell had proven himself more than worthy before, and she was confident that he would continue to be useful—in any capacity she chose. The theatricality behind his transference had been wholly unnecessary, but as she saw it, it was a means to an end. She had long recognized the look of pure adoration on his face whenever she spoke to him, and she decided that as long as she lived up to his perceptions of her as some sort of benevolent sponsor, that he would do anything and everything that she asked of him.

She smiled despite the pain. The men in this century were far more indiscriminate when it came to being charmed by a woman. In centuries past, things like one's wealth and upbringing were what it took to enchant them; nowadays, all they needed was a pretty face and a hint of a bosom.

She had been considerably more generous in his creation than with the other newest progeny as a result of this, and she was now feeling the effects. If any more of her children—either the oldest or the newest additions—were to die, she might not be able to shake the feebleness as easily as she had done on prior occasions. The sheer determination and strength of will which had served her so faithfully over the past two centuries had its limits, which made dispatching the woman imperative. The plan she had set in motion would ensure that the two of them would meet. One way or another victory would be hers, and only one of them would walk away from the inevitable confrontation.

# Chapter 7

Andrew sat on the examining table feeling like the world had suddenly opened up in front of him. One false move in either direction would spend him spiraling downward, and there wasn't a damn thing he could do about it. The nagging little voice in his head that had shown up weeks ago reached a fever-pitch, and was mercilessly taunting him. *Told you so, told you so, told you so. . ..*

*Shut up, shut up, SHUT UP!*

Bruce sat on his stool over by the cabinets and was trying his best to appear calm and reassuring.

It wasn't working.

The longer Andrew sat there saying nothing, the more anxious he was becoming. He tried not to fidget with the papers on the clipboard and forced his feet to remain still. Finally he'd had enough.

"Say something, Andy."

Andrew scoffed and ran his hand up through his hair. "What do you want me to say? That I can't believe this is happening to me? That I'm only twenty-six years old and can't possibly be suffering from something like this? What, Bruce? What could I *possibly* say that will make any of this better?"

Bruce had had a similar reaction when he had first received the results of Andrew's lab work the day before. The lab had confirmed his fears that Andrew was suffering from something far more serious than a recurrent infection or prolonged stress, and while it *did* validate his decision to consult with Dr. Torres about his suspicions, it came as small comfort. Nevertheless, he was determined that his friend would not sink down into despair even if he had to force him to see reason. No way was Andrew going to give up now when the battle had only just begun.

Time for some tough love.

Bruce stood up from the stool with enough force to send it skittering backwards, and his voice trembled with just the slightest trace of anger. "You could say that you're not going to give up, that's what you could say. More importantly, you can get rid of the defeatist attitude and listen to the rest of what I have to say before you decide to lay down and die."

He swore and whirled to face the counter. "Look, Andy," his voice was softer now. "I realize that this is somewhat of a shock for you. I understand that you're freaked out of your mind right now, but for God's sake do not—*do not*—give up on me. You hear me? I hate to be the one to have to come down on you like some sort of hard-ass, but the worst thing you can do right now is give up and give into despair. That's an automatic death sentence no matter what you're suffering from. No one deserves to go through this—not even that asshole of a boss you have, or Gary your co-worker for that matter—but it happens."

He set the clipboard down and leaned his weight on the counter. "I know things seem pretty bleak right now, but trust me when I tell you that there *is* hope. I've taken the liberty of consulting with a colleague of mine, a Dr. Miriam Torres who's an expert on oncology. She says that while your symptoms and lab work— the depressed levels of platelets and red blood cells, the elevated lymphocytes, unusual bruising and enlarged liver— *do* point in the direction of some type of leukemia, it is possible to treat it. It all depends on how early you are diagnosed and the treatment options you pursue, but more than anything else, it depends on your outlook. If you go into this with a 'woe is me, all is lost' attitude, then you're looking at a self-fulfilling prophecy. Dr. Torres has agreed to take you on despite the short notice, not only because you're my friend, but because she's one of the few decent people left on this planet. She does need to perform an analysis on your bone marrow to determine exactly what type of leukemia if any you are suffering from, and the earliest she can do this is Tuesday of next week. I'll be honest with you—it's not something I would want to go through myself, but it's the only way we'll get a clear picture of what's ailing you. It's your choice how you want to pursue this. I hope that whatever you decide, that you also realize your life *is* worth fighting for regardless of what's happened or is happening in it lately." His breath gusted out in a loud exhalation of air and his fingers drummed against the edge of the counter. It wasn't easy playing the role of Doctor and Friend all at the same time, but he had given it his best shot. He was a lousy speaker when it came to pep talks, but honesty was the one tool in his limited arsenal that he could depend on. Lack of bedside manner or not, it was better than nothing.

*Your life* is *worth fighting for regardless of what's happened or is happening in it lately.* Andrew sat there weighing the worth of his friend's words against the all-consuming panic that beat a frantic counter rhythm to his heart. Bruce stood there staring down at him waiting for him to respond. The look of raw panic in his eyes was plainly evident, and as the seconds continued to tick by, the look intensified. Pushing back his own urge to run screaming from the room, Andrew considered what his friend must be going through. As his physician, perhaps Bruce could afford to take a detached view of the diagnosis, but as his friend, that was a luxury he could not indulge in. Guilt over this added to the maelstrom of emotions roiling and heaving within him, and he hung his head in equal parts of shame and weariness.

Staring down at the toes of his shoes—shoes recently purchased with money earned from his job—Andrew felt slightly disgusted at his behavior. True, the diagnosis had effectively blindsided him, but in the larger scheme of things there were people out there who had far worse things happening in their lives. He had a job, received a paycheck each month, and had a roof over his head with food on the table. Never mind that his boss was overbearing and abusive of his staff, or that his apartment was little bigger than this examining room—all of these were inconsequential details. With the economy in the toilet like it was these days, he had no right to bitch and moan. People had lost their entire life savings, had lost their homes, their livelihood, and here he was seeing things as half-empty.

He knew that the root cause of all his anxiety was the possibility that he may be dying. He had never once considered the possibility of his own mortality, had never considered the possibility that perhaps he was fallible. He was twenty-six years old—no twenty-six year old ever really considers the possibility of their own death. In the modern age where death was continually kept at bay by prescription drugs, innovative technology, and an innate knowledge of the human body that previous ages could never conceive of, death had no place in the minds of the populace. It was only until the possibility of a terminal illness entered the picture that things were different. It was only when the possibility of death entered the picture that any allusions to perpetual youth and health vanished into obscurity.

Staring at Bruce's anxious face as the silence continued to stretch out, Andrew knew that his own feelings would have to take a backseat to those of his friend. He couldn't let Bruce worry at the situation like a dog with a bone—like he knew he would. The inability to let anything go without picking it to pieces had gotten him through medical school as surely as his intelligence and drive to help others did. He had to say something to convince him otherwise. He didn't know how long he could keep the anxiety at bay, but he was fairly sure that a definitive diagnosis would smash any illusions of normalcy to smithereens.

He sighed and ran his hand up through his hair again and then shifted his weight on the examining table. "You do know that my boss is going to have fits about me taking off another day for personal reasons, right?"

Bruce nearly collapsed against the cabinets with relief. For a minute there it looked as if his friend was about to plunge headlong into the abyss, and he had little to no idea how to drag Andy away from the edge.

Whatever he'd said or done had apparently done the trick.

He smiled and turned to face his friend. "If he does, tell him he's a self-righteous, sanctimonious bastard. I'd be happy to write it up on my prescription pad too. Seeing *is* believing, you know."

"Bob Garrett wouldn't know the truth if it came up and bit him on the ass—you should know that after reading the trash that he insists on printing."

They both laughed.

Andrew scoffed and felt himself starting to feel better. "I don't know how you do it Bruce. One minute I'm convinced that my life is for all intents and purposes over, you more or less berate me for feeling sorry for myself, crack a joke at my boss' expense, and then I'm back to my old self again."

"It's one of my many talents." He clapped Andrew good-naturedly on the back. "So it's safe to say that your appointment next week with Dr. Torres is a go, then? She's one of the best in her respective field, not to mention a half-way decent person." He grinned. "We used to give each other hell during our residency, but she's a good sport. She's the only one to ever beat me in an arm-wrestling contest over who gets the last donut in the box."

"That's definitely an incentive to meet with her then." Andrew suddenly grew serious. "Bruce, you're certain that I'm just overreacting and that this may still turn out to be nothing? That even though it may turn out to be leukemia like you and Dr. Torres suspect, that it *can* be managed?"

It was impossible to promise such a thing given the unpredictability and utter randomness of life at times, but rather than rub salt in a wound still fresh and bleeding, Bruce decided to go for ambiguity. "Dr. Torres is very good at what she does, Andy. I promise that whatever your results are that she will do her best to get you on the road to recovery."

Some part of him loathed the deception in that statement, but another part felt justified. It wasn't a blatant lie, but it wasn't exactly the truth either. Only time would prove the extent of the truth and deception.

# Chapter 8

"Hey, Andaaaay!"

Andrew groaned under his breath as Gary Simms noticed him coming through the front doors of *Elysium's* headquarters. He resisted the urge to flip him off and settled for cursing the miserable wretch under his breath. He was generally an easy-going sort of person, but Gary and his holier-than-thou attitude set his teeth on edge. His stories invariably made the front page of each issue even though it was the collective opinion around the office that they weren't worth the paper they were printed on. Bob Garrett—who may have been many things according to his employees—was anything but stupid, and there was no denying that crappy reporting aside, sales had a tendency to increase when this formula was applied. Andrew had tried for years to rationalize their friendship, but he had ultimately come to the conclusion that like attracted like. They were both self-centered egomaniacs, so it did make a certain amount of sense that they gravitated to one another.

Gary was sandwiched between Mrs. Azumi and another man whose name evaded him. Was it Dave? Derrick? Andrew decided it really didn't matter one way or the other and headed towards the group. They were all crowded around the office's lone television screen that had been set up on a little cart with wheels. The ancient v.c.r. had been hooked up and one of the employees pressed the Play button on the remote. The screen sputtered to life as the film started—a report by the looks of things that had undoubtedly been taped off the evening news—and the assembled parties settled into their seats. The picture quality on the t.v. was sub-par and faded in and out, crackling and flickering sporadically. Mrs. Azumi stood up and whacked the side of the set with the palm of her hand, and the image flickered in and out of focus before righting itself. A small chorus of cheers erupted from the assembled party and Gary grinned up at her as she sat back down.

"I had no idea you knew Karate"—he stretched out the syllables until it sounded more like *Karatay*—"I love a woman who can hold her own. What are you doing Friday night?"

Mrs. Azumi, who had been happily married for over thirty-years and was old enough to be Gary's mother, didn't miss a beat. "I'll be practicing my Kung Fu Death Punch. It's an ancient Japanese technique specifically designed to disable annoying, self-absorbed assholes who can't take no for an answer."

Mrs. Azumi had been born and raised in the United States and had evidently had enough of Gary's ethnic stereotyping and relentless flirting. She turned her chair around until Gary was left staring at her back. As Andrew sat down in the empty chair behind him he turned and whispered behind his hand, "Ooh, feisty."

Mrs. Azumi said something sharp and clenched her hand into a fist. Andrew found himself wishing that Gary would continue to press his luck, and Death Punch or no, that Mrs. Azumi would knock him down a few pegs. Someone had to.

"So how'd the check up go? You dying or what?"

Apparently Gary lacked tact as well as ethnic sensitivity and any discernable morals. Andrew didn't feel like rehashing the events that had only recently transpired, so he decided to dodge the subject.

"What's all this?" He motioned towards the screen where a reporter was interviewing a uniformed police officer who kept speaking into the microphone in a dull monotone, answering each of the reporter's questions with one word answers. He didn't volunteer any extra information when pressed about the condition the bodies had been in when they were initially discovered, but the haunted look in his eyes spoke volumes—he was thoroughly and completely spooked. Something had rattled him to the point that he was practically jumping at shadows, and when the reporter thanked him for his cooperation, he hurried out of camera range as quick as his feet could carry him.

A grunt came from somewhere to Andrew's left. It was Dave/Derrick. "Well *that* was helpful," he snorted sarcastically. A few people mumbled assent. He got up from his seat and addressed the group. "I mean, how does Bob expect us to do a story on *that*? The only information we have is from the local news stations, but they're just as clueless and in the dark as the rest of us." There was more agreement, louder this time.

Gary merely sat there with an odd smile on his face. Andrew had seen that smile before and it usually meant that he was privy to information that no one else was. It was the same look he got when a particularly gruesome and sensational cover story was within his grasp.

Dave/Derrick continued. "I mean seriously, did you see the look on that guy's face when they asked him about the bodies? He looked like he'd seen a ghost or something. I don't know about the rest of you, but I'm betting it's bad. Real bad."

Several heads bobbed up and down in agreement and the conversation reached a fever pitch. Gary stood up. Everyone braced themselves for what was undoubtedly coming next.

"Well, I don't know about the rest of *you*," his eyes swept the group smugly, "but *I* am going to find out. I have a source down at the M.E.'s office that's been invaluable to me in the past, so if you'll excuse me," he paused dramatically for emphasis, "I'd best be on my way." He strode confidently towards the exit, his chin jutting out at a haughty angle.

Someone scoffed behind him. "A source down at the M.E.'s office? You don't mean that little creep that got arrested last year because he liked his job just a little *too* much, do you?" The voice belonged to Gerald Hynes, who had been working there for the past three years. He was an older gentleman who had worked at a professional, legitimate publication years ago, and he shared Andrew's belief that journalists owed a certain amount of responsibility towards their readers.

Gary turned and leaned casually against the exit until he was facing him. "No, this is a *different* source," he said in a voice dripping with condescension. "And might I add, that just because a man is clearly in need of professional help, it doesn't automatically mean that he's an unreliable source."

He turned and left the building with that remark hanging in the air. A smattering of catcalls and witty retorts ensued as the group broke up and headed towards their respective desks. Only Mrs. Azumi and Gerald Hynes remained seated around the television set, which continued to go in and out of focus. They appeared to be engaged in a deep and slightly-animated conversation— either about the ambiguous news report, or Gary's latest high jinks—and Andrew decided to join them. Mrs. Azumi smiled up at him as he sat next to her, and Gerald nodded in greeting.

"How did your appointment go? We all missed you at this morning's debriefing."

It was common knowledge around the office that he had been in and out of the doctor's office more than once over the last few months, but he had been decidedly guarded about the details. No one knew of the results of his CBC or the possibility that he had leukemia—a possibility he himself could still scarcely believe—and at the very least, were under the impression that he was being treated for something minor.

He shifted uncomfortably in the chair. The spot where the marrow had been extracted was beginning to ache despite the local anesthetic that had been applied, and he did his best to conceal his discomfort. Dr. Torres had clicked her tongue disapprovingly at him as he had insisted on returning to work right after the procedure. Bob Garrett was already up in arms over his having to be gone all the time for personal reasons, though exactly *why* Andrew didn't know. Bob never actually *liked* anything he wrote, so what was the big deal anyway? Andrew supposed that a control freak like Bob would naturally feel that way. After all, it's hard to control every aspect of a person's life if they're not there for you to observe and scrutinize. The fact that he was scheduled to meet with Bruce again to discuss the results of his most recent procedure would only make the situation worse.

He smiled politely. "Great. Right now everything looks fine." Best to keep it simple and to the point. The more information volunteered, the more questions said information could generate.

Mrs. Azumi patted him reassuringly on the arm. "I'm glad to hear it dear. I'm sure that whatever you've got going on will clear up in due time and that it's nothing to worry about."

Gerald made a small noise of apparent agreement and then they became silent for a moment. Andrew jumped at the opportunity to steer the subject away from his health to the news report and the morning briefing.

"So what did I miss this morning? Did Bob get on his soapbox about deadlines and profits, or did he do his usual thing and trash everybody's contributions?"

Gerald spoke up. "You're partially correct. Bob spent nearly twenty-minutes reminding all of us in not-so-subtle terms that the publication is in danger of going under." He snorted disdainfully. "Frankly, I'm surprised it's lasted this long. Bob's got his head so far up his own derriere that he hasn't bothered to notice that it's been limping along for the past three years. He should thank his lucky stars or whatever it is he has that it didn't crash and burn on impact. Other than that, he spent the remainder of the time praising Gary's piece on the alleged Chupacabra attacks across the border."

He and Mrs. Azumi rolled their eyes.

Gerald continued. "Needless to say, his ego inflated exponentially and he's been on a tear all day, as Mrs. Azumi can attest to."

Andrew had to carefully conceal a grin as her hands subconsciously balled up into fists, no doubt remembering her comment about the Kung Fu Death Punch.

Dave/Derrick sauntered casually up to them, his coffee mug clutched in one hand. He had evidently been on his way to the coffee machine when the sight of the assembled group caused him to take a detour. He sneered at the mention of Gary's name and then joined the conversation. "What'd you make of that crap-story the local cops are trying to sell the public about that murdered couple? Gary's articles actually make more sense then that guy did." He took a noisy swig from his mug and waited for his colleagues to respond.

Mrs. Azumi spoke up first. "It sure is a shame that that couple was murdered. They were so young." Her words trailed off as Andrew wracked his brain for anything concerning a murdered couple in the news recently. There had been plenty of unsolved homicides in the city lately, but try as he might, he couldn't seem to remember this particular case.

"Murdered couple? When did this happen?"

His three co-workers turned to stare at him, but it was Dave/Derrick who answered his question.

"Dude, where have you been? This story has been in the news for over a week now! Apparently this young couple was out for a night on the town last week, when they just up and vanished. No witnesses, no shady business dealings that would make them fake their own deaths, nada. They just disappear into thin air." He paused for emphasis, clearly enjoying his audience. "Two days ago the cops get a 911 call from a garbage man who's having hysterics. Apparently he found the missing couple, but what the media won't reveal is what caused him to freak out like he did. It's like I said earlier: something bad happened to them— something that goes above and beyond your average kidnapping and murder case."

Everyone was silent as they contemplated this newest development. Andrew vaguely recalled seeing something in the news a few days ago concerning the ongoing investigation, but his health and the stress of his job had made him less attentive to his surroundings.

"So how does *Elysium* factor into all this?" He gestured at the television screen that continued to blink in and out of focus.

Dave/Derrick drained the last of the coffee in his mug. "Well, you know *Bob*. He saw the story on the evening news and figured we could work it into this week's issue." He said it as if that explained everything, but Andrew knew that there was more to this investigation than just idle curiosity. Bob Garrett had the uncanny ability to smell a story even when there wasn't one. The unexplained disappearance of an apparently happy and carefree couple for nearly a week was no doubt troubling to the local authorities and their families, but once Bob got wind of it...well, there was no telling what twisted path the story would take.

Andrew nodded knowingly. "So what sort of spin was he hoping to put on this one?"

Dave/Derrick grinned. "Doomsday Cult Murders. Can you believe it? Like that hasn't been done a *million* times over. Either that or something similar to what happened to Oliver Larch or other people who just up and vanished without a trace. A 'rip in time,' he called it. 'Course when the bodies were discovered yesterday morning, it looked like those angles were sunk. That is until he got wind of all the secrecy concerning what state they were in, which everyone is being really tight-lipped over. Gary naturally offered to uncover the truth of this with the help of his *sources*"—he made a face before continuing—"so there's no telling what's gonna come of all this."

Andrew nodded again. He understood Bob and Gary's mutual enthusiasm about digging deeper into the case, which with any luck might dredge up some dirt or anything else that could be sensationalized for the sake of increasing sales.

"Such a pity."

Mrs. Azumi's comment broke through his reverie and Andrew shook his head to clear it. The conversation gradually dwindled away and the group scattered towards their respective work stations. Andrew scoffed at his co-workers' blasé attitude towards violent murder, trudged slowly towards his desk, and prepared to resume the week's work. Bob had assigned him a follow-up piece three days ago concerning the alleged alien abduction of a prominent politician's wife. She had been found in a seedy motel with a man nearly half her age and was claiming that the aliens must have done something to her, because quote, "she would *never* engage in such activities otherwise." This was ignoring the fact that she had been found in a similarly-compromising position four years ago, *before* her alleged abduction. The story was complete bull corn and the press was just eating it up by the spoonful. Bob Garrett had immediately jumped on the media bandwagon and had assigned it to him, insisting that it was "the biggest story of the year." It was big all right. A big waste of his time.

Andrew sat down heavily in his chair and stared balefully at the pile of notes waiting to be organized into something that Bob considered print-worthy. The spot at the back of his leg throbbed dully, but he ignored the pain. The cursor blinked and appeared to be counting down the seconds as he sat there with his hands poised above the keyboard, waiting for something to pop into his head. He began typing the introduction and then after skimming over it, erased it. He stared up at the large, black utilitarian-looking clock mounted above the bullpen, or at least the small rectangular room that passed for one.

11:34 a.m.

On the upside, he would be able to break for lunch in less than half an hour. On the downside, he wouldn't be able to clock out until another six hours had passed. He sighed and began retyping his introduction. Before long his brain kicked into high gear and the words started flowing onto the screen at a rapid pace, almost like magic. He smiled as he typed in the final words and sat back to admire his handiwork. It was a solid piece of journalism regardless of how absurd the subject matter was, and he felt confident that there was no possible way that Bob Garrett could thrash it.

He attached the two pages with a paper clip and headed towards Bob's office at the other end of the building.

His confidence in himself and in the inherent goodness of people was shattered a few minutes later.

"It's crap."

Andrew opened his mouth to protest, but Bob Garrett cut him off with an emphatic wave of his hand. "No excuses. Start over." He glared at Andrew pointedly and when he didn't immediately leave to obey the command, he crumpled the draft up and tossed it into the trash can next to his desk.

"Give me something useful I can print!" This parting shot was delivered as the door to Bob's office banged shut behind him. The attention of everyone in the bullpen had been riveted on the door as Andrew had entered. To them it was part spectator sport, part train wreck: you knew that a fiery crash was inevitable yet you couldn't quite seem to drag your eyes away from the carnage.

His co-workers quickly became interested in what was on their desks as he exited the office. There were a few tentative peeks as he made his way back to his workstation, but eventually they lost interest. There was always the hope that one of these days someone would either go into hysterics or threaten to blow the place and everything in it straight to Kingdom Come. So far the reactions had been limited to defeat or bitter resignation.

The office had been entertaining the idea of setting up a plaque outside Bob's door that read, "Abandon all hope ye who enter here," but they doubted that he would appreciate the humor. Based on the nearly-identical experiences that each and every staff member had undergone under Bob Garrett's unyielding scrutiny, the plaque seemed better suited above the entrance to the building instead.

# Chapter 9

"Gary."

"Jake."

Gary shook hands with the lanky man who leaned casually against the stone façade of the coffee house that had become their unofficial meeting place. Jake Arnold had been working at the Medical Examiner's office for just under three years, but he was a bevy of information. Gary often wondered how he acquired his information, but when it came down to useful facts or interesting tidbits that would make a good story, he honestly didn't care about the specifics. They had an unspoken agreement between them that summarized their partnership in so many words: ask and you shall receive. The exact details of how the answers to Gary's requests were obtained were of little consequence, and never entered the conversation.

Gary bounded up the short flight of concrete stairs that led to the entrance, and the man followed silently behind him. Gary chose a booth closest to the far end of the building. With its windowless walls, this section was considerably more private than the rest of the place. They skipped ordering at the counter and settled into their seats knowing that no one would bother them. At nearly noon on a Tuesday, the place—which catered more to the after-five crowd—was relatively empty.

Gary opened the yellow legal pad that he had brought with him and uncapped his pen. Jake had made two stipulations at their first meeting years before: he preferred cash, and he insisted that no electronic recording devices be used during their conversations. He seemed almost intensely paranoid that these tapes might find their way back to his employer, and he had made it plain that if he went down, so would Gary.

Gary respected Jake despite the overt threat, and when it came right down to it, he would have done the same thing if their positions had been switched.

Jake sat opposite him with his hands folded on the table, a small smile twitching at the corner of his lips. He liked an audience, and judging by the eager little glint in his eye, he had one hell of a gem for Gary today.

Gary made a notation of the day and time in the right-hand corner of the first sheet, and then produced a plain white envelope from the depths of his pockets. He pushed it silently across the table. Jake took it and placed it in the pocket of his jeans jacket. This was more or less a cue to begin, and he motioned towards the legal pad.

"You ready?"

Gary grinned. "I was born ready. I want to know everything, every grisly little detail. You did say that it was going to be grisly, right?"

To most people, the casual and almost callous way that his eyes lit up at the possibility that the unfortunate victims had died gruesomely would have been unnerving, but not to Jake. He got paid in cold, hard cash to deliver the goods—grisly details and all—and by golly, was he going to earn his keep today.

"Oh, no worries on that my man. The stuff I seen lately," he looked down at the palms of his hands, "I don't ever wanna see that again. I wouldn't doubt it if I have nightmares after this." He picked absently at a hangnail on his thumb and then continued. "The couple they brought in yesterday—they weren't just murdered, they were *butchered*."

Gary's pen stopped racing across the page. He glanced up at Jake and the grin widened. "'Butchered' as in cut up, or 'butchered' as in hacked to pieces?"

Jake shook his head slowly. "More like *ripped* apart by the looks of things. The ME can't quite figure out what was used to do this kind of damage, or for that matter who would want to, but I have my own theories." He leaned forward after glancing around conspiratorially. "One of the arms flopped out from under the sheet while I was wheeling the bodies down to cold storage, and as I went to put it back I noticed something odd." He paused and his eyes met Gary's. The lanky streetwise façade had been replaced by something else: fear.

Gary repressed the urge to shudder at the haunted look in his eyes and kept scribbling. This was definitely going to turn out to be a better story than he originally anticipated, but he knew that the best was yet to come.

Jake leaned in and his voice was barely a whisper. "There were fingerprints bruised into the skin. I could hardly believe it at first, but when I looked closer, sure enough, there were fingerprints—sometimes whole handprints—bruised all over their bodies. The ME noticed them too, but he didn't comment on them. My guess is that he was just as creeped out as I was by the whole thing, but I'll tell you something he did comment on—something that hasn't been leaked to the press—is that the victims seemed to have been killed at the same place that they were found at. From what I overheard, the blood spatter at the scene is consistent with that idea, but the weird thing is, they should have bled more than they did. I mean think about it: your average person has about two gallons of blood in their whole body, but the blood found at the scene was barely half of that, and we're talking about *two* people here. Something ain't right."

An idea had been blossoming in Gary's mind for some minutes, something so wildly fantastic that he didn't dare breathe a word of it until he was absolutely sure that he could make it stick. Never mind that it was totally asinine or implausible, if he could just mold the facts in this case to work in his favor, there was no limit to how these murders could be sensationalized—all for the sake of sales, of course. Another cover story to his credit would be mighty sweet, and he was sure that once he worked his magic this goal would be within his reach.

He looked down at his notes and read them back to Jake to make sure that he didn't miss anything that had the potential to break the story wide open. "So here's what we have so far: the victims vanished about a week ago, but their bodies weren't found until early Tuesday morning; second, they were ripped apart—as in no weapon was found at the scene, or was positively identified as the culprit—at the location they were found at; three, the bodies—despite the violent manner of their deaths—had bled relatively little, almost as if they had suffered blood loss elsewhere. Mind you this is purely speculation on my part, but I'm sure you'll agree that the facts support this."

Jake nodded as each of these points was listed. "You catch on quick, Gary. I agree with you that they must have lost blood elsewhere or by some other means, but I shudder to think why that would be."

Gary chuckled, clearly enjoying himself. "Well, that's the difference between you and me Jake. I *don't* shudder to think why. In fact, I have a pretty good idea of what is responsible, but I want to hear what else you have to say first."

Jake shrugged. He wasn't about to get into a pissing contest with one of the city's most ruthless and unscrupulous journalists—professional or not—so he let it go. "Fair enough. There are a couple of more things that you might find interesting. The bodies had some injuries on them that had scabbed over, things that looked like scratches, more bruising, and defensive cuts. Also, quite a few puncture wounds were found on various parts of both bodies. My guess is that this is where the majority of the blood loss occurred."

Gary nearly fell to the floor in unadulterated jubilation. The missing piece of the puzzle that would make his story stick had just landed in his lap, and he was going to play up the drama for all it was worth.

Jake stared at him warily. "You okay, man? You look like you're gonna be sick or something."

"Hardly. But tell me more about these puncture wounds."

Jake shrugged. "Not much to tell. They were just normal punctures—like anyone who does this kind of shit can be called normal."

Gary looked slightly deflated, but he refused to give up. "Are you sure about that? Nothing that looked out of the ordinary? Abnormal? *Fang*-like?"

Jake's brow furrowed in confusion at this sudden fixation on the puncture wounds. What was Gary all worked up over anyway? And what did he mean by "fang-like?" He was smart enough to know that Gary was fishing for more information than was available, but that didn't help with the confusion.

He shook his head. "Like I said; normal."

"Huh." Gary finished scribbling a final line of notes and then replaced the cap on his pen. He gathered up the legal pad and stuffed it back into the depths of his satchel. He extended his hand and Jake took it, though he didn't like the look on Gary's face as he bid him farewell. There was no telling what was brewing behind those glittering eyes, and he honestly didn't want to know.

As they exited the building and parted ways, something half-formed popped into his head, but the idea was so ludicrous that he dismissed it with a derisive snort. Nah, even Gary wouldn't try to sell that kind of trash to the locals, but still... something about the way he seemed to latch on to the missing blood and the puncture wounds was making him uneasy.

He shook his head and dug his hands into the pockets of his jeans jacket. The weight of the envelope was slightly comforting, yet he couldn't shake the feeling that he was an unwitting player in some yet-unknown drama, and that by revealing what he knew of the murders, that he had set a chain of unstoppable events in motion.

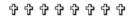

"All hail the conquering hero!"

A collective wince rippled throughout the bullpen as Gary strutted confidently to his workstation with the yellow steno pad held triumphantly over his head. He plopped down into his chair with a contented sigh and motioned for his fellow employees to come closer.

When it became apparent after a few moments that no one was going to fall over themselves to hear what he had to say, Gary went on the defensive. "Okay, fine. If all of you are too *intimidated* by my journalistic prowess to come hear my story, then I'll talk loud enough that you don't have to strain anything to hear me!"

*How dare they*, he fumed, glaring at the impassive faces around him. *After everything I've done for this publication, this is the thanks I get! If it weren't for me, every single one of you would be out of a job—my front-page features are the only reason anyone in this pissant burg reads our publication to begin with!* He crossed his arms over his chest and glared smugly at everyone. "My source has informed me that we have a vampire on our hands, who is stalking this city *as we speak*, and who has already killed two people—two innocent people who never had a chance against this monster."

The silence that followed that statement was so profound you could quite literally hear a pin drop. Someone in the back of the room snorted derisively. It was Dave/Derrick.

" *'As we speak?'* " He imitated Gary's overly-dramatic tone of voice. "Come off it Gary, this is the twenty-first century. That kind of half-baked superstition went out decades ago." He nudged the people next to him as if he'd scored a point.

Gary refused to have his moment of triumph spat back in his face. He stood up and faced Dave/Derrick, and a ripple of excitement went through the assembled crowd. Something interesting was going to happen around the workplace for once, and a battle of wits no less!

All eyes were riveted on the pair as they prepared to do battle.

"Alright *Dave*," Gary sneered. "Answer me this: what other explanation can you come up with that accounts for two victims that have been ripped—not cut or hacked, mind you—limb from limb?" He tore a piece of his steno pad into shreds for emphasis. Dave blanched, but recovered quickly.

Gary wasn't finished yet. "Not only that, they had fingerprints bruised onto their skin, were drained of blood, and had puncture wounds on them as well. Hmm? Answer me *that!*" The look on his face and the attitude exuded by his posture practically screamed "checkmate."

For a moment Dave looked uncertain, as did a few other staff members. From his vantage point a few desks away, Andrew was taking all of this in stride. Vampires? In San Antonio? It just didn't quite have a ring to it, and it was beyond ludicrous. The fact that divisive lines were being drawn in the office over the whole thing was even more ridiculous.

Mrs. Azumi stood up suddenly from her desk—all five-feet-two inches of her—and wagged her finger at Gary and Dave. "Enough, both of you! Gary has a right to his opinion—*however misguided it is*," she amended quickly "—as does Dave, but I will not tolerate you acting like children when it comes to expressing them! You are both adults and this is a place of business, so for Pete's sake, start acting like it!"

Dave looked down at the floor in equal parts of shame and relief. He really didn't have a reasonable counter argument to Gary's theory, and Mrs. Azumi's outburst helped him save face for the moment.

Gary interpreted her intervention as something entirely different. He grinned wolfishly at her. "I knew you had a thing for me, and you backing me up is proof of it. You know, you really are incredibly cute when you're angry."

Mrs. Azumi held up a clenched fist. "Remember, bucko: Kung Fu Death Punch."

Gary laughed and returned to his seat, sure in his belief that he had emerged the victor. The argument and accompanying antagonism fizzled away, and there were more than a few disappointed faces as everyone got back to work.

Gary whistled softly as he began to assemble his notes to begin typing. It didn't take him long to hammer the piece out, and as he passed by Andrew's desk on his way to Bob's office, Andrew felt a twinge of jealousy. The fact that he felt this way at all was even more unsettling. Sure, Gary's features invariably made the front page of every issue, but the man himself was pathetic. Hitting on a woman who was old enough to be his mother day after day, not to mention every skirt within a ten-mile radius? That was beyond sad. Filling his stories with lies, exorbitant claims and half-truths to sell copies which contributed to his overall sense of self-worth? Even more sad.

His feelings were justified nearly an hour later when Gary emerged from Bob's office with a self-satisfied smirk on his face. Andrew sighed and began reworking the piece on the politician's wife and her bogus alien-abduction-slash-infidelity-scandal. He could sit here tweaking it all day and it would still be crap regardless of how well it was written.

Bob Garrett came striding into the bullpen at that moment and made a beeline for Gary's desk. The two talked in animated tones as Bob discussed the layout that he had in mind for

next week's issue—a "sure-fire crowd pleaser" as he called it—
that wouldn't fail to capture the public's imagination. From
what Andrew could make out, it appeared that Bob wanted to
dedicate the whole issue to vampires. There would be columns
dedicated to ways of protecting yourself from attacks, famous
actors who have portrayed them in movies, and for the coup de
grace, a column on Dracula, the most famous vampire of all.

My God, but it was amazing how the two fed off each
other's bullshit.

Just as Andrew was in the middle of this little reverie, the
two parted company and Bob passed by Andrew's desk on the
way back to his office. The friendly look on his face faded.

"How are we coming along, Mr. Crossman?" He nodded
curtly towards the computer screen where the blinking cursor
seemed to be taunting Andrew about his inability to finish the
piece.

Andrew managed a weak smile. "Fine, sir. I'll have it into
you by the end of the day."

Bob glanced up at the clock and then back at the screen.
His eyes crawled slowly over the print and his lips screwed up
like he had a mouth full of lemon juice. "It still needs a *lot* of
work. "Gary," he waved the other man over towards the desk.
"You mind helping Mr. Crossman here with his feature? It
could use a *professional* touch."

Andrew forced his face to not betray his emotions. This
was beyond adding insult to injury.

"Sure thing, Bob." Gary looked just a little too happy
for comfort, and the knowing look he flashed at Bob wasn't
missed by Andrew or the rest of the office. There were a few
tentative peaks over the tops of their cubicles, but eventually
they lost interest and returned to their work. One or two shook
their heads, and the thought behind the action was the same:
those two are it again. It was more than obvious by the way
that Andrew tailored his actions around the two of them that

something had and was going on between them. Speculation ran rampant around the workplace, but every single theory thrown out for public scrutiny came circling back to the same conclusion: whatever had happened between the three of them, Bob and Gary were the aggressors, and Andrew—who was too mild-mannered for his own good—had become their own personal punching bag. Every little belittling comment, every conspiratorial glance and half-concealed glare of antagonism was slowly chipping away at that calm exterior, and eventually something had to give. It was only a matter of time before that happened, and despite everyone's mutual desire for a little excitement in the place, neither one of them would have wished such a fate on their worst enemy. Andy was a good guy, and contrary to what Bob or Gary believed, was too good a writer to be working in a rat box like *Elysium*. It was a shame that his talents weren't realized and put to good use by the owner, but it was an even bigger travesty that Andrew hadn't come to the same conclusion years before.

Gary stood looking over Andrew's shoulder while he read through the story. He muttered to himself as he read, and the critique sounded far from impressed. "You remember the story I did a couple of years ago about the Elvis sightings in the area and the way that the issue's profits soared through the roof? *That's* what we need to aim for on this piece."

Andrew did indeed remember that particular story. He had been working at *Elysium* for just over a year, and as inconceivable as it was now, he and Gary—not to mention Bob Garrett— were actually on good terms. All of that changed after Andrew and Gary's exchange in the office that day, an exchange that had gone something like this:

*"Oh, come on Gary. Elvis has been spotted near the dumpsters outside of Giovanni's Italian Bistro? That's beyond crap, and might I add, has been done before."* Andrew leaned back in his chair and rested his feet on the desk. *Gary was an okay guy—quirky but harmless. While he frequently tried to*

push the envelope when it came to feature stories, this seemed just a tad out in left field even for him.

"Who cares if it's crap or has been done before? Or for that matter that it may not even be true?" Gary wiggled his eyebrows conspiratorially and leaned closer. "The only thing that matters is selling copies. Trust me"—he winked at Andrew over the brim of his coffee mug—"this is going to drive the schitzos and conspiracy theorists ape-shit. They'll be falling all over themselves to buy a copy." He had then noisily drained his mug and laughed long and hard over his own joke.

Up until that moment Andrew had no idea just how low Gary could stoop to sell copies. Naïve as he was at the time, he felt that it was his duty to report Gary to Bob Garrett. It just seemed awfully irresponsible—not to mention unethical—to deceive the publication's readers like that. So what if more than a few of them were a little off or were convinced that the government was out to get them? As loyal customers, they deserved better than that.

The ensuing conversation with Bob Garrett had been short and to-the-point: mind your own damn business and do your job. As an employee of *Elysium*, your job was to sell the publication for all it was worth, and if fudging the details is what it took, then so much the better.

Andrew couldn't believe what he was hearing and went into something of a tirade, denouncing Bob and Gary as charlatans who dealt in cheap entertainment. Bob had fixed him with an icy glare and told him through gritted teeth that if the policies in place offended his delicate sensibilities *so* much, then he was free to walk out the door and seek employment elsewhere. He knew perfectly well that Andrew couldn't afford to call his bluff, and had made it his personal mission to make his life a living hell since then.

Things had been made worse when Bob had confided to Gary about Andrew's opinion of him. Things had cooled significantly between them in the days following that little incident, and if anyone could hold a grudge, it was Gary. He didn't do anything inherently illegal or unethical, although the hairs being split were extremely fine. It was a series of little things—a snide comment here, a conspiratorial glance there, the constant trashing of his contributions at every given opportunity, and always underneath it all, a sense of nauseating superiority. Andrew was still in no position to quit his job and the harassment continued unabated. This little collaborative effort with Gary was just one more kick in the groin after years of abuse.

Three hours later, Gary finally stood back with a satisfied smirk and proudly proclaimed the article to be a work of art. To Andrew it barely resembled the original piece and was so chock-full of "Garyisms" that his own voice was lost in the mix. As soon as Gary returned to his desk and was out of earshot, Andrew exhaled loudly and buried his face in his hands. "Surely the day can't get any worse.

# Chapter 10

"The bodies have been disposed of?"

The small assemblage nodded their heads fervently and cast wary glances at the three men who stood with them, yet who seemed apart from the group as a whole. They were the only ones aside from Darnell who met her eyes without flinching, and when she spoke she appeared to be addressing them alone.

"So it has begun. The next move is hers, and we need only wait until she comes to us."

Some silent communication seemed to pass between her and the three men, and they turned and silently exited the room. The rest of the group bowed awkwardly, unsure of the proper way to exit the drawing room, and hurriedly trailed after them. When they entered the foyer with its pair of ornately carved armchairs, the three men stood with their backs to the room and were gazing out of the blasted windows at the street outside.

The group shivered and shifted uncomfortably. When they had initially been approached and systematically entranced and seduced by the strange and wonderful world that their mistress had offered them, they were blind with lust and eagerness in equal amounts. Some desired power of the magnitude that she possessed, while others were criminals or budding sociopaths—murderers—who saw in the opportunity that she presented them with the chance to indulge their darkest fantasies unchecked. Each of them had sworn their undying allegiance to her in exchange for what she had offered them: strength and stamina beyond their wildest dreams, unlimited power and potential, immortality itself.

It was a dizzying and intoxicating combination, but now, as they exited the drawing room and stared at the unmoving and statue-like countenances of the three men who were her second in command, they were afraid. Even the most hardened and sadistic of them were forced to admit that perhaps the deal they had accepted was too good to be true, that perhaps it was rife with consequences that they hadn't even considered before. They had since come to the conclusion that they were expendable, mere pawns in some twisted and yet-unknown game that she was playing against an equally enigmatic assailant. Reggie had been the most recent of them to suffer such a fate, but they doubted that he would be the last. Escaping to parts unknown was not an option. She would make her displeasure known when she found them, and running away would merely speed up the inevitable.

Darnell was the only exception to these misgivings. It was more than obvious that he was hopelessly enamored by their mistress, and it seemed that reason had taken a back seat to his affections. All of them felt that it would ultimately be his undoing, but if they had a choice they would rather be blinded by love than aware of her deception—at least then the inevitable wouldn't be so unbearable.

The ambient sounds of the street floated back to them through the gaping holes that served as windows. The house had been abandoned for years and was practically falling down around them, yet the interior was decorated in lavish and expensive furnishings. Large gilt-framed portraits, abstracts, landscapes, and the occasional bauble that hailed from a bygone era covered every available surface. It was a strange mixture of the contemporary and the past, but it suited the respective inhabitants well.

Outside, several teenagers laughed and shouted jubilantly as they passed the house, undoubtedly daring one another to go in and prove their bravery. They were young and had their whole futures ahead of them, were full of promise and unrealized potential. The sound conjured up images of a young couple out for a night on the town, laughing and talking in slightly-hushed tones as they made their way down the street towards their parked car. They had walked hand in hand completely oblivious to the danger that lurked around and in front of them, but the sound had died away as this realization hit them too late.

The woman had held out her purse with trembling fingers, so sure was she that this was only a mugging, and the man had done the same with his wallet. Their eyes were round and glazed with fear—like deer in the woods after catching the predator's scent—and as the steel-like arms bound and restrained them, they practically bulged out in terror. Their eyes had retained that same look of hopeless resignation as they were brought back to the house and brutally tortured for days. Now and then small, pitiful sounds would punctuate the silence and break the monotony of their screams, and when they were finally, mercifully torn limb from limb, they were silent.

The three men had overseen the whole operation and they had laughed at their victim's pleas for mercy. Their mistress had reassured the couple in her soothing, velvety voice that they were not going to die in vain—quite the opposite. Their deaths would polarize the city and would be on the front page of every publication—whether professional or independent—and would galvanize the populace into action. What she neglected to inform them of was that the only individual that she sought to incite was the mysterious assassin who continued to prowl the streets, hell-bent on destroying her children.

"If she insists on hiding in the shadows while picking us off one by one, then I will give her a reason to come out into the light."

The bodies had been dumped as instructed, and now all that was left to do was wait.

# Chapter 11

The three-inch headline stamped on the front page of *Elysium's* latest issue stopped me dead in my tracks.

## TRANSYLVANIA, TEXAS?
## LONE-STAR VAMPS SLAY LOCALS
**By Gary Simms**
*Elysium* **Features Writer**

I shook my head to clear my vision, but the headline remained unchanged. I handed the bored-looking cashier seventy-five cents and hurried out of the little corner market across from my apartment. I kept the paper folded neatly in half under my arm until I was safely behind my own door. I carefully spread it out across the coffee table and examined it under the light streaming in through my window.

I already knew that my kind were in the city, so why was I so upset over the article? *Because apparently they've killed people while you were supposed to be watching over the inhabitants,* my mind taunted me. I bent down and began to read.

*November 13, 2008*
*SAN ANTONIO—we've all heard of vampires in popular fiction and multi-million dollar Hollywood productions, but here in Texas? Don't be so quick to judge the merits of that statement*

before you hear all the facts. The disappearance last week of twenty-one year old David Summers and nineteen-year old Rebecca Stocks seemed to be yet another random, senseless crime committed against the innocent. A spokesperson for the police department stated in an interview with the local news stations that "every resource is being exhausted and every lead is being thoroughly looked into." The families of the missing couple held a press conference last Thursday pleading with the captors to "return their loved ones safe and sound." Sadly, those pleas seemed to fall on deaf ears.

This past Tuesday, 911 dispatchers received a frantic call from a waste management employee who spotted something suspicious in an alleyway while making his daily rounds. Upon closer inspection, the previously-unidentified mass turned out to be the remains of two people which were later positively identified as the missing couple. Details as to the apparent cause of death are sketchy, and not much has been revealed to the general public. However, an anonymous source has contacted this publication and provided us with exclusive information detailing the medical examiner's preliminary findings. According to the source, the couple wasn't merely murdered, they were "butchered."

The grisly details are straight out of a horror movie. The bodies were apparently ripped limb from limb, and at the time of this writing, the medical examiner has been unable to determine the type of weapon used, if any. The source went on to state that fingerprints and sometimes whole handprints were bruised onto the skin of the victims, almost as if they had been restrained by someone with superhuman strength.

Perhaps the most tell-tale sign that the murders are indeed the work of a preternatural assailant is that the victims experienced significant blood loss prior to their death. This is further compounded by the presence of puncture wounds on various parts of the body. It is entirely plausible that someone or something drained the victims' blood through these puncture wounds, but as to what caused them or for what purpose the blood was drained remains to be seen.

*So are the murders the result of some blood-sucking nightmare straight out of a gothic novel, or is it merely the work of an overly sadistic and imaginative killer? It is the opinion of this author that the evidence speaks for itself. The victims were ripped apart by someone with incredible (dare I say "inhuman" strength?), which is evidenced by the presence of fingerprints bruised onto the skin. Factor in the strange blood loss and the puncture wounds, and the evidence is even more compelling.*

*The source left this author with these parting words: "I wouldn't doubt it if I have nightmares after this."*

*I am inclined to agree with them.*

I stopped reading and quickly scanned the rest of the article for any more useful information. The location of the murders stood out in bold black and white like an accusation, and I felt my blood run cold.

I set the paper down and went to stand by the window. The traffic cruised by in its ceaseless rhythm, winding down the Interstate and axis roads that crisscrossed the city like silver snakes. I wrapped my arms securely around my elbows and willed the trembling in my limbs to subside. I didn't tremble out of fear—that was ridiculous, despite the truth of what the article had stated—but from anger. I was angry at myself, but more than that, I felt immeasurably guilty for what had befallen that poor couple. Their bodies had been dumped in the vicinity where I had systematically dispatched the five progeny, and where I suspected their Font and the rest of their brood were holed up. I had patrolled the area with renewed conviction since the night of my last kill, but things had been quiet.

Too quiet.

I had been waiting anxiously for months for the Font to finally take notice and confront me, but they had been unwilling to do so. I had wracked my brain for a possible ulterior motive behind this reluctance, but I had come up empty. The discovery of the two bodies that had been horribly mangled and apparently been drained of blood presented a problem for several reasons, even though I agreed with the article that they were the work of a preternatural assailant. For one thing, while my kind is perfectly capable of ripping a human limb from limb, they seldom do. They can kill and feed from their victims without having to expend that kind of energy or go to such extremes. There were those who have an affinity for torture, but they aren't in the habit of leaving the body in an area where they are sure to be found. They conceal them so that no trace remains, as I knew only too well with regards to the sinkhole on my country property.

The missing blood was perhaps the most perplexing aspect of all. While my kind could be characterized as vampires from the standpoint of being perpetually youthful or incredibly strong, we don't drink blood to survive. We like to taste it, to roll the texture of it around on the tips of our tongues, but it does nothing for us nutrition-wise. Blood serves the more practical purpose of establishing a bond between us and our prey. Blood opens up their aura, their life force to us so that we can feed. Whoever had killed the couple hadn't fed from them in this manner.

Perhaps the most significant aspect of blood was that it was the medium of transference, a primal, almost-alchemical substance that bestowed a semblance of immortality upon the recipient. It was imbued with power that Fonts alone possessed, and when it inundated a human's body it transformed them into progeny, into something more and less than human: monsters.

It seemed odd to me that someone or *something* had gone to a lot of trouble to make the murders look like one thing—in this instance, the work of a vampire—despite the fact that it clearly was not, or at least not in the sense that the people over at *Elysium* thought that it was. No, these murders looked like they had been *staged*, but for what purpose? Were they designed to draw me out? Was this the inevitable confrontation that I had been anticipating?

My hand went to the knife on my right and gripped the bone handle convulsively. I forced my fingers to relax as the handle creaked ominously, and I considered a second option. Was it merely a coincidence that two murders designed to look like vampire kills to the casual observer were committed in the very same area as the one that I had killed five progeny in? Something in my gut told me that the odds in favor of this were astronomical. I wasn't a firm believer in coincidences and I wasn't willing to bet on it.

I turned away from the window and stared at the article on the table. Either way it was worth looking into, and I honestly couldn't forgive myself if I didn't and more people wound up dead. Even if it turned out to be nothing more than some psychopath with a vampire fixation who was really methodical about what weapons they used, I was still obligated to dig deeper. It was enough that these people had died on my watch in an area I frequented.

I would not let it happen again.

The author of the article was Gary Simms, and I decided to pay him a visit at his workplace later that day. The details in the article were scanty, and I knew that there must be something more that he was holding back, either due to censoring or with the mindset of doing a follow-up piece. I was going to do my best to get that information for myself, and I was confident that he would be willing to share with me.

With any luck I wouldn't even have to break a sweat or threaten him with my knives.

The man stumbled through the entrance of Vasquez Liquor and gripped the door frame for support. Black spots danced in front of his eyes as he struggled to make them focus, and he was dimly aware of someone shouting from a distance. Annoyed, he straightened up and stared around him at the shelves full of shiny bottles and felt the longing tug at his bones. He took a tentative step towards the counter, one foot placed carefully in front of the other as he held his hands out to either side for balance.

The shouting appeared to be growing louder and more animated the closer he got. A shaft of sunlight streaming in through the windows hit him squarely in the eyes and he swore and blinked furiously to erase the brilliant afterimages. He made it to the edge of the counter and braced himself against it with one hand, the other rubbing at his tender eyelids. The shouting increased in volume and a rhythmic tremor went through the countertop that seemed oddly in sync with the shouting.

"…not out of here in five minutes, I'm calling the cops!"

He blinked and stared up as the muddled hoots and clicks suddenly tuned into plain English. Mike Vasquez, proprietor and current-cashier, waved his arms towards the exit to illustrate his point.

"You know I'm good for the money…I just…need a few more hours…." The world tilted slightly and he nearly fell over. His head felt like he was trying to balance an egg on a toothpick, but somehow he managed. He had had plenty of practice in the last few years and the effort had become second nature by now.

Mike wasn't having any of it. "That's what you always say and I'm not falling for it anymore, Wendell. If you want something, you pay for it just like everyone else." He crossed his arms over his chest as if to illustrate the fact that he wasn't going to be his enabler today. Wendell had been coming here for the past two years, and at first Mike had been happy to give him liquor on credit, despite the fact that he was homeless. Wendell always managed to pay him back with the money he got from panhandling or the few bottles and cans that he recycled for cash, but lately he had been falling behind on his payments. Mike apparently didn't appreciate that in the slightest.

Snatches of nightmare images flickered past his closed lids, and he screamed softly and buried his face in his hands. *No, no, no, no, no!* His mind kept desperately trying to shield itself behind an alcohol-induced haze that no longer existed. *No, not that; anything but that!*

He moaned miserably and stood rocking from side to side in the bright spill of light that flooded in from the windows. In here he was safe. In here, away from the confines of the darkened alleyway with its terrible secrets, he would be fine. His mind however, presented a problem. However horrifying and traumatic the memories he sought to escape, they kept bubbling up to the surface and he was desperate to keep them in check. His first and best line of defense was to get blind drunk, but the effects were dissipating much quicker than he would have liked. He needed just a little more to finish pushing him off the edge into blessed oblivion.

*Just a drop*, he thought. *My kingdom for a drop....*

He laughed harshly. Now *that* was ironic. Everything that he called his own in this world was on his person or was in the dirty black backpack that he carried with him everywhere. The greasy trench coat, tattered jeans, and shabby flannel shirt that he wore were the only clothes he owned. Somewhere in the depths of his backpack was a post card from South Dakota and a few letters creased and smudged beyond recognition. These, along with an empty wallet that held nothing but pictures of his ex-wife and children, were the only tangible memories he had left of his family. His daughters Leah and Cassidy, who were now five and seven, hadn't seen their father for nearly two years.

His ex-wife Virginia had taken them with her to live with her mother in Sioux Falls after the disastrous fallout of his latest—and last—financial investment. He had sunk everything that they owned into a budding new business venture that had seemed like the answer to their prayers, and when it went under it took him and his family down with it. Virginia left and took their children far away so that they could start over after Wendell hadn't handled the news all that responsibly and took to drinking heavily. The only contact that he had with his daughters was the postcard and a few letters that stopped as abruptly as they started arriving. Wendell had read and reread them so many times that the ink was badly smudged and the writing was indecipherable, but they meant the world to him. He had memorized every line of their child-like scrawl and could almost envision their voices as they read over what they had written. The memory of what he had lost brought with it a peculiar mixture of pain and longing—pain over what was certainly irreparable damage to his relationship with his family, and a longing for the days when their lives had been simple, yet happy.

The loss of their life-savings, home, and car he could deal with, but not the loss of his wife and children. He considered going after them and trying to patch things up with his wife, but Virginia flatly told him that he was a negative influence on their children, and that his presence would only upset them more. There was no doubt that she had put a stop to the correspondence between him and his daughters, and the weekly letters he sent were never answered. By this point he was drinking constantly and he was slurring so badly on the phone that his wife could barely understand him as he begged her to reconsider. Matters had come to a head during the shouting match when he had overheard his daughter Cassidy in the background.

"Who are you talking to, mommy?" His heart nearly broke at the sound of her voice. She sounded so innocent and was completely oblivious to the turmoil that her mother was currently embroiled in. As he overheard his wife explain to her who it was, he felt the burden of his loss like a crushing weight on his chest.

"It's no one, sweetheart. Go get your sister and get ready for bed. I'll be up to read to you in a little bit."

Cassidy's answering squeal of delight jabbed fresh shards of glass into his heart. "Leah, time for bed! Mommy's going to read us a bedtime story!"

There was another squeal as she and Leah rushed off together. Wendell heard the patter of their feet racing up the stairs, and he felt a wave of shame and revulsion wash over him. His children were happy and he had no right to barge back into their lives in the state that he was in and compromise all that. What was more, his children were happy without *him*; they hadn't even asked their mother about their father as if he no longer existed even to them.

He made his decision before their conversation could pick up where they left off. "You're right, Virginia." He knew in that moment that he had forfeited any chance—however slim—of coming back into their lives. The only comfort he had was the knowledge that his daughters were happy with their mother and grandmother and didn't appear to want for anything.

There was a momentary pause on the other end as the implications of what he was saying slowly dawned on her. "Goodbye, Wendell." He heard the finality in her voice and knew that there was nothing left for them to say to one another. The phone disconnected with a slight *click* and that was the end of it.

It was the last time that he had spoken to her or heard his daughters' voices.

When his meager resources had finally run out after months of fruitless searching for a steady job, he could no longer afford to stay in a cheap motel and it was then that he took to living on the streets. The first night was terrifying and bewildering, and he felt as if the city was leering down at him, mocking him and his demoted status. He had no idea where to go or how he would manage to fend for himself, and the prospect of spending the rest of his days stuck in a sort of limbo were beyond disheartening.

The first time that he had approached passerby for change was the most humiliating and demoralizing thing he had ever had to do in his life.

He was surprised to find that he had enough for at least a meal or two at the end of the day when he counted his earnings. His stomach growled audibly at the thought of food, and as he headed down the street to the nearest restaurant, he saw an advertisement printed on orange neon for the grand opening of Vasquez Liquor. The store seemed all shiny and new despite the rough neighborhood, and he found himself pushing open the door and staring wide-eyed at the rows upon rows of sparkling wine and liquor bottles. His favorite brand of whiskey sat on the shelf nearest him—almost as if it had been placed there as a temptation—and was surprisingly cheap.

He felt the weight of the money in his pocket and stood wrestling with his conscience. The money would be better spent on a good meal, which is what his body demanded of him with another growl of his stomach. On the other hand, the liquor was cheap and would dull his senses enough that he could get through the next couple of days without the feeling of worthlessness and self-loathing that seemed to follow him like a shadow. The liquor would keep him warm in the freezing temperatures long after the food had been digested, would make him feel safe and euphoric as he dreamt of the family that he had had to leave behind. The food would only fill his stomach and not the aching chasm that was his soul.

He made his decision and walked out of the store, bottle in hand.

After that, the days and weeks flew by in a blur. Whenever he managed to scrape up enough cash, he would hurry to the store and restock before the illusion the liquor created around him faded away and was beyond his reach. Lately he hadn't had much luck when it came to donations, and he was growing more and more desperate every day. Mike had taken pity on him and despite his reservations about enabling the man's addiction, allowed him to buy liquor on credit. Wendell wasn't sure if it was greed or pity that ultimately convinced Mike to do this, but he was grateful and had kept up his side of the bargain up until a few days ago when the money had abruptly run out.

The surrounding neighborhoods had been thrown into a panic by the gruesome discovery of the murdered couple in one of the back alleyways, and as so often happens in such instances, the homeless and anyone else who seemed only slightly suspicious or out of place was avoided like the plague. Wendell hadn't been able to earn a single cent in nearly three days, and his body was experiencing severe withdrawals. The aches, pains, and debilitating headaches made it nearly impossible for him to walk around the corner to the liquor store, much less haul up stakes and move on elsewhere.

He was in a panic now that he had a much-more pressing reason to drink himself into a stupor that exceeded the guilt he harbored over his long-lost family. A little over a week ago, sometime in the late evening or early morning hours—he couldn't quite be sure of the time—a van had pulled up and dislodged a group of men into the alleyway that Wendell called home. He was lying in a pile of cardboard boxes and paper refuse trying desperately to generate enough body heat to live through the night, when he heard sobs and mocking laughter. Curious, he peeked out from under the garbage concealing him and saw a group of eight men surrounding a pair of terrified teenagers who lay cowering on the floor of the alleyway.

Three of the men were shouting orders at the other five who seemed to hang back, unsure of what to do. The two teenagers on the ground held up their arms in supplication, as if pleading with the men to not harm them. Their arms and exposed skin were horribly marred by extensive bruising and was spattered with dried blood. The female looked like she had been crying for some time, and the man beside her was trying his best to shield her with his body. The three men who had been shouting orders began to stalk around the couple, their movements lithe and oddly gracefully for men of their size.

The female began to babble and tears streamed down her face as she attempted to track their relentless pacing around them. Wendell was frozen in terror over what he instinctively knew what was going to happen, and it seemed as if his breath was frozen in his lungs.

One of the men suddenly dragged the woman to her feet. Her voice caught in her throat and her eyes bulged from the sockets. The man beside her jumped to his feet and attempted to pry her away from the other man, and the other two moved in swiftly. All at once there was a wet, ripping sound and his face went blank with shock. The woman seemed to find her voice then and screamed, but the sound was abruptly cut off as a hand closed over her mouth.

The man beside her never had a chance.

When it was over, he lay shattered and broken at her feet as she continued to scream, the sound muffled behind the hand at her mouth, her fists drumming a mindless rhythm against the man who restrained her. The other two men laughed and teased her as they gathered around and began gently stroking her face and hair. Her eyes showed too much white around the edges as one of them turned and ordered the other five closer.

They encircled her as Wendell watched. Their dark forms blotted out the pale and bruised planes of her skin, and their hands reached out towards her. A sharp cry pierced the night, but it was cut off in mid-scream by the same wet, ripping sounds as before. Wendell squeezed his eyes shut so tight that his head throbbed, but he was unable to cover his ears from the horrible sounds and dull *thumps* that echoed throughout the alley.

The sound seemed to go on forever and then all at once it was eerily silent. He cautiously cracked one eye open and then the other. The alleyway was empty except for the scattered white limbs that his mind instinctively kept shying away from. The moon glinted off the glazed and lifeless eyes of the woman who only moments before had been a living, breathing creature.

He lurched violently away from his hiding place and retched till he was empty. He gulped down great lungfuls of the cold air and somehow managed to stagger away. Tears marred his vision as he ran in a blind panic down the familiar streets where he was sure that monsters lurked around every corner. He had no conscious awareness of where he was headed, only that he had to get *away*....

"C'mon, man, don't make me do this."

Wendell glanced up and saw that Mike had the phone in his hand and was preparing to dial. He shook his head to clear the visions away and Mike took it as a sign that calling the cops was unnecessary, and that he would be leaving.

He turned to go without a word and stepped out of the warm, safe confines of the store and back out into the nightmare reality that had become his world. A cold wind whipped through the trees and wormed its way through the holes and tatters in his clothes. Rubbing his hands together to warm them, he put his back to the wind and headed away from the liquor store towards the bank of privately-owned businesses that lined the street. There was a nail studio, a carwash, a Laundromat-slash-convenience store, and a Vietnamese restaurant that was boarded up. He dug into the lining of his coat for the money that he kept for an emergency, and came up with four dollars and some change. He sighed and looked back towards the convenience store. At this rate all he could afford was a cup of coffee. While it wouldn't exactly help keep the nightmare visions away, it would at least keep him warm.

The bells tied to the door jingled merrily as he stepped inside. He knew that loitering wasn't tolerated, so he headed straight for the coffee machine towards the back. As he set his coffee down on the counter to pay for it, a stack of newspapers lay next to the register. His eyes crawled over the top page and the headline glared out at him: *Transylvania Texas? Lone-star Vamps Slay Locals*. They widened in undisguised horror as he read the first page, and the nightmare images were suddenly made reality in bold black and white.

The cashier saw him eyeing the paper and after informing him that reading it before buying it wasn't allowed, he managed to mumble that he would be buying one and turned to leave. He exited the store and settled down out of sight near the dumpsters and began to read, his coffee long-forgotten by his side. By the time that he was finished reading, he knew what he had to do. He had to tell someone about what he had seen—someone who wouldn't automatically think that he was just some crazy old drunk.

He hurriedly fished out the rest of his change and went to the pay phone at the front of the store. He dialed the hotline number listed on the back of the tabloid and waited impatiently for someone to answer.

The phone picked up on the third ring. He sighed and prepared to speak.

# Chapter 12

The woman who answered the phone listened politely while the man on the other end began describing in breathless detail events that corroborated Mr. Simm's article. She sighed discreetly and rolled her eyes. This was the first of what was sure to be many calls related to the article in question. Already the phone lines had been tied up with readers wanting to know more information about protecting themselves from the "walking undead," and she'd missed her mid-morning smoke break. Needless to say, she wasn't exactly in a good mood by the time she answered this call.

She turned her face away from the phone and snorted derisively. She had to hand it to Gary. Despite his apparent shortcomings as a card-carrying member of the human race, the man had a talent for stirring up the schitzos and alienating his colleagues.

The voice continued on the other end and she stared up at the clock mounted above her workstation. About twenty minutes to noon.

She had a lunch date with a guy she had just met off one of her chat rooms, and she didn't want to be late. This guy actually had a job and didn't appear to be a psychopath, but then again her track record wasn't the best. She didn't want to chance it by being late and making a bad first impression. She decided that if Gary's article was what the man on the phone wanted to talk about, then it made a whole lot of sense to have him talk to the person who had written it.

"Excuse me, sir?"

The man stopped in mid-sentence and she jumped in to fill the momentary silence. "If you would prefer, I can connect you with Mr. Simms directly. I'm sure he'd be *more* than happy to discuss your experiences in person." She smiled evilly.

The man sighed in what was apparently relief, and for a moment she almost regretted pawning him off on Gary.

"I appreciate that, but I don't exactly have a way to get to your office. You see, I'm...homeless."

Somehow she managed to make her response sound as professional as possible, despite the overwhelming urge to laugh herself silly. My God, but Gary had fans in the strangest places! "Sir, I *assure* you that that won't be a problem. Just give me the address of somewhere close to you that you would like to meet, and I'll forward the message to him as soon as possible. Is there a phone number that he can contact you at?"

The man rattled off the name of a Mexican restaurant in an area that she was familiar with, and read off the number to the payphone that he was calling from. She thanked him for his interest in *Elysium*, promised to give Gary the message, and then hung up.

She got up from her desk and crossed the room with quick, purposeful strides. Gary was sitting at his computer screen typing up some other piece-of-garbage feature, and she dropped the message on his desk.

"Message for you." She tried her best to hide the smirk behind her hand as she discreetly pushed her hair back from her eyes.

He opened it without a word and as his eyes crawled over the message, his face lit up like a kid on Christmas morning. "So I'm getting fan mail already," he crowed and stretched casually in his chair. "I had a feeling today was going to be a good day. I'm never wrong about these things you know."

"Really." *Yeah, fascinating, but I got a date, so moving along now. . ..* She smiled politely and nodded at the appropriate moments while Gary expanded on that statement. She glanced at her watch several times during the course of the conversation, but Gary didn't seem to notice. For a journalist, the man was woefully unobservant and couldn't take a hint if it meant the firing squad. After five full minutes she finally had to break him off in mid-sentence and excused herself. Gary assured her that he had to follow up on this lead as well—as if she genuinely gave a shit—and reached for the phone on his desk. Seizing the opportunity to escape, she walked away, grabbed her coat off the rack near the entrance, and left Gary alone with his ego.

✝ ✝ ✝ ✝ ✝ ✝ ✝ ✝

Wendell sat next to the payphone with his back pressed up against the wall of the convenience store. An odd sense of peace hung about him. Now that he had confided in someone else about what he had seen, the sense of fear and isolation that had plagued him for days seemed to be melting away by the second. He counted cars as he waited anxiously for the phone to ring, and he sipped his now-cold coffee absently. Soon he would be able to lay out all the details. Soon he would be able to let the truth of what he had seen be made public knowledge.

He drained the last of the coffee, crumpled the Styrofoam cup in his hand, and got up to toss it into the dumpster. The phone rang just as he got to his feet, and he fumbled awkwardly with the receiver before bringing it up to his ear.

"Hello?"

"Mr. Bowers? This is Gary Simms, Features Writer for *Elysium.* I understand you have some information that may be of interest to me."

"Yes, that's correct. If we could perhaps meet somewhere?"

"Excellent. You mentioned Tia Juanie's in your message. Is that okay with you, or would you prefer somewhere else?"

"No, no. Tia Juanie's is fine. It's actually not that far from where I am, and I can meet you there in about fifteen, twenty minutes."

"Great. See you then, Mr. Bowers."

The line went dead and Wendell hung it up with slightly-trembling fingers. He picked up the crumpled coffee cup from where it lay seemingly forgotten on the pavement and tossed it into the dumpster before he headed up the street. His destination lay two blocks away, but even as his muscles protested loudly with each step, each step took him that much closer to peace of mind.

# Chapter 13

The drive from my apartment to *Elysium's* headquarters was not as long as I had expected, considering that it was on the other side of town. This actually worked to my advantage in that the less time I spent in traffic, the more time I had to get some solid information that I could work with.

The parking lot designated for both employees and visitors was located at the rear of the building. As I exited the car, I readjusted my coat so that the knives around my waist were properly concealed. There was no sense in stirring up trouble before I had even gotten what I had come here for.

There was nothing about the place that gave any indication that it was the veritable nerve-center of an independent publication. The walls of the building were painted a sunny, almost pukey yellow that reminded me of egg yolks, and only a faded window decal that was peeling away at the corners identified the building as *Elysium's* headquarters. There was a medium-sized terracotta pot near the entrance filled with geraniums that had seen better days. They had undoubtedly been placed there to try to make the place seem more cheerful, but they actually had the opposite affect.

I pushed open the door and stepped into a rectangular room that was better suited for kid's parties or low-grade banquets, rather than a make-shift bullpen. The mismatched desks, chairs, and semi-cubicles took up every available space.

Battered filing cabinets, an ancient Risograph, and a couple of fake fichus trees were crammed in haphazardly to complete the chaotic scene before me.

I headed towards a desk set a little bit away from the rest. Judging by the fax machine set off to one side and a pile of manila folders and assorted memos on the other, this had to be the receptionist, though if I wasn't mistaken, the girl seated at the desk couldn't be more than eighteen.

I approached her and smiled brightly. "Good afternoon. My name is Katrina Armentani, and I was wondering if I could speak to Gary Simm's, please—if he's available, of course."

"Oh. Hi. Uh, lemme see what his schedule's like…."

I kept the smile on my face while the girl—who looked slightly bewildered at my request—started rummaging around the desk. After a moment she produced a large burgundy daily planner and began slowly flipping through it.

I tried not to drum my fingers against the counter as she continued to casually flip through the pages, her eyes crawling sluggishly across each one. I may be immortal and have all the time in the world, but people were dying—*had* died—and every second was vital. The girl finally heaved a frustrated sigh and yelled out across the bullpen. "Hey, has anyone seen Gary today?"

There were a few groans and a muttered "Unfortunately," and then one man spoke up towards the back. He was an older gentlemen somewhat overdressed than the rest of his colleagues in pressed jeans, boots, and tan blazer. Salt and pepper hair added to a face that was attractive for his age.

"Gary stepped out to interview a witness to the 'vampire murders' "—he made air quotes as he said the last two words—"and he won't be back until after lunch, I believe."

"Thanks Gerald," the girl called out and he nodded in acknowledgment.

She turned to face me with an apologetic grin. "Sorry 'bout that, but Gary just can't seem to resist witnesses who can back up his...stories." The look on her face and the momentary pause spoke volumes about just what she thought of Gary's quote "stories."

"If you want, you can have a seat over there and wait till he comes back. He shouldn't be that much longer...with any luck." Again, the momentary pause spoke volumes about just what she thought of Gary, but phony sincerity aside, I really didn't care.

Someone had witnessed the vampire murders and could potentially corroborate his article. If this was true and the witness was reliable, then that meant that I had my work cut out for me. It also lent itself to the possibility that a Font was behind the murders. It was possible that by being directly involved in such activities that they were trying to draw attention to themselves, and by the same token, were willingly trying to draw me out. Granted, this whole theory hinged on the validity of Gary's witness, but my instinct was telling me that I was on the right track. The murders were just too gruesome and too brutal to be anything but vampire kills, and ulterior motives aside, they had to be stopped.

"Miss Armentani?"

I blinked and turned back to the girl seated behind the desk.

I smiled as reassuringly as I could and said that I wouldn't mind waiting for him to return. She motioned towards a set of plastic chairs—the kind that one finds so often in hospital waiting rooms—and said that I was welcome to the coffee and donuts that sat on a little table nearby. I thanked her and sat down in the chair nearest the door so that I would know the instant Gary walked in. I ignored the offered refreshments and didn't even bother with the magazines, which seemed at least two months old. I needed to think and gather my thoughts so that when Gary walked in I would be prepared to ask him all the pertinent questions.

The seconds on the clock ticked on as I thought about hapless victims being torn apart in darkened alleyways, and I tried to keep my thoughts from showing on my face.

1:08 p.m.

The minutes dragged on but still I waited. And waited, and waited....

✞ ✞ ✞ ✞ ✞ ✞ ✞ ✞

The lab printout trembled slightly in Dr. Ackerman's hands as he stood with his back pressed firmly against the fax machine. The past week had been filled with nearly unbearable anxiety as he awaited the results of Andrew's bone marrow analysis, and now that he had them he was almost afraid to look. Miriam had graciously agreed to fax Andrew's results to his offices as a courtesy to him as the primary physician. It made up for him not being directly involved in the procedure that he had left in more capable and qualified hands. It was of no consequence that they had arrived in his office just prior to Andrew arriving for his follow-up appointment. The fact that the technicians had been able to run and examine the specimens in just under a week was more than he had a right to ask for. With the caseload Miriam's offices typically operated under, this was the favor to end all favors.

Bruce sighed with resignation. There was no point in dragging out the anxiety any further.

His gaze flicked across the printout.

The clock slowly ticked away the seconds as his eyes continued to crawl over the page. As he neared the bottom of the printout, they lit on the items in question and the carefully composed façade slipped for a fraction of a second. "Christ, Andy." His lips formed the words in a silent negation.

The world took on a dull, surreal quality as he made his way through the hallway back to his own office. Up until this point his office had been a veritable refuge from the harshness of reality. It was the place where he dispelled doubt and allayed his patient's fears, reassuring them that he would do everything in his power to get them on the road to recovery. Now he felt powerless.

The results of the lab work had confirmed his worst fears.

He had a name for what was ailing his friend, but as far as treatment was concerned, he was out of his league on this one. He knew that Miriam would treat Andrew's case as carefully as the others. Like him, she believed that friends and their health took top priority, and a colleague's friends were no exception. It was the least he could do at this point, notwithstanding being there for Andy every step of the way. Andy was like a brother to him and he would not leave him out in the cold to find the answers alone.

He entered his office without noticing the faces around him and shut the door firmly behind him. He sat at his desk for as long as he was able to and listened intently to the clock faithfully ticking the seconds away. He glared at the polished face and it seemed to glare back.

*Tick tock. Your friend's life is slowly ticking away as we speak, and there's no stopping it. Tick tock.*

He smashed his fist against the desk and the clock toppled over.

He got up and headed out the door to deliver the news. Andy's follow-up appointment was in thirty minutes, and time was of the essence. The sooner he broke the news to him, the sooner he could get on the road to recovery. He only hoped that Andy wouldn't see through the act and realize that it was deceptively simple. Nothing in this world ever was, but by God he was going to make it as easy on his friend as he could.

# Chapter 14

Andrew walked down the crowded streets completely oblivious to everything around him. He plowed into more than a few people and was rewarded with angry shouting and venomous glares, but he didn't pay them any mind. His mind spun with the memory of what had recently transpired in Bruce's office. Words like "CBC," "oncology," "thrombocytes," and "bone-marrow aspiration" rattled around uselessly in his brain. He desperately needed a distraction, *any* distraction to drown them out.

A group of men wheeling several cartons of supplies into a pub passed right in front of him, and he weaved sharply to avoid crashing into them. One of the cartons tipped dangerously to the side and nearly fell off the cart, and the men rushed forward to right it. One of them swore angrily at Andrew and got right in his face as he yelled one obscenity after the other at him.

Andrew stared at the man, unblinking.

His friends managed to calm him down and persuaded him to leave Andrew alone. The man waved his hand in disgust and stalked inside the pub. His companions finished pulling the cart through the doorway and disappeared into the building's smoky interior. One of them hung back and approached Andrew. He laid a tentative hand on his shoulder and stared down at him.

"You okay, man?"

Andrew stared up at him and finally shook his head. "No. No, I'm not." He laughed harshly and the tears that had been threatening all morning were suddenly let loose. He stood there in the doorway of the pub as his shoulders heaved with the intensity of his sobs. The stranger looked on and shifted uncomfortably, unsure what to do.

"Look man, lemme buy you a beer, huh? I'm sure whatever it is, it's not that bad." He let go of Andrew's shoulder as if he didn't know what else to do.

Andrew wiped his nose with the back of his hand and removed his glasses. His world blurred around the edges momentarily while he rubbed the foggy lenses against his coat, and then he settled them securely on the bridge of his nose. His vision righted itself and the world swam back into focus, but Andrew knew that the sense of perfection was an illusion. His body was being eaten up from the inside while everything around him remained unchanged, unaffected by time or the elements. He glanced around and felt the cold wind ruffle his hair and chase its way down the nape of his neck.

He realized that he had never really watched the changing of the seasons before, and armed with this latest news, it struck him that he may never have the chance to again. So much of his life had been taken for granted, so much of his life had passed before his eyes with the barest of acknowledgments.

He shut his eyes and couldn't believe it, refused to believe it, but the lab report in his pocket was more than confirmation. The numbers didn't lie even if he couldn't make heads or tails out of them. It was entirely possible that all he had ever been or had ever hoped to be would soon be reduced to a plot in the ground and an epitaph carved in stone.

The news was was almost too much to bear, and he had stood mute with disbelief as Bruce had explained the results in his office. Words like "blasts" and "Basophil granulocytes" had been liberally peppered throughout the conversation, along with an impressive but altogether meaningless amount of statistics concerning survival rates.

All of this was of no consequence to Andrew. The confirmed diagnosis of leukemia had been the final straw in a long chain of events that had been steadily driving him towards the breaking point. Bruce had tried to reassure him that the accompanying chemotherapy and radiation treatment may be covered by his insurance, and Andrew had nodded without really comprehending anything. The office with its stark white walls and plastic models of human organs seemed stifling, and he wanted desperately to escape. Running away from all things medical may have only created an illusion of being able to run away from this new reality, but as it was, an illusion was far easier to handle.

He made an awkward move for the door and hastily mumbled an apology to Bruce. "I can't…not right now. I need some fresh air and some time to think about all this. I just need some time…."

*Time,* he thought as he shambled clumsily through the waiting area, *is the one thing I* don't *have.*

The delicate balancing act that he had been maintaining for days suddenly tipped in the opposite direction, and the old fear over his impending mortality returned in a rush. He had to get out of here, had to get away from these rooms that reeked of alcohol and death. Anywhere was preferable to the smothering confines of these rooms.

Bruce reluctantly allowed him to leave in such a state and made him promise that he would call him as soon as he reached his workplace. He wasn't sure if Andrew was in any condition to drive anywhere, and he wouldn't be able to live with himself if he caused an accident.

The fresh air was a welcome relief after the antiseptic-ness of the building, and the throbbing in his head subsided briefly. Once he was alone with his thoughts, the reality of what was wrong with him hit him with full force and he had to pull over after he found himself weaving erratically in and out of traffic. He had then gotten out and started walking without any sense of where he was going.

"Look man, if you don't like my offer, just say so." The man's voice drowned out Andrew's reverie and he turned to join his friends in the pub.

"I would love a beer."

The man paused and then motioned for Andrew to follow him inside.

He did.

# Chapter 15

"Are you *sure* I can't take your order, sir?"

Wendell sighed and tried to smile up at the young waitress who stood across from him with her pencil poised above her notepad. He could never figure out why these places insisted on having their staff dress in neon pink or green t-shirts, especially when they clashed, rather than complimented the décor. Surely these places had no need to attract such attention. To their loyal customers and people in the know, the quality of their food far-exceeded that of the more upscale or big name chain restaurants. And it was cheaper.

He sighed again. That was a moot point as far as he was concerned. He had used up his meager store of emergency cash on convenience store coffee and this little jaunt with *Elysium's* Features Editor.

*If only he'd show up. . ..*

It had been over half an hour since he had spoken to Mr. Simms on the phone, and he was getting increasingly nervous and apprehensive as the minutes continued to crawl by. Was Mr. Simm's reassurance merely a ruse to placate the crackpot calling in with his wild fantasies and delusions? Or perhaps he had something come up and was trying to reach him on the payphone, which was two blocks from where he now sat?

Crap.

Perhaps he had better leave while he could still save face. When he had initially walked in, the wait staff had exchanged wary glances and had whispered behind their hands at him. He chose the seat nearest the front door by the windows so he would be sure to know when—and *if*—Mr. Simms showed up.

One of the waitresses had finally approached his table to take his order. He explained that he was waiting for someone and that he would order when they arrived. The girl had nodded in understanding and had brought him a complimentary serving of chips and salsa. He had wolfed those down within a few minutes, and realized that he was hungrier than he'd initially thought. He tried not to stare at the plates of food coming and going out of the busy kitchen area out to the waiting tables, but he couldn't silence the rumbling in his stomach—a fact which hadn't escaped the attention of the young waitress.

He smiled politely. "In a few minutes. I'm sure my friend won't be much longer."

She returned the smile and stuck the pencil behind her ear. "Just holler when you're ready."

Just as she turned to leave, the front door opened and Gary Simms swept into the room with his yellow steno pad in one hand. He spied Wendell in his seat over by the windows and approached him confidently, his free hand out in greeting.

"Mr. Bowers, a pleasure to meet you. Please call me Gary." He turned to the waitress who had paused in mid-step on her way back to the kitchen. "Two Juanie's Specials and two Dos Equis, one ticket." He turned and flashed a shark-like grin at Wendell before he had a chance to protest. "Now, now, Mr. Bowers. I make it a point to treat my sources the best I can, and if buying them lunch in addition to the money I usually pay out for their services is what it takes, then so be it."

He settled down into his chair and began making a notation on his steno pad. He then produced a plain white envelope from his shirt pocket and pushed it across the table towards Wendell who merely stared at it.

Gary chuckled. "I assure you it won't bite, Mr. Bowers. It's just my way of compensating you for your time."

Wendell visibly blanched at the attempt at levity. Gary noticed his reaction, and recognizing his faux pas, said apologetically, "Oh. I guess given the circumstances that 'bite' was not the best phrase to use, now was it?"

Wendell shook his head and attempted to push the nightmare images to the back of his brain. "No, no, it's fine... Gary. I just wasn't expecting to be paid for what I have to say is all."

His hands closed around the envelope and he tucked it into the depths of his back pack. It seemed rude to count it right in front of him, so he decided to wait until they had parted ways. If he didn't concentrate and get his facts straight, Gary may very well insist on taking the money back. He couldn't allow that to happen, especially now that the money could be put to the more practical use of drowning out the images that were plaguing him once again.

*First things first*, he thought as their food arrived and the smell of enchiladas and refried beans filled his nostrils, *tell your side of the story to earn your keep, and then the moment he's gone make a beeline to Mike's.*

✜ ✜ ✜ ✜ ✜ ✜ ✜ ✜

I found the heels of my boots tapping out a rhythm in sync with the ticking of the clock mounted above the bullpen. It was now nearly 2 p.m. and there was still no sign of Gary Simms. I was getting impatient, and I felt like a lion pacing the length of its cage over and over again until it had finally worn a smooth path in the floor.

I got out of my seat and approached the receptionist seated at the front desk. The regular receptionist had since come back from her lunch break and had relieved the pre-teen girl who'd kept staring at me out of the corner of her eyes. Occasionally I came across individuals whose hindbrains seemed more attuned than others, who instinctively knew that I wasn't human even if the more rational part of their mind refused to entertain such an idea. Judging by how wary she was of my presence, it seemed safe to assume that she was one of these people.

I smiled at her when I caught her staring the first time, but it just seemed to make her more nervous, so I stopped. When the other receptionist showed up just after 1:30 p.m., the girl hurried back to her workstation and seemed visibly relieved.

I approached the other woman and introduced myself and explained why I was there. She rolled her eyes when I mentioned Gary's name and then snickered under her breath. Obviously she knew something that I didn't, and seeing as how this wasn't the first time one of the employees had reacted this way whenever he was mentioned, I was glad that I'd brought my knives with me.

*Not* that I'd actually planned on using them, but I still felt comforted by their presence.

I settled back in my uncomfortable plastic chair and listened to the receptionist fielding calls. Most of them were for Gary and I laughed quietly to myself at her growing frustration. It seems I wasn't the only one in the city who was interested in his article, but I was sure that I was the only one who could actually *do* something about it.

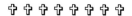

Gary pushed himself back from the table with a contented sigh. "Oh, man that was good. I know it's sinfully high in fat and cholesterol, but who cares when it makes you feel this happy?" He patted his full belly and stretched slowly, feeling extraordinarily pleased with himself. His article had made the front page of the latest issue once again, and before the day was even half over he had received vital and exclusive information that had the potential to make this one of the longest running stories in *Elysium's* history. Yes, indeed folks, Gary Simms was on top of the world looking down his nose at the other peons as they scurried around, destined to forever be in *his* shadow. He grinned and finished stretching.

Wendell sat across from Gary and was staring at him like he was an interesting yet frightening species of insect. He had just finished reliving one of the most horrifying and traumatic incidences in his life to a virtual stranger—a stranger who had scribbled madly while he talked, and had egged him on for more grisly details while he shoveled forkful after forkful of food into his mouth. Gary seemed to be enjoying himself a little *too* much, and lack of conscience aside, Wendell was concerned what Gary was going to do with the information that he had imparted to him.

The waitress came and cleared the plates and empty beer bottles away, and Wendell felt the urge to leave with her. The little alcohol that the beer had infused into his system had long-since worn off, and the nightmare images were once again threatening on the periphery of his mind. He began to tap his feet restlessly while Gary continued to read over his notes, and he reached in and out of the pockets of his coat—his old nervous tick—just for the sake of doing *something*.

Finally Gary spoke up. "Hmm, yes, this is *perfect!*" He clicked his tongue and the grin tugged at the corners of his mouth even more. "Everything you told me corroborates what my other source revealed to me, but just for clarity's sake...." He flipped through several pages of notes until he found the section that he was looking for. "You said that there were eight men, but that three seemed to be in control, correct?"

Wendell nodded.

Gary's pen lit on a spot further down the page. "Now, you said that once they started to uh…..,"—he made a ripping motion with his hands to illustrate what he was talking about. The restaurant was nearly empty once the lunch rush had ended, but Gary wasn't taking any chances with having his story leaked before it could be printed—"that the men took off in their van and fortunately didn't notice you in the corner."

Wendell shook his head. "I *assume* that they took off in their van, even though I didn't see or hear them do this. As I said, I had my eyes closed during the…..," he couldn't bring himself to say it. "But it seems reasonable that if they drove up there, then they must have left by the same means."

Gary nodded. "A reasonable assumption. As for this van, any chance you could provide me with a color, make, model, or even a partial license plate?" His eyes glittered greedily while he waited for Wendell to respond.

"It was dark. The most I can tell you is that it was large enough to hold around ten people, had a sliding door on the right-hand side, and the brakes were bad and squealed when it came to a stop."

The pen made a scratching sound as it raced across the page, and then Gary stopped, replaced the cap on his pen, and closed his notepad. He stood up, laid a twenty on the tabletop, and then pushed his chair back in.

Wendell stood up as well, and his mind instantly strayed to the vision of Mike's store and its glittering shelves of liquid courage.

As they exited the restaurant the wind whipped across their faces and chilled them to the bone. Wendell buried his hands in his coat pockets while Gary fished out his car keys and began juggling the notepad in one hand while unlocking the door of a pale blue Toyota with the other.

"Well, I do thank you for your time again, Mr. Bowers." He shook his hand once more. "I'm going to run this by my boss once I get back to the office, and it should be out by next week. If for some reason I need to get in contact with you again, is there anyplace I can reach you at?"

He gave Gary the location of the alleyway that ran near Vasquez Liquor, and he made a notation on the corner of his notes.

"Are you sure I can't give you a ride? It's awful cold out."

Wendell shook his head. "I'm used to it." Truth was, he wanted whatever minute traces of alcohol that remained in his system to be burned away as he walked, because once he hit Mike's he was going to inundate it like there was no tomorrow. If he only had one shot at this before the money ran out again, by golly was he going to give it his all.

Gary waved once as he pulled out of the parking lot, and the two parted ways as they went about their respective missions.

✛ ✛ ✛ ✛ ✛ ✛ ✛ ✛

"You have a visitor waiting to speak with you." The receptionist motioned towards the bank of plastic chairs reserved for visitors near the front entrance.

Gary paused in mid-step on his way through the front door and craned his neck in the direction that she had indicated. From his vantage point, the most he could make out was a set of denim-clad legs wearing calf-length brown boots—a very attractive set of legs.

He grinned wolfishly and turned to the receptionist who was staring at him with a look of slight apprehension. She knew Gary was a self-styled ladies man and that every female who had ever passed through the doors of *Elysium*—whether co-worker, reporter, or fresh off the streets—had all been given the once-over. A few found it flattering, but more than a few had found it irritating. Based on the way the young woman carried herself, she was betting on the latter.

"Now Kerri, you know my birthday is not until next March, so why all the eye-candy?"

The receptionist scoffed and waved a disapproving finger at him. "You get your filthy mind out of the gutter, you hear me? Miss Armentani is here to speak with you about your latest article; it's strictly business."

Gary stuck his lower lip out and pouted, and then his eyes lit up. "*Miss* Armentani? Well, perhaps I can take a few moments out of my *very* busy schedule to talk to her." He swaggered over to the woman and introduced himself. "A pleasure to meet you, Miss Armentani. If you will just follow me into my *office*, I'll be more than happy to discuss my latest article with you." He motioned for her to follow him, and he practically skipped across the bullpen towards Bob Garrett's office.

The receptionist's eyebrows drew together in a frown. Gary was laying the charm on extra thick for this one, and since when did he ever take visitors behind closed doors? The answer was never, but she had a sneaking suspicion that this was going to be the first and last time he did this. There was just something about the young lady that was slightly unnerving, yet she seemed polite enough.

She scoffed. It was probably nothing more than her desperate desire for something exciting to happen in this joint that was giving her false hopes. Lord knew that her social life was coming up equally empty. Her lunch date proved to be yet another loser that she seemed to attract like flypaper, and her mood—which hadn't been particularly good all morning—was getting progressively worse as the day dragged on. Seeing Gary all fluffed up like he was increased the desire to see him knocked down to size, and if anything would bruise his pride beyond repair, it would be to have that young lady do the honors. Gary wasn't exactly conspicuous about his appraisal, and judging by the look on her face, the young lady wasn't flattered in the slightest.

# Chapter 16

Sometime after Andrew had first entered the pub, he lay slumped over the edge of the bar. He had no conscious awareness of just how long he'd been there, or for that matter, when his companion had left. The area around him was littered with empty beer bottles and scotch slopped from shaky hands as the will to drown his sorrows proved stronger than his motor coordination. His senses were dulled from the liquor and he felt light and fuzzy, at ease for the first time in months. The myriad and altogether meaningless conversations of the clientele seated around him created a lulling backdrop to his own disjointed and chaotic thoughts. Some part of him berated himself for being such an irrational self-indulging coward, but another part—the dominant part of his personality that invariably crumbled under heavy stress—didn't give a damn.

A wave of darkness washed over him and his vision swam in and out of focus. Scrabbling clumsily for anything solid, his hands slipped and skittered along the slickness of the bar.

That was when gravity took over.

He vaguely remembered a momentary sense of weightlessness, which was soon swallowed up in an angry red tide of pain. Then all was blackness.

Little by little the darkness receded and he awoke to find that a cab had arrived to take him home. After a few failed attempts to understand his mumbling, the bartender had finally pulled out his wallet and had given the driver his address. Andrew sat up too fast and his vision suddenly went black as they tried to pull him to his feet. When he regained consciousness for the second time that afternoon, he recognized the familiar scenery whizzing by and realized that he was in a cab headed towards his apartment. He frantically pounded the back of the driver's seat with his fists to get his attention, and startled, the driver swore and told him to keep it down. Somehow he managed to understand his slurred speech as Andrew insisted that he drive him to his workplace instead. He gave him the address to *Elysium's* headquarters and settled back against the musty and dirty upholstery.

An idea had taken root in his mind back at the pub and had been strengthened by the alcohol flowing in his system. It was a fool's errand, but Andrew was a man on a mission. As he had sat at the bar downing one drink after another, he had reflected on how unrewarding his life had been of late: his editor hated everything he produced and he had to fight for every word of his that was printed. His co-worker Gary didn't share his passionate pursuit of the truth, yet his articles were the gold standard over at *Elysium*. Every word he produced was treated as gospel by his boss and apparently the public based on the fan mail that he regularly received. The fact that Gary received these accolades under false pretenses—in this case journalistic integrity and an unwavering adherence to the truth—was despicable beyond description. More than that, Andrew hated the fact that he had wasted his precious, but all-too-limited time being jealous of that miserable excuse for a human being, not to mention being too chicken-shit to call his boss on the way he treated him and the other employees. Three years of constant harassment was going too far, and he'd dealt with it like a coward.

*But not anymore,* he thought as the cab pulled over to the curb and came to an abrupt stop. *After today things will be different.*

Andrew tossed some money at the driver and told him to wait for him to reemerge from the building. What he had to say wouldn't take long, and with any luck Gary would be chatting it up with Bob in his office—that way he'd kill two birds with one stone.

He had to fumble with the latch several times before he was able to open the door, and he nearly stumbled and fell onto the sidewalk as he exited the cab. He began to make his way towards the front entrance in small, shuffling steps, his gaze fixed on his feet as he fought gravity every step of the way. As he pushed open the door and stepped into the reception area, he had no way of knowing that his path was about to be crossed by someone who had the potential to change his entire future. He also had no way of knowing that by crossing her path, that *her* future would be equally changed as well.

# Chapter 17

"So, *Miss* Armentani: how can I help you?"

Mr. Simms—Gary, he'd insisted—sat leaning back in his chair and was staring at me in a way that made my skin crawl. I'd been looked at that way more times than I cared to remember, but I couldn't treat Mr. Simms like I had treated all the others. After all, you can't kill a person just for being a creep, so I decided to encourage him as little as possible.

I stared back at him as neutrally as I could manage and crossed my arms over my chest to appear standoffish. If Mr. Simms was half as intelligent as he thought he was, he'd recognize a rebuff when he saw one. "I want to know who your witness is—the one who saw the vampire murders being committed." There it was: no pretense, no small talk, just down to business.

He looked surprised for a moment and then he gave a shout of laughter. I retained my posture and stared at him unblinking, my expression never wavering. The laughter gradually faded away and the humor in his eyes was immediately replaced by deep suspicion. He leaned forward and pointed his finger at me accusingly. "You're a reporter, aren't you?"

I almost laughed at the illogical but not altogether unexpected conclusion he'd drawn, but I was fairly sure that he would throw me out of "his office" if I did. The name *Bob Garrett* on the front placard hadn't escaped my notice as we'd filed in, but despite his attempt at deception, I couldn't leave before I got what I had come here for. I swallowed the laughter down and forced my mouth to relax.

When I didn't immediately respond, he swore and stood up from the desk.

"Goddamn it, I told that nitwit to do a check on everyone who came in here looking for me!"

I assumed that the "nitwit" in question was the woman at the front desk—the very nice and *helpful* woman at the front desk—and I felt the anger rise within me. It was one thing to treat women like an object to be possessed, but to speak against them when they weren't present to defend themselves? Not on my watch.

"Sit down, Mr. Simms."

His eyes showed too much white around the edges as he turned to stare at me. Apparently something in his hindbrain kicked in and informed him that there was more than one predator in the room.

He started to say something, stopped, but remained standing. I knew that his inability to obey my command had nothing to do with courage—he was scared stiff, virtually paralyzed with fear. This time I did smile and some of the anger vanished from my expression. I spread my hands and tried to appear genial. "Mr. Simms, let's put aside your own glaring personality faults when it concerns the appropriate treatment of women, and get one thing straight: I'm not a reporter, and I'm not trying to steal your sources. I want the name of your witness for my own personal reasons and for those reasons alone."

He kept staring at me and then he licked his lips. He chuckled nervously and made his way back to the chair and sat across from me once again, the old sense of cockiness returning as the fear faded away. He smiled condescendingly. "And what would a pretty little thing like you do with that kind of information? My sources are my sources, Miss Armentani. I gave them my word that they would remain anonymous and I won't give them up—unless of course you have something for me in return."

He let his eyes rove over my body and I found my hand instinctively going for the knives hidden under my jacket. I had to remind myself that I was in a public place and that this wasn't the time for knife play.

I forced myself to breathe and reconsidered my options. It wasn't fair that Mr. Simms take the fall for my own stupidity. I had assumed that he was smart enough to recognize danger when he saw it, but apparently I had been giving him too much credit. Now that this option had been eliminated from the equation, it was time to move on to option two.

I never got the chance.

At that moment there was a terrific amount of noise, shouts, and what sounded like chairs being pushed away from desks too quickly. The sound seemed to snake its way from the front entrance right up to the threshold of the office that we were in. Something thumped against the door and the doorknob twisted from side to side as someone tried to get in. From the frosted pane of glass set in the middle of the door, several amorphous shapes bobbed and jerked from side to side. Obviously someone *really* wanted to get in here, but apparently a few others didn't think that that was such a good idea.

This time I did go for my knives. I kept one palmed at my side to use the moment the door flew open.

There was one more bang against the door and it burst open with a loud *smack* as it struck the wall behind it. Several bodies tumbled through the door all at once in a tangle of arms and legs—men, women, young, and overweight—and I stood up from my chair at the same moment. My eyes swept over the scene and dissected it in seconds.

In the center of the fray stood a young man, mid to late twenties with dark hair and glasses, and he was *very* sick. His aura sputtered and flickered like a fire in a rainstorm, and the border was eaten away and pockmarked with black spots. The light that normally would have emanated from it was almost completely extinguished. I cringed despite myself and hurriedly tucked the knife away. Not one of these people—this man in particular—was capable of inflicting harm on me or anyone else in the room. The auras of the other people present flared brilliantly around them as the adrenaline coursed throughout their system. The contrast between theirs and the man in the middle was astounding, and I felt a stab of sympathy for him as the reek of alcohol wafted across my nostrils.

He turned away from the arms simultaneously attempting to comfort and haul him out of the room, and then his bloodshot eyes fixed on Gary. He stopped struggling and raised his right arm, index finger pointed directly at him.

"You."

I didn't think it was possible for a single word to carry such a multitude of roiling emotion behind it, but there it was for all to hear.

Gary was looking slightly bewildered at the melee that had spilled into the office. One minute he had been giving me the once over, smug in his belief that I would actually *consider* his offer, and the next he was the center of unwelcome attention. The eyes of everyone in the room were riveted on the two as they stood there facing one another. The noise in the bullpen had dwindled away to an eerie silence that was laced with an air of expectancy, and I heard more than a few phones being taken off the hook.

Maybe putting my knife away wasn't such a good idea after all.

At that moment, the man shambled unsteadily into the room until he was standing next to the desk. He placed one hand on the edge for balance, and the verbal grenades started up with a vengeance. The words were so badly slurred and spilled out so fast that I barely understood half of what was said, but from what I did manage to pick out, it was apparent that the man who had barged in had a bone to pick with Gary.

Gary barely had time to duck the first few shouted accusations before he fired back a few of his own. "How dare you come barging into my office when...!"

"*Your* office? When the hell did Bob die and make *you* king?!"

"You're just jealous because you're still at the bottom of the totem pole, and I'm moving up the ranks!"

The other man grew silent and the people who stood with bated breath in the doorway and out in the bullpen all heaved a collective gasp.

The man shook his head and smiled ruefully. "You know what? You're right. You're absolutely right. I *am* jealous of you. I'm jealous because you've somehow managed to convince yourself that this *job*," he gestured around the room with his arms outstretched, "this *joke* of a publication, is as good as it gets. I've spent the last few years of my life hoping that someday I might come to think of this job in the same way, but I never have. I *wasted* those three years, but today my eyes have been opened. I *finally* see beyond the bullshit that you and Bob Garrett spew around you on a daily basis, and I pity you. You're both too helplessly inured by the world that you've built for yourself here, that you're afraid to break free. But not me. I'm breaking free as of now." He took a step towards the door and looked back over his shoulder. "As soon as I prove to everyone around here that you're nothing but a washed up old reporter who fills his stories with lies and paranoid delusions just to sell copies, I'm out of here."

Gary's face turned a brilliant shade of puce and I found myself silently applauding the other man. Everyone within earshot bore identical expressions of unabashed glee, and their eyes sparkled with delight. It seemed safe to assume that this little exchange was about the most exciting thing that had happened here in....well, ever.

"You wait just a goddamned minute!" Gary thundered. He stepped back from behind the desk and blocked the other man from leaving. "You can attack my personal character all you want, but one thing I won't tolerate is being called a liar! Everything I've ever reported from my sources is as true and accurate if they had written it themselves! What, you think that I just made all of this stuff up?" He gestured around him to the framed issues that graced the walls on all four sides.

I had to admit that the display of righteous indignation *was* impressive, but judging by the amount of eye rolling that the assembled crowd was engaging in, I was betting it was just a defense mechanism against a well-deserved reproach.

He continued his little speech and punctuated the air with dramatic gesturing. "You think I just sat there in my car during my lunch break and fabricated witness testimony? That I paid that homeless man over by Vasquez Liquor to say what *really* happened to that couple who were found butchered in an alleyway? Hmm? You think I just pulled the name 'Wendell Bowers' out of a hat or paid someone to call here and leave me a phony message to meet with them today?"

My ears pricked up at the mention of the murdered couple, and I realized that I had gotten exactly what I had come here for. I had the name and location of the witness. All I needed to do now was confront them to see if they were legit.

The man seemed un-phased by Gary's outburst. "Yeah. That's *exactly* what I think. And I'm gonna prove it." He shoved past the crowd gathered in the doorway and stumbled awkwardly towards the front entrance. I decided to take my leave as well.

"Mr. Simms, thanks again for your time. It's been... interesting."

He barely had time to blink before I was out the door and through the crowd. The whole office was erupting in applause and excited babbling as I raced across the bullpen. Mid-way across the room, I heard Gary swear and bang his fist against the desk. "I knew that woman was a reporter and I just let my source slip!" Two more bangs accompanied a volley of expletives.

I caught a glimpse of the man sliding across the seat of a taxicab idling by the curb just as I reached the threshold. It took off in the direction Gary had mentioned and I shot around to the parking lot in the back. I was in my car and screeching around the corner in a matter of moments, and I caught sight of the cab's rear bumper right before the light turned from red to green. I tailed them as inconspicuously as I could, despite the urge to burn rubber all the way towards our destination. The culprit behind the murders was within my sights, and they were not going to escape without paying for what they had done.

Mark my words.

☩ ☩ ☩ ☩ ☩ ☩ ☩ ☩

The brakes of the battered gray van screeched in protest as it slowly pulled away from the building it had been parked next to, and made a wide U-turn onto oncoming traffic. Horns blared and several drivers flipped them off amid shouted curses, but the three men in front paid them no mind.

*She* was within their sights. *She* had made the connection between the articles in the paper and had come to the source for more information. Their mistress had hoped that the grisly murder splashed on the front page of the newspaper would spur the woman into action, and it had done exactly that. Never mind that the local paper treated it as nothing more than another murder—a sadistic and *bizarre* murder no less— but what mattered was that the independent publication had made the connection regarding the true identity of the killer. It was of no consequence whether the writers actually believed that vampires were stalking the city and were preying on the innocent or not; what mattered was that *she* believed it. The fact that she had come to the very source of this connection was testament to this.

It appeared that for all her expertise and prowess as a killer, that this woman was entirely predictable. Predictable was good. Predictable eliminated all the guesswork and made tracking her down easier. More importantly, predictable was killable.

The man in the cab was an unforeseen element, but no matter. He was obviously bound for the same destination as the woman, so perhaps his presence wasn't all that inconvenient. The fewer people who were aware of their mistress' presence in the city, the better. If a little more blood had to be shed in the name of anonymity and security, then so be it. They would be happy to shed it when the time came.

# Chapter 18

The bottle fell from nerveless fingers and lay forgotten and partially empty on the floor of the alleyway. Blessed darkness descended upon him in a rush and the nightmare images were silenced. Wendell was at peace despite the cold and the filth, and he would have welcomed oblivion with open arms if he hadn't been too drunk to move.

"Hey buddy!"

Andrew was rudely jarred awake by the blaring of a horn that sounded too close for comfort. When he finally surfaced from unconsciousness, blinking owlishly in the glare of the sun coming in through the bug-spattered windshield, he had no earthly idea where he was.

The horn sounded again and he reached out and swatted at the empty air. *Where was the damned alarm clock?!*

A blast of cold air ghosted over him and he reached for the comforter that should have been there but wasn't. Two hands gripped his shoulders and hauled him unceremoniously out of bed and set him against something hard and cold.

Andrew groaned and swore as the sudden movement sent white-hot bolts of pain stabbing through his brain. His eyes felt glued shut, and he forced them to open completely. His vision swam in a hazy mass of colors and semi-solid shapes before righting itself, and he found that he wasn't in his bed like he had originally assumed, but was standing outside with a very pissed-looking man staring down at him.

"C'mon man, I ain't got all damn day to be babysittin' your ass! Lot's of people in this city have places to go and are happy to pay for my services. And speaking of," he held out his hand. "You owe me twenty-eight dollars."

"Wha…?" Andrew blinked again. Was this some sort of bizarre nightmare where figments of his imagination actually charged him for disturbing his sleep? He shook his head and immediately wished he hadn't done that.

"Hey!" The man shook him none-too-gently. "We're right in front of Vasquez Liquor and you owe me twenty-eight bucks for driving you here!"

Little by little, bits and pieces of the day's events began to come back to him. They were hazy at first, but gradually they strengthened in clarity: his visit with Bruce, the pub, his wanting to tell his boss and Gary exactly what he thought of them…all of that came back in a rush except for the reason why he was *here*.

"Vasquez Liquor?"

The man scoffed. "Yeah, just like you asked me to. And if you ask me, the *last* thing you need is another drink. If I were you I'd be looking into AA soon before you wind up dead in the gutter somewhere."

"Oh. *Ohhh*…." Andrew suddenly remembered the reason why he was here and how he'd obtained the information. Well, looks like his promise to break free from *Elysium* wasn't so far-fetched after all. Once Bob Garrett got wind of his drunken tirade, it was a sure bet that a pink slip with his name on it would be waiting for him.

"I'm still waiting for my money. Either you got it or I'm gonna have to call the cops, your choice."

Andrew dug out his wallet, pulled a twenty and a ten from the depths, and slapped them into the man's upturned palm. "Keep the change."

The man walked back to the driver's side muttering under his breath and sped off in a spray of gravel.

The neon façade of Vasquez Liquor blinked and buzzed as he walked up to the front door. In the fading light it threw broad orange shadows all around him and created the illusion of daylight. He had no idea what he was trying to prove by tracking this Wendell Bowers down—hell, for all he knew, the man didn't even exist—and even if he *did* exist, what then? He couldn't very well go back to *Elysium* and apologize to Gary and then beg for his job back. If he was to feel any vindication for the stink he'd caused, then groveling was out of the question. He'd made his bed and by golly, he was going to lie in it.

To his surprise, Mike Vasquez the proprietor knew exactly who he was talking about, and even pointed him in the direction of the alleyway that ran parallel to the store.

"I gotta warn you that he left here a few hours ago with a bottle of whiskey, so no telling what state he's going to be in when you do find him. My advice is to let him sleep it off and come back in the morning." He stared at Andrew with a mixture of pity and confusion as he wavered slightly on his feet.

Mike's expression inched closer to pity.

Wendell often came in here in a similar state and if this young man didn't watch himself, he was in danger of going down the same road.

Andrew thanked the man and began making his way to the alley. He'd already come this far so might as well see this through—whatever *this* was.

The man exited the liquor store and began heading towards the alleyway nearby, his pocked and sputtering aura visible even from across the street. I watched the exchange between the man and the cab driver—not the friendliest person on the planet, but the brutal honesty he'd leveled on him about the drinking won points in his favor. I felt slightly guilty for allowing him to lead *me* to the witness, but based on what I'd seen back at *Elysium*, this man had something to prove—both to himself and to his co-workers. It just didn't seem right for me to interfere.

I took comfort in the fact that in the highly-unlikely event that things did get out of hand, that I was close enough to be able to jump in and save him. I watched as he turned down the alleyway and headed towards the redbrick Victorian that I knew lay at the end, and then I opened my door. A curious tingly feeling rippled down my spine and wormed its way into the pit of my stomach as I climbed out of the car.

Nerves?

Hardly. I was fairly certain that neither he nor the mysterious Wendell Bowers were any threat to me, so perhaps the sensation was due to something else.

Anticipation?

That seemed plausible. After all, I was considerably closer to discovering who—though I already knew *what*—had murdered that poor couple. The only thing left to discover after that was *why*.

I planned to be as unobtrusive as possible and would watch their exchange from a distance while listening in for the pertinent information. I would stay long enough to ensure that the man got safely into a cab, and then I would make a monetary donation to this Wendell Bowers. He need never know the real reason behind the charity and I hoped that he put it to good use, especially now that the weather was growing bitter.

I set off across the street to follow him.

✟ ✟ ✟ ✟ ✟ ✟ ✟ ✟

They realized where they were headed long before they actually entered the street in question. The three men in the front of the van grinned ferally as they anticipated the ensuing attack. The five other men—with one exception—had some reservations about what was to be asked of them, but they didn't let the fear show on their faces.

If this woman was capable of taking down a progeny who was a hundred years old or older, then *they* didn't stand a chance. They were months or weeks old at best, and had never seen real carnage. Some of them suspected that when the shit invariably hit the fan that *they* would be part of the ensuing bloodbath—not as aggressors, but as victims.

✟ ✟ ✟ ✟ ✟ ✟ ✟ ✟

Andrew strained to see in the gathering gloom that permeated the space around him. He'd passed one crumbling and dilapidated house after the next along with innumerable trash heaps, but there was no sign of the mysterious Wendell Bowers. He picked his way carefully over the ground that was littered with broken bottles, dirty baby diapers, plastic bags, and cigarette butts. The last thing he needed was to stumble and risk an injury.

At that precise moment his foot caught the edge of a pothole and he pitched forward. He managed to break his fall with his hands and they came away bloody.

Great. Just great.

A small noise to his right caused his head to swivel instinctively around. A smaller path led away from the main alley and passed behind a sagging white Victorian that was swathed in shadows. About midway against the rickety metal fence that bordered the house, a vaguely-human-shaped mass was in the process of rolling onto its side. Glass clinked as the figure curled into a fetal position, and a bottle rolled momentarily into view.

This either had to be Wendell Bowers in the flesh, or one hell of a coincidence.

He approached the figure tentatively and peered down at him. It was impossible to tell the age of the man because his face was buried in the folds of the dirty trench coat that he wore. A half-empty bottle of whiskey lay nearby just out of reach.

This *had* to be Wendell Bowers.

He knelt down and gently shook the man. He grunted and curled up tighter against the intrusion and clutched at a dirty black backpack. Andrew persisted and shook him harder, and he finally seemed to come to.

"Okay Cassidy, Daddy's on his way, he just...needs a few more minutes of sleep...." He started to drift away and Andrew shook him again. This time his eyes snapped open and they stared blankly out at Andrew with a mixture of confusion and anger.

"What have you done with my daughter?" He sat up and stared wildly around him at the darkness, his head whipping from side to side.

Before Andrew could feel sorry for the man and explain who he was or why he was here, something heavy crashed to the ground near them with a loud *slap*. As the dust cleared, it appeared that some shingles from the house nearest them had come loose, and as Andrew's gaze flicked up to discover the cause, he saw several forms leering down at him. At that moment a woman's voice rang down the narrow space and ordered them to get down.

Then all hell broke loose.

# Chapter 19

I hung back out of sight as the man veered off down the narrow path worn into the grass between the sagging remains of two houses. He had apparently found who he thought was Wendell Bowers, but the man was equally if not more drunk than the other.

Birds of a feather, I thought and edged closer.

I surveyed my surroundings out of habit and kept flicking my gaze around constantly. The space was relatively open on my right and afforded me an unobstructed view. It was nearly impossible for someone to be able to sneak up on me, so I didn't pay it much mind and chose to concentrate on what was directly in front of me.

Something red flickered in my periphery just above eyelevel as I watched the two men. My head whipped upwards and I saw four distinct profiles standing on the roof of the house. All of them were surrounded by a hazy nimbus of red and gold, and I immediately knew that we were about to be ambushed. A small sound behind me caused me to whirl around instinctively, and I saw four more profiles—all with the same aura around them—headed straight for me.

I had a split second to decide what to do.

I started sprinting for the two men crouched on the floor of the alley and opened my mouth to scream at them to get out of there as fast as they could. Some part of me knew that the effort was futile, but I had to try regardless of the odds stacked against us.

One of the man-shaped figures on the roof tensed as if to spring. Several loose shingles went tumbling down to the ground and landed a few feet away from the two men. The sudden intrusion gave them a few seconds of warning before all hell broke loose, and I screamed at them to move.

"Get down, now!"

I had a knife in each hand by the time I reached them and I shoved both of them against the fence. I got into a defensive crouch and blocked them with my body as the four men in front of me launched themselves directly at us. One of them tackled me to the ground and we went down hard, but I had anticipated the move and was ready for it. I brought the knife around and it sheared through the thin fabric of his leather jacket and plunged into the flesh below. He screamed and made the mistake of rolling over onto his back to throw me off, but I hung on for dear life. His eyes widened as he realized his error, and I brought the knife down and struck him again.

Blood splashed against my palm and I felt the urge to lick it clean along with the knife. It had been nearly a month since I had last fed, and the sight of him struggling and thrashing while he bled out brought the hunger rushing forth. I quashed it firmly down and threw everything I had into the remainder of the fight.

He brought his left arm up to protect himself and I yanked it away from me at an impossible angle. The bone snapped effortlessly and the sound echoed like a shotgun blast in the confined space. He cried out and struggled harder, throwing his weight from side to side. I responded by leaning my full weight against the knife, and as I watched, the blood pulsed out in a crimson torrent. His good hand fluttered uselessly against my arms as I wrenched and twisted the knife in deeper, and his aura begin to sputter and dim. Small, inarticulate noises escaped his lips as they drew back over his teeth, and his back arched up off the ground as the death agony began to overtake him.

A high, keening scream echoed off the walls of the house and sent chills down my spine. Strong hands gripped me by the collar of my coat and flung me away from the man as he lay dying. The metal fence groaned as I went flying into it, but it held strong despite the onslaught. Wendell and the other man were cowering in obvious terror as I smacked into the fence with bone-rattling force, but I sprang to my feet un-phased before the metallic ringing had subsided.

Two of the men knelt by their fallen comrade, and the fourth man—who seemed bewildered by this sudden turn of events—stood there alone and unprotected.

Easy prey.

The two men seemed wholly oblivious to what was going on around them and I began to stalk him slowly. He backed up in response to my advances, and his gaze switched anxiously from my face to the backs of his companions, as if he half-expected them to come to his rescue any moment.

When he was no more than a foot away from the opposite fence, he was trembling in obvious terror. He shot his companions one last desperate glance. "Castillo! Daman, help me!"

The two men ignored him and were cradling the body of the dead man in their arms and were weeping openly.

I was momentarily struck dumb. Not once in my three-hundred and forty-seven years did I ever observe progeny react this way to the death of one of their own. If I had been asked yesterday if this were possible, I would have said with certainty that it wasn't.

Now I wasn't so sure.

I could reconsider this belief after I had dealt with them and they were all safely dead and disposed of. I turned my attention back to the man in front of me. He whimpered as the betrayal set in, and he raised his hands in a supplicating gesture.

"No."

He continued backing up until his body was pressed firmly up against the fence. I stepped closer and steadied the knife in my hand.

"Please, no!" He raised his arms in front of his face as I sprang forward.

It was over very quickly.

His body slumped slowly down to the ground and then fell over on its side. I backed away and felt slightly uneasy. Maybe it was because he had used the word "please" that unnerved me, or perhaps the fact that like the others before him, he was weak and relatively new to this life. His aura had been marginally brighter than the one from a month ago, and I found myself once again pondering the motives of the Font behind their creation. Either way I had executed him as quickly and mercifully as I could. I would deal with these new-found emotions later.

I turned to face the remaining attackers. The two men who were grieving over their fallen brethren stood up in unison and turned to glare at me with undisguised malice. The one closest to my right wiped the blood that stained his palms on the front of his shirt and flexed his muscles. The one on the left shouted an order in the silent alleyway, "Take her down!"

I barely had time to brace for the attack before the four men on the roof descended silently to the ground with cat-like reflexes. My attention was distracted by their frontal assault, and as a crushing blow knocked me to the ground from my left, I realized that it was a diversion. The two grieving men were the obvious muscle in this little group, and the rest were there to provide a distraction.

Instinct took over, and fighting furiously for my life, I lashed out with the knife in my right hand. There was a snarl of rage as the blade sliced through the flesh of my attacker's face, and I quickly drew my hand back to strike again. I managed to inflict a matching wound on the same side of his face before an elbow was slammed into the side of my head. Stars rocketed in my field of vision and the world tilted dangerously to the side. Fingers dug into my arms as I was pushed face-first into the dirty ground. I instinctively curled my hands around the knives and tried to roll onto my side, but I was pinned by his weight. His hands clawed furiously at my fingers, and just as I felt him beginning to wrench the knives from my hands, something remarkable happened.

Something remarkably stupid and reckless.

There was the sound of glass smashing against something hard, which was followed by a startled scream of pain. The man holding me down lifted his head to shout at the others to help restrain me, and I managed to shift my face upwards. Wendell and the other man stood wavering on their feet and were brandishing the remains of a liquor bottle and what looked like a length of pipe. Apparently enough alcohol still thrummed throughout their system to make them feel brave enough to ignore the danger before them. One of the progeny knelt on the alley floor, his hair slick with blood and amber liquid, looking a little worse for wear. The others stood around him and were casting wary glances between him, Wendell, and his companion.

"Destroy them!" Hot breath ghosted over my ear as the man pinning me down struggled to control the situation from all angles. It was obvious that he had to compensate for the relative lack of experience and cooperation on the others' part, and I used it to my advantage. I knew that I only had one chance to gain the upper hand again, and I was going to take it.

I went limp and stopped resisting. The pressure slowly eased up on me as I allowed him to relieve me of my two knives. It was a small price to pay in order for the two humans and me to get out of here alive, but I was confident that by the end of the night I would get them back.

The man holding me down handed my knives over to his companion and he took them wordlessly. In a scene parodying the one from a month ago, I was flung back against the fence and was pinned there by his body. Blood pulsed dark and thick from the ragged wounds in his face, and followed the curve of his cheek and chin before finally dropping off into the collar of his shirt. His eyes bulged out of their sockets as we stood face to face, but unlike his predecessor, his aura blazed with power. He was at least a century or older, but he wasn't powerful enough to be a Font. Perhaps another century or so would result in that, but I had no intention of giving him the luxury of time.

The corners of his mouth twitched as his eyes roamed my face, the gaping wounds pulling grotesquely with his every movement. He motioned to the man at his side and one of my knives flashed into view. Gripping it tightly in his hand, he pushed the hair plastered to my face away with the tip and then ran the blade slowly over my eyelids. I forced myself to breathe as normally as possible—one false move and he'd gouge my eye out.

There was a brief scuffle as the four progeny dragged Wendell and his companion towards us. Both of them had blood running down their faces—mainly from the nose or across the brow—but the other man, the journalist, was virtually unconscious.

My reaction must have shown on my face because the man pinning me down laughed. He gestured towards the two of them with my knife. "It pains you to see them like that, doesn't it? Good. I *want* you to suffer." He leaned forward until his mouth lay at my earlobe. "Take a good look at what you did to my brother." He pointed towards the still form on the ground. "By the time I'm done, you'll be begging me to do the same thing to you. But first," he snapped his fingers and Wendell and the other man were forced to their knees, "you get to see these two die, then *you* get to die knowing that you were powerless to protect them, your precious *innocents*."

Brother. So *that* explained the bond between them and accounted for the intense grieving. I flicked my gaze over to the left and realized that the other man was the mirror image of the one in front of me and the one that I had just killed. They were triplets.

The last word was barely a snarl as he shifted his weight over to my left, affording me a view of Wendell and the other man. It also afforded me an opportunity that hadn't been present moments before. I had just enough room to cock my head back and I smashed my face into his without hesitation.

It hurt, but it hurt *him* worse.

He let go of me and stumbled back, and then I drove my knee into his gut, knocking the breath out of him.

Panic ensued as the four progeny scrambled away in an effort to avoid being next. I didn't give either brother a chance to react, and my reflexes kicked into overdrive. I drove my elbow into the man's back as he knelt on the ground, and he went down hard for the final count. In that same instant I had my other two knives out and readied. His brother was still gazing at the scene in shock when I sank both blades into him and twisted them in to the hilt. His eyes bulged from their sockets and he opened his mouth to scream, but no sound came out. I had just enough time to notice that his aura was equally as strong as his brother's before he collapsed to the ground. I watched as his life force began to ebb away as the blood flowed from his wounds—one in the neck to ensure certain death, and one in the chest just for good measure.

It took every ounce of will to ignore the hunger screaming in my veins that demanded that I bend down and feed from him before his life faded away, but I managed. I stood up from the alley floor and rolled my head back on my shoulders, flexing my muscles for the ensuing slaughter. I turned with deliberate slowness and smiled as the four remaining progeny gaped at me in horror. They immediately scattered in all directions and began frantically scaling the roof of the sagging white Victorian.

The third brother was slowly getting to his feet, and I stood my ground waiting for him to regain his composure. He winced as he finally stood up and I couldn't help but smile at my handiwork. "Take a good look at your *brothers*." I made sure to emphasize the plural form. "You should know that I'll be taking my knives back very soon," I gestured to the two knives that were still clenched in his palm. "By the time I'm done, *you'll* be begging *me* to do the same thing to you." I spat his words back at him and his face contorted with animalistic rage.

The sound of a siren screeching up the road drowned out the man's reply. The sound was growing louder and louder and I realized that we had seconds to leave the scene before the authorities arrived. There wasn't enough time for me to attack him, retrieve my knives, and spirit Wendell and his companion off to safety. The same applied to him. He couldn't kill me, kill the two witnesses, and escape with his dying brother either.

It seemed we were at a standstill.

He made his decision first and flung my knives down to the ground and raced towards his brother. He slung him up effortlessly and then tossed him limply over his shoulder as he began to scale the wall of the house. I hurriedly scooped up my knives, shoved them loosely back into the sheath, and then rushed towards Wendell and his companion. I wrapped an arm around the other man and hauled him to his feet, and then slung him over my shoulder just as effortlessly.

Wendell scrambled backwards, but there was no time for me to explain myself. "Hurry, there's no time!"

With my free arm, I helped Wendell to his feet and we made our way down to the end of the alley and then veered right. My car had been parked nearby, and I practically dragged him towards it and shoved him in the backseat. He scooted over as I set the unconscious man down beside him, and then I was behind the wheel in a matter of moments.

I burned rubber the length of the street as I drove like a bat out of hell towards my apartment.

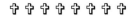

The man lay cradled in his brother's lap as he struggled to breathe, his feet drumming the floor in a mindless tattoo as the blood bubbled up from the wounds in his chest and neck. His hands grasped at the empty air as he fought against the pain and crushing darkness that was attempting to suck him under forever. His brother clasped his hand and held him closer, his eyes hard around the edges. The wounds on his face throbbed with the memory of her cutting him, of her slicing his flesh with the knives—the knives that had killed one brother and mortally wounded another. There were no words to describe the intense hatred he felt for the woman who had done this to them, no words to describe what he planned on doing to her the moment their paths crossed again.

"Daman…." The man gasped and his back arched off the floor as the blood began to fill his lungs and impaired his speech.

The other man shushed him and gently stroked his hair. "Save your strength, brother." He shut his eyes as the wet sounds continued to fill the room, but he couldn't shut out the reality of what was happening. His brother was dying and there was nothing he could do about it.

"Alec is….is de…," he gave a choking gasp and his feet kicked the floor once more.

"Yes, Castillo—Alec is dead." The words were alien and inconceivable all at once and sounded like they were being spoken by somebody else. Their mother had promised them that they would be together forever, but their mother had been wrong. She couldn't have known that this woman would set foot in her city and would destroy everything that they had ever known and loved. She couldn't have known that when she ordered them to bring her into custody. Now it was too late.

Castillo sobbed and then his breathing became erratic as the blood filled his lungs completely. His eyes stared wildly around the room as he thrashed helplessly in his brother's arms, and his grip tightened on his hand.

Daman couldn't bear to look at him while he struggled in his arms. He didn't want to remember his brother reduced to a whimpering mass of blood and pain, so he averted his eyes. It was a cowardly thing to do, but at least his brother wouldn't notice it. He had to be strong for him. He had to be strong for them all.

Castillo's struggles slowly began to cease as his feet stopped their mindless dance upon the floor. His whole body went slack as a final susurrating pulse of air escaped his lips and then he was still.

Daman threw back his head and screamed in anguish as his brother's life force was violently expelled into the air. The police car tore around the corner and barreled down the alleyway outside the house at that precise moment, and the sound was lost in the din of the siren squall. The force of the outburst left his throat raw and bleeding, but it was nothing compared to the agony he felt over the loss of his brothers. Where there had been three, always three for decade upon decade, there would now be only one for the rest of eternity.

He looked down at his brother and saw that his eyes were open. He gently brushed them closed with the tips of his fingers and slowly stood up. Castillo's body slipped silently to the floor and his knuckles rapped against the dusty wood. He strode across the floor and exited the tiny attic room that had become his brother's makeshift tomb, and then headed out to hunt down the four cowards who had abandoned them in their time of need.

# Chapter 20

The man moaned and tossed restlessly as the car flew down the street. I kept glancing at my rearview mirror every few seconds to make sure that we weren't being followed. All the other cars seemed to be headed towards their own destinations, and no one tailed us as I exited and took a right towards my modest apartment. Wendell sat with his back ramrod straight against the seat with his eyes fixed on mine in the mirror, one hand steadying the other man's shoulders as his head lolled from side to side. Fear radiated off of him in waves, and for the first time since all this madness began, I noticed his aura shining like a beacon in the dark. Despite his apparent history of hard drinking and the fact that he lived on the streets, he was remarkably healthy.

I couldn't say the same about the other man.

His aura continued to flicker in and out of focus, and once again I found myself wondering what could possibly be eating him alive from the inside. He whimpered as my car bottomed out on the steep driveway that led to my parking space, and Wendell flashed him an apprehensive look. His eyes immediately flicked back to mine, and they widened as the car began to slow down. The dirty black backpack that he had been carrying with him when I had tossed him into the back of my car was clutched tightly in front of him, almost like a shield to ward me off.

It was obvious that he was afraid of me. He had seen what I could do back at the alley and my flinging him into the back of my car without an explanation hadn't exactly helped any. The fact that we were now coming to a stop only made things worse; for all he knew I had driven them here to kill them.

I turned off the ignition and placed my hands on the steering wheel to show that I was unarmed. I looked at him in the rearview mirror and I spoke to him reassuringly. "I know you're probably frightened out of your mind right now, but I swear I'm only trying to help. As soon as you help me get him"—I jerked my thumb at the man next to him—"up to my apartment so that I can tend to his wounds, I'll explain everything."

His expression didn't register that he'd heard me, but after a moment he slowly nodded his head.

"Okay." I reached over and opened the door and then got out. I went around to the back of the car and the door opened before I could touch the handle. Wendell was leaning over the other man as he pushed the door open for me. He undid his seat belt while I ducked down and gathered the man up into my arms.

"Thanks."

"You're welcome."

He slid across the seat and then shut the door behind him while I hefted the unconscious man over my shoulder and began to walk towards the complex. He trailed silently behind me and we went inside.

"Andy? Come on, Andy pick up the phone."

There was a slight hiss of air as Dr. Bruce Ackerman exhaled slowly. The answering machine continued to whir away the seconds as he stood debating what to say next. This was the fifth call he'd made in the last two hours and he was growing increasingly concerned. Andrew hadn't answered his cell phone since he'd left his office hours ago, and a call to his workplace had confirmed his suspicions that his friend wasn't handling the news of his diagnosis very well. Andrew had shown up drunk and had gone into a frenzied tirade in front of God and everybody, and had then stormed out and gotten into a cab. No one had seen or heard from him since. Short of calling every cab company in the city to track him down, Bruce was effectively stuck at square one.

He sighed and rubbed at his temples. "Call me as soon as you get home. I don't care how late it is just...call me back. Please."

The dial tone sounded as he hung up.

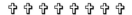

The radio squawked and beeped as Officer Bryan Rhodes and his partner Anthony Cepeda began to cordon off the scene of the city's latest homicide. Two males—one Hispanic and one African American in their early twenties—lay dead in the alleyway. The scene itself was one of intense violence: blood was spattered on the filthy ground and had pooled beneath the two bodies, the two bodies that had each sustained massive trauma to the neck and chest. The coroner's technicians waited patiently on the sidelines for the crime scene photographer to finish up.

*And what would be rush*, he thought as the photographer snapped another series of shots. *It's not like the bodies are going anywhere*. Officer Cepeda scoffed and kicked at the edges of a pothole near his feet. It had already been a long day, and now with a double homicide on his hands, it was going to be an even longer night.

A broken whiskey bottle lay a few yards away and the shards were stained with minute traces of blood. It had apparently been used as a weapon and the tech guys were busy placing the pieces in evidence bags to be tested for prints back at the lab. Few if any clues were left behind at the scene, and there were no witnesses to the crime except for an anonymous caller who had heard screams coming from the area. They had hung up as soon as the dispatcher took down the location and hadn't called back. Given the jump in brutal, unsolved homicides in the area lately, it was no wonder they didn't want to become involved.

His partner Bryan Rhodes stood next to the yellow police tape with his back to the scene. He had been the first one out of the car as they had skidded to a stop at the sight of the bodies illuminated in the cruiser's headlights. He had checked each victim for a pulse, but they were both beyond saving. Cepeda had then called in for backup and the scene had been turned over to the technicians.

He sighed and ground the heels of his boots against the dirty asphalt. They were going to have a shitload of paper work to fill out because of this.

As visions of triplicate and shoddy filing systems filled his head, he was motioned over to the sidelines by his superior.

He knew what they were going to find even before they reached the scene and the headlights revealed the grisly carnage before them. The dispatcher had radioed in with an assault or possible homicide in a neighborhood less than two blocks from where he and his partner sat parked in their cruiser. Anthony had immediately radioed back and sped off in the direction that the call had come from. Bryan recognized the street and location and felt his stomach churn. For months, his mistress' brood had been systematically picked off one by one by an unknown assailant, and the location that the call had come from was the very same one that they had gone missing in. His mistress had set a trap for the woman based on Darnell's intell, and now that she had effectively taken the bait that had been provided, her sons and five other progeny were dispatched to accost her. Based on the urgency he heard in the dispatcher's voice, he knew that whatever they found at the scene wouldn't bode well with her.

When her children had first started to disappear and it appeared that someone or something was challenging her hold on the city, his mistress had charged him with recruiting replacements to replenish their ranks. His position within the law afforded him access to all sorts of violent and questionable characters who were looking to get ahead in this world, but not necessarily by the most honorable means. His mistress could provide such opportunities in spades for the right price, a price many were willing to pay.

He had provided her with no less than a dozen potential replacements, but only the most vicious and hardened of them were selected to join the ranks. He didn't know why she had asked him to do this—despite the fact that their numbers had dwindled down considerably—and he was at a loss to account for why she would want to replace them now. Now was not the time to do so, especially when there was an unknown assailant out there steadily picking them off one at a time. Each death had impacted her and the energy that she had expended during their creation was stripped away when they died, energy that would take a considerable amount of time to replace. Many victims and many feedings would gradually see her strength restored, but creating new progeny was effectively a fool's errand. She just didn't have the resources to spare to accomplish this, and she was better off protecting what few children remained.

As it turned out, that is exactly what she had in mind.

Once she had overlooked the potential replacements and listened to his rationale for selecting them, she called him behind closed doors and revealed the reason why she had sent him on such an errand. She explained that she had spent many nights contemplating a plan of action in order to discover the identity of the assailant, but the issue was *how* to go about discovering their identity; if she could not risk her children for fear of risking herself, then how could she hope to obtain this information?

The answer emerged from the very root of the problem.

The loss of her children meant the loss of considerable strength and energy for her, so to avoid this she would have to prevent any more of them from being killed. That seemed simple enough, but again, there was the issue of them cowering in the shadows like cowards. That was simply unacceptable. She hadn't lived for nearly two centuries to be forced into hiding by some vigilante and their misguided mission. No, a more proactive approach had to be undertaken.

She knew instinctually that she wasn't weakened unto death yet by the deaths of three of her children. It was feasible for her to create more of them, but they were just as likely to be killed—perhaps more so due to their relatively young age and inexperience. While this would temporarily swell their ranks, it would defeat the overall purpose. Perhaps, she reasoned, there was another way to increase their ranks while protecting her interests and discovering the identity of the killer. It was possible for her to create a small arsenal of spies that could patrol her territory and relay information back to her, and while they would be utterly expendable, their services would be invaluable to her. The issue of how to procure such potential replacements fell on Bryan's shoulders, and he had recruited more than enough to replace those that had been lost. The most promising individuals—those who proved their commitment to her and to the other children—would undergo a rush-version of the transference and would then be turned loose on the streets to feed at their discretion. The bond between them would be strong enough to allow her to gain sustenance through them by virtue of the transference, but it would not be strong enough to drag her down into death with them should they be killed by the assailant.

This was a delicate balancing act to perform, but she was confident that she could accomplish it. She would start out with only six to test the effectiveness of her plan, and if it proved fruitful then there was no need in transforming the other replacements, who would better serve as sustenance for the rest of them if it came down to that.

His admiration for her increased as he listened to this explanation, and while it was a pragmatic, albeit under-handed tactic, it appealed to the predator within him. It was one of the reasons that had attracted them to one another all those decades before.

Reggie, Marcos, Stephano, Djimaldin, Thomas, and Augustino were chosen as the first six replacements, and underwent the transference days apart. Even with the minimal amount of energy that she expended to transform each of them, the effort still took a toll on her. Too weak to feed herself, she granted them free reign throughout the area in which she and the others had taken up residence. Feeding was allowed at their discretion, and the only thing that she asked of them was to keep watch over the area that they frequented. They were undoubtedly so enthralled with their new lease on life that they didn't even question the command, and the threat of certain death never once entered their thoughts. They were equally unaware of the fact that her oldest children—the ones who had been nurtured extensively by her and who had accompanied her for decades—were kept closely guarded. These children were not allowed to hunt amongst the population as they had done on previous occasions—that was too risky. They couldn't very well remain sheltered indefinitely, and as their Font she was obligated to provide them with free passage. The city was hers and by rights was theirs as well. As long as this assailant compromised their safety and sense of security they would have to remain close by.

Bryan and his mistress's three sons were the only exceptions to this rule, Bryan because his position as an officer of the law afforded him protection by his fellow officers, and her sons due to their desire to protect their mother and her interests. Based on what little they did know of the assailant, assaulting and killing a uniformed officer of the law would have been a major blunder. Her sons were not content to remain idle and useless, and as her second in command, they were obligated to look after their mother's interests. The city was theirs by virtue of this relationship, and they felt obligated to secure their power base. Having walked the earth for nearly one-hundred-and-fifty years, they were considerably more capable of handling themselves than the others, and they took it upon themselves to guide the newest replacements in their mother's mission.

It was a simple enough plan, but the flaws in it became painfully apparent after the number of deaths had risen to four. The toll that the latest death and the numerous transferences had taken on her was readily apparent, and in desperation she was forced to feed off of the remaining human replacements to restore her strength.

With one exception.

Darnell had been immediately taken with her the first time that he had laid eyes on her, and she decided to use this to her advantage. She had encountered others like him before and recognized a fawning sycophant when she saw one. A few brief tastes of what she could offer him had cemented the bond that he felt existed between them, and as she watched him succumb to the inevitable swoon, she knew that he would serve her until the death.

But first a test.

If he was truly worthy of eternity, then he had to prove his loyalty. The five remaining replacements were dispatched with the same instructions, and Darnell was to accompany them. Reggie was by far the most violent of them all, and she reasoned that if Darnell could witness him in action without running away in terror, then he was fit to join the ranks.

While Reggie consequently became the fifth casualty of this little war, Darnell had given his mistress the information she needed to strike back. He had been brought into the fold as a reward for his services, but his achievement was decidedly short-lived.

Bryan recognized Alec as he lay on his back towards the right of the alley. A quick glance to the left revealed the remains of Darnell slumped against the opposite fence. His stomach clenched as he realized what his mistress's reaction would be. Darnell was expendable despite his prowess as a spy, but not Alec. Alec was her son, her reason for living, part of her soul even. Now it appeared that he was going to be part of her reason for vengeance as well.

There was no sign of Castillo, Daman, or the others, and it appeared that they had fled the scene in a hurry. This certainly didn't bode well for his mistress, or her plans to accost the assailant and deal with her in earnest. The fact that two were dead and six were presumed missing or had fled the scene entirely, meant that the woman was a formidable adversary.

The car had barely come to a stop before he opened his door and was sprinting towards Alec. His partner was busy radioing for backup and his attention was momentarily distracted. That was when he had spotted the wallet lying in a pool of what smelled like whiskey. The remains of the bottle lay scattered nearby and he gingerly picked the wallet up and shoved it into his pocket. None of the three brothers or the others carried wallets with them. None of them existed on paper and they had no need for money or identification.

The air around the two men was devoid of any semblance of their auras, and although he knew that they were dead just by this alone, he would have had a hard time convincing his partner how he knew this without checking for a pulse. Blending in with the human population was as much a defense mechanism as it was a way to maintain a position of authority without the benefit of being a Font—it would be several more hundred years before he would earn such a distinction.

He quickly placed his index finger on the side of Alec's neck and felt for a pulse. There was none just as he expected. Darnell's body revealed the same results, and from what he could tell from their injuries, the wounds were clean and deep. Knife wounds.

When the crime technicians and backup began showing up in droves, he had excused himself down the alley as if he were going to be sick. No one paid him any mind and as soon as he was out of sight he removed the wallet from his pocket and opened it. The smiling face on the driver's license tucked inside proclaimed that it was the property of Andrew Crossman.

*Andrew Crossman.*

The name sounded familiar, and it struck him where he had seen it before. His partner Anthony frequently left copies of an independent tabloid called *Elysium* lying around in the cruiser or on his desk back at the station. In Bryan's opinion it was a waste of perfectly good paper and ink, and he recognized the name as one of the columnists that was featured in it from time to time. He also realized that he held an invaluable piece of evidence in his hand. It seemed that Mr. Crossman had had a hand in all this, though exactly how and to what extent remained to be seen.

He would present his mistress with this little token—a consolation for the grief that she would be experiencing—and the rest would be up to her. The bond she shared with all of her children had no doubt alerted her to the death of her son the moment his life ended, and by now she would be screaming for vengeance. The wallet would give her a place to start.

He placed it in his pocket and headed back towards the crime scene.

# Chapter 21

I set the man down on my bed and quickly propped his head up on the lumpy pillow while Wendell looked on silently. He groaned and tried to roll over onto his side and then his hands flew up to his face, quickly covering his mouth. I recognized the symptoms and immediately grabbed the wastebasket near the bed. He lurched violently and began to retch as the contents of his stomach were emptied into the trash. When he was finished, he clutched weakly at his sides and rolled onto his back. I quickly drew the worn coverlet over him and tucked it in around him. His face was slick with sweat and dried blood and he looked terrible, truly sick.

"There should be a washcloth in the bathroom," I motioned towards the room at the end of the short hallway. "Could you please run it under some cold water and bring it to me?"

Wendell nodded and hurried away. I turned back to the man and gently smoothed the hair that had fallen over his eyes away from his face. His glasses hung at an odd angle on his nose, and I readjusted those as well. His face was young and quite pleasant to look at despite the dirt and blood.

Wendell returned with the damp washcloth and handed it to me wordlessly. I thanked him and began to wipe away the grime on the man's face. He whimpered softly and gradually the strained look on his face faded away. I was relieved that the worst of his injuries was a swollen lip and a cut above his right eye—both of which I could easily fix.

I dabbed at the cut above his right eye and his eyes flew open and then slowly slid shut.

His eyes were a warm hazel-green and were the mirror image of my beloved Nicholas—Nicholas, who had been dead for over three-hundred years. All at once the colors of the room swam together and I inhaled sharply. The washcloth slipped from my fingers and landed on the floor with a dull *plop*, and I quickly buried my face in my hands.

The face of Nicholas—his face drawn and slicked with sweat as the fever ravaged his body—was so vivid that I found myself reaching out for him, determined that we would touch once more. Through the haze of my memory I saw my hand connect with the side of his face and I hurriedly pulled back, afraid that it would vanish as if in a dream. The image remained and I tentatively laid the palm of my hand against the soft down of his cheek. He was warm but not feverish, and for the briefest of moments my heart rejoiced at the prospect that he might recover, that his injuries would not prove fatal as the doctor had insisted.

"Are you all right?"

A light pressure on my right shoulder caused the image to shimmer and finally dissolve away. Nicholas once again vanished into the cursed abyss that was my memory, and the present scene took its place. The man still lay unconscious, but his breathing was noticeably calmer. My palm lay against his face and I hurriedly withdrew my hand. I turned towards the voice that had startled me from my reverie, and I saw Wendell staring down at me with a curious look on his face.

I finally managed to nod my head yes, and then I turned my face away. I wasn't capable of shedding tears anymore because my nature prevented it. Even if that weren't the case however,

I had lived through enough hardship that I no longer had any tears left to cry.

# Chapter 22

The gilt mirror shattered into hundreds of pieces as the ornately-carved chair smashed into it with terrific force. The glass tinkled to the floor and reflected the drama playing out in the room as a beautiful face—a face rendered hideous and terrifying with wrath and anguish in equal amounts—stared out from each glittering shard.

The four men knelt in terror in the middle of the room as their mistress continued to rage like a whirlwind destroying anything and everything in its path. She screamed and tore at her hair as she sent a vase flying into the opposite wall, and then her nails sheared through the canvas of a multi-hued landscape like paper. The frame was barely recognizable and lay twisted and broken off to the side.

Her sons were dead. Dead, dead...

Her mind refused to wrap itself around that realization. Not once in her one-hundred-and-sixty-five years could she have ever conceived of such a thing happening. Her sons Daman, Alec, and Castillo were her reason for living, were the reason why she had chosen the path that she was currently on.

If it hadn't been for them she would have died on that plantation along with the rest of her people. She would have passed on into history as anonymously as the rest of the slaves, and would have never experienced life outside of the cloistered existence that their master enforced with an iron fist and a stinging whip. She wouldn't be who she was today—a Font to eight children, a mother grieving for her two sons, a woman just on the verge of desperation and insanity—if it weren't for *her*. All of this traced back to that *woman* who had stepped into her city and who had forced her to take drastic measures, drastic measures that had resulted in the creation of four miserable excuses for progeny, progeny who had betrayed her sons in their time of need. Alec and Castillo had paid the ultimate price for their betrayal, a price that Daman would continue to pay throughout eternity. His face was permanently scarred where the woman had slashed at him with her knives, and while he had fed as quickly and as furiously as he could following Castillo's death, it was too late to reverse the damage. The damage would have reversed itself all on its own if he had only been older and stronger.

Two long, puckered scars now marred the beauty of his face, each one a constant reminder of what he had lost, of what they had both lost.

Someone was going to pay for these injustices, *must* pay— starting with the four traitors.

When the contents of the room had been reduced to broken timbers and ruined silk, she turned her blazing eyes to them. They flinched and one or two whimpered in fear.

Daman stood behind them with the left side of his face carefully hidden in the shadows. He was flanked by the two bodyguards who had their hands on the shoulders of the two men near the far end. He had one hand on each of the other two men and his face was utterly blank as he watched his mother's rampage. A roiling tide of emotions chased themselves in the recesses of his mind, but he watched the scene with cool detachment. Soon enough he would be able to dole out punishment as he saw fit. His mouth twitched up at the thought of their torment, but the puckered scars twisted his expression into a shadow of a smile.

Officer Bryan Rhodes stood with his back to the wall nearest the front door and looked on the scene with the same cold indifference. The four traitors in the middle of the room were about to be punished for their betrayal, and while it wouldn't bring his mistress's sons back, it was the least they could do—they owed her that much for the loss of their lives.

Bryan opted to approach her with Andrew Crossman's wallet after the inevitable cruelty had been justly dealt out. Perhaps this newest development would help to ease hers as well as *his* suffering; the loss of the other children had been felt by him as well, and the fact that it could have easily been him made the issue of revenge all the more personal.

A collective cry of anguish went up from the four kneeling figures as she closed the distance and stood before them.

The cries of anguish turned to agony as Daman moved to stand by his mother. It was hours before the sounds finally died away.

# Chapter 23

I sat on the edge of the bed watching the rhythmic rise and fall of the man's chest as he slept. His aura continued to flicker in and out of focus, but it was largely infrequent. It was still pocked and indistinct around the edges, yet it burned like a low-grade flame in the dim room.

Wendell emerged from the bathroom wearing the borrowed t-shirt and sweats that I had loaned him, and the steam from the shower followed him out of the room. I could tell by the way that he kept casting furtive glances in my direction that he wasn't entirely convinced that I was human. I decided to let him bring it up if and when he wanted to. As it was, I had more pressing matters to attend to—like the man asleep in my bed.

My mind refused to relinquish its hold on the seemingly-random association it had drawn between him and my long-dead husband, and I was plagued by a sense of déjà vu and something else that I couldn't quite put into words. Concern? Pity? My maternal instinct re-emerging after centuries of lying dormant? I had no idea. It could be all or none of these things.

I got up from the edge of the bed and went to stand by the window. The traffic flowed by like a line of fireflies marching in the night, and I stared out at its ceaseless rhythm for a long time. I knew with absolute certainty that the Font behind the creation of the weakened progeny was thinking about me at this precise moment. How could they not? They had sent eight assassins to accost me and my two new companions—somehow *friends* didn't seem appropriate—in an alleyway, and I had sent five of them running for their lives. Three of them were dead because of me. That brought the grand total to eight progeny that I had permanently removed from their ranks, and I was betting that they were beyond furious at this point. Fortunately, they didn't know who I was and were ignorant as to my location and the identities of Wendell and the other man.

It occurred to me that I was still referring to him as "the man" after all this time, and I had no earthly idea what his name was. It also occurred to me that neither of them knew my name, and there was no telling what Wendell was referring to me as in his thoughts.

There was a deep intake of breath and the man stirred in his sleep. He snuggled under the covers and nestled into the pillow, and it seemed as if he was going to continue sleeping through the night. His brow wrinkled as something alerted him to the fact that he was not in his own bed, and he sat up abruptly, eyes staring wildly at the room before him. He blinked owlishly and his gaze flicked from me to Wendell and then back again. Then it flicked to the bed that he was in.

I could almost hear the wheels in his head turning as his mind reviewed the night's events along with the truth of what his eyes revealed to him.

"I must have been dreaming." He blinked and then shook his head as if trying to clear the visions away. "I'm still dreaming."

I didn't know how to proceed. How could I break it to him gently that this wasn't a dream and that he had been part of a very-real nightmare only hours before?

"You're not dreaming." I got up and took hold of his hand and placed it above his right eye just over the cut that was slowly scabbing over. He winced and the slight pain seemed to shock him back to reality. He gasped and scrambled backwards, but the headboard impeded his progress.

I stood there debating how to continue and I finally settled on a diplomatic approach. "My name is Katrina Armentani." I approached him slowly and extended my hand.

His response was slightly-hesitant. "Andrew Crossman."

I nodded at him. "Pleased to meet you Andrew."

Wendell followed our lead and introduced himself. "Wendell Bowers." He shook both of our hands and we exchanged the same pleasantries.

Now that we all knew who we were, it was time to move on to *why* we were here. That was a tricky one, because I didn't know for sure how much either of them knew about any of this. I knew that I had my own interests to protect, and I was sure that that applied to them as well.

I sighed and ran a hand up through my hair. "Look, I don't really know how to go about explaining to you what happened tonight, so if you could give me a few pointers...?" I looked hopefully at them.

Andrew spoke first. "Well, the beginning is usually a good place to start."

I had to admit that made a certain amount of sense.

✞ ✞ ✞ ✞ ✞ ✞ ✞ ✞

I gave them the annotated version of how I had come to be in the alleyway at the same time that they were, sans any details as to what had led me there, what I was, or how I had managed to overpower eight full grown men. I could tell that neither of them— especially Andrew—was buying what I was attempting to sell them, but it was the most they were going to get out of me.

I crossed my arms over my chest to signify that I was through speaking and that the conversation was effectively over. I should have known better, especially with the way that Andrew kept shaking his head when I glossed over the details or when I became dodgy in my account.

My suspicions were confirmed a few seconds later.

"And here I thought that Gary had cornered the market when it came to bullshitting people." He scoffed and drummed his knuckles against the nightstand. The noise made a rhythmic staccato and underscored the sounds of the late-night traffic rolling by outside my window. Wendell remained just as silent as ever. I sighed and leaned against the wall.

"What else can I say? That's exactly what happened; you can take it for what it's worth. As for Mr. Simms...," I frowned as the memory of how his eyes had appraised me popped into my head. "While he may not win any popularity contests, he still retains that distinction."

Andrew straightened and looked me straight in the eye. "How do you know Gary?"

I blinked and opened my mouth, but I didn't know how to proceed. If I told him that I had met with Gary earlier in the day, he would want to know when and why. As far as *when* was concerned, I could skimp on the details, but *why*? I just didn't have a reasonable explanation that didn't involve vampires and mutilated bodies—a quandary.

He eyed me suspiciously. "You're holding something back and I want to know what it is."

I kept my position against the wall. "Look, Mr. Crossman, I've been more than cooperative when it came to explaining to you how you wound up here and there is nothing more to tell."

"The hell there isn't." His brows drew together in a frown and then he winced as the cut above his eye protested the movement. "The only thing you've given either of us," he motioned to Wendell still sitting in the armchair, "is some half-ass story about how you just 'happened' to be out for a walk on that particular street, heard the commotion in the alleyway, and then came to help. Forgive me if I seem rude, but you don't look like you can even handle a heavy gym bag, much less a group of full-grown men."

When I didn't answer, he stood up from the bed and reached for the telephone. "Fine. If you don't feel like telling me what really happened, then maybe having the cops question you down at headquarters will help get you in the talking mood." He picked up the receiver and began dialing.

I reacted instinctively and snatched the phone away from him. It cracked into several pieces and went dead after making a low whining noise.

We all froze where we were in that instant. Andrew's eyes were round with astonishment and his hand clutched at the phone that was no longer there. A quick glance in Wendell's direction proved that he was in even worse shape, and his eyes were glassy with fear. His hands reached in and out of the pockets on his—*my*—sweatpants, and I had a momentary flash of recognition. I had seen that exact same gesture nearly three weeks ago when I had saved a homeless man from certain death. I remembered the way that his trench coat had flared around him as he stumbled down the street and the way that his hands reached in and out of the pockets—undoubtedly some sort of nervous tick. My mind flashed to the alley scene from earlier this evening, and lit on the dirty trench coat that Wendell had wrapped around him to block out the cold. It was the same one. The trench coat, the nervous tick, the two homeless men who had a weakness for drinking, they were both one and the same. Wendell.

The room spun momentarily and I opened my hand and let the remains of the phone drop to the floor. They bounced off the cheap carpet with a dull *thud*, and I turned my back on the two men who sat there gawking at me like I was some sort of freak—a dangerous freak.

I walked back to the window and stood there debating on how to proceed. Things had progressed past the point of playing human—the broken phone was testament to that. More than that, things had progressed past the point of quirky coincidence to plain unnerving. My actions from three weeks ago had set me up to not only reunite with Wendell later on, but apparently Andrew and I were meant to meet as well.

I couldn't conceive of the significance of such a thing. Not once during my lifetime did my path ever cross another's in the manner that it had Wendell's or Andrews. For too long I had lived my life under the impression that my sole purpose was to slay those guilty of crimes against the innocent. I had sworn to protect them and exact revenge when they could not, but not once, not *once* did it ever occur to me that perhaps I was meant for something more, even if it only included a homeless man and a journalist barely out of his teens.

I closed my eyes. The memory of the people whose lives made this night possible—however forced and errantly justified—threatened to overwhelm me. The realization that Wendell, Andrew and I were meant to meet—towards what ends I knew not—was close to being the final straw.

Andrew's voice pierced the awkward silence. "What the hell is going on here?"

"She's one of them."

I turned in the direction of Wendell's voice. He was standing near the armchair and the fear on his face was replaced by certainty.

Andrew whirled around and stared at him, the look of astonishment giving way to confusion. "What are you talking about? What do you mean, 'one of them?' "

Wendell kept his gaze level with mine. "Vampires; she's a vampire."

Andrew scoffed and rubbed at his temples. "I don't know how you found Gary or how he found you, but I can assure you Mr. Bowers that there is no such thing. I don't know how much he paid you to say those things earlier, but that doesn't mean that you have to keep on with the lie. Vampires don't exist. Nothing that we write about over at *Elysium* exists; it's just a way to sell papers." He hung his head as if ashamed of himself, and perhaps he was. No matter what he or his other co-workers had done over the years, the truth of it was that Wendell and Gary were correct: vampires *did* exist, and they were out there in this very city. More than that, Wendell and Andrew had become unwitting players in this little drama and were now firmly entrenched in the very epicenter of danger. It seemed only fair that they be adequately informed in order to protect themselves.

"He's not lying." I continued speaking before Andrew had a chance to protest and turned back to face them and the room. "Perhaps you'd better sit down—what I have to say could take awhile."

Some part of me demanded to know just what I thought I was doing confiding in two complete strangers, but another part—the more vocal and rational part—was anticipating the ensuing conversation with a mixture of apprehension and relief. Since the night of my own transference, I hadn't engaged in meaningful conversation with another soul, whether mortal or immortal. The only person in the whole world who had any knowledge as to the pain and trauma that had preceded this turning point in my life was me, and truth be told, it was more than any one person should have to bear. I considered the fact that perhaps I was being a tad selfish in wanting to unleash some of this burden on someone else, but I knew that that wasn't the truth, or at least not the whole truth. These men deserved to know what was happening. They were already involved in what was and had been happening in the city, and there was no changing that. Their innocence and sense of security had already been violated beyond repair and the truth would help assuage the fear they must be experiencing.

Knowledge is power. Knowledge is yet another means of protecting oneself against ignorance and the unknown. Protecting the innocent is what I do best, and this was yet another extension of that. By confiding in them, I was upholding my end of the bargain.

I opened my mouth and began to speak.

# Chapter 24

"I was born in the year 1661 in the village of Holloko, Hungary. It was and still is a beautiful and idyllic place to live. Maize and sunflower fields dot a rolling landscape which seems perpetually lush and green. The soil there is dark and fertile, and life seems to spring out from everywhere. In the springtime the trees and flowers are in bloom, and one can truly gain a sense of the earth's amazing ability to renew itself after the harshest of winters. Every tendril and tender bit of foliage is a testament to this, a living tribute to sheer tenacity and the will to live. The people themselves are like this, and despite the hardships that accompany every facet of life, they always manage to eke out a comfortable living from the land and from the fruits of their labors. Life in Holloko was simple yet fulfilling—a good life—the kind of life that my family and I should have had, but were cruelly robbed of."

My voice sounded small and unsteady. After nearly four-hundred years of shunning all human contact, recounting the story of my life to virtual strangers was more than a little awkward. I didn't quite know how to situate myself within the room: should I lean casually against the windowsill as far away from my audience as possible? That seemed like the most practical thing to do considering I had no idea how they would react to what I had to say.

I turned my back to them and stared out at the traffic. It was a familiar yet oddly soothing sight, a flowing and predictable constant in an otherwise chaotic existence, and it provided the perfect medium to help me organize my thoughts. I knew that giving my memories voice was undoubtedly going to be excruciating if not downright unbearable, so I felt justified in facing the window. I knew that the mask of civility I usually wore could be stripped away in the blink of an eye, and more than once it had set others on edge. The pre-teen receptionist from this afternoon as well as a host of nameless souls I'd encountered over the centuries was testament to this.

I continued my narrative in order to fill the absolute silence that followed my initial statement. Now was not the time for reflection or for dealing with what may or may not happen. I had an eternity's worth of days ahead of me to sort through the specifics of tonight. I had no doubt that this night would stand out from the rest—for better or for worse—but for now I had to contend with the past as well as the present—the future could wait.

"Holloko was a very simple town. It couldn't boast a sizeable population such as Budapest, which lay a hundred kilometers to the northwest. It was known as the gateway to the town of Paszto, and the only notable feature was a thirteenth-century castle perched atop the Szar Hill.

"Historically, it was just as noteworthy. The Mongol hordes razed the town in the thirteenth-century, and it was later re-burnt by the Turks in the sixteenth-century. The overall layout was relatively unimaginative: a single cobblestone street traversed through the center of town and was lined with houses in the Paloc style. All of them were whitewashed with embellished facades and wooden balustrades, had tiled roofs and tiny windows. Every house had their own garden surrounded by low wooden fences, and they were designed for extended families. Perhaps the one thing that I have had the most difficulty accepting in this new age is the advent of nursing or convalescent homes. In my day, one room was reserved for the parents and their children, and the grandparents had their own on the other side of the house. The central living room was the heart of any home and it was frequently filled with friends and family. No one would have dared nor even entertained the idea of sending their elderly family members off to the care of strangers. The idea was as unthinkable as it was distasteful, and to do so would have brought shame and scandal upon the whole family.

"Family and our faith were perhaps the two most important facets of our existence, and while our homes were where we honored our family, the fifteenth-century whitewashed chapel located at the end of the street was where we honored our Lord. Easter time was perhaps the most celebrated holiday next to Christmas, and indeed even today, the Hollokoi Husveti Fesztival is still quite popular among the residents and tourists. In those days we celebrated the resurrection of Christ with a festival that attracted musicians and entertainers from the neighboring towns and cities who would ply their trade for the locals. I can still remember the way that their campfires lit up the night as they bedded down near the outskirts of town in their brightly painted wagons, which were so unlike anything that we had ever seen before. Holloko was small enough that it did not have an inn or any place for these people to stay, so they had to make do with what they had. In any event, it didn't discourage them in the slightest, and every year more and more would participate in the festivities. My family and I would count the days until it was time for the next year's celebration, and we frequently attended it together. When I was younger my parents would take me and my siblings with them, but as we grew older this pattern changed.

"My older brothers and sisters had married, borne children, and established their own households years before, but not me.

No, love and marriage were two things that I wanted absolutely nothing to do with. This was unheard of for a woman living in the seventeenth century. There may have been the occasional woman who for some reason or other did not marry, but they either entered a convent or remained a spinster, much to their family's shame. I don't want to leave you with the impression that love is or was beyond me. It was only that love had caused me more pain during my mortal years than I could endure, and I vowed to steer away from it at all costs. I had the distinct disadvantage of falling in love with the wrong person for what I felt were all the right reasons. I loved them so completely and utterly selflessly that I unwittingly set myself up for disappointment every step of the way. Just the mere thought of them would lift me to such incredible heights of joyousness that I could scarcely breathe, but my downfall was that these sentiments only went one way. I was unfortunate enough to find myself the victim of unrequited love, and I could not for the life of me discern why that person did not feel the same way that I did. I couldn't imagine what it would feel like knowing that they felt the same way about me as I did them. All I knew is that when my affections were not returned, I withdrew into myself and became cold and indifferent. The capacity for love that I had in my heart soon became a burden—a horrid, excruciating weight that was only minimally assuaged by my indifference. There was no available avenue for this love to go to, and it soon turned to bitterness.

"My father, in a paroxysm of anxiety over the prospect that I would become a spinster, could not understand my reluctance. He had no knowledge of what had transpired and was convinced that I was merely being stubborn in my refusal to be courted. My mother, who had always been particularly close to me, was content to have me remain close by. She herself had married young and had borne many children before the age of thirty. She didn't need to tell me that there were things in her life that she regretted not having the opportunity to complete. I saw it in her eyes whenever my father attempted to bring up the prospect of marriage to me, and there was no mistaking the resentment in her expression. She was devoted to my father and loved her children, but it was more resentment over the attitude that dictated a woman's destiny in those days than anything else. It was more a resentment towards the mindset that women had to be married before a certain age, and any behavior to the contrary was looked down upon. It was resentment over things that were beyond her ability to change. She knew that I was torn between my own insecurities and a desire to respect his wishes, but she could not see the logic in marrying anyone just to put his own fears to rest. If I was to marry, it would be out of genuine love for that person. If I didn't marry, then at the very least I could live out my days to the fullest extent allowed in those times. My parents only wanted what was best for their children, even if they couldn't quite agree on what that was."

I smiled wistfully in the reflection staring out at me from the window. "Fortunately for all of us, the right circumstances came along and cleared up our respective conflicts in their own way. My father's fears were vanquished, my mother saw me married to a man who loved me as deeply as I loved him, and I had effectively found the missing piece of my soul, the one part that completed me and made me feel whole and alive: Nicholas Armentani.

"I still lie awake most nights and contemplate the circumstances that brought us together—the circumstances that while seemingly-mundane to the casual observer, resulted in something extraordinary in its own right. Nicholas had suffered much during his life prior to our first meeting, and I—sheltered as I was at the time—could not conceive of how he carried on in spite of the odds dealt to him. His parents had passed away years before due to illness and the accidents typical of our day and time. It may have been a common occurrence to succumb to something as simple as the flu or to step out onto a frozen pond thinking that the ice was stronger than it really was, but it was still unfortunate. In Nicholas' case it was extremely unfortunate. His youngest sister was only a few months old when their father died, and when their mother took ill she was only four years of age. That left Nicholas and his two older brothers to care not only for a toddler, but to care for the land and the household.

"I knew of their plight from the town gossip, but had never spoken to either of them directly. There was no inherent reason why we didn't associate with one another, it was merely that the right circumstances hadn't facilitated this. It wasn't until the summer of my sixteenth year that these circumstances presented themselves and we became something more to one another.

"I had gone to a neighbor's house to borrow some thread for mending and was on my way back home. The sky had been threatening rain all day and I was about halfway home when the deluge began. I didn't want to get soaked and risk a fever, so I decided—rather stupidly—to run the rest of the way home, when my foot caught a loose cobblestone and I stumbled. I barely remember my head striking the ground, and the next thing I knew I was being lifted by strong arms and carried down the street. I could hear a voice asking me if I was all right, but I was disoriented from my fall and could not respond. I vaguely remember being carried into my room amid the concerned faces of my family, and then nothing.

"I had passed out.

"When I came to, I was lying in my own bed and my mother immediately flew to my side. I reassured her that I was fine, but that I had no idea how I had gotten home.

"It was then that Nicholas, who had been standing at the back of the room, came forward and informed me that it was he who had brought me home. He had been in town when the storm hit and had seen me fall. He told me that when he reached me I was barely conscious and he feared that I had been severely hurt. He had then carried me home to my family and the doctor was called in.

"I sat up from the bed—a little too quickly—and immediately regretted it. I closed my eyes against the pain and waved the prying arms of my mother away. I wasn't so hurt that the logical progression of facts was completely denied to me.

"I tentatively cracked one eye open. The faces of my family were all etched with concern, including Nicholas'.

"I looked straight at him. 'How did you know where I live? We've never spoken until this moment.'

"The attention of everyone in the room suddenly shifted towards him, and his face flushed a brilliant crimson. He stared down at his feet and didn't look at me as he spoke. 'I've seen you around town before but had never gathered the courage to speak to you. This afternoon I happened to see you emerge from your house and I made up my mind to introduce myself. I saw you enter another house and waited for you to leave, and that was when you fell.'

"It was impossible to miss the implications in that statement, and the expression that my father wore at that instant—a mixture of hope and relief—wasn't missed by my mother or me. Nicholas had more or less admitted his interest in me, and circumstances seemingly beyond my control had brought us together.

"Was it coincidence? I found myself reluctant to believe in this, but when I looked at him—*really* looked at him—I felt a curious sense of completion.

"In that instant as my father shook his hand and my mother insisted that he stay for dinner, I knew that something special had happened.

"As I watched the way he interacted so naturally with them and the manner in which they responded to him, I saw him then not as Nicholas Armentani—a virtual stranger—but as someone who had the potential to further change my life. He caught me staring at him and I hurriedly averted my gaze. Even with my cheeks burning I couldn't resist the temptation to look again, and I found that he was staring at me with the same look of wonder and...honestly, I have no words for it. It was as if we hadn't really seen each other up until that moment."

I found myself smiling at the memory. "He and I were virtually inseparable from that moment on. Our families would frequently gather together for meals and celebrations, and the sense of warmth and joy was undeniable. During the course of our courtship I asked him about the day that we met and the circumstances that had led up to that event. He blushed and admitted that he had admired me from afar for quite awhile before we actually met face to face. He had been steadily working up his courage to approach my father to ask permission to court me, when a loose cobblestone had quite literally sent me tumbling into his arms. It was a neat and otherwise effective solution to a problem that had been nagging at him for some time.

"We were sitting beneath the dappled shade of a great tree outside my father's house and the air was filled with the sounds of birds chirping and insects chirring in the grass. He took my hand in his and gently traced the lines of my palm with his finger. I shivered involuntarily and hastily cleared my throat. He stopped tracing and smiled up at me. 'You're hand is almost perfect, but it's missing something.' I was a little confused by what he meant, but the next moment he had produced a small object from his pocket. As the sunlight glinted off of it I knew immediately what it was and my heart sped up. He knelt in front of me and took my hands in his. 'I have loved you since the first moment I saw you, and I promise you that until my dying day my feelings for you will not change. I can't provide you with wealth or riches, but I can provide you with love. If you will do me the honor of becoming my wife, you will make me the happiest man alive—nothing that life throws at us can change that as long as we have each other.' He slipped the ring onto my finger and it fit perfectly. My mouth felt dry as he continued to speak. 'Will you do me this honor?'

"I met his eyes and saw the truth of his words reflected in them. I smiled and the look of pure, unadulterated joy on his face was undeniable. We embraced and remained locked in each other's arms for the longest time. I found myself reflecting on the remarkable chain of events that had brought the two of us together as we knelt there under the tree. For so long I had steadfastly refused to search for love, convinced that it was something unattainable for me. What I had failed to realize was that while *I* may have not been looking for love, love was looking for me. It had found me in the arms of a stranger trying to save my life, a stranger who was now not a stranger at all but was the missing part of my soul, the other half that completed me.

"When we announced our intentions the following evening, our families were overjoyed. I can't tell you how indescribably happy I was during this time and I knew that the only thing I wanted more than anything else in this world was to settle down to a long, happy life together."

I laughed bitterly. "It seems I got part of what I wished for. I've lived for a long time, and by all accounts I'm going to live forever, but my life has seldom been happy. If anything it has become a burden, and I have no one to blame for that but myself." I did not look at Andrew or Wendell as I spoke because I was afraid of what I would see.

Would I see fear or confusion reflected in their eyes? Either one would have made the pain that I was feeling all the more unbearable, but I also feared what I might *not* see: sympathy.

Sympathy is a very human emotion, but I wasn't human anymore. I hadn't been human for over three-hundred years. I had managed to convince myself that I wasn't like the rest of my kind, had managed to convince myself that I didn't kill the innocent in order to survive. I was different in that I was the killer of killers, the protector of those who had been victimized. I had managed to convince myself that this distinction is what not only set me apart from them, but which had accorded me some measure of humanity, however minute. To see an absence of this acknowledgment in their gaze would shatter such a deception, and I knew that I wouldn't be able to accept it. This belief had sustained me as surely as the burning desire for revenge in my heart did, and the loss of it would destroy a part of me that could never be replaced.

I shook my head to dismiss these doubts, and continued. "In a town as small as Holloko, a wedding was a grand affair and everyone came out to help our families celebrate the union of their children. The church was decorated simply with garlands of wild flowers and candles, and I wore my mother's wedding dress. I can still remember the way that she hugged me and told me that even though I would soon be a bride that I would always be her daughter. Nicholas positively beamed at me as we took our final vows, and when we exited the church as husband and wife we were full of hope over the life that we planned on building together.

"That night when we settled into our new home together, he presented me with a small box. A single smooth stone lay on the bottom. It was a good size cobble—about the size of an apple—and I wondered what he was up to.

"He smiled at me and took it from my hands. 'You don't recognize it?'

"That was when it hit me: it was the very same cobble that I had tripped over months before, the very cobble that had sent both of us on the path that we were currently on.

"It had pride of place on the mantle in the days that followed.

"The first two years were the happiest of my life. We shared our home with his youngest sister Amelie just outside of Holloko. Nicholas' two older brothers left to parts unknown soon after the wedding, and wanted nothing further to do with a town that they had long considered a burden. I think they were relieved that their younger brother had finally taken a wife, because it freed them from the sense of guilt and responsibility they felt over wanting to leave him and their sister behind. The work of any household—the cooking, cleaning, mending, tilling, plowing, and harvesting of the fields—would have been a strain on even an able-bodied man, but with Nicholas and I there to take over the responsibilities, they saw no reason for them to remain in Holloko any longer.

"The work was hard and oftentimes back-breaking, but it was rewarding in its own way. We never did have any children, but his younger sister Amelie was like a daughter to me. The fact that she hadn't had any sort of maternal contact for some years may have had something to do with this, but Amelie identified with me on a level that surpassed any maternal affection. She was given to bouts of silent contemplation and introverted behavior much like I was, but Amelie and I understood one another. We knew that our emotions ran just as deep as anyone else's, and we didn't need to wear our thoughts on our sleeve like other people. We also knew that doing so was not an indication of their absence. We were of the same ilk as it were, and it was natural that she gravitated to me like she did. I would frequently lie there at night gazing at my sleeping husband while reflecting on the life that we shared, and I would thank God for being so generous to us, for giving us more than anyone could hope to have during their lifetime. I gave thanks for every day, every hour, every minute that we spent together. But when tragedy came to our household and left death in its wake, I cursed those days. I cursed them because they caused me indescribable pain now that they were lost to me, cursed them because they left an aching chasm in my soul that could never be filled.

"It was in January of 1680 that my life changed forever. Nicholas had gone off by himself to gather firewood in the forest nearby. Amelie and I stayed behind to take care of the place and we set about preparing a hot meal for him when he returned. I remember watching him as he cleared the rise leading to the edge of the woods, and the way that the sun played along his hair. His hatchet lay slung over one shoulder and glinted in the light. He carried a club and knife with him in case he ran into predators, who starving in the harsh conditions, wouldn't hesitate to attack a full-grown man. He promised me that he wouldn't be gone long, kissed me on the cheek, and headed out the door. Amelie stood beside me watching him leave, and when he disappeared over the rise we set about preparing dinner. She helped me prepare dough for bread and in a moment of childhood pique, asked me if she could shape it any way she chose. I told her that that would make her brother smile, and she immediately set to work. I glanced outside the window and was slightly alarmed to see that the shadows were steadily creeping closer to the house. The sun was beginning to dip below the horizon and I knew that Nicholas had been gone longer than he'd promised. Perhaps he'd encountered trouble or was injured? That was entirely possible, but I knew that he would never venture too far away from the house. If he was in need of assistance, he need only yell and we'd hear him.

"Another hour passed, and still there was no sign of him. I was now in a blind panic but I forced myself to appear calm for Amelie's sake. It wouldn't do her any good to see me in such a state, so I told her calmly that I was going to go search for her brother and that she was to stay here and look after the place. She didn't question me and merely sat there at the wooden table rolling a small ball of dough between her fingers.

"I wrapped my thickest shawl around me, made sure that the lantern was full of oil, and went outside. It was bitter cold now that the sun had almost set, and I begin to shiver. Nerves had as much to do with it as the cold, and as I cleared the rise and began to make my way into the woods, I remembered that animals may be on the prowl. I snapped a sturdy limb off the nearest tree and continued on. No sooner had I made my way down to the bottom of the rise when I saw a dark shape sprawled on the ground to my right. I immediately rushed forward, and in the soft glow of the lantern I saw that it was Nicholas. A dark pool had spread out and frozen beneath his right knee, and protruding out from it was the handle of the axe. I could only surmise that it had slipped and then embedded itself in his knee while he gathered wood, and I knew that if I didn't get him indoors soon that he risked not only bleeding to death, but freezing to death as well.

"It took every ounce of will not to panic, but somehow I managed to heave him into a sitting position. He was dead weight in my arms as I struggled to heft him to his feet, and more than once he sagged back to the ground. I shook him vigorously and called his name, pleading with him to wake up, but he remained unresponsive. I finally had to slap the side of his face in a last ditch effort to revive him, and he came to with a sharp cry of pain. I shushed him and spoke in a soothing tone, telling him that he needed to try and stand up—I simply couldn't carry him out of there on my own. He understood what I was asking of him and slowly rose up. He bit back a scream and gripped my arm almost painfully for balance, and gritting his teeth fiercely, he managed to stand up. He couldn't bend his right leg very well, so he had to lean on me in order for me to drag him along.

"We made our way back to the house with agonizing slowness. When we reached the rise, he sagged to the ground in sheer exhaustion and had to crawl the rest of the way. I remained by his side helping him as best I could, and when we reached the other side, I yelled for Amelie. She emerged from the house and as she took in what had happened, I saw the fear in her eyes. I told her to go inside and start boiling some water, and to tear up a sheet for bandages. I knew that as long as she was kept busy that the panic would be kept at bay.

"We finally staggered onto the porch and Amelie had to help me finish dragging him the rest of the way in. By the time that we had gotten him in front of the fire, he was shivering violently and was fading in and out of consciousness. I knew that a fever had begun to set in, but I was confident that things hadn't progressed past the point of hope. Once I cleaned the wound to stave off infection, he stood a good chance of recovery. I sent Amelie into the kitchen to fetch me a bowl while I stripped away the leg of his pants. The wound was deep and the blade had sunk in at least an inch or two. I knew enough to know that removing the blade would only make the wound bleed more freely, but it couldn't very well remain in there.

"My heart sank as I realized that I would have to cauterize the wound, and that I would need Amelie's help. She stood just behind me as if she sensed my hesitation. I could stand here and debate the merits of involving her further in the night's events, but it was time that could be better spent tending to his injuries. As calmly as I could, I told her to place the end of the poker into the coals and to step aside. She did as she was told, and with a quick prayer for strength, I took hold of the handle and yanked upwards. The blade slid loose with a sickening squelch, and I breathed shallowly to stave off the nausea. Nicholas' back arched off the floor and he screamed, staring wild-eyed at the room before him. I hurriedly pressed a clean cloth against the wound as the blood flowed out in a torrent, but I knew that it was necessary to bleed out any contamination. He moaned softly as I spoke to him soothingly, and Amelie gently held his hand. When his breathing became less erratic, I removed the cloth and moved the basin of hot water closer to me so that I could wash the wound clean.

'Cover his eyes. No matter what happens, do *not* let him see.'

"She nodded obediently and I reached over and removed the poker from the fire. The tip glowed red-hot, and quickly so as not to lose my nerve, I pressed it against the gaping wound. There was an audible hiss as the edges of the wound puckered up, and Nicholas's agonizing cries filled the room. He bucked violently off the floor as I continued to seal the wound, and when it was finally over, I tossed the poker aside and pinned him down with my weight. He continued to thrash around helplessly but his movement was limited. Finally, mercifully, he lost consciousness and sank down to the floor. I quickly washed the dried blood away and bandaged the wound up. Amelie brought blankets from the bedroom and helped me wrap him up, and we kept the fire going throughout the night. He remained unconscious for the majority of the evening, but he tossed and whimpered in his sleep. He burned with fever and we took shifts re-applying cool clothes to his forehead. As the first rays of sunlight snuck in through the cracks in the shutters, I rose and went to fetch the village doctor. I had no choice but to leave Amelie behind to watch her brother, and I hurried to town as fast as I could, my thoughts never straying from the poor, wasted form of my husband.

"The doctor brought two men from the village with him, and together they carried my husband into the bedroom and laid him on the bed. He was sweating profusely and was delirious with pain and fever, and when the doctor examined him I saw a look cross over his face. He carefully examined the wound and then changed the bandages without saying a word. When he stood up to go into the next room, I followed him and demanded to know what the look had meant. He stared at me and tried his best to reassure me that it was of no importance, and that my husband would be fine. I knew he was lying because he refused to look me in the eye, but I didn't persist. I couldn't conceive of my husband dying so young and over something so careless. It was an accident—he didn't deserve to die because of a mistake.

"The rest of the day passed slowly as the doctor and I took shifts tending to Nicholas. His condition did not improve but seemed to worsen by the hour. By the afternoon of the third day when the bandages were being changed, the first signs of infection were present. Pus was beginning to build around the edges of the wound and Nicholas' fever grew more severe. I was effectively numb by this point and went about tending him in a daze. I had gone without sleep since the doctor had arrived, determined that if my husband did take a turn for the worse, that I would be there with him. As evening fell fatigue tugged at me and I couldn't remain on my feet any longer. The doctor reassured me that he would watch over Nicholas while I got the rest that I needed, and if there was any change in his condition, he would wake me immediately. It was with a great deal of reluctance that I agreed to this, and after kissing my husband goodnight, I lay down to sleep."

I wrapped my arms around myself to steady the trembling that had started up without warning. "That night Nicholas took a turn for the worse. I had fallen asleep in the rocking chair with Amelie nestled snuggly in my arms when I heard him calling for me. I left her in the chair and reassured her that everything was fine and that I would be right back, and then I ran for the bedroom. I ran as fast as I could, even though some part of me knew that I was already too late. When I entered the room, the doctor was bent over my husband and was attempting to restrain him as he thrashed around in his delirium. I shouted at him to get me a basin and a damp cloth, and then I threw myself into his arms. His complexion was a sickly gray color and his eyes were glassy with fever. I choked back a scream as I felt how hot his skin was, even though he shivered as if he were freezing. I shushed him and smoothed the hair back from his forehead and applied the damp cloth that the doctor hurriedly placed in my hands. He moaned and called my name, thrashing weakly on the bed. I soothed him and reassured him that I was there, but he didn't respond. He kept calling my name over and over until he finally lost consciousness, and then he never woke up. My husband was dead, and I was a widow with a seven-year old girl to care for at nineteen years of age."

A lone car passed by outside my window and with taillights flashing, vanished out of sight. "After my husband's funeral, Amelie and I packed up our belongings and boarded up the house that was now more a tomb than a home. The livestock had been sold off and the fields were left to lie fallow indefinitely. I wanted nothing further to do with the house, and by rights it should have gone to his brothers. They had been born and raised in it, but despite my best efforts they could not be contacted. It was almost as if they did not want to be found, so with Amelie and a few belongings that had sentimental value in tow, we moved into town with my parents. It was a bittersweet homecoming but they were immediately taken by Amelie and life seemed to return to normal—or at least a semblance of normalcy. I grieved for my husband in private, never in front of my family, and certainly never in front of Amelie. I knew that she missed her brother terribly, but I never once saw her cry or express her grief in any way. It seemed that both of us had had to become strong for the other. She really was an extraordinary child: loving, precocious, wise beyond her years, yet she still retained a child-like innocence to her despite the cruelties that life had already dealt her.

"Amelie turned eight in March of the following year and my parents and I presented her with a gift that had great sentimental value, a doll that had belonged to my older sisters and I that would now be passed on to her. Amelie was immediately taken by it and spent long hours embroidering tiny aprons and dresses for it. When Nicholas and I had first been married, I had spent many afternoons mending garments and bed sheets, anything that showed signs of wear and tear within the household. On more than a few occasions Amelie had kept me company and would take a needle and thread and stitch together scraps of fabric that I had left over. For a child of her age she was quite adept at it, so I began to tutor her in embroidery. By six years of age she was a virtual prodigy and I watched her antics over the years with great pride."

I paused and stared down at my own hands. They were small and delicate—a woman's hands—but the appearance was deceptively simple. Nearly four centuries ago they had been used to comfort and instruct, but now they were instruments of destruction. They didn't seem whole without the feel of the knives in my palm, and it was nearly inconceivable that at one time the most dangerous object they had ever wielded was a needle and thread. Their appearance didn't seem to suit the task that they had undertaken; they should have been hideous, battle-scarred, not smooth and dainty looking. They were frozen in time—mired forever in the characteristics of my seventeenth-century life—and would always remind me of simpler times.

I took a deep breath and steeled my nerves. I had gotten this far without going into hysterics or smashing the contents of the room into pieces, however much I longed to rage against the wrongs committed against my family. The effort would have been as pointless as it was destructive, and it wasn't going to accomplish anything, much less change the past. I knew that if I was to do my family's memory any justice that I had to maintain an iron grip on my control. The rhythmic ticking of the clock faithfully counting away the seconds was the only sound in the room as I warred silently with my turbulent emotions. Even the flow of traffic outside seemed to have tapered off as if in anticipation of what I was to reveal next.

"It was some weeks later that the annual Easter festival was to be held, and the four of us decided to uphold the tradition of going together as a family. Spring was in the air, the flowers and trees were in full bloom, and the symbolic representations of Christ's Resurrection were everywhere one looked. It was a time of renewal, of new beginnings, and my family and I were determined to leave the past safely behind us.

"We left the house early on the morning of the festival and headed down the cobblestone street towards the church grounds. The air was cool and damp with early morning dew and all around us were the sounds of children running and laughing in anticipation. The sounds of hammering and men's voices punctuated these familiar and comforting sounds as the traveling performers set up their shops for the day. Amelie had brought her doll with her and was pointing out the sights and discussing which stand we should visit first.

"I smiled down at her as she walked slightly ahead of me, as if she had no fear of anything and was sure of her place in the world. My parents walked arm in arm beside me and watched Amelie with tenderness. From this perspective, it occurred to me that this is what they must have experienced when I was her age as we headed towards the festivities. It was a curious experience that left me feeling like an outsider looking in, and it brought everything into sharp relief, that even in the midst of tragedy new beginnings are possible. I had no way of knowing just how prophetic and ironic this revelation would be in the coming days, but these words are as true now as they were then.

"Amelie's attention was immediately arrested by a trio of puppeteers that had set up shop near the center of the festivities. I couldn't recall ever seeing them there in previous years, and it was doubtless that I could have forgotten them. Two men and a woman made up the group, and they were beautiful beyond description. They were dressed in exotic silks, velvets, and embroidery in a riot of colors, colors which I had no names for at the time. The woman, whom I later learned was called Griselda, was like an angel. Her perfectly oval face was ringed by a mass of golden-brown hair and her skin was like cream—smooth and absolutely flawless. The tint of her lips and cheeks was the softest shade of rose, and her eyes were like twin skies. The men were equally beautiful but they lacked some degree of perfection that the woman possessed. There was something about the way that they schooled their gestures and expressions around her that seemed to further set her apart, and it was almost as if she was superior to them in ways that exceeded her extraordinary beauty.

"The children pressed eagerly around their wagon and edged as close as they could. Amelie tugged at my skirt and practically dragged me with her in her eagerness to get a closer look. I'd never seen her so enchanted by anything—indeed the way that her eyes sparkled with delight made my heart swell with happiness. Since Nicholas' death she had never once cried or shown any signs of grieving, and to see her like she was now made me realize just how much she had kept inside. She was now like the child that she should have *always* been, so I allowed her to run ahead of me and be exactly that.

"She turned back once as she ran and her hair flew out of the sides of her bonnet in a spray of ribbons. I remember standing off to the side watching her as she joined the other children, pleased with how well she was getting on and envisioning a future of possibilities. The puppeteers were smiling down at the sea of eager little faces that surrounded them, gazing at each with apparent adoration. The men were taking down several large chests from the back of the wagon and set them down out of sight behind the velvet curtain and its tiny stage. The woman held out her hands and the men hurriedly clasped each one and helped her stand on a small box set off to one side. In a loud, clear voice that was almost musical, she greeted the assembled crowd, dipped gracefully at the waist, and bowed. Silence seemed to fall all around her and then she rose up slowly and smiled. A low, admiring murmur went up through the crowd as her beauty shone forth in all its glory and more than a few men blushed and averted their gaze. The woman's eyes sparkled as they swept over the crowd, and there was just the faintest tinge of something else behind those blue orbs—something sinister, almost predatory.

"I shook my head. Surely the sun was playing tricks on me. The woman was merely playing to the crowd to draw them in to make a profit. She had done nothing inherently threatening for me to mistrust her, and neither had her two companions. A quick glance at Amelie and the other children showed that they were just as enthralled.

"The woman continued her introduction while the men behind her disappeared behind the confines of the stage. She announced that the puppets they had in their care were magical and that in order for them to come alive, they would need a volunteer who truly believed. It was all very theatrical and was undoubtedly geared towards the children, but even a few adults in the crowd smiled wistfully. A volley of hands shot up in the air as the children begged to be picked, each of them shouting above the din of their companions that they were the best one suited for the task. The woman watched their antics with amusement from her perch and then her eyes lit on Amelie— Amelie who stood quietly but slightly bewildered in the center of the melee. She was clutching her doll almost protectively to her chest as the other children shouted and jockeyed around her, and perhaps this is what caused her to stand out. The woman's eyes glittered triumphantly and she raised her hand for silence. She then pointed a delicate finger directly at Amelie, and all eyes instinctively followed. Amelie looked slightly taken aback, but then a smile spread over her face and she rushed headlong towards the stage.

"I found myself instinctively moving from my place near the back of the crowd to intercept her as something that went beyond maternal instinct screamed at me that danger lay ahead. The woman's gaze flicked towards me and the angelic façade slipped for a moment.

"Amelie had reached the edge of the stage and was gazing up at her. A frown creased her small face as she followed the woman's line of sight, and when her eyes met mine there was nothing but confusion. I was now only a few yards from where they stood and all eyes had turned to stare at us. I immediately cursed myself for acting so impulsively, for reacting to a threat that didn't exist anywhere except in my own mind, and I met Amelie's questioning gaze. The woman glanced down at Amelie and then back at me. Understanding crossed her features and she smiled.

" 'It's all right mother, your daughter will not come to harm here.'

"Something in the way that her smile didn't quite reach her eyes caused me to take a step forward. Amelie stared at me with huge eyes, glanced back at the woman, seemed to come to a decision, and then turned back towards me. She strode slowly but purposely away from the stage and into the thick of the crowd, her small shoulders hunched in defeat.

"The woman watched Amelie's every movement with hawk-like intensity, tracking her progress until she reached my outstretched hands. I immediately enfolded her within the protective cage of my arms. She turned her face up to peer into mine and I knew that behind her neutral gaze lay deep disappointment. I cursed myself and my actions, cursed myself for denying her a moment of childish glee. Yet I couldn't shake the nagging feeling of danger that tugged at my heart. I glanced back at the woman still standing on her perch, and she gazed back levelly. The crowd at her feet was all staring at us and an excited murmuring was rippling through the sea of bodies. The woman had said that no harm would come to Amelie here, and it occurred to me that if either she or her two male companions were to try anything that the crowd would turn on them in an instant. As long as they had an audience, perhaps Amelie was safe after all.

"My grip loosened the tiniest of fractions. Amelie gazed up at me hopefully and I found my arms unwinding from around her. I inclined my head towards the stage and she hugged me briefly before scampering off through the crowd. The woman smiled triumphantly and the two men led Amelie behind the stage. I maintained my position outside the laughing, wildly clapping audience with my eyes fixed on Amelie for the remainder of the performance.

"When the show ended and the trio stood Amelie upon the box while the crowd roared and clapped, I approached the performers. When my body was pressed up against the lip of the stage I reached up for her and the two men gently lowered her towards my waiting arms. I clutched her tightly and headed away from the crowd towards where my parents stood some yards away. I set Amelie down on the ground and she immediately ran to them, shouting excitedly that she and her doll had brought all the other puppets to life. They were naturally impressed and patted her reassuringly on the shoulder, but all I could do was stand there feeling like a great danger had been narrowly averted. Amelie turned to look at me and something must have shown on my face because she tugged at my apron. I reassured her that I was just tired from the day's events and that she did a wonderful job during her performance. She beamed at me and stroked her doll's hair. Any lingering questions she may have had over my earlier behavior seemed to have vanished in the wake of her exuberance, and we headed off hand in hand towards the other booths.

"Throughout the rest of the day I found my gaze traveling almost compulsively towards the direction of the puppeteers, but each time there was nothing out of the ordinary to be seen. More than once I found myself questioning my own actions, and I began to wonder if perhaps the stress of the past year was beginning to affect me. Towards dusk as the shops began to close down one by one, Amelie insisted that we stop by the puppeteers one last time. I naturally balked at such a notion, but my parents were curious to meet these people. The crowds from earlier in the day were long gone and I was keenly aware that we were the only people around. The two men were packing the last of their equipment into the back of their wagon and the woman was seated on the box, almost as if she were expecting us. Amelie immediately sprinted towards her and I once again found myself propelled forward. My father caught my arm and said reassuringly, 'Let her be, she's enjoying herself.' I stilled and watched as the woman laughed at something Amelie must have said, and once again she stared at her like she was something precious. Amelie tugged at the woman's hand and practically dragged her over to us. She was even more striking up close and once again I felt the hair on the back of my neck stand up.

"Amelie babbled excitedly and began to introduce the woman. 'This is Griselda, and the two men back over by the wagon are Dimitri and Kristof.' The woman dipped her head gracefully and then began to carry on over Amelie's performance from earlier in the day. She indicated the doll in her hands.

" 'She seems quite attached to it, doesn't she?' My parents nodded and explained that it was a birthday present as well as a family heirloom. The woman nodded knowingly and said that Amelie must be mature beyond her years to be trusted with something so valuable. Amelie immediately spoke up and said that yes, she was. Everyone laughed at that, and then Amelie spoke the words that would forever seal all our fates:

" 'Griselda and her companions have nowhere to stay tonight. Can they come home with us?' "

I could see Wendell and Andrew's reflections in the window before me, and their expressions bordered on rapt, horror-struck attention. I turned and faced them.

"That night the peace and tranquility of our home was forever shattered, and I became then what I am now."

I spread my hands and held them out to my side. "As Wendell so accurately stated earlier this evening, I am a vampire. I underwent the transference less than a fortnight after encountering the three strangers, but I did not do it willingly. I was forced into it, but not before I was forced to witness the slaughter of my family." I reached for the sheath around my waist and took hold of one of the knives. My hands felt complete now that they were wrapped around the bone handle, which was so smooth and harmless-looking. The old horror and revulsion I felt over my actions centuries ago was only a dim memory compared to the bitterness I now felt.

I spoke clearly and my voice sounded sure and strong in the tiny room. "I may have been a victim, but I did not stay one for long. I exacted my revenge on my tormentors and the fact that I've outlived all of them is an extension of that revenge. I made sure that they would never do what they had done to my family and me ever again."

I let go of the handle and stayed facing the two men. It was impossible to read their expressions, much less guess at what must surely be racing through their minds. I was certain that they were thinking I must have killed my tormentors, and they were partially correct. But truth—much less reality—is seldom that simple. Or that clean. No, I had done much worse than merely kill them, but I had never lost any sleep over my actions.

"That night—despite the voice screaming in my head that our lives were in mortal danger—my parents acquiesced and allowed the three strangers to enter our home. Amelie was practically beside herself with joy and childlike glee. My parents were perplexed and troubled by my sullen mood and chided me that I was being petty, jealous even. I had tried to dissuade them from allowing them into our home, but my father cut off my protests. He was the head of the household and could invite anyone he saw fit inside. My mother looked at me as I was effectively put back in my place, and I desperately wanted to tell her what I knew in my heart was true, that these strangers were more than what they appeared. There was just something about them—the woman in particular—who kept setting off alarm bells in my mind. They had done nothing inherently threatening, so what defense could I level against them? I had nothing, nothing but my own gut feelings to back me up, so I bore my fear and suspicions silently.

"The trio declined dinner and contented themselves by sitting around the fire telling stories and singing songs. At some point during the evening conversation Griselda fetched one of the puppets from the wagon and began to play with Amelie on the floor. I sat with my back to the front door and had an unobstructed view of the living room before me. The puppet was a wondrous thing made of gilt painted wood, silk, embroidery, and ribbons. From what I could make out it resembled a man in princely garb replete with a small crown and scepter, a king of some sort. Amelie's doll had assumed the role of princess, and their antics cast animated shadows around the small room as the two small figures danced by the firelight. The evening progressed in this manner for some time and as so often happens at the end of an eventful day, there was an inevitable lull in the activities. The conversation gradually drifted off and even the sounds of the crackling logs seemed to dwindle away. Fatigue tugged at my eyelids, but I forced them to remain open. Dimitri and Kristof were now seated at the large wooden table that dominated the room, one on each side of my parents. Griselda knelt on the floor with Amelie dozing in her lap. The puppet and Amelie's doll lay off to one side with their small limbs arranged haphazardly around them. I felt a twinge of jealousy as I watched the two of them like that, but I forced myself to remain where I was. I tried not to stare directly at them, but I kept casting sideways glances every few seconds. Before long my head grew heavy on my shoulders and my eyelids drooped closed. I had no conscious awareness of falling asleep and I had no idea how long my attention had lapsed. What I do know is that I was jarred awake by a scream that was quickly stifled by a sharp warning: make another sound, and your family will die.

"I swam rapidly up towards consciousness and was on my feet in seconds. I blinked in the harsh glare of the fire and saw Griselda standing over it with Amelie's doll dangling limply by its feet. The fiend—for there was no longer any doubt in my mind as to what she was—was taunting Amelie by threatening to incinerate it if she didn't stop screaming. I made a move to block Amelie with my body and the woman turned and smiled coldly at me.

"She gestured with her free hand at something behind me, and as I half-turned, I found my parents being restrained by the two men. Sharp blades glinted against the sides of their necks and their eyes were round with fear, confusion, and something else—perhaps betrayal.

"There was a curious lack of sound in the tiny room as all parties involved froze in an apparent standoff. Instinct screamed at me to throw myself in front of Amelie to protect her from further harm, but it also insisted that I save my parents as well. I was squarely in the middle of a set of impossible choices: whose life do I choose to save? If I make a move towards one do I condemn the others? If I do nothing do I risk losing them all, or if I do act, do I risk losing them all to the carefully-orchestrated attack?

"All I could do was stand there numb and in shock over the terrible turn of events. Through it all I cursed myself for not acting on my earlier suspicions, and I was fervently praying to God that He would allow my family to live long enough to learn from this experience.

"Griselda's eyes blazed with maniacal triumph and she dropped softly to one knee. Her hand kept the doll dangling perilously close to the flames but she spoke low and soothing to Amelie. 'If you wish to save your family, you will stop screaming and come with us.'

"I made a sound of negation and her eyes flicked towards me. It was monstrously unfair to offer a mere child such a choice, if you could call it a choice. It was little more than a threat cloaked in the guise of a choice, and I knew that no matter what Amelie decided that things could not possibly end well.

"Griselda kept staring at me as she continued speaking to Amelie. 'It is your choice, child, but remember that their lives are in your hands.' Amelie's eyes were round with bewilderment and tears streamed silently down her cheeks as she considered the woman's words.

"I knew that when she turned to look back at the woman that she had made her decision, as had I: I would not allow her to be taken anywhere by these monsters.

"Amelie nodded ascent and cries of anguish erupted from my parents. There was a brief scuffle as my father was forcibly subdued by the smaller man, Dimitri. He shoved him roughly against the table and forced him down until he was sprawled halfway across the top. Amelie screamed and begged the man to stop, and Griselda's free hand shot out and tangled itself in her hair. Griselda forced her closer until Amelie's weight lay against her and then she forced her head back, leaning in closer to bury her nose in the side of Amelie's neck. Her eyes were shut so tight you could practically see the tension singing along her jaw, and the fingers clutching the doll tightened convulsively. She seemed utterly lost in some sensation known only to her, and that was when she reached into the folds of her skirt. A long blade was withdrawn and laid against Amelie's skin with such lightening swiftness that it seemed it had appeared there by magic. The men's voices cut through the terror-filled silence as her skin dimpled under the edge of the blade.

'Amaris expects them whole and alive.'

"Griselda's eyes flew open and she snarled at the two men in fury. The look of raw hunger on her face was bestial in nature and the angelic façade that had graced her features earlier in the day was completely stripped away. I realized that she hungered for Amelie's blood just like the creatures in our legends did, and I knew now that evil—*true evil*—wore many guises, but its most clever deception was to appear as human as the rest of us.

"When it became apparent that blood was what she wanted, I offered myself to her, to all of them. I took a tentative step closer with my arms outstretched to show that I was unarmed.

"I felt a curious sense of peace even though I was sure that I approached certain death. If my sacrifice would spare the lives of my loved ones, then I could bear whatever tortures they had in store for me. I saw the knife hesitate over Amelie's skin and I offered up a prayer of gratitude.

"Griselda approached me with the knife in her hand. I closed my eyes as I felt her draw closer and I steeled myself against the inevitable pain. It was then that a vicious blow struck me on the side of the head and knocked me to the ground. A brilliant display of colors danced behind my eyes as I hit the floor, and through the roaring in my head I heard similar blows landing behind me. My parents were being harmed such as I was, and when I managed to force my eyes open, Griselda loomed over me, mocking my feeble attempts to save them. I tried to push myself up to strike at her but her right foot lashed out and knocked the breath from me.

"The next few moments took on a nightmare-like clarity as Amelie and my parents were similarly bound and forced to the floor. I realized then that the choice offered to Amelie had been nothing more than a cruel joke. Griselda and her companions had no intention of allowing either of us to escape the situation, sacrifice or not.

"One by one the large wooden chests containing the trio's puppets were unloaded from the wagon and carted into the house. One by one the contents of the trunks were emptied into the roaring inferno that had been built up in the fireplace, and one by one the beautifully-painted puppets were reduced to blackened stumps. When the last of the chests had been emptied, the two men took hold of my father and hefted him into the chest. The lid cut off his muffled protests and brought any hope for a peaceful resolution to an end. Hot tears stung my eyes as I watched my mother and Amelie being treated in the same manner. My hands were bound behind me with a length of coarse rope and my mouth was cotton-dry from the gag that had been stuffed in there. I was helpless, defenseless, completely at their mercy.

"As the lid shut on my own chest, I knew beyond a doubt that we were doomed. The chests were then loaded one by one into the back of the wagon, which lurched forward after a series of whip lashes punctuated the air. Beside me I could hear the quiet weeping of my parents and Amelie. I desperately wanted to talk to them, to reassure them that whatever the trio had in store for us that it would soon be over. I didn't believe for one second that this was true, but if I could make *them* believe it, then I could bear the pain of my own death with that much more grace and dignity."

# Chapter 25

The sound of flesh being torn was the only sound in the room as she struck again and again at the still forms at her feet. Neither of them moved to defend themselves, and it further infuriated her, further solidified the fact that her plan—which she was sure had been so carefully constructed—had gone horribly wrong. Neither of these miserable wretches were worthy of what she had offered them, of what she had given them. The only thing that they deserved was to be punished.

Her face twisted up in a parody of a smile. The energy she had expended in their creation may have been conservative, but she would be more than generous with regards to their torment. Her strength had been waning for some time but she refused to be beaten, refused to surrender what she felt was rightfully hers to that *woman*.

The woman—the one who had murdered her children.

A sound that was more a howl of rage rather than a cry of grief echoed eerily around the room. The silence retreated in its wake and was replaced by the sounds of renewed torment.

# Chapter 26

"I don't recall exactly how long we traveled before reaching our final destination, but I do know that it was long enough to make one day blend seamlessly into the next. The complete and utter blackness of the trunk made judging the time of day impossible, and for miles upon miles the only sound I heard was the clattering of the wagon and the horses' hooves. I burned with hunger and thirst and my limbs had long since gone numb in the confined space days before.

"I thought that I would go mad if this torment didn't end soon.

"I knew that my parents and Amelie must be in a similar state, and I found myself wishing that they had succumbed to these tortures days before. I knew in my heart that we hadn't been on the road long enough, but still I hoped. God only knew what lay at the end of the road.

"Towards the end of our journey the wagon began to slow and the sounds of the whip biting through the air grew more and more frequent. The horses had been driven mercilessly through the winding countryside and were undoubtedly near the breaking point, exhaustion having set in days earlier. Presently the wagon began to creak ominously and then came to a shuddering stop as the horses finally collapsed from the strain. I heard one of the men jump down from his perch to whip them to their feet, but it was useless. The horses were dead.

"Griselda's voice punctuated the sounds of cruelty and began to speak to him soothingly. I strained to make out what was being said and managed to catch only a few syllables: '...here already.'

*Holy Mary Mother of God, pray for us sinners now and at the hour of our death...*

"I didn't get the chance to finish my benediction, because at that moment the back of the wagon was forcibly opened. Wood shrieked against the metal hinges and I heard the trunk next to mine being dragged out. There was a muffled scream as the person inside thrashed against the confines of their prison in a last ditch effort to escape, but ultimately it proved fruitless. I had spent as much time as I was able to during the journey attempting to do just that, and the only thing I had to show for my efforts were bruises and splinters. My heart thudded painfully in my chest as the box I lay in began to scrape across the pitted and uneven floor of the wagon. There was a momentary sense of being weightless before the box was tipped downward and then fell flat against the ground. My forehead smacked the inside of the lid and stabbed fresh shards of pain through my head. I gritted my teeth against the urge to scream and tasted the staleness of the gag on my tongue.

"Griselda laughed and kicked the side of the box, which caused me to flinch in the confined space. 'Are you still alive in there?'

"Another kick to the box nearest me. I heard Amelie sobbing quietly beside me and I vowed that as soon as the lid was lifted, that I was going to claw the woman's eyes from her face.

"Someone stooped beside the chest and lifted it up. The change in altitude made the bile rise up in my throat but I swallowed the nausea back down. I would meet my doom with resolve and I would *not* scream, especially since I knew that it would give my captors pleasure. The box jerked and bobbed from side to side, but all too soon it was lowered to the ground.

There was a faint clatter as it came to rest, almost as if it were lying against heavy stone. The locks on the chest were thrown back and as the lid swung slowly upwards, I shut my eyes against the searing brightness. Strong arms hauled me out of the box and flung me hard against the floor. I lay there hunched in a fetal position, my limbs still too numb to untangle themselves. I gingerly cracked one eye open the tiniest fraction to allow them to grow accustomed to the change in light. When I could fully open them the sight before me froze the breath in my lungs.

"We were in a huge stone antechamber. The vaulted ceiling was adorned by arches and sharp angles that resembled the rib cage of some great beast. Torches burned in each corner in tall, black sconces, and a few smaller ones were set into the far wall. I craned my neck to see where my captors were and all three of them were prostrated before a great stone chair. A man dressed in a flowing robe of the purest blue I'd ever seen emerged from the shadows and stepped lithely into the soft glow of the torches. The light caused a riot of movement in his hair as the highlights seemed to swell and breathe with his every movement. The colors in his robe shimmered and shifted from indigo to blue to silver. His skin bore the same flawless beauty as Griselda's, and his eyes burned with the light of the torches. Heavy gold rings glittered on his tapered fingers, and at the center of one, a ruby winked and sparkled. The adornments seemed wholly unnecessary given the extraordinary presence he radiated. He wasn't strikingly beautiful like the three forms before him— indeed his face was unremarkable in every respect. The face was rounded with a short, almost squat forehead. A long, straight nose and prominent chin completed the whole of his features. His eyes were a dark brown that seemed to catch and hold the light reflected before them, but there was something about him, something that radiated authority, charisma even. His every movement was infused with this undeniable magnetism and it was nearly impossible to drag your gaze away from him. The faintest hint of a smile touched the corners of his eyes as he took in the three forms before him, and when his gaze flicked over the forms of my family and I the smile grew wider. He raised his right arm and Griselda immediately stood up and moved closer. She clasped his hand in hers and bestowed a gentle kiss upon his knuckles.

'Amaris.'

"*Amaris expects them whole and alive.* A ripple of fear wormed its way into the pit of my stomach as the men's words came back to me. Terror wrapped cold fingers around my heart as the prospect of what awaited my family and I here in this dark chamber slowly set in.

"He leaned forward and murmured something into her ear, whereupon she leaned closer and motioned towards Amelie.

" 'The little one's life burns the brightest—she is my gift to you. That one,' her finger pointed directly at me, 'was less than cooperative and got in my way. She wronged me Amaris, and by the same token she wronged you as well. Her insolence must not be tolerated.'

"His gaze left her face and came to rest on mine. Torchlight glinted off the dark orbs of his eyes as they roamed over me. He nodded slightly in apparent approval, and Griselda's face immediately lit up with vulpine triumph. There was a brief scuffle as Dimitri and Kristoff rose to their feet and forced my parents to their knees. I strained against the ropes that bound me and flung my weight from side to side. Amelie had gone very still beside me and was mute with fear. Griselda and Amaris stepped down from the stone dais and approached us with their hands clasped tightly together. They moved in tandem as if they were one mind in the same body, their every action perfectly choreographed.

"When they were inches away from us they separated and closed the distance. Griselda bundled Amelie up into her arms and she screamed and thrashed violently. I instantly recoiled from Amaris' touch as he knelt beside me and wrapped his arms around my upper torso. He lifted his head to stare at Griselda who knelt demurely with the still-struggling Amelie in her arms. His gaze then traveled once more to the figures of my mother and father, and his eyes narrowed slightly. It was almost as if he was appraising them in some manner, and it was evident by the look on his face that he was not pleased by what he saw. He said something to the two men in a language that I did not understand and they forced my parents' heads back in unison. Amaris turned towards Griselda and repeated a similar phrase that had the lilt of a question to it, as if he were asking her opinion of something. She shrugged her delicate shoulders as if she were ambivalent towards what was about to happen, and then her gaze flicked back towards Amelie.

"I struggled against him and cursed her through the gag in my mouth. I was so completely enraged that I wanted nothing more than to see that beauty marred by my hands. I fought against the arms that restrained me and threw my entire weight against his chest, but he was as unmovable as stone. Amaris laughed and remarked that I was spirited for a woman—even a lowly peasant one such as myself—and then his hands tightened painfully around my arms. I could feel my skin bruising under the pressure, but I gritted my teeth and refused to scream. He lowered his face and whispered in my ear that soon enough I would give in, that eventually everyone reached their breaking point—he had only to discover mine and he had all the time in the world to find it.

"He spoke my mother tongue perfectly, but there was an accent to each syllable that I could not trace. His appearance alone seemed to confirm that he was not native to the area, but his origins were of no consequence to me. The only thing that mattered was getting my family out of here unharmed.

"Griselda's mocking laughter echoed eerily around the stone room like shrieking birds. 'Is it not obvious what her weakness is?' She gently ran her fingertip along the inner curve of Amelie's cheek. 'It is her family.'

"My heart hammered in my chest and I struggled despite myself. I was completely overwhelmed by the basic instinct to save those that I loved, and my actions confirmed what she had said. I couldn't comprehend why she wanted to see me suffer so. Surely I had done nothing to harm her, though I wished that I had. The only thing I had done that was even remotely confrontational was my attempt to shield Amelie from her during their performance. As I looked at her mocking gaze through the tangled sweep of my hair, I realized that this was exactly what I had seen reflected in her eyes that day. She was surprised that someone had not only suspected that she wasn't human, but that they didn't hesitate to get between her and her prey. By protecting Amelie I had challenged what she felt she had a right to take by force.

"I realized this too late as Amaris removed the gag from my mouth with enough force to cause my lips to bleed. I ran a tongue that was equally dry over them and coughed once before speaking. 'Mark my words: one way or the other I will see you pay for this. All of you.'

"The laughter died away and her face became very serious. Her eyes narrowed shrewdly as she spoke. 'A strong threat, but a threat means nothing without the means to back it up. You have the will—I have seen this myself, but you are incapable of carrying it out, will or no.'

"My voice sounded unnaturally calm. 'No. I am not powerless.' Conviction chased away the tremor that fear had created and I raised my head up to meet her gaze. 'I challenged you that day at the fair—your quarrel is with me. Release my family.' To my left, my mother sobbed and struggled against the arms that restrained her. My father's eyes shone in the torchlight and the fear in them was plainly evident. I couldn't imagine what was going through his mind in those moments.

Was it anger? Fear? Regret? Certainly some small part of him regretted welcoming the three strangers into our household, which surely added to the terror he felt for his family. He had been born and raised in a time where the man of the house was the provider as well as the protector of their family. By showing kindness to the three strangers, he had endangered everyone's lives. I wanted to tell him in those moments that he was not to blame. How could he be? He had no way of knowing what he invited into his house. Even with my suspicions there were moments when logic dictated that the strangers in front of me couldn't possibly be more or less than what they appeared to be.

"Griselda seemed to consider my offer. She turned to look at Amaris and I felt him shrug against me.

" 'It is your choice.'

"Her reaction could have meant any number of things. She sat there with Amelie still nestled in her arms, one finger absently stroking the soft down on her arms. Her fingernails made a slight rasping sound as they passed over the skin, and I gasped involuntarily. Griselda's hands stopped in mid-motion and she spoke without looking at me. 'You're right. My quarrel *is* with you.' She stroked Amelie's hair and a small shudder ran through her tiny body. I heard the smile in her voice when she said, 'Dimitri, Kristoff: release her family.'

"A scuffle ensued as my parents were wrenched apart. My mother wailed behind the gag in her mouth, and my father grunted and struggled against his restraints. He struck out at Dimitri and managed to regain his freedom for a fraction of a second. He half crawled, half hobbled to where Amaris and I sat. He had managed to work part of the gag loose and he was frantically trying to reason with them. 'No, take me! Take me!'

"Dimitri tackled him and dragged him back across the room. He tightened the restraints and replaced the gag, cutting off any further attempts at escape. I cursed and fought to get free of Amaris' arms, but it was useless. Blind panic and rage overrode any other emotion, and I screamed in my fury.

" 'You said you'd release them!' I kept screaming the same thing over and over again, as if by saying it enough times I could make it true. My pleas fell on deaf ears, and I finally slumped against my captor and sobbed miserably. Sheer exhaustion and humiliation left me feeling defeated. There was nothing more I could do to save my family. Threats, reason, sympathy, all of these were useless against these beings. They were immortal and death held no power over them. It seemed reasonable that life had no value to them as well. Humans were nothing to them but sustenance and sport. We never once stood a chance and everything in between had been nothing more than a cruel charade.

"Griselda was unaffected by my cries of injustice. 'I am true to my word. I will release your family, but it is *you* who failed to specify in what condition.' She giggled. The fiend actually giggled as if she'd said something clever.

"She turned towards the men restraining my family and nodded once. I had just enough time to see the glint of a knife as it arced downward towards my father. High, piercing screams bounced off the walls of the room in a hellish cacophony as my mother watched her husband being murdered. The gag did little to muffle the sound and she continued to shriek, her eyes wide with horror. Amaris said something sharp, and nodding his head in acknowledgement, Kristoff raised his own hand to strike. As I continued to stare at the horror unfolding before me, I saw the faces of my mother and father—frozen in the agony of their death—slump silently to the floor.

"Amelie was staring at the nightmarish scene around her without really seeing it, her small hands clutching at her doll for dear life. The arms that restrained me released me suddenly and as I scrambled away, I realized that the screams were coming from me. They welled out of the very depths of my soul, and all the horror and pain that I had lived through in the past year—the death of my husband, our abduction, and now the murder of my parents—was given voice. I screamed until my throat was raw and bleeding because it was the only thing that I *could* do."

"Time seemed to stand still in those moments following the murder of my parents, yet I kept seeing their death replayed over and over again in my mind. Over and over again I saw their faces contort in a mixture of shock and agony as the knife struck home, and over and over again I realized that I was powerless to stop what had happened. I remember the feel of the cold, damp stone under my hands and the smell of the torches in their sconces, but underneath it all, the harsh, coppery smell of blood is what drove me back to reality. I remember scrambling to my feet and sweeping Amelie up in my arms, and then the awful sense of us being torn from each other's embrace. I dug at the fingers that held us apart and by then I was raving and crying hysterically. I was disheveled and utterly miserable as we were forced away and the space between us seemed to stretch out into infinity.

"Dimitri and Kristoff each had me by an arm and Griselda and Amaris cradled Amelie between them. She was still staring at the scene before her without really seeing it, which I still consider a mercy even now. She looked as lifeless and immobile as the doll she still clutched in her hand, an ode to stark terror rendered in flesh and bone. They were both running their hands lovingly over the smooth skin of her arms and were utterly entranced by something evident only to them. Their eyes shone as they traveled over her small form and low murmurs of content and something else I didn't want to identify emanated from them. A knife emerged from the folds of Amaris' robe and the blade winked in the torchlight. I realized that it was identical to the ones that Griselda, Dimitri, and Kristoff carried, and as I watched, the skin of Amelie's left arm dimpled under the blade. A single crimson drop slid into the crook of her arm and her eyes rolled sluggishly in their sockets. The small pain seemed to jolt her back to reality, and I realized that if I didn't do something soon that she would be aware of her inevitable death. I went very still in the arms of my captors and spoke soothingly to her, my voice carrying unnaturally loud in the stone chamber.

'Amelie, listen to me. You've had a nightmare, that's all. Go back to sleep now; everything will be all right.' I willed the tremor in my voice away as I saw her eyes roll slowly towards me. She blinked but did not seem to take notice of the two kneeling forms beside her. I forced myself to smile reassuringly. 'Close your eyes, darling. Everything will be better in the morning.'

"The pair watched the spectacle silently, their eyes glittering with triumph and a mixture of something else that I couldn't identify: a mixture of arrogance and supremacy that only the criminally insane or the truly evil possess? Perhaps. But underneath all this was the sense of raw, unadulterated need, of a hunger so great it threatened to consume the bearer if it wasn't adequately satisfied. To say that their eyes burned with this need is an understatement—they were complete and utter slaves to it.

"Comforted by the truth in the spoken words of a loved one, Amelie closed her eyes without question.

"My breath caught as the knife was lifted towards her throat. I forced myself to meet the gaze of the still-smirking pair and they returned it with cold indifference. I opened my mouth to plead with them one last time and to appeal to their better nature if indeed they had one, but even before the first words could tumble from my lips, the knife slashed downward with brutal, lethal precision. The hand clutching at the doll with its tiny plaited hair and embroidered apron went slack and it slipped silently to the floor. The painted face stared blankly out at the scene of carnage, its dark eyes mercifully blind to what lay before it. I was dimly aware of my own mind struggling to block out what it instinctively knew was before me. For the longest time the only thing I seemed to be able to focus on was the doll. It seemed to hold some strange fascination to me, but in hindsight I knew that it was a subconscious effort on my part to avoid acknowledging the truth: my entire family was dead, and if there was any sense of justice or mercy in this world, I would soon be joining them.

"A sense of movement to my left dragged my eyes away from the doll, and the spectacle that awaited me nearly drove me over the brink. Amelie's tiny form struggled and twitched feebly within the prison of Griselda and Amaris' arms, her chest rising and falling in a frantic effort to sustain life. The blow hadn't killed her but had merely wounded her and cast her into a hellish sort of limbo between life and death. I could see from her expression that she was aware of what was going on around her, and she was in a paroxysm of fear and agony. Torchlight glinted off the blood pooling at their feet and off the blade of the knife lying just out of reach. Amaris caressed Griselda's face and she mimicked his actions, their eyes locked on each other with an intensity reserved for only the most intimate of lovers. Each of them dipped a finger into the pooling blood and gently, tenderly traced the contours of each other's lips. Their fingers slid into each other's mouths as they began to slowly suck the blood away, relishing the taste of it. Low moans of pleasure mixed with Amelie's hitching gasps and added to the sheer horror and perversity of the situation. Their eyes squeezed shut as they continued to savor the blood, and as Amelie whimpered and began to thrash helplessly in their arms, they threw their heads back with violent force. Their arms came up in unison and clawed frantically at the air as some unknown sensation held them in its grasp. Amelie's back arched off the floor and as her head lolled slowly to the side, her eyes met mine. I saw reflected in them the horror she felt as she realized what was happening to her, of what she was sure was undoubtedly going to happen to me. I saw the light dim from her eyes as her face twisted up with the final agony, and the confusion and sorrow she felt vanished into the abyss.

"I screamed.

"I kept screaming even as I wrenched myself free from my captors with a strength and ferocity that I wasn't aware I possessed, and as my hand closed around the knife lying at the feet of Amelie's murderers, the screams continued. The pair was still so utterly caught up in the aftermath of the kill that they didn't even notice me until I lashed out at them. I reserved the brunt of my fury for Griselda—the demon with the face of an angel—and I slashed at her face in a blind rage. Her snarls and screams of pain rent the air and even as hands struggled to wrench the knife away from me, I kept slashing at her. Blood coated my hands as I was forcibly thrown back, and even through the haze of pain that obscured my vision, I saw that streaks of red marred her face and breast. Blue eyes blazed behind the mask of blood, and I laughed. I was consciously aware that my mind was effectively broken, but it was of no consequence to me. The only thing that mattered was that I had accomplished exactly what I had sworn I would do. It was a small comfort in those dark moments, but a comfort no less.

"No sooner had I come to this realization when Griselda launched herself at me in a blind fury. Blows came at me from all sides, and through the wildly-swinging limbs, I saw that her hands had been hooked into claws. The first swipe caught me on the right cheek but the stinging pain barely registered. I was numb in those moments and neither cared how or when I died, so long as I eventually did. My relative lack of reaction further infuriated her and she snarled savagely in frustration. As she drew her arm back to strike at me again, Amaris' voice rang out in the stone room.

" 'Griselda.'

"That one word stopped her cold, but the arm remained poised in midair. Tension sang along her limbs as she trembled with silent rage. He walked up to her and gently lowered the arm to her side and she offered little to no resistance. Her breast continued to heave from her exertions and he placed a reassuring hand on her shoulder. One hand came up to cup the side of her face, and I could see in the torchlight that the knife slashes had healed. His thumb wiped the last traces of blood from her face, and once again that striking, radiant flawlessness shone forth in all its glory.

" 'You see?' He pushed the hair back from her face. 'She cannot harm you.'

" 'It is of no consequence.' She turned her hate-filled gaze to me. 'She *meant* to harm me and should be punished.' She made a move to approach me, but he stopped her with a firm grip on her arm.

" 'Would it not be better to make her suffer for what she did rather than merely punish her?'

" 'I don't understand.' She was still glaring at me but confusion had chased away some of her anger.

"Amaris smiled indulgently and spoke softly. 'Consider this: you may punish her—torture her, maim her—but she is human, fragile. She cannot survive the level of pain that I know you desire to inflict on her. Death would come fairly quickly and would be a blessing to her. But to have her suffer—*truly* suffer as one such as we can if the proper methods are applied—now *that* would be punishment indeed.'

"A slow, devious smile spread across her face. He saw her expression and matched it with his own. My mind was too broken to recognize the look for what it was, and I merely sat there on the stone floor with my captors leering down at me. Even as the four of them moved towards me with slow, calculated precision, I made no move to defend myself. *This is it,*

I thought as Dimitri and Kristof each took an arm and forced me to my knees. *I will soon be reunited with my family. Every wound that I receive and every drop of blood that I shed will bring me one step closer to them.*

"The forms of Amaris and Griselda flashed into my field of vision, but again I gave no indication that I was aware of their proximity.

" 'She is in shock.' Amaris wrenched my head from side to side in an attempt to elicit a response, but the most I could muster was a low whimper.

"Griselda's voice was a snarl behind me. 'I can remedy that.'

"A searing pain shot through my scalp as her hands grasped my head and forced it back. Whole clumps of my hair were ripped away as she yanked my head back towards the floor. My spine bowed at an excruciatingly painful angle and I couldn't stop the scream of pain that tumbled from my mouth. Griselda's mocking laughter drowned out my struggles as her left hand came up and pinched my nose closed. I fought against the panic that overtook me as I realized that they were going to smother me. My mouth instinctively opened to draw breath, and it was then that Amaris' wrist flashed into view. I saw him raise the knife and he drew it across his wrist in one quick motion. Blood so dark and viscous that it appeared to be black rather than crimson welled out of the wound and splashed against my face. I struggled to force my face away from the blood spilling over it, and it was then that he pressed the wound directly over my open mouth. I choked and gagged and continued to throw my weight violently from side to side, but the three of them restraining me made it impossible. My mind screamed that I was being contaminated by the evil that was animating them and that I was going to be condemned to an eternity of bloodlust such as they were.

"*No*, I thought as Amaris pressed his wrist tighter against my mouth, *if I become such as they then Paradise is forever lost to me—all that remains is Hell.* I bucked and writhed as the blood continued to flow unimpeded down my throat. I could feel it working its way into the very depths of my being, could feel it invading every pore of my body. Hot tears stung my eyes as I moaned and whimpered in my wretchedness. My eyelids fluttered frantically as the lack of oxygen gradually took its toll on me. I was dimly aware that Griselda's grip on my nose relaxed, undoubtedly in order for me to remain conscious throughout the ordeal. I involuntarily drew in a great lungful of air and I felt my vision begin to come back into focus.

"Amaris—his expression almost beatific in its serenity as he loomed over me—was surrounded by a swirling nimbus of red and gold. It was like nothing that I had ever seen before, and as my head slipped slightly to the side, I noted that my left arm was surrounded by the same film. As I watched, it swelled past my field of vision and then snapped back on itself. The films rippled and contracted in unison as they began to meld into one another, gradually dwindling away to a single crimson strand that stretched out between us. The sight of that single strand connecting the two of us together only added to the horror and revulsion I was experiencing. I felt violated in the most horrific and unspeakable way and I wanted nothing more than to rid myself of this evil that had entered my life.

"Time once again seemed to stand still as they continued to violate me in this manner, and gradually I was aware of them allowing me to slip to the floor. I had managed to partially block out what was being done to me during this time, but as the pain of the transference began to ravage my body, I was aware of what was happening to me. I remember clawing at the ground in a frenzy as the world seemed to tilt and the colors of the room took on a nightmarish clarity that left my eyes tearing. Wave after wave of excruciating, unimaginable pain shot through my body and left me flailing in my agony. I threw my head back and cried out miserably for my parents, to my God, anyone that could possibly save me from this torture. I remember the way that my fists slammed into the stone floor again and again as my back arched at an impossible angle. Every fiber of my being seemed to be stretched to the absolute limit and seemed to expand and collapse upon itself as the blood permeated and invaded each one in turn. Then suddenly as it began, the pain vanished as if in a dream. I remember collapsing to the floor in a heap with my breath coming in great, heaving gasps. Footsteps echoed around me and as I cautiously opened my eyes, the figure of Griselda came into focus.

" 'Now your punishment has truly begun.'

"I coughed and struggled to prop myself up on my elbows. 'Say what you want; you may have violated my body and sanity, but my soul you can not touch—not as long as there is life and breath in my body.'

"She bent forward. 'Not only will you will live long enough to see the irony in that promise, but you will live long enough to regret your words. Oh, yes you will.'

"Her foot lashed out in a blur of movement, and then I was spiraling down into darkness. I knew no more."

"I awoke to darkness so complete that for a moment I was sure I was dead. Little by little a dull ache started up in my head where Griselda had viciously kicked me, and I knew that I wasn't. Sounds echoed back to me from seemingly far away: the sound of water dripping rhythmically, the sound of tiny feet scrabbling against stone. Rats or some other small vermin were squealing and crawling over my bare feet. I hurriedly kicked out at them and they moved away from me.

"I gingerly stretched my arms out to either side and felt damp stone under my palms. The air around me was damp as well and had a curious, earthy smell to it, of a place seemingly unaffected by the civilized world—a primal smell that could only come from the very bowels of the earth. I strained to see in the gathering gloom, but the darkness was firmly wrapped around my surroundings and obscured my vision. I sat up slowly and tentatively stretched out my legs to test the confines of this place. They connected with another wall of stone, and further experiments in either direction produced the same results. I surmised that I was in a cell of some sort, and my heart sank.

"*My heart.*

"I gently laid a hand upon my breast and had to stifle a cry of negation. My heart beat, but the rhythm was slow and barely noticeable. I cautiously flexed my limbs as much as I was able to and found that I felt lighter, boneless, somehow detached from my own flesh. The pain that had wracked my body earlier was only a dim memory and there was a curious lack of sensation throughout. The blood that Amaris had forced on me was undoubtedly responsible for this, and I felt sick with horror. I felt contaminated and unclean and I clasped my hands firmly in prayer. The sound of my voice raised in supplication was the only sound in the tiny room, and when I finished my benediction, I sank to the floor in grief. The faces of my family and of their death unfolded with frightening clarity, and I wailed in my misery. I knew then that they were lost to me and that the doors to Paradise would be barred to me forever. The legends of my people stressed that one such as I was damned and would never be able to enter God's house again. All signs and symbols of Him would forever repel me, yet I had managed to successfully offer up a prayer without harm. If this was so, was I truly damned as my people believed or was I merely forsaken and cast aside?

"My body was wracked by uncontrollable sobs but no tears trailed down my cheeks, and it was the final indication that I was no longer human. But yet the issue remained: if I felt grief over the death of my family then surely I wasn't evil even if in the eyes of the Church. The damned feel no such things, yet the pain in my heart was palpable. Perhaps redemption *was* possible for one such as me.

"The sound of a heavy door sliding open echoed loudly in the room before I could dwell on the issue further. A slash of light illuminated the doorway and the two figures that came into the room. I recognized the first form as Griselda as she gracefully dipped her head to enter through the low doorway. Dimitri and Kristoff trailed behind her carrying torches, and they immediately set them in sconces buried in the wall. They then left the room as abruptly as they had entered. The sudden illumination was harsh after the prolonged darkness and I raised an arm to shield my eyes. Griselda's mocking laughter filled the room and I found myself tensing to spring. I vowed that when all of this was over that I would see her dead—I would see all of them dead even if I had to wait for eternity to accomplish it.

"She must have seen these thoughts reflected on my face because the look she flashed me was full of scorn. 'I see the desire for revenge in your eyes. I see the anger and the injustice of it all peering out at me and it pleases me. It pleases me to know that you are suffering. You thought that you could take what was rightfully mine, thought you could slash my flesh without consequence. You were mistaken.' She paused and leered down at me, her eyes flicking greedily over what was undoubtedly my disheveled appearance. 'Amaris was right. It is *far* sweeter to prolong your punishment—death *would* have been a blessing for you.' She turned towards the doorway and nodded her head.

"Kristof and Dimitri reemerged with a struggling human in their arms. They were roughly hustled into the room and were forced to kneel on the cold stone floor. They were crying and whimpering, begging with their captors to please not harm them and their daughter.

"*Daughter?*

"Confusion added to the look of shock on my face and when Griselda saw it, she smiled darkly and exited the room. She re-emerged a moment later carrying a little girl in her arms, a little girl with dark curls and deep, inquisitive eyes—eyes that rolled in their sockets in terror. Griselda saw me staring at the child and when the horror of it all dawned on me, she laughed shrilly.

"I cried out in dismay when I saw their features illuminated clearly in the torchlight. Each of them—the man, the woman, and the little girl—were almost identical to those of my family.

" 'I thought that this would surely please you.' She set the girl down on the floor and the mother immediately scooped her up and held her protectively. 'I thought that surely you missed your family and would want to see them again. To think that I went through so much trouble...' Her full lips turned down in a mock pout but the humor did not leave her eyes. She was enjoying my torment, but worse still, she was enjoying the family's torment as well. Hell could not be any worse than this.

"I flung my arms over my face and scrambled clumsily against the opposite wall to put as much distance between us as possible. I collapsed onto my side and lay there huddled in the corner hugging my arms to myself to keep from clawing at my eyes. I couldn't bear to see the family kneeling there—lambs led to the slaughter—knowing that this was going to be the place of their execution, and that *I* was to be the executioner.

"I wouldn't do it, I couldn't do it. I would not become the monster that Griselda and Amaris wanted me to be. I would not lose my sense of self and succumb to the hunger that I knew lay dormant within me. I would not embrace this side of me no matter how painful the consequences.

"I heard Griselda and the others retreating towards the door and I tentatively looked up. My eyes had finally adjusted to the darkness and I could make out the forms of the family in front of me. They were all huddled together in the center of the room, and when they saw me move, a cry of terror went up from them. Griselda's laughter followed her out the door as she bade us farewell with the admonition to 'enjoy our time together.'

"The hatred I felt for her and the others then was complete and overwhelming.

"When I turned to face the people in the room with me and saw the fear in their eyes, it threatened to consume me.

"They had no right to do this to them. The injustice I felt over what had been done to my family and I was overshadowed by the injustice towards these people. They were innocent and had nothing to do with Griselda and her apparent quarrel with me. They had nothing to do with my family save for an uncanny resemblance to them, a resemblance that had effectively sealed their fate.

"I tried to speak to them, to reassure them that I would not hurt them in any way and that I would figure out a way for us all to get out of here. They were leaning against the opposite wall with their arms linked around one another and refused to meet my gaze. Only the man dared to glance in my direction, and I saw the challenge in his expression. *Come near my family, and I will risk life and limb to defend them.*

"I had no intention of testing his resolve.

"The woman and child finally fell into a restless sleep as the hours passed. The man remained ramrod straight, determined to watch over them at all costs. When I was sure that the sleeping pair was truly deep in slumber, I whispered softly to him. 'Stay as far away from me as possible. Do not let your family out of your sight for even a moment, and do not for one second believe anything I tell you.'

"I saw him nod slowly in understanding, and he tightened his grip on his wife and daughter. For the past several hours I could feel the hunger gradually building up within me. It was a strange sort of sensation, almost as if I was being drawn deep down and away from myself. All emotions were leeched away as the hunger took over my thoughts and actions. It was all I was, was all I knew, and was all that I wanted to embrace.

"I gritted my teeth and squeezed my eyes shut. I would *not* give in. Yet every time I stole a glance in their direction, I envisioned myself coaxing them closer with promises to not hurt them, all with the opposite intent. I longed to run my hands over their smooth flesh and to taste the coppery blood running in their veins. I longed to take them into me and to fill myself to bursting with their life. I actually smiled when I envisioned the terror on their faces when I wrenched them apart and took them one by one.

"I found myself on the verge of rising to my feet to close the distance between us. The man glanced apprehensively in my direction and when our eyes met, the hunger raged within me and slammed against the wall of restraint that I had fought for hours to maintain.

" 'God help me,' I whispered. The man hurriedly crossed himself and edged closer to the wall.

"The hours, days passed without incident. I was maddened by unimaginable hunger, ravaged beyond comprehension, but still I did not give in. The family was in a similarly worse shape, as no food or drink was ever provided for them. They made do with the little water that dripped from the stones in the ceiling, but it wasn't enough. As I saw them succumb to hunger and thirst, I found myself rationalizing their murder: would it not be more humane to put them out of their misery with only a minimal amount of pain? Surely that was better than languishing in this cell day after day while slowly starving to death. I couldn't bear to see the look of hopelessness in their eyes as we stared at each other across a seemingly unbridgeable chasm. The divisive lines that had been drawn on that first day were still being enforced, but the man's resolve was slipping. He was consumed by grief over what was happening to his family, was consumed by grief at his apparent inability to protect and save them. Every time my breath hitched from the pain that the hunger was causing me, I saw his eyes flick towards me expectantly. It was several days before I realized the significance of this: he was asking me without words to put him and his family out of their misery. They had no way of knowing how long they would be forced to endure this torture, so rather than face such a daunting prospect, he had decided that death was infinitely more preferable. I was aghast at this realization, but my own constant struggle with the hunger was waning. It wouldn't be long before I would give into my baser nature and take them by force, so perhaps it was better to take them now when they were willing sacrifices. I would be doing them a great mercy, I told myself. There needn't be any guilt attached.

"Only the thought of feeding off of the child like Griselda and Amaris had done to Amelie was enough to send me scrambling back towards my corner. So the days continued to pass in this manner and the looks the man shot me from time to time grew more and more resentful.

"Eventually I slipped into a sort of twilight state where fantasy and reality intersected, where I was almost blissfully unaware of what was happening. I knew that the family was still suffering a few feet away from me, but I was comforted by the fact that my resolve had not wavered. Never mind that it was grossly self-righteous, but in those moments where I drifted in and out of consciousness, it was the one tenuous thing I had to cling onto in the abyss.

"This conviction held strong until the door was once again opened and horror was heaped upon horror, when my conscience was brutally and violently assaulted by the savage murder of the family, a murder committed by my own hands, and which I have sought absolution for the past three-hundred-and-twenty-eight years."

# Chapter 27

The four bodies lay crumpled on their sides, whimpering and twitching feebly. She merely stared down at them with cold indifference. She knew that no matter what sort of cruelties she leveled on them that the aching sense of loss would never be quelled. The faint echoes of her sons' death still resonated deep in her soul and she clutched at her sides to keep from screaming. When the knife had slashed through their flesh, she had felt it; when their last breath had wheezed painfully from their lungs, she had fallen to the floor gasping. She knew the pain and terror that was their last moments, and she had been powerless to stop it. The bond she shared with them went beyond the transference—they were her flesh and blood, her children whom she had nurtured from birth.

And now they were gone. Gone, but certainly not forgotten. As their mother, their Font, she would always feel the pain of their passing.

She swayed unsteadily as the world seemed to tilt sideways. Several pairs of hands reached out to assist her, but she angrily swiped them away. The four traitors would live, but they would suffer for what they had done—for what they had *not* done. They had not come to her sons' aid and were paying the price for their cowardice, a price they would continue to pay for centuries. As her progeny, she couldn't risk killing them for their transgressions. She had no desire to experience the pain and momentary disorientation that followed the death of a progeny again that night, much less that discomfort magnified fourfold. Considering her adversary was still on the loose, she couldn't afford such a blunder and needed to be at full strength. No, she would have to wait until the threat had been eliminated, but patience was a virtue she had in spades.

It seemed she had underestimated the woman after all. That was unforgivable, and part of her knew that she was just as guilty over her sons' death as the four cowering forms on the floor were. She could destroy the guilty parties but the guilt she harbored over her own short-sightedness would haunt her into eternity—*that* she could not abide.

Bryan had come forward after the screaming had finally given way to strained silence, and had knelt reverently at her feet. He held a small leather square out to her and explained that it belonged to one of the people responsible for Alec and Castillo's death. Daman, who had been watching the whole spectacle from his position against the far wall, strode forward and corroborated Bryan's findings. His voice was barely a growl through clenched teeth, but his mother placed a reassuring hand on his shoulder and told him that they would soon have their revenge.

*And so the noose tightens.* She stood there swaying slightly on her feet and grinned ferally. It seems that the whole debacle wasn't a complete failure after all. The woman had undoubtedly ferried the two men off to her place of residence, whose location had been made known to her thanks to Darnell's intell. If for some reason Mr. Crossman was not with her, the address on his license coupled with Bryan's knowledge of where he worked left them several options. Either way her quarries were cornered like rats.

She gazed down at the bloody forms at her feet. One of them crawled slowly towards her with its hands held out in supplication. She kicked it away from her.

The man bit back a scream and shrank away from her while she smiled at his pain. She motioned to Daman and Bryan. "They will need to heal as soon as possible; you know what to do."

They nodded slowly and turned to leave. They knew that she was even weaker now after the torture her progeny had endured, but she had been remarkably pragmatic about the whole thing. She could have easily killed them, easily in the sense that her fury was great enough that she almost lost herself and had to be held back more than once. She had shown remarkable restraint and presence of mind by sparing them and her from certain death. By allowing them to live, she had placed them in a situation where they would have to feed furiously to heal. As their Font, she would garner the lion's share of whatever energy they obtained from their victims. Even as they fed to keep themselves alive, they contributed to her overall strength and supplied her with the energy that she needed to kill the woman once and for all. A double-edged sword no less, but she was aware of which edge could do the most damage to her person and avoided it accordingly.

It seemed these sniveling progeny had a purpose after all.

# Chapter 28

My hands gripped the windowsill tightly and the metal groaned under my touch. I forced my fingers to relax as I continued my narrative. "I was awoken by screams and cries of horror. I hurriedly glanced towards the door of my prison and saw Griselda and Amaris leering down at the family. Awareness had not abandoned them and they knew that death had come for them at last. Griselda turned to smile at me as she picked the screaming child up by her ankles and dragged her away from her parents. The mother wailed and scrambled towards her, but her husband thrust her away and tried to shield her with his body. They struggled momentarily as he tried to protect both his wife and child from further harm, and I knew even as he managed to push his wife behind him that his efforts were doomed to failure.

"Amaris swept behind the man and grabbed his wife by the arm, pinning it behind her so she couldn't move. With a bellow of rage, the man launched himself at them without any regard for personal safety. The sharp crack of bones being splintered echoed loudly off the stone confines of the room.

"The man lay writhing on the floor with both of his arms twisted away from his body at a grotesque angle. He flailed miserably, trying desperately to reach his wife who was sobbing and praying hysterically in Amaris' grip. The little girl was screaming for her parents, and Griselda pressed her hand against the girl's mouth. The skin dimpled under the pressure and she whimpered in pain. Griselda shushed her and began to hum softly as Amaris forced her mother's head back. The woman's eyes were wide and the white showed all the way around as he bent over her, smiling haughtily at her terror.

" 'All of this could have been avoided if you had just fed from them yourself.' He glanced up at me and his voice dripped with mock sorrow. 'To think that your stubbornness and self-righteousness could cause all this pain.' He gestured towards the man who was moaning in agony on the floor. 'To think that your stubbornness and self-righteousness could cause all this sorrow.' The little girl's sobs, though muffled behind Griselda's hands, drove spikes into my heart. He sighed heavily and looked back at the woman who was praying fervently. 'I suppose that if you want something done, you have to do it yourself.'

"He ran the tip of his index finger along the line of her throat, tracing the artery that pulsed maddeningly under the pale skin. I stared transfixed at the throbbing pulse and felt the hunger swell and expand within me. It roared forward in a frightening burst of lust and savage need, and my knees buckled beneath me. I scrabbled desperately at the damp stone walls and gritted my teeth so tightly that my jaw throbbed with the effort. My whole body shook violently with this undeniable need but I refused to give in, refused to look at the family who were now more food to me than people.

" 'Yes, feel the hunger—embrace it!' Griselda's impassioned voice cut through the roar of the pulse pounding in my head. 'Do not fight it. It is what you are, and these,' she gestured curtly towards the family, 'are nothing more than prey, fuel for our immortal bodies. They live only to serve our needs, the need you refuse to acknowledge.'

" 'How can you say that?' I avoided looking at her as I spoke. 'They are human beings. They have feelings—by God can you not hear their screams?'

"She scoffed. 'God? What does God have to do with any of this? We are beyond God, and time and the elements cannot affect us. We do not age, we do not die. Why then should it matter if they suffer before we feast? You speak of their suffering as if it were a sin against God, a sin that we must surely pay for. If God truly exists, why then was this allowed to happen to you, to your family—*this* family?' She stroked the girl's face with the tip of one finger. 'No, God is only a myth. There is no ultimate goodness or justice in the universe. Death is the only certainty of humanity. *We* are forever, and God has no place in our world.'

"I stared at her and Amaris in horror and they gazed back at me with impassive eyes. They truly did not feel any remorse for what they were putting the family through, and they felt no remorse over the deaths of my family. Pity was foreign to them, guilt had never affected them, and mercy was beyond them.

"Amaris' voice cut across the room like a blade. 'The woman and her husband are of little consequence to us,' he pulled her head to the side, exposing the pulsing artery. 'The child's life, however,' he inclined his head towards her, 'is like a beacon in the dark. Her parents' by contrast, pale in comparison. We would be doing them a mercy killing them here and now. There is so little life left to them that they would be dead within a few short years. Time would ravage their bodies and leave them frail and feeble. Would it not be better for them to die quickly rather than suffer a slow death stripped of all dignity?'

" 'Are you trying to justify your actions?' I didn't even attempt to keep the scorn and disgust from showing in my voice.

"He shrugged his shoulders and the colors of his robe shifted with his movements. 'I was merely making an observation.'

" 'The same held true for your family. Amelie was the one we wanted because of the strength of her life force. At the most, your parents could have lived for another decade each.

They were already old and time would not have been kind to them.' The matter-of-fact tone of Griselda's voice infuriated me beyond reason, and for a moment it overpowered the hunger raging within me.

" 'You fiend—it wasn't your place to decide such a thing!' I scrambled awkwardly to my feet. The world tilted dangerously to the side and I hurriedly reached out for the wall for balance. My pulse roared in my head, but the sounds of remembered screaming and cries of agony steadily drowned them out. My body trembled with emotion as I shuffled towards them. Rage quickly burned away any last traces of fatigue I was experiencing and propelled me forward. 'You had no right to interfere in their lives, no matter how you try to justify your actions! You murdered my family in cold blood and then you turned me against my will!'

"My voice had reached a near-hysterical pitch. 'You talk of killing as if it were a mercy you bestow upon your victims, but your actions suggest otherwise. You tortured and killed my family because you wanted to, the same as you are doing with this family!' As if for emphasis, the woman sobbed in Amaris' arms. He didn't seem to notice or care.

" 'What justification is there for what you did to me? Why didn't you kill me along with my family and save me from this…this…' I couldn't find an adequate enough term to describe the living hell that I was currently embroiled in.

"I stood there in the middle of the tiny room and looked from one to the other. 'I have to know why you did this.' I swept my arm around the room, indicating that this included the family as well. 'Did you do it because you can?' My emotional state had no obvious effect on Griselda, and she continued to stroke the child's hair absently.

" 'That is not the only reason.' The corners of her eyes crinkled up. 'We did it because we can as you so bluntly pointed out, but mainly we did it because we enjoy it.' She nodded towards Amaris. 'In your case, we did it because it was entertaining. In all the centuries that Amaris and I have walked this earth, you and your family have given us something that no other family has: a challenge. See,' she readjusted the girl's weight in her lap and spoke conversationally, 'after a thousand years or so, things tend to get predictable regarding prey— there are only so many types: quivering, feeble, pathetic, but you...you were fearless, *confrontational*.' Her eyes blazed with passion and the torchlight reflecting off of them was lost in the drowning darkness. 'You recognized that there was something different about me, knew that I was not human and that I had designs on your little Amelie.'

"I flinched at the mention of her name, but she ignored it.

" 'You not only fought to save your family, but offered yourself as a sacrifice in their place—*astounding* for a mere mortal. Generally your kind is so concerned with their own miserable little existence to think of anything but themselves, but you proved to be the exception to that rule.'

" 'And what of *your* kind?' I stuck my chin out indignantly. 'Your actions are just as selfish as anyone else's—human or otherwise.'

" 'That is of little consequence. We kill to live, as you yourself are about to learn.'

" 'No.' The weight of my entire conviction was carried in that single word. I would not become like them no matter what. I had no say in my creation, but I would be the architect of my own destiny. I would not become the thing I hate.

"She shrugged. 'So you say. But in time you will no longer be able to resist. The hunger will be too great and will consume you.' She sighed and shook her head sadly. 'Your intentions are as honorable now as they were then regarding your family, but they will not save you. Suffice is to say that your actions made what would have been an otherwise predictable and routine hunt so much more gratifying.'

"I stared at these beautiful, alluring creatures and knew that evil lurked at their very core. There was no sympathy behind their dark eyes and their hearts were a barren place devoid of all emotion. As for their souls, there was no doubt that they had none.

"I turned to stare at the whimpering and cowering forms of the family and came to a decision. My family's murder had been nothing more than sport for these creatures—there was no denying that. The deaths of this family would also be sport if I didn't do something about it. I knew that the odds were stacked against me, because in my weakened state I was simply no match for Amaris and Griselda's combined strength. Unless I fed—which every fiber of my being rebelled against—I would continue to grow weaker. I had to be strong to confront them and there was only one way for me to accomplish this. I knew that no matter what was decided in the confines of the stone room that the options left available to the family were far from favorable. There was no conceivable way that Amaris and Griselda would release them. If I didn't give in to my nature and kill them, then *they* would. It would be a slaughter.

"I couldn't allow an injustice like that to occur when I had the means to prevent such atrocities, yet I couldn't conceive of committing such an atrocity myself. I considered a second option: if the family had to die, then this did not necessarily mean that they had to suffer. It was possible to give them a quick, relatively painless death. Mercy was beyond Amaris and Griselda, but not for me. Was it possible to be damned for all eternity because I committed murder under the auspices of mercy? Was mercy itself an apt justification for what I was about to do? Was I truly immortal and need not concern myself with issues of God, sin, or salvation? I didn't have a reasonable answer for any of those questions at the moment, but I knew that time was of the essence. Amaris and Griselda would not wait forever for me to reach a decision. I had to act now.

"I drew myself up to my full height. God forgive me for what I was about to do, but it was all I *could* do given the state of things. 'I will not have you make a spectacle of their deaths; they've suffered enough.' I gestured towards the man lying prone on the floor, his breathing labored from the pain. 'I will embrace the hunger and what you have made me for no other reason than to save them from further torment.'

"I silently vowed that I would not lose my sense of self while I committed these unspeakable acts. I knew that to take even the smallest amount of pleasure in the family's torment meant that I had reached the point of no return, and while I vowed to abstain from this, I also vowed that Amaris and Griselda would not derive any as well. I knew that if I fed I would live. As long as I lived I would thirst for revenge against my tormentors. Every breath that they had denied my family would eat away at me if I didn't avenge them, and if committing murder was a means towards this end, then God help me I would do so for as long as necessary.

"I watched as the pair considered my proposal, and when they shoved the family closer to me and retreated into the background to watch, I knew that there was no going back— one way or the other."

My throat constricted as the memories of what inevitably transpired threatened to overwhelm me. I couldn't bring myself to voice the horror of it all, but I forced myself to. Confession, after all, is the balm of the soul. I couldn't remember who had said that to me or where I had heard it, but it didn't matter anymore.

In a voice curiously devoid of emotion in direct contrast to how I felt, I told of how I had numbly taken the knife that Amaris offered me and slit the man's throat as mercifully as I could. I chose to start with him because he was the one with the worst injuries and had suffered the most. The man thrashed and gasped for breath as the blood poured thickly from his wounds. I watched his struggles without really seeing them, without allowing myself to feel anything but detachment.

"Amaris' eyes had shown with pride as he gently guided my hand towards the dark pool spreading slowly on the floor. He dipped my finger into the blood and raised it my lips, instructing me to taste it, to open myself up to the life that flowed within it. I did as I was told and was immediately overcome with the most intense ecstasy that I had ever experienced in my young life. The force of it bowed my spine as it drove me to my knees, causing me to cry out. The blood left a searing trail down my throat, and as my tongue greedily licked all traces of it from my hand, I could feel the life flowing within it, could feel the strength that had been the man's, could feel it working its way into the marrow of my bones and the very core of my being. He—it—was becoming a part of me, and as I watched the man's chest frantically rising and falling, I could feel his life slipping away into mine. When he gave his last breath, the force of his life slamming into me drove me to the floor and I writhed with the intensity of it. Time itself seemed to be suspended as my body reacted independently of my mind, and when the swoon finally ended, I lay limp and unresponsive.

"The sounds of the room slowly began to filter back into my consciousness, and with it, the alertness and sense of exhilaration that accompanies the kill. The woman was cursing and swearing wildly at me as I took her into my arms, and her nails clawed uselessly at my hands. I held her as effortlessly as a child, and with the same swiftness that had dispatched her husband, I feasted on her life as well. Even as the ecstasy began to overtake me for the second time I tried desperately to cling to my sense of self, but it was swiftly buried in the surging red tide of oblivion. When I regained consciousness, I saw that Amaris stared at me through half-lidded eyes. His pupils had dilated and were glazed over, almost as if he were experiencing the effects of the feeding as well. I couldn't conceive of how this was possible, but I didn't dwell on it for long. The little girl who looked so much like Amelie was huddled in the corner with her face buried in the crook of her arm, her sobs barely muffled by the thin cloth of her dress. She screamed as I gathered her up into my arms, fighting me with everything that she had. It wasn't a fair fight, but fairness had long since been replaced by detachment. I forced myself to see her not as a hapless victim fighting for her very life, but as the means to help me achieve revenge in the long run. This was the mantra that I kept repeating over and over as I managed to pin her down on the floor, and when I struck the final blow with swift, brutal precision, it drowned out her cry of pain.

"The force of her life slammed me bodily towards the wall, and I found myself clawing at the air in a frenzy. Snatches of memory filtered through the red haze that wrapped me in a thick blanket of indescribable bliss, images of Amelie lying stretched and lifeless between the kneeling forms of Amaris and Griselda, their arms raised in unison towards the heavens.

"I knew now what I didn't know then, that the taking of an innocent life was the greatest pleasure that my kind could possibly experience. I opened my mouth to scream in horror, but all that came out was a strangled moan.

"Amaris lay slouched against the opposite wall, his face beatific with leech-like satisfaction. Griselda knelt beside him and was lovingly stroking his face and smoothing the waves of hair back from his forehead. He turned his head towards her with almost exaggerated lethargy, and then he reached out and drew her forward. The kiss was heated and passionate, and as I slipped in and out of consciousness, the two forms blurred and became one. I closed my eyes against the wanton depravity and wanted to weep. My body thrummed with the lives that I had consumed, but my soul was cold and barren. My humanity had been washed away in the blood of my victims, and I knew that I was damned. I may live forever and never know peace in death, but damnation would follow me wherever I went. Nothing could ever erase what I had just done, but I prayed that my intentions—however misguided—would ultimately be for the benefit of all. I had committed the sin of *non facias malum ut inde fiat bonum*—you should not make evil in order that good may be made from it. I hoped to God that I would be granted the opportunity to prove the validity of such an endeavor.

"He must have heard my prayers, because I did not have long to wait.

# Chapter 29

"When I awoke I found that Amaris and Griselda were gone, but that Dimitri and Kristoff were in the room with me. Kristoff was pawing through the clothes of the family and when he found a small pouch around the man's waist, he quickly cut it free with his knife. Dimitri was dragging the body of the little girl by the ankles towards the door, and I shut my eyes against the horror of her death. I swallowed the scream that threatened to rip its way up through my throat as I took in the girl's expression. Despite my best efforts her death had not been peaceful, and the pain and suffering that had brought her to that point had followed her to the grave.

"Dimitri grunted and struggled to drag the body out through the door, shouting at Kristoff to stop what he was doing and help him. Kristoff ignored him and was busy untying the leather cord that fastened the bag closed, greedily examining the contents. Dimitri cursed at him but continued on his way, leaving the door open behind him.

"*The door was open.*

"Hope flared in my heart as I heard him making his way down the stone corridor, bumping and cursing his way along. Kristoff took no notice of me, nor did he seem to care that I was even in the room as he set his knife down and began to remove the woman's jewelry.

"*His knife.*

"Surely he couldn't be so careless, I thought, but as I watched him struggle with the dead woman's hand, I knew that his greed overshadowed common sense. I may never have another opportunity like this again, and I moved to take it.

"I sat up slowly and let my eyes focus in the dim light. I could see perfectly despite the flickering light of the single torch, and I rose silently to my feet. He continued to wrench and twist at the ring and as I crept stealthily behind him, he never even noticed as I knelt down and took his knife up in my hands. The ring came loose with a final tug and he held his treasure up to the light.

"I tightened my grip on the knife and closed the distance between us.

"I saw him reach over to retrieve his knife, and when his hands closed around empty air, he spun around on one heel. In the same instant that his eyes widened in surprise, I drove the knife into his gut. A strangled groan escaped his lips and he toppled forward on his knees. His eyes rolled in their sockets as he watched me loom over him, and when I took hold of his jaw and forced his head back, they stared at me in terror. I pressed the edge of the blade against the smooth column of throat. 'For my family.' The blade sliced into the flesh effortlessly, and the blood splashed warm and wet over my hands. I had no desire to bend and feed from him and I left him where he fell.

"Griselda had said that we could not die, but she had been wrong. We *could* die if the proper methods were applied, and I couldn't wait to see the expression on her face when she discovered this for herself.

"All at once I heard footsteps echoing down the corridor, and I knew that Dimitri must be returning. I quickly took hold of Kristoff's ankles and dragged his body along the wall behind the door. I stood with my back pressed against the damp stones and waited for him to come into my line of sight. Kristoff's knife was a reassuring weight in my hands, and I braced myself for the kill. A moment later the back of Dimitri's head came into view and I saw him pause.

" 'Haven't you finished with them yet? Where…?' His hands instinctively flew to the knife on his hip, but I was already moving towards him. With a snarl of rage that was more animal than human, I leapt onto his back and straddled him as he attempted to throw me off. I dug my knees and feet in as hard as I could, and then I drew the knife back and sank it into the side of his neck. He screamed, but even before the sound could fully emerge, I withdrew the blade and struck a second time. Like Kristoff before him, Dimitri sank heavily to the floor and struggled briefly while he bled to death. I knelt beside him and rolled him onto his back, taking care that I was in his direct line of sight. He glared at me with a mixture of surprise and hatred as the death agony overtook him. I watched his movements with mild curiosity, and when his back arched off the floor as death took him under, I smiled at his pain.

"The silence that followed his death was so profound it was almost deafening. I had killed five beings in the past day but only three of them merited remorse. I removed Dimitri's knife from the scabbard around his waist and stood up. I knew that I had only so much time to make my escape before their absence would be noticed. I made my way towards the open door and tentatively peeked around the corner. Torches had been spaced intermittently along the stone corridor which appeared to veer off to the right. A bright smear of blood led from the prison to this alcove, and I hurried past it. Undoubtedly this is where the bodies were being disposed of and I had no desire to revisit the horror my earlier actions had caused. The rest of the corridor stretched out in a long, dark line, and there were no twists or turns to confuse me. I followed it until a small set of stairs jutted out into the light streaming in from the floor above. I came out into a lavishly appointed set of rooms decorated with the most unusual and elaborate furnishings I had ever laid eyes on. The room with its sharp stone arches and the cells themselves must have been part of the same complex, which had been partially built underground. Large, triangular shaped windows looked out over a dense wooded field, and from what I could see this was the only structure for miles. No road was visible from my vantage point, but I knew that if my family and I had been brought here by wagon that one existed. If there was a road leading to this place then it could easily lead away from it.

"I stared around me at the low-slung benches with their intricate carvings. The light streaming in from the windows glinted off of various swords and pieces of armor that adorned the walls, and in carved niches, delicate and graceful statues of maidens frolicked. The place was like a junction where two worlds collided. The rough-hewn stone prison and antechamber that my family and I had been brought to were in stark contrast to the cultured and civilized appointment of these rooms. I knew that the paint and gilt was camouflage against an evil as old as the world itself, a primal evil that knew no bounds and that had swept countless innocent victims up in its wake.

"To my left the rooms stretched down a length of corridor that turned sharply to the right. Directly in front of me was another corridor that snaked sharply to the left, and I surmised that they were connected and led to the same place. The right side of the room ended abruptly at the bank of oddly-shaped windows, and behind me, the passageway that led to the prison and all its remembered horrors loomed out of the darkness.

"I turned and headed to the left. I had no way of knowing where I was headed, but I knew that my tormentors had to lie at the end of the passageway—there was no other place for them to go.

"I passed room after room full of the same strange and wondrous decorations. When I finally reached the end of the hall a small set of stairs led down to another room that faced out over the south side of the building. This room was even more lavish than the ones before it, and a massive bed held court in the center of it all. Gauzy curtains billowed softly in the cool breeze blowing in from the open windows, and a veritable sea of embroidered cushions littered the floor around it. A discarded robe with tiny jewels worked into the fabric of the cuffs and collar lay next to the collection, and as my eyes scanned the rest of the room, I spied a doorway off to one side. Soft light spilled out from underneath the door and the sound of splashing water drifted back to me. I stood there with my senses straining and my heart pounding slowly but loudly in my ears, listening to the water sloshing back and forth. The faint odor of a delicately scented soap wafted across my nostrils, and I realized that the water must be coming from either a tub or a basin—a tub or basin that was currently in use by at least one of the two occupants that I sought.

"Keeping close to the wall with the knives held in readiness at my side, I crept forward on the balls of my feet ready to spring forward or jump back as the situation dictated. The door was ajar just the faintest degree, and I slowly pushed it open with my right hand. Inch by inch I eased it open until there was enough room for me to crane my head to see what lay in the room. Griselda lay soaking in a large marble tub surrounded by a galaxy of glittering bottles of oils, perfumes, and small golden platters heaped with softly burning candles. She reclined languidly against one end of the tub, and her head and shoulders were the only parts of her that was visible above the rose-tinted water. Her eyes were covered by a damp cloth that had small flowers embroidered along its edges, and she didn't appear to notice that she wasn't alone.

"This was more than I could have hoped for.

"I was about to spring forward and exact my revenge, but in my eagerness I grew careless. I neglected to see a small urn at my feet, and as I swept into the room with my arm pulling the door closed behind me, it toppled over.

" 'Dimitri? Kristoff?'

"I froze, fearful of discovery. To be so close and not see revenge realized would have been too much for me to bear, so I concentrated on remaining absolutely still.

" 'I've been calling you for some time now. How long can it take to dispose of the bodies?' Griselda heaved a frustrated sigh and settled back down under the water. 'Never mind,' she said flicking at the edge of the tub with one finger, 'hand me a towel.'

"I bent down and retrieved the first thing that my hand closed around. I approached the tub and reached down to hand it to her. Muttering under her breath, she reached up and clasped the object that I held—a bejeweled slipper tossed carelessly to the side—and her face twisted into a frown underneath the damp cloth.

" 'I said towel, you imbecile! What...?'

"She never finished the thought. The knife sheared effortlessly into the flesh right below her left breast and she gave a startled gasp. The rosy water immediately darkened to a deep, rich crimson, and as she frantically scrambled to sit up and put some distance between us, I pushed her under the water and held her there. Her fingers dug at my hands as she thrashed helplessly in the tub. Water soaked the floor and my clothes, but still I held on, my face set in a hard line that felt immobile as stone—and just as cold.

"I didn't care who heard us as we struggled—I just wanted her dead. Her movements began to slowly grow sluggish. She kicked feebly at the other end of the tub, and with a convulsive snarl, I heaved her up into a sitting position. The washcloth fell away from her face, and through the scarlet water streaming in rivulets down her face, she recognized who held her, recognized who was going to kill her.

"I saw the azure orbs widen in horror, and I shoved the blade up under her ribs and into her heart. She grunted with the force of the blow and threw her head back, eyes lolling in their sockets. One hand came up and brushed lightly against my arm, but I wrenched the knife in deeper, twisting it savagely from side to side. Blood that was nearly black welled up from her mouth and she began to choke. Small, helpless sounds added a counter rhythm to the slow, calm beating of my heart, and I let her fall back into the water. She gave a final, heaving gasp and was still.

"I stepped back and let the knife tumble from my hand. The other one in my left hand was clutched savagely like a talisman, and as I stumbled away from the carnage, a howl of rage that lifted every hair on my body ripped through the air. I only managed to turn a fraction before the blow sent me sprawling to the floor. I crashed into the candles that had managed to survive the deluge, and several caught in the curtains surrounding the tub. With an audible whoosh, the flames began to lick at the flimsy material, and before long they had caught the edges of the thick tapestries that hung from the ceilings. Embers danced away from the main inferno and created blazes of their own in the baskets of soft, white towels and bits of clothing scattered around. The edge of my dress began to smolder and I hurriedly rolled onto my side. Strong arms gripped me around the waist and wrenched me to my feet. Cold breath lapped against my face as another inarticulate growl reverberated through my head, lifting the tiny hairs on the back of my neck. I was forcefully swung towards the bank of gilt mirrors that adorned the far wall, and as my head connected with the glass, the identity of my assailant was reflected in a thousand glittering shards.

"Amaris' face—his expression a mask of rage and grief—threw himself at me and dragged me by the legs back to the edge of the tub and its grisly contents. Bits of burning curtain drifted down and sizzled as they made contact with the water, reflecting orange before finally burning out. Flames lapped at my hands as I was dragged along the floor, and I gritted my teeth against the pain. Amaris lifted me up and carried me bodily towards the edge of the tub, and then he began to climb in. Crimson water soaked the edges of his robe and turned the material amethyst. I threw my weight against him and his balance, already compromised by the burden my weight presented, toppled backwards. His face disappeared for an instant in the depths of the water, but he quickly swam up and grabbed at the hem of my dress. With a scream, I fell against him and his arms latched around me with an iron grip. I drove my elbow into an area in the general direction of his face, and he let me go with a howl of pain. I scrabbled desperately for the two knives which lay discarded on the floor, and just as my fingers closed around them, I was dragged back into the tub.

" 'You'll burn for what you've done.' His fingers threatened to crush my hands and the knives slipped a fraction of an inch in my grip. 'I may burn with you, but at least I die knowing you did not escape.'

"Fighting back the terror that statement evoked, I threw everything I had left into the fight, and with a fearsome yell, I managed to twist my right hand free of his grip. The blade slid along the back of his hand and the flesh offered little to no resistance. Amaris screamed and momentarily released his hold on me.

"It was all the time I needed.

"I whirled around and sank the first blade into the hollow of his throat. His left arm shot out and shoved me back against the edge of the tub, dislodging the blade in the process. Fingers dug into my own throat as he attempted to choke the life from me, and as my vision began to darken, I slashed out with all my remaining strength. The blade connected with his flesh and sheared effortlessly through it, striking the bone beneath with a satisfying *crunch* before continuing on through to the other side.

Amaris shrieked in pain and fury, cradling the bloody stump tight against his chest. Not giving him a chance to recover from my attack, I slammed the remaining blade into his chest. The slickness of the tub prevented me from being able to gather enough momentum, and it struck him just shy of his heart. Dark eyes rolled up in their sockets, and as his face went slack he toppled face forward into the bloody water.

"The room had by then become an inferno and the flames danced and whirled around the entrance to the room, nourished by the steady breeze that fanned them from the open window. Without thinking, I snatched up Amaris' severed limb and threw it over the side of the tub. I cannot describe what exactly was going through my mind in those moments, or for that matter if I was even thinking clearly. All I knew was that I had to get out of this room before the flames consumed it, but not before I had taken something from my enemies. They had taken so much from me already, and it seemed justified that they repay the favor in some way.

I removed the knife lodged in Amaris' chest and pushed his body away as I groped for Griselda's arm under the water. Finding it, I pressed the edge of the blade down and applied all of my weight to it. Skin, flesh, muscle and bone succumbed to the onslaught and surrendered ownership of the limb. I grabbed it up and heaved myself out of the tub just as a blazing timber beam came crashing down. Crawling on my hands and knees, I snatched up the three knives and my grisly relics and headed for the doorway. Coughing and choking from the thick smoke that billowed around me, I exploded out into the bedroom just as the bathroom ceiling caved in, sealing the room off forever.

"I staggered across the room in equal amounts of exhaustion and relief. I saw the edge of a blade winking out of a pile of clothes that had belonged to Griselda as I neared the door. I stumbled on the hem of my dress and went down hard on my knees. I was so tired, so very tired, and the reality of what I had just done began to set in: I was a murderer, a killer of killers, a butcher.

"I don't know how long I knelt there in the room with the greasy smoke swirling around me as I vacillated between horror and grim satisfaction, but the thick, pungent odor of roasting flesh wafting out from the blazing room brought me sharply back to the present. Heaving and dry-retching miserably, I crawled awkwardly along the floor until I reached the pile of clothes, tugged the knife free, and added it to the collection.

"My sanity in those dark moments hung by a thread, but sheer instinct and self-preservation propelled me forward. I knew that there was still work that had to be done, so I made my way back to the dungeon with all its horrors that awaited me.

"The damp coolness of the dungeon was a welcome relief from the stench of burning flesh that seemed to follow me through the brightly furnished rooms, and I made quick work of Dimitri and Kristoff. Slinging my burden over my shoulder in a makeshift sack fashioned from the bottom edge of my dress, I made my way out of the cell and to the small alcove set off to the side. Even without the benefit of the torches, the sticky trail of blood easily led the way as I pushed open the door. Bright, golden sunlight fell across my face and the sweet smell of the trees and the grass stroked cool, comforting fingers across my nose. I tilted my head back and breathed deeply, clearing the smoke from my lungs.

"This was freedom. This was life. This was the start of a new beginning, all things considered. I followed a well-worn path up the steep slope of a hill past the visible structures of Amaris' lair. The blood trail led to the edge of a sheer drop off with a river flowing in the valley below—the last resting place of my family and Amaris' victims.

"I stumbled over a rock in my path and pitched forward. The sack slid off my shoulder and landed with a dull thump near my face. Ignoring it and the small pain that had accompanied my fall, I lay there with the wind blowing my hair around me in matted tendrils and watched the cleansing flames as they went about their work."

To my left I could hear slight movement coming from my audience, but I ignored them. I was unsure how they would handle the story I had just imparted to them, and even less sure how *I* would handle it. Would I try to stop them if they threatened to storm out, convinced that I was suffering from paranoid delusions? Would I stop them if they ran screaming for the nearest exit, entirely convinced that I was some blood-sucking monster straight out of a nightmare? They already knew that I was a monster, as my little recollection had so perfectly illustrated, but I was a monster in so many other ways. Not only did I kill my tormentors as brutally as they had killed my family, but I had taken a memento of my deeds and had harnessed them into a weapon. To me, it was justice embodied, because the very limbs that had restrained, tortured, maimed, and killed were now put to the more practical use of preventing such atrocities.

I slowly undid the sheath around my waist and removed one of the knives. The blade glinted dully in the moonlight streaming in from the window behind me, and I caught a glimpse of my own reflection on its polished surface. My expression was utterly blank and I felt completely detached, as if the actions I had just described in no way pertained to me, as if the misdeeds of my past were not my own.

I held the blade face up on my palm as I spoke. It was perfectly balanced, perfectly sharpened, and perfectly lethal while in my hands.

"It is safe to say that in those moments following the deaths of my tormentors that I was mad with grief, consumed by the desire to keep on slashing at their corpses. It seemed wholly unfair to me that their deaths were relatively easy deaths, because they had not suffered near enough as my family had, nor had the process been drawn out. They were accorded considerably more mercy than they had bestowed upon their victims, and I screamed and raged in fury. I wanted them to suffer as I had suffered, as my family had suffered. I wanted to see their faces twist up in agony as the blade was plunged in again and again. Again and again I wanted to see their life slip away in a wash of blood. I wanted all of these things, but they were not to be. They were dead and no force on this earth could restore them so that justice would at last be mine. I felt cheated, betrayed, every negative adjective you can conceive of. I was left standing there in the smoldering ruins with the prospect of eternity before me—an eternity of bitterness over what had been lost to me—an eternity of bitterness over what *should* have been mine. I couldn't conceive of it.

"The prospect of such a cruel and terrible fate drove me further down into crushing despair and I considered doing away with myself, considered using their knives to end my suffering. But as I stood there shivering and alone with the smoke stinging my eyes, I caught sight of something familiar in the wreckage. I found myself stooping to get a closer look—though I don't remember having moved at all—and then my fingers closed around something soft. As I brought the object up to eyelevel, I saw that it was Amelie's doll, whole and undamaged in the inferno, still spattered with blood. It was then that I fell to my knees and clutched the doll to my breast, as if by doing so I could hold onto some semblance of my former life.

"I knelt there in the rubble and rocked the doll gently in my arms. I don't know how long I stayed there locked in that embrace, but eventually I came to my senses. I stood up slowly and kept the doll pressed tight against me. The cloth bag with its grisly relics dangled loosely from my left hand, and it was then that an idea occurred to me. I set the doll in the crook of my left arm and bent down to retrieve the four blades at my feet. The metal handles were thick with blood and gore in equal amounts and were sticky to the touch. I wiped them on the folds of my dress and stared at the ornate handles. Thick scrolls had been worked into the metal and were embedded with precious stones, but the beauty of the knives could not hide the horror of what they had been put to use. No, these instruments deserved something befitting their purpose. The weight of the cloth bag seemed to provide just such an avenue, and in the temporary madness of those dark moments, I knew what I had to do. I had the power to turn these instruments of destruction into something more, into instruments of salvation. In my hands they would never again kill with a complete disregard for life. In my hands they would slay only those who threatened the innocents, the innocents whose blood still stained the blades.

"I swore right then and there that I would spend the rest of my long life avenging my family and the lives of all innocents who had met death at the hands of my kind. I turned away from the ruin of Amaris' lair without so much as a backwards glance, but I made one stop before I attempted to leave the memories of what had transpired there behind me, one stop that I had a moral and familial obligation to make. The weather was beginning to turn from late summer into early fall, and as the brisk wind swirled my hair about my face, I selected a spot under the dappled shade of a great tree on a peaceful hill overlooking the valley below. I used the knives to dig out a shallow impression under the tree, and then I placed Amelie's doll into the earth. The bodies of my family had been disposed of by Amaris and his children, and I had nothing left to remember them by, nothing to bury or grieve over except memories of our time together. The blood that stained the tiny, embroidered apron of Amelie's doll belonged to all of them and would have to do.

"I gently smoothed the loose earth over the painted face and whispered a prayer that their souls might rest in peace for all eternity, and then I stood up. The small mound looked like a dark blemish over the uniform greenness of the grass, a symbolic representation of the blackness that now stained my soul. I lusted for revenge in every conceivable way and if my tormentors could no longer provide me with solace, then others like them would have to. I bowed my head and hugged my arms around me. '*Nemo malus felix*,' I whispered on the empty hill. 'No peace for the wicked. For as long as there is breath and life in my body, I will spend my days dispatching those who threaten the innocent. For as long as there is breath and life in my body, I will have them fear me as their victims once feared them; for as long as there is breath and life in my body, I will never forget you and the oath that I have sworn upon your memory.'

"I said goodbye and then walked off towards the horizon and into eternity. I kept the knives clutched in one hand and the cloth bag in the other. If I had encountered anyone along the road I was sure that they would have fled from me in terror, convinced that I was some sort of revenant raised from the grave. My clothes were filthy and stained with soot and blood, but I had extraordinary clarity of mind. I knew that I had to fashion new handles for the knives that would not only befit their new purpose, but which would also serve as a constant reminder that my tormentors had *not* won and that *I* had had the final word."

I smiled ruefully. "There is an old saying about keeping your friends close but your enemies closer. I have kept my enemies close to me ever since then. I swore that I would not become the thing that I hated most in the world, and would never relinquish the last tenuous hold I had on my humanity by creating another of my kind."

I held the knife up for emphasis, blade pointed towards the floor, handle pointed heavenward. The bone gleamed dully and the initials carved near the hilt stood out in startling contrast. "What you saw in the alleyway tonight was a just a taste of the life that I've lived over the past three centuries. Any of my kind who seeks to do harm to the innocents of this or any other city will have to go through me first. I'm not saying that my actions are right or wrong, but it's my way of coping with eternity."

From somewhere down the hall the faint echo of a child's laughter floated back to us and seemed strangely out of place. The traffic flowed by in its ever-ceaseless rhythm outside, and a phone rang one floor beneath me. It seemed in this moment that the past and the present had intersected, and at the very epicenter of this juncture stood myself, unchanged after nearly four centuries. Wendell and Andrew were completely still, and as I glanced briefly at their expressions, I saw the undeniable hint of sympathy reflected in their eyes.

It amazed me how calm the two of them continued to be even after everything that I had told them. Perhaps the modern world—which had managed to conquer forces that were deemed inexplicable in centuries past—had never been touched by a genuine mystery. Perhaps the arrogance that so often accompanies such power and discovery does not allow fear to enter the equation. Perhaps wonder and curiosity overshadowed fear and uncertainty and left the observer primed and receptive. For all I knew it could be all or none of these things, but that wasn't relevant at the moment. I did not want to do or say anything that would compromise the serenity I felt right then. This was very nearly my first moment's peace in centuries, and I wanted to cherish it for as long as possible. Equally strange was the desire to not frighten the two men who had been thrown headlong into my path tonight, and I attempted to wade through the tide of confusing and disquieting emotions that I felt. I realized that I felt strangely protective of them, not merely in the sense that I would do anything to save them from bodily harm, but from mental and emotional pain as well.

I couldn't understand why I felt this way. Not one of the people that I had saved over the centuries had created this desire within me, and I never once sought to form a lasting relationship of any kind. To the person being saved I was almost a ghost who was never seen or heard, and I disappeared as quickly as I appeared. The parameters that I enforced upon my involvement with mortals were smashed to bits with Wendell and Andrew, and the tide of emotions that accompanied such a shift threatened to overwhelm me. The centuries of loneliness stretched out behind me like a dark and dreary road, and at the end of this road stood my two new companions, a shining beacon of light in an otherwise solitary and desolate existence. Wrath and revenge had been my constant companions, but they had never offered me comfort. Wendell and Andrew were the embodiment of all that I lived and stood for, were the embodiment of all that I had lost and desired to possess again.

But I knew that it was not meant to be. How could it? I was immortal, impervious to the passage of time and indifferent to the elements, and they were mortal, human. At the most they would live fifty years—sixty, seventy—perhaps more, but what then? Time would strip them down to their barest essentials, would rob them of their sense of self and cloud their memories of our time together. Time would take them away from me as it had taken everything else away from me, and I would once again be left barren and alone. I would carry their memory alongside those of my family with me for all eternity, and in time the weight of them would threaten to crush me. In time I would come to resent them for this, and the memories of our years together would become twisted and grotesque.

No.

I had to let them go. I had to let them live their own lives to whatever ends they chose. I would stay with them long enough to see the danger dead and buried, and then I would move on and leave them to their own devices. Their mortal lives must not be tainted by my own miserable existence, and I cursed myself for having involved them in it thus far. I should never have told them my life story—that had been selfish of me to share my torment with another living soul, and it was entirely unforgivable. Loneliness was not a viable excuse for my actions, and there was no taking it back. The most that I could hope for was to let them down easily and stop their involvement before it was past the point of reversal. Their lives may never be the same again given the knowledge that they now held, but it was the best I could do. I may be immortal, but I was human in my flaws and limitations.

"So there you have it. You know how I came to be here as I am, and you know why I have chosen to live the life that I do. Now it is time to go." It was a clumsy summation and did little justice to my recollection, but I had said more than I should have.

I made a move towards the door and a small commotion erupted behind me. Andrew looked flustered and kept insisting that there was so much more to be told. I agreed with him, but I wasn't going to budge in my conviction that more harm than good was being done involving them further in my life. Wendell sat very still in the armchair as emotions chased themselves across his face. I would drive Andrew home and order him to stay away, to not pursue this further, but Wendell had no place to go. I couldn't just dump him back on the streets to continue living the life that had been his for years, so arrangements would have to be made for him. I knew that Andrew's training as a reporter would not allow him to let the issue die so easily, so I would have to disappear for the time being and relocate elsewhere in the city. The threat would have to be eliminated as swiftly as possible so that I could once again vanish as I had always done. It seemed cruel to treat them like this after they had shown me such compassion, but it was the way things had to be.

"Wendell can wait here until I find him a place to stay." I grabbed Andrew's shoes up off the floor and tossed them to him. He fumbled for them awkwardly, his young face twisted in a mixture of confusion and anger. He grabbed my arm as I swept by—not aggressively, but comforting. The gesture made the loneliness rush forth in a torrent, but I angrily shoved it aside. No one had touched me like that in centuries, and the aching desire to explore it twisted spikes into my heart.

I gently pried his fingers loose. "No."

He shook his head, fighting for control. "But why? Why won't you finish your story? I don't understand why you are sending us away like this...?"

"My story *is* finished. You know how it ended and there is nothing left to say." I stood by the door with my keys clenched tightly in my hand. The small pain helped to distract me from the pain I felt over having to exile the two of them, but I knew that once the door was opened and the apartment was mine once again, that the pain would not be so easily vanquished. The most I could do was harness it into a weapon and feed it to the rage within me to further fuel my desire for vengeance. Amaris had taken away my mortal life and had given me a new one fashioned of blood and despair, and in so doing, he had ensured that it would be devoid of another's love or understanding. Though long dead, the consequences of Amaris' actions had effectively denied me the gift of forging a friendship with Wendell and Andrew.

The rage intensified, and I channeled it into my desire to find the Font and finish them off once and for all.

Andrew stood up slowly. I held the door open and he walked through it down to the other end of the hall. He didn't look at me as he went past, and I kept me eyes carefully averted. I didn't want to see the look in his face because I knew that it would make the situation that more real. Wendell sat there clutching his backpack as if unsure what to do.

"I could go too." He stood but I gestured for him to stop.

"I can't let you go back out there on the streets. That would be…"

"Cruel?" He scoffed and set the backpack down on the floor. "Be sure you know what that means before you send us away." He turned away from me and stared out the window.

I didn't know how to respond to that, so rather than make a strained situation that much more awkward, I closed the door quietly behind me. Andrew was standing at the end of the hallway staring at the opposite wall, and when he heard me approaching, he walked on ahead of me without saying a word.

# Chapter 30

The woman's back arched off the floor as the swoon caught and held her in its embrace. She stretched out her hand and touched the smooth flesh of her children who were crouched around her. Flesh writhed against flesh as the swoon overtook each of them in turn, their bodies twisting and turning like snakes. Power in all its myriad forms coursed throughout her veins and thrummed through her flesh as yet another life was extinguished, as yet another one of her children took in the sustenance that would feed and strengthen her. Her fingernails dug into the ancient wood and a sound between a sigh and a moan escaped her full lips as the last of the victim's lives was absorbed.

Through half-lidded eyes she surveyed her children's handiwork and smiled with satisfaction. To her left lay the remains of the two bodyguards who were no longer of use to anyone. They had been an extra set of eyes and ears in the days following the slaughter of the first of her children, but their services were no longer needed now that the enemy was within her sights.

She slowly stretched her limbs to test her new strength, and finding it more than satisfactory given the events of the past few months, sat up in one languid movement. In a series of perfectly synchronized gestures, each of her children crawled to her and helped her to her feet. The four wounded traitors—who up until this moment had fed against the far wall for fear of further punishment—slowly began to make their way towards their mistress. The compulsion to wind their arms around her—to touch and be touched by her—was purely linked to the bond they shared. No matter how tenuous, this desire was independent of their minds and could not be ignored.

They kept their eyes downcast and maintained a submissive posture until they were a few feet away. They weren't entirely sure if she had forgiven them or not, yet despite their misgivings they didn't want to destroy any chance of being accepted back into the fold. Each of them had come to the conclusion that things would be forever strained between them due to their cowardice earlier in the evening, but there was hope for at least tense civility.

She saw them approaching and held her arms out to either side. The other children shifted around her to accommodate the four of them, and when they finally reached her, they fell at her feet and groveled.

Daman felt his lips peel back from his teeth in a snarl as the audacity of it all enraged him beyond reason. It took every ounce of will to not lash out and strike at them, to rend and maim. The only thing that held him back was the realization that it would hurt his mother, who only moments ago had barely regained a fraction of the strength she had lost. He watched as she gently laid her fingertips against the tops of their heads and stroked them lovingly, her fingers carefully avoiding the still-bleeding wounds that marred their flesh. Their bloody hands tentatively clutching at her legs and ankles as they continued to fawn at her feet.

Daman knew that the display of benevolence was a carefully contrived smokescreen. There was always the slim possibility that the four traitors would have refused to feed and preferred death rather than save themselves—to have them do so would have further weakened her. He knew that she could not afford to have that happen, especially now when the woman was within her reach. He knew that for the sake of self-preservation alone would she be willing to play the merciful benefactor if only for the time being.

She stood there with the eight forms entwined around her absently stroking arms, faces, and hands. "Now is the time for action. The enemy is within our sights and we have the means to bring her to us. My children will once again be safe." She paused to gaze at each one in turn, and the four wounded ones felt relief and love flood through them.

She had forgiven them and would fight to protect them. They had been wrong to doubt her intentions before, but now they knew that she cared for all of them.

They would fight until the death if necessary. They would fight for *her*.

"Today the enemy dies, and with her, her two companions." She reached into the folds of her dress and withdrew Andrew's wallet, stroking the worn leather lovingly. "Today the enemy will have seen her last sunset and will trouble us no more."

# Chapter 31

Andrew sat in the seat next to me without saying a word. The silence was broken only by his giving me directions towards his car, which had been parked a few blocks away from a pub downtown. I didn't offer anything in the way of conversation as well, so we rode down the streets in silence.

I knew that he was angry at me. Angry over my refusal to finish my story, angry over my hasty and less-than-refined dismissal? Perhaps.

The sputtering and flickering of his aura spoke volumes where words were absent, and I knew that his emotions ran much deeper than that. The set of his jaw and his steadfast refusal to meet my gaze made a living barrier between us, and it was painfully obvious in those moments that more differences than commonalities existed among us. Friendship could never be forged or hope to flourish under such circumstances, or at least that is what I kept telling myself over and over during the seemingly endless drive.

I had to keep resisting the urge to close the distance and open myself up completely and unconditionally to him. I was almost desperate with this desire but I quashed it down and replaced it with the old and familiar rage.

I knew that I had hurt him in ways that no one else could have, but I was at a loss to explain what they were or how to go about repairing the damage.

"Turn left here at the light."

I steered the car smoothly down the street in question and kept my gaze fixed on the road in front of me.

"Go up about a block and half and then drop me off."

My heart sank as I realized that I had so little time left to feel even remotely close to normal. I could pull over right here, lock the door, and demand that he listen to what I had to say. I could gently take his arm the way that he had taken mine back at the apartment and beg him to stay, beg him to please not leave me alone with my guilt and loneliness. I wanted to tell him that he made me feel human, that he brought out the old warmth and love that had always existed within me but that I had kept dormant and hidden for years. I wanted to tell him that I had forgotten what it felt like to need and be needed in return, and that he and Wendell reminded me of what this felt like.

I never wanted to be alone no matter how well I had managed to convince myself of this over the centuries—it was simply that the life I had chosen to pursue didn't leave me any other choice. To have taken a companion and subjected them to the danger that I lived and breathed on a daily basis would have been unfair to them, and when time had finally taken them away from me I would be the one left behind picking up the pieces of that relationship. I knew that the desire to draw the only human beings that I had come into this close a contact with stemmed from my loneliness. I knew that it was wholly irrational and desperate of me to even consider such a thing, but it didn't matter if he didn't understand, I just wanted him to stay with me.

I wanted him to stay with me forever.

The force of my reaction to such a sentiment threatened to send the car careening into a light post, and I hurriedly stomped on the brake. I leaned my head against the steering wheel breathing in quick, shallow gasps. My hands gripped the molded leather so tightly that it creaked.

Andrew turned in his seat and I felt the air currents shift.

"Don't." I felt rather than saw him withdraw. My breath whistled as I slowly let it out and I turned away from him.

"Just go—please," I said as if it would make everything better. After a moment's hesitation he got out and shut the door behind him.

I backed out without really looking for oncoming traffic and laid a quarter inch of tread down the street. I knew that he was staring at the car as it wove erratically away from him, but I didn't dare look back. To do so had the potential to be disastrous—for Andrew as well as myself.

✞ ✞ ✞ ✞ ✞ ✞ ✞ ✞

Andrew stood there watching the car drive away and didn't know what to think or feel. His mind still reeled with the incredible story that the woman had told him, the incredible story which some small part of his mind kept insisting could not possibly be true. Vampires just did not exist—that was insane. They were a staple of badly-dubbed foreign films where the production companies that cranked them out had less tact than they did funds for special effects, and they had no place in reality. Didn't they?

The woman—Katrina Armentani—didn't seem insane, and Andrew had had plenty of experience over the last three years when it came to judging the mental shortcomings of delusional sources. She sure as hell didn't look like she was trying to pull one over on him in order to make a profit or garner a headline in *Elysium's* upcoming issue, but that seemed a moot point considering that he didn't even work there anymore.

*Which is a shame, because for once I actually have a story that is worth publishing.*

The journalist in him saw the innate potential of the situation, but the more rational part of his mind—the kind linked to his sense of justice and morals—felt ashamed. Here was something extraordinary that had been imparted to him in good faith and he had been tempted to profit from it. He would be no better than Gary, perhaps worse if he did this.

The woman had just validated his belief that there were things out there in the world that defied all explanation, that there were things out there in the world that science, mankind, and even religion had said could not be. Here was validation after years of chasing shadows on the job, validation that extraordinary things *were* possible.

Here was living proof that death *could* be conquered.

*No.*

He had no aspirations of living forever. The thought brought with it a nightmarish collage of his family and friends crippled by age and ravaged by disease shuffling past him, their rheumy eyes filled with envy over his perpetually youthful form. Worse than that was the knowledge that everyone you ever loved and cherished would one day be gone, and what then? Did you file those memories away forever and attempt to create new ones? Or did you find yourself replacing all that you had lost again and again, doomed to never really find it?

He shivered and dug his hands into the pockets of his jeans. No, such an existence would be a fate worse than death. His religious upbringing had taught him that death was not merely the end of one's life, but was the start of a new existence. You were surrounded by your loved ones for all eternity, not separated from them forever. Your physical form may have died, but your soul lived on. It was free of all the cares and worries that made up a minimal part of human existence, not trapped in the prison of its own flesh for all eternity.

The confirmed diagnosis had revived his old fear of death—everyone had at least some reservations about what it would mean to die no matter their religious upbringing—and despite the poor judgment that he had made after he received the news, the woman's recollection had made the prospect of his own death that much easier to bear. He realized as he listened to her story, that human life was precious. While it may be temporary or relatively short in the larger scheme of things, that is precisely what made it precious. Each day would never be repeated and every incident no matter how small was a reminder of the fleetingness of life, a constant reminder that once it was over the memories were all one had left. In the murkiness of old age where time seemed suspended, those memories would sustain him until his life came to an end. In the case of the woman Katrina, her life would never end, and the memories she had of her younger years would only torment her rather than comfort.

The pain of what had transpired all those centuries ago was evident in her voice even if he couldn't see the look in her eyes. The guilt she felt over the murdered family was eating her up, but he wanted to tell her that she needn't feel that way. She was undoubtedly torn between the belief that she was inherently corrupt or evil over her actions, but her every action since that fateful night seemed to indicate otherwise. Her life had been in the service of a greater good no matter how much she saw it as vigilantism. The fact that she felt guilt at all over the deaths of the family was not an indication that she had lost her humanity, but was actually a *testament* to it. She said it herself when she remarked that the damned feel no such things, and he wondered why she hadn't realized it long before.

He felt a stab of sympathy for her as he realized that she would continue to live her life under this impression, and that she would continually feel the need to justify her actions by cloaking them in a mantle of righteous vengeance. He wanted to tell her this, but she had effectively and abruptly severed all contact with him and Wendell. He couldn't understand why she had been so accommodating and open one minute, and had then been uncooperative and guarded the next. Did talking about what had happened to her and her family suddenly make it seem more real? Were the memories simply too painful to relive once again? He had no answer.

He realized that the initial resentment he felt was misguided anger over her dismissal, and that it was geared more towards his feeling cheated of the remainder of her story rather than anything else. He was upset that a genuine mystery was within his grasp and that he had allowed it to slip away. The last three years of his life had been spent putting every conceivable spin on lies and half-truths for the sake of selling copies, and now that something tangible was within reach he was reluctant to let it go. It was a petty and selfish reason, but what it all boiled down to was that he was curious about her and her kind. There were so many unanswered questions, and he simply wanted to *know.*

He dug for his car keys and debated what to do next. He could go home, but home was the last place he wanted to be. It was filled with too many memories of Rachel and their time together, filled with too many nights spent alone after she had left for what she felt were bigger and better things. He could go to his work place, but he doubted that he would even have a job waiting for him once he got there. Weighed against each other like that, neither option seemed appealing.

*On second thought. . .*

His little tirade over at his work place had been less-than-satisfying given that Bob Garrett had decided to make himself scarce that day. There were still plenty of things left unsaid and now would be the time to do it. On the other hand, he was stone-cold sober and wasn't in the mood to pick at that particular scab, so he settled for driving over there to clean out his desk while retaining what little dignity he had left.

*Too bad he could always sense trouble brewing from a mile away,* he thought as he began driving towards his workplace. *There are so many things left unsaid between Bob and me, so many loose ends that I won't ever get the chance to tie up.*

He had no way of knowing that the comment would soon prove prophetic in the coming hours.

# Chapter 32

She watched as the two vehicles—a gray van and Officer Rhode's cruiser—took off in opposite directions. The noose was getting progressively tighter as she and her children began to close it around the woman and her two companions. She may have proven difficult in the past to accost, but that was before innocent persons had been dragged into the situation. Now the stakes had been raised, innocent blood had been spilled as more inevitably would, and it was only a matter of time before the woman realized that the situation was no longer in her hands. It was only a matter of time before she realized that the hunted were pulling all the strings, and that the hunter had long since become the puppet.

✣ ✣ ✣ ✣ ✣ ✣ ✣ ✣

The radio blared as I drove away from the drive-thru window. The young woman who had taken my order could barely hear me over the squall of electric guitars and screeching vocals, but I wasn't about to lower the volume. I couldn't afford to hear what my thoughts were saying to me, what that tiny part of me that I kept carefully locked away was urging me to do.

*You needn't ever be lonely again*, it crooned. *All you need do is tell him that he's dying, offer him your blood, and your loneliness will end.*

I turned the dial of the volume up with enough force that the knob cracked in protest.

I couldn't conceive of any circumstances that would drive me to bridge that final chasm between human and inhuman, couldn't conceive of anything or anybody that would make me take that leap. Perhaps loneliness is what eventually drove all of us to create more of our kind. Perhaps it was as much love rather than necessity or a show of power that drove us to seek out eternal companions. Perhaps it was none of these things and it was all geared towards selfish intentions, or in the case of Amaris, was out of a desire to see others suffer.

I *was* lonely—I could admit that—but I wasn't lonely enough to condemn another being to this kind of existence. I could never place my feelings before another's no matter how I approached the situation, because the words I would use to entice them would be tainted by deceit. I would either have to lie to them or play on humanity's instinctive fear of death to draw them further into my world, or I would be lying to myself as to the reasons why I did it. Perhaps I was drawn to Andrew because he resembled if only superficially, my beloved late husband. Perhaps if you live long enough eventually everything and everyone will remind you of something from your past. But Nicholas was dead and no force on this earth could ever restore him to me. To attempt to substitute another in his place, to see his features reflected in a man born centuries after his death and pretend that he *was* that person, that would be the ultimate betrayal—for all parties involved.

I would *not* do it. God forgive me for even considering such a thing.

I set the bag of food on the seat next to me and thought of Wendell alone in my apartment. Would I find him where I left him seated in the armchair by the window? Or would he be gone, content to live the rest of his life as he chose, rather than have someone else attempt to change it for him? I knew that it was misguided guilt as much as anything that made me want to save him, but I wouldn't hold it against him if he decided to leave.

I thought back again to the night when our paths had first crossed, of how blissfully unaware he was that he was being followed by a murderous progeny who only saw him as food, rather than as a person. How strange it was that our paths kept crossing as a result of the murders. Perhaps it was better that I had not asked him for the details—he seemed shaken up enough by what was happening, and having him relive the trauma would be asking too much of him. It would have further involved him in my life, and seeing as how I was determined to prevent this at all costs, it seemed like the most practical thing to have done. I thought back again to the previous night's activities when I had followed Andrew down the darkened alleyway where Wendell's path and mine had first crossed and set this bewildering chain of events in play. I knew instinctively that the Font I had been hunting was behind the murders, and while I was still no closer to finding out their identity, they were aware of my presence. That little display in the alleyway signified their acknowledgement, and it was only a matter of time before I closed in on them.

I stopped.

The music blaring out of the speakers and the sounds of the traffic rolling by outside dwindled away until I was left with only my panicked heartbeat roaring in my ears.

Followed.

We had been followed to that alleyway—how else to explain how the progeny had come to be there at the exact same time that we were, how to explain how orchestrated the attack was?

I was a fool to ever let the two men out of my sight. Odds were good that all of us had been brought to the attention of the Font behind the killings, and it was only a matter of time before they came for us again. The fact that all three of us were separated made my blood run cold.

I stomped on the gas and ignored the angry shouting and bleating horns behind me as I weaved and wrenched my way through the traffic. I had to get home. I had to get to Wendell before anything happened. As for Andrew, I had no idea where he lived although I knew where he worked.

*Had* worked.

My heart sank. How was I supposed to find him in a city teeming with over a million and a half people? I didn't have an answer right then and there. I only prayed that I wasn't too late to save either of them.

# Chapter 33

Andrew shut the engine off and sat there staring at the yellow façade of *Elysium's* headquarters. The steady ticking of the engine as it cooled off was the only sound he heard, and after contemplating and systematically discarding nearly a dozen ways to approach the current situation, he sighed and opened the door. The cool November breeze ruffled his hair, and underneath the stench of smog and car exhaust, it smelled faintly of rain and fall leaves.

"Let's get this over with." He placed the car keys in his pocket and his fingers brushed the very bottom lining.

He frowned, realizing that something was missing.

His hands dug through the rest of the pockets, but there was no sign of his wallet. He kicked the tire nearest his foot and rested his head on the roof of the car. *I really don't need this right now...*

He let his head rest there for a moment before the sound of approaching footsteps made him look up. A young policeman was walking towards him and before he could wonder what he was doing in the parking lot, the man waved in greeting.

Andrew waved back.

"Good morning. Having some trouble with your car there, sir?" The man smiled politely.

Andrew scoffed and shook his head. "No, I just misplaced my wallet is all." He stared around him and then dug out his car keys. "Knowing me it probably fell out on the floorboards or something."

The policeman was now standing beside the car and continued to smile politely. "Perhaps I can help."

The pain knocked whatever Andrew was going to say next out along with his breath, and with a wheezing grunt, his legs folded underneath him. He was dimly aware of the policeman yanking his hands hard behind his back, and then the metallic *click* as the cuffs snapped closed. A second pair of hands hoisted him roughly to his feet, and as his eyes slowly came into focus, the face of a hideously-scarred man leered down at him.

"Help me get him gagged." The policeman tied a rag around Andrew's mouth and cinched it tightly behind his head. Andrew grunted but couldn't offer much in the way of resistance.

*Stun gun*, he thought as the pair lifted him like he weighed nothing and carried him over to a gray van parked nearby. *Had to be a stun gun. . .arms and legs are useless.* And on the heels of that: *Oh, God what's happening to me! Don't let them put me in the van!*

He tried to scream, but the gag and lack of motor coordination made his attempt little more than a low moan.

He was dumped unceremoniously onto the musty upholstery with his head twisted painfully to the side. The scarred man leered down at him once more and then got behind the wheel. Three other individuals were seated in the van with him, and from what he could tell they were of varying ethnic origins. The one on his right was Hispanic and the one seated in the front passenger side was of Asian descent. The third man who leaned over the back of the seat that he lay on was fair-skinned and blonde, most likely Caucasian or possibly Russian.

Andrew really couldn't understand why he was even thinking of such things at that precise moment, but his best guess said that he was scared shitless and that this was the mind's way of helping him not panic.

It wasn't working.

He tried to roll off the seat, but the policeman was there beside him still grinning politely.

"Don't make me hit you again." He smiled as if he would enjoy doing exactly what he said.

It was a good threat and Andrew had no intention of testing the man's resolve. He lay still and tried to make his eyes focus on the man's face. He was young—probably no older than he was—with dark hair cut short just above the ears. His nametag was partially obscured, and the most that he could make out was the name Rhodes.

*Rhodes. I'm going to have to remember that once I get out of here—if I ever get out of here.*

The van roared to life and lurched forward.

✝ ✝ ✝ ✝ ✝ ✝ ✝ ✝

I heard the ambulance even before I saw it, and I screeched to a halt outside the parking lot of my apartment complex. Crowds of tenets and passerby were milling around the cramped space, necks stretched at painful and awkward angles to see what was happening. It struck me again how odd it was for people to be intrigued by death; they all knew that their own was inevitable some day, more than a few were terrified by such a prospect, yet not one of them could quite seem to tear their eyes away from it. Maybe it was the spectacle of it all that enthralled them. Maybe it was a need to see just how bad it could get, or maybe it was the sense of relief they felt when the body was wheeled into view. Better you than me seemed to be the standard mindset in this instance.

I neither knew nor cared what they thought or felt. I only cared about who was on the stretcher being wheeled out of the front entrance of the building.

I ran through the crowd and ignored the venomous glares and startled exclamations I left in my wake, and practically threw myself against the gurney. It rocked to a shaky halt and the technicians flanking it on either side stepped back with the impact.

"Hey, who the hell let this woman through?!"

I ignored the shouting and stared down at the still form lying prone against the starched whiteness of the sheets. Wendell, his face bloody and barely recognizable underneath the bruises, cuts, and abrasions, stared at me through one half-swollen eye.

"Wendell?" I took his hand and clasped it gently. Something thick and smooth was hastily pressed into it before the technicians, their ranks increased by the presence of a police officer, moved me away.

"Ma'am, if you don't step aside, I'm going to have to charge you with obstruction." The burly policeman's face was red and flushed with anger, and I was guessing that it was equally geared towards the perpetrators behind the crime as well as my own actions.

"I know this man. His name is Wendell Bowers, and he was staying with me while he found himself a new place to live." That was more or less the truth so I kept at it. "I had just run into town to pick him up something to eat, and he was alone in my apartment."

The policeman eyed me suspiciously. "And you are?" He pulled a notepad and a pen from somewhere on his person.

"My name is Katrina Armentani. I live in Unit 401." I handed him my I.D. and he glanced at it briefly before handing it back to me. It occurred to me that giving the officer my name was not the smartest thing to do given the circumstances, but I knew that being evasive would only make things worse. Eventually the police would find out who the apartment was registered under, so it seemed that I had no choice either way.

"You'll need to come down to headquarters to answer a few questions."

I nodded, though I had no intention of doing any such thing. My worst fears had been confirmed by what had happened to Wendell, and I could only speculate as to what was happening to Andrew at this time.

"I just need to go back to my car to get my purse."

"You do that." He jotted down a few more notes and then turned his attention back to the scene.

I made my way casually over to the side of the gurney and bent down towards Wendell's face. He was breathing hard and was evidently in pain. His lips moved as if he wanted to tell me something, and I leaned in closer.

"Two of them...they were so strong..." His face constricted with pain and he whimpered, head lolling on the pillow. "Left a message for you...said you'd know what to do...said that now you would come out of hiding and face them on their own ground."

I clenched my hand into a fist. The object in my hand crumpled under the onslaught, and I hurriedly relaxed my grip.

"Miss Armentani?" I looked up to see the policeman glaring down at me. "If it's not too much *trouble*," he ground the word out through clenched teeth, "the technicians would like to get Mr. Bowers to the hospital as soon as possible."

I stepped back and allowed them to load the gurney into the back of the ambulance. I shrugged my shoulders apologetically and made my way through the crowd, keenly aware of the policeman tracking my every movement. I intentionally wove my way through the thickest part of the crowd, and when I was sure that he had lost me in the sea of bodies, I sped off on foot.

The Font behind the killings had upped the stakes when they went after Wendell.

Time to add some counterweight.

# Chapter 34

The cab seemed to be traveling at a snail's pace and I was past the point of patience. I had already asked the driver to speed it up, but apparently he either hadn't heard me or didn't care that a man may be dying. I reached into my pocket and drew out a small roll of bills. I handed them across the seat.

"Drive faster."

He glanced at the bills and then back at me. "What the lady wants, the lady gets." He stuffed them in his pocket and lay rubber all the way to the address that I had given him. The object that Wendell had handed me back in the parking lot turned out to be Andrew's driver's license with a plain card taped to the back. The only writing on it was an address to a house within the very area that I had been hunting in since my arrival in the city. I didn't recognize it as one that I had passed during my patrols, but it was of no consequence. I would soon enter that house in search of Andrew and would no doubt lay waste to the inhabitants.

"Alright, here you go." The cab pulled over to the curb in front of the remains of a once-grand house. Huge, soaring columns graced the façade, but their grandeur was compromised by large wooden braces that had been set up in an X-pattern between them. Undoubtedly they were placed there to support the sagging weight, but they were more a scar on the face of the building than anything else. It was difficult to tell what the original color of the house had been, but it was evident that it had been painted and repainted several times during its lifetime. The top portion of the house resembled a large triangle and was trimmed in a garish array of purples and greens. The sides with their boarded-up windows were a dreary, peeling gray. It looked for all intents and purposes like the ideal haunted house, but I knew that very-real monsters lurked within its walls.

I casually adjusted the sheath underneath my coat and then stepped out into the cool morning air. It was still early—barely nine o' clock—but the sun was beginning to peak out from behind the steely clouds, and there was a very good chance that the temperature would be heating up by noon.

The cab pulled away and I stood there staring up at the rambling structure. A wrought iron fence ran the length of the property, now thick with rust and corrosion. I circled the house to find the best and most inconspicuous place to enter, but my options were limited to the front door. Every window on the ground floor along with the back door had been nailed shut with heavy boards, and there was no way to pry them off without attracting attention.

It seemed I had no other choice, so I took the only one offered.

The front door opened silently on well-oiled hinges, and at first the rooms looked like they were strewn with garbage and scattered refuse. Upon closer inspection I found that the floor was littered with the remains of once-beautiful paintings, furniture, mirrors, and assorted bits of pottery. My boots crunched in the remains of a graceful celadon vase, and I was reminded of the strange and lavish furnishings that Amaris had decorated his lair with. Shoving the image aside, I made my way from room to room searching for any sign that Andrew was in the building with me. This could all very well be a trap, but if it guaranteed me a confrontation with the Font behind his abduction, then so much the better.

There seemed no point in my attempting to be stealthy in my inspection—they had to know that I would come and face them—so I called out softly in the quiet rooms.

"Andrew?"

Nothing but silence. I rounded the corner and stepped into what must have been the dining room. A large crystal chandelier hung suspended from the ceiling in solitary splendor, and at the far end of the room was a large fireplace stained with soot. The light was so dim in this room that I found myself making my way cautiously across the floor, one tentative step at a time.

An open doorway set into the opposite wall led down a short flight of stairs into what I could only surmise was the basement. I stood at the top of the stairs peering down into the inky blackness and knew that I had to go down those steps. Why else would the door be kept open if not to indicate that what I sought lay within its depths? I withdrew one of the knives from the sheath and gingerly placed one foot on the topmost step.

I paused, ears straining for the faintest sound that would alert me to danger. There was nothing.

I took another step and then another until the faint light streaming in from the cracks in the dining room windows barely illuminated the stairs in front of me. When I was now more than halfway down the short flight, I let instinct be my guide. When I reached the very bottom and the light from upstairs vanished into the darkness, I paused and looked around me. Shadows seemed to lurk in every corner and more than once I was sure I heard breathing next to me. I bit down hard on the fear and anxiety that set my heart pounding, and hurriedly crossed into the center of the room.

My foot thumped against something soft and heavy and I stepped back quickly in alarm. Cautiously, I bent down and gingerly touched it with the tip of my finger. The object was cool to the touch, fleshy. Breathing shallowly with my eyes fixed on the amorphous shape before me, I ran my finger over the object, tracing its contours.

An arm.

Without thinking, I rolled the body onto its back and brought the face up as close as I dared to. Like a blind man, I let my fingers trace the curve of the jaw, the shape of the cheeks, and finally the texture of the hair. The hair was cropped in a buzz cut and the jaw was just a tad strong and obstinate.

It wasn't Andrew, and while I *was* relieved, I felt pity for this individual. They had been dead for perhaps a few hours based on the rigidity of the flesh, and I gently set them back down on the floor. By this point my eyes had begun to adjust more to the room, and as I glanced up and around me, I saw that there were bodies—at least a dozen or so—scattered around the area. Most of them lay on their backs staring blankly up at the ceiling, but a few were face down, their limbs twisted out and away from them at grotesque and unnatural angles.

It was a massacre.

I stumbled back and smacked into something hard and immobile. I managed to make a half turn before a fist smashed into my face and I went reeling back. Waves of red danced before my eyes as a dark form loomed over me, its face twisted in a snarl. One cheek was marred by two long, puckered scars, and just before the darkness swallowed me up, I thought I saw a flash of recognition in those hate-filled eyes.

Then all was darkness.

Little by little the darkness began to recede. Little by little my limbs remembered how to work and as consciousness swept me up and buoyed me forward, the pain returned with full-blown force.

I grunted and tried to sit up. A foot pressed into the back of my spine and pinned me to the floor.

"I see you're awake."

I craned my head to stare at the person speaking to me. The room was bathed in a crimson glow thanks to the massive twin candelabra standing in the far corner. Several bodies lounged and reclined languidly on the floor and several more knelt at the feet of a woman, a woman with the most extraordinary eyes I had ever seen.

She was tall in stature, all curves and long, sleek limbs. She was dressed in a blouse the color of stormy skies that was fringed in soft, dark fur. It was cinched tightly around a slender waist and the ends of her tapered fingers were barely visible under the bell-sleeves that hung in diaphanous waves at her side. The cut of the blouse was tailored in such a way that it automatically drew your eyes upwards, and in the soft glow of the candles her skin was the color of burnished copper. Eyes slightly darker than the fur fringing her blouse peeked out underneath a thick sweep of lashes and her full lips were a deep, rich crimson.

She smiled at me and there was nothing human in the gesture.

"We meet at last." Dark eyes glittered triumphantly as they swept over me lying on the floor. A hazy nimbus of swirling red and gold pulsed rhythmically around her and created a halo-effect. The auras around the eight forms gathered around the room paled in comparison—four of them were so dim that the glow coming from the candelabra actually outshone them. These auras were exactly like the ones that I had encountered in past months, exactly like the one that I had dispatched in the alleyway last night. This could only mean one thing.

Here was the Font that I had been pursuing for the better part of half a year, the Font who I felt was behind the deaths of the murdered couple, the Font who had abducted Andrew and sent her children after Wendell. I was as sure of this more than anything else in my life. The desire to finally confront the Font mixed with the fury I felt over the very senselessness of the murders, and I struggled under the weight of the foot holding me down. I was so completely enraged by her indifferent attitude that I wanted to cut the look of smug superiority on her face away with my knives.

*My knives.*

My right hand instinctively went to my waist but even before my hands grasped nothing but air, I knew that I had been disarmed.

The woman laughed—a high, keening shriek that was hard and grating like the tinkling of glass. I resisted the urge to wince and settled instead for glaring venomously at her.

"Who are you?"

"My name is Aloysius. Aloysius Rey."

"Rey?" I had never heard that particular surname before.

"Rey is Spanish for *king*. Seeing as how this is *my* city, the term seems fitting."

She nodded curtly at one of the forms crouched at her feet and a man dressed in a policeman's uniform stood up. She must have seen the expression on my face, because she reached out and stroked the side of his face lovingly. Her finger trailed absently down the length of his chin and came to rest on the badge on his chest. "There are few places in this city where my power is not felt."

The man raised his arms and reverently handed her my sheath. She took it from him with an indulgent smile and began to work one of the knives free.

"So these are what killed my children."

The pressure of the foot on my back intensified, and I gritted my teeth against the pain. "You're the one that I've been hunting—the Font behind what's been happening in the city."

"I thought that would have been obvious by now." She ran the tip of the blade along one slender finger, mocking, teasing.

I licked my suddenly dry lips and shifted my weight on the floor. It was obvious that she thought highly of herself and that she seemed confident that she had me exactly where she wanted me. Over the centuries I had encountered similar Fonts that had shared her sense of superiority, and without exception it had proven to be their downfall. I may have been relieved of my weapons but I was hardly defenseless.

I allowed the rage to boil over, allowed the cynicism that shielded me from the pain of my loneliness and despair to come rushing forward. I used it to strike at the one glaringly-obvious fault she had: vanity.

"I wasn't sure at first; your aura's a little weak." I motioned towards the four men with the dim auras who sat on the floor away from her. "A true Font would have never allowed such weaklings to be born from them under any circumstances. Their auras are so dim that they can't be more than a few weeks old, and they are hardly capable of defending themselves. But I'm sure that you knew that already, considering that you've lost eight of them in the last six months."

She stiffened and the look of triumph in her eyes was replaced by hatred. "A true Font, as you put it, would have done *exactly* what I have done. A true Font would have done anything and everything in their power to protect their interests, which *I* have done. Because of you I have had to do that and more."

She motioned to the person behind me.

The foot that was on my back lifted up momentarily and then slammed down with bone-rattling force. The heel ground into my lower vertebrae and crushed my pelvis against the floor. I ground my teeth harder and refused to be beaten.

She began walking towards me. The air in the room was thick with a mixture of fear and expectancy, but I refused to let either emotion show on my face.

She moved directly in my line of sight and stood towering over me. I craned my head upwards and met her gaze without flinching.

"You owe my son a scream after what you did to him."

"I don't owe him anything." I spat in the dust at her feet and it spattered off the side of her bare foot.

No reaction registered on that beautiful face, and even before I felt the pain I knew that it was coming. The force of the blow smashed me face-first into the floor and left a searing trail of fire down my spine. I shut my eyes against the white-hot pain but still I did not cry out. Angry snarls roared in my ears as I was lifted bodily by strong arms and flung hard into the wall. Ancient plaster cracked and crumbled under the onslaught, and the air took on a strange, misty quality. The dark, lumbering form of my attacker seemed to emerge as from a fog, and a fist caught me in the kidneys, driving the air from my lungs. Plaster dust coated my hands as I slid down towards the floor and I sank down heavily on my knees. My attacker hauled me to my feet by the collar of my coat, and as they spun me around to deliver yet another crushing blow, I saw their face clearly for the first time.

Dark, hate-filled eyes bulged out of a once-handsome face that had been marred by two large, puckered scars that ran from the corner of the left ear to the fullness of the upper lip. It was the face of the man in the alleyway from the night before, the man whose brothers I had killed—the triplets. I knew what had made those scars, and I also knew exactly how he planned to get his revenge on me. He had started to get his revenge the night before but the sudden arrival of the police had forced him to abandon that plan.

Now he had the luxury of time.

I knew that I had to do something in order to get the situation back under my control, and if he was anything like his mother, then vanity was his Achilles heel as well.

I coughed and tasted blood. "You may kill me for what I've done to you, but it won't reverse the damage; you'll still have to walk through eternity looking like that."

His face twisted up in a snarl, and with a bellow of rage, his fist rocketed forward at lightening speed. I saw it coming towards me in slow motion, the fist clenched so tightly that the knuckles threatened to break through the skin at any moment.

"Daman!"

The man paused and turned to stare at the woman behind him. I couldn't help but smirk. All that power and rage-filled potential and he still had to answer to his Font—yet one more reason I was glad that I had killed mine.

"We don't want to hurt her too badly before she gets what she came here for." She moved to his side and gently pulled his arm back and away from my face. He said something between clenched teeth that was unintelligible, but it had the cadence of a cheated whine.

"Patience, my son. I promise you that she will get what she deserves." She turned to stare at me with eyes like drowning pools. "She will get what she deserves and more."

The man spun me around and shoved me forward. He grabbed me around the waist and molded his body against mine, pinning my arms to my side. The woman knelt beside me and smoothed the hair back from my face. I fought the urge to recoil from that touch, that simple gesture that under different circumstances would have been comforting.

There was nothing comforting in that action. She wanted me to see what she planned on doing to me.

"By rights your life should be mine, but my son seems quite taken by you. As my second in command he has equal claim to this right."

I shook my head. Why did she keep referring to the man as her son? Progeny were often referred to as children by their Fonts, but never anything specific like this.

"He has no right to anything and neither do you. No one, especially a sniveling little progeny like him…"

I didn't get to finish the sentence. She slapped me so hard that my head whipped violently to the side and stars rocketed in my field of vision. She grabbed my by the chin and forced me to meet her gaze.

"He is borne of my flesh as surely as my blood, and you *will* show him respect!"

I stared at her with slowly dawning horror. *No, it's not possible. He can't be more than thirty years old, so how…?*

And then I knew. Knew the way I knew Wendell was in trouble, knew the way that the murdered couple had been the work of vampires rather than a sadistic and imaginative human. She *was* his mother, and by some monstrous quirk of fate or her own actions, had managed to accrue enough strength to be able to turn him and his brothers before they reached thirty years of age. She had managed to become a Font in less time than the space of one human lifespan. Impossible.

She leered at me and stepped back. "Now you know what you are up against. Now, we are equal."

She snapped her fingers and two of the forms lounging on the floor got up and retreated across the darkened room. They reemerged a minute later with the limp and bloodied form of Andrew sagging between them.

Multiple cuts and shallow wounds crisscrossed his body, and heavy bruising made Rorschach patterns across his upper torso. Blood had seeped heavily into the waistband of his jeans from the numerous and randomly spaced punctures, punctures which seemed eerily familiar:

*"The source went on to state that fingerprints and sometimes whole handprints were bruised onto the skin of the victims.…Perhaps the most tell-*

*tale sign that the murders are indeed the work of a preternatural assailant is that the victims experienced significant blood loss prior to their death. This is further compounded by the presence of puncture wounds on various parts of the body."*

I stared intently at the bruising that marred Andrew's body. Angry purple welts were molded around his wrists and arms, almost as if someone with incredible strength had restrained him while he was being tortured. The characteristic bruising and the tell-tale and well-placed punctures that the source had mentioned in Gary's article were all a perfect match.

I had found the killer that I had been hunting. Where I had once been working with instinct and speculation, I now had irrefutable proof that Aloysius and her progeny were the culprits behind the murders.

The men released him and he toppled heavily to the floor.

A confusing jumble of images from the night that my family was murdered mingled with the scene before me, and I threw my weight against the man restraining me as the past and the present seemed to intersect. For the third time in my long life I was powerless to stop the people that I cared about from being hurt. Andrew was still a virtual stranger to me, but once I protected someone I felt responsible for their lives until the danger was eliminated once and for all.

The woman laughed and strode casually over to Andrew's limp form. She knelt before him and drew him up into her lap, cradling him like a child. Blood smeared on her blouse and arms, but she paid it no mind. She had eyes only for me.

"It seems that there is more about you than meets the eye. I had long thought that you were nothing more than a cold-blooded killer intent on taking my territory away from me by force—apparently I was wrong." One long, tapered finger gently traced the edge of a shallow cut and toyed with the sticky blood, smearing it in thick lines. "For someone that you have just met, it would appear that Mr. Crossman means something to you, something important enough for you to risk your own safety for; how very curious."

The finger circled the wound once more and then gouged through the tender flesh. The wound gaped like a lipless mouth and Andrew screamed as consciousness returned to him. He fought against the strong arms that restrained him and she indulged his feeble attempts, smiling coldly at him.

"Quiet yourself now. Your friend and I have much to discuss and we can't do that with you screaming like this," she soothed, stroking his chest.

Andrew's face was a mask of terror and pain as he turned in her arms, his eyes wide and frightened. He stared wildly around the dark room as if unsure where he was.

"My children and I had a very interesting conversation with Mr. Crossman this morning." She continued stroking his chest and he whimpered each time that her hand made contact with his skin. "He told us everything about you. Every. Thing." She paused and seemed thoughtful. "Well, almost everything. It seems that Mr. Crossman neglected to inform me what his relationship with you is. It appears that more is going on here than he initially let on." The tip of her finger brushed against his lips, and he jerked away from her.

"Stop it."

Her expression was one of polite interest. "I beg your pardon?" She continued to stroke the side of his face, her eyes daring me to get up and put a stop to the torment.

"You heard me. Let him go—your quarrel is with me."

She shook her head and the long curly locks of her hair gently brushed the top of Andrew's head. He squirmed and tried to turn his face away. One hand absently came up and gripped him tightly around the chin, forcing his head back towards her. "And if I don't? What do you propose to do about it? You're hardly in a position to make such demands."

"No, you're wrong. I'm exactly where you want me to be. I'm unarmed and am completely at your mercy. There's no need to torture him when he has nothing to do with what's going on—this is between you and me."

She scoffed daintily. "You're still trying to play the selfless martyr after all these years. Haven't your past experiences with your family taught you anything?" The fingers of her left hand dug into a wound above his ribs. Andrew hissed in pain and squeezed his eyes shut. "You can't save him anymore than you could have saved your family. You can't even save yourself from what you are becoming." She seemed almost wistful when she said this. "Such power and potential and you waste it feeling sorry for yourself. You've wasted the last three centuries trying to run away from what you are, have spent the last three centuries denying the very basic principle of your existence: you are a killer, a hunter, a predator."

"I slay those who threaten the lives of innocent humans, humans who have no way of protecting themselves from monsters such as you."

"And you are so innocent yourself?" She shook her head. "I think not. You kill out of vengeance and because you enjoy it. You kill because it gives your actions some semblance of righteousness, when in reality feeding should be devoid of such emotions. It is the most natural thing in the world—it is what we do, what we are, and you have managed to pervert even that."

I refused to have my actions and beliefs twisted by her inane logic. "It's one thing to kill to live, and I'd be a hypocrite if I said that my hands were free of innocent blood, but it is another thing entirely to torture them before you kill them. That *is* evil, pure and simple." I let my gaze shift over to Andrew to emphasize my point.

She looked at me and smiled. "Ah, but that is the very root of the problem isn't it? You killed three people for what you believed were selfless actions, but which were not. How did you put it? 'I committed the sin of *non facias malum ut inde fiat bonum*—you should not make evil in order that good may be made from it?' You killed those people in order to save them from a cruel death at the hands of your tormentors, is that it?" She laughed and wrapped her arms securely around Andrew's torso. "Such a paradox of emotions; you hate what you are yet you insist on living long enough to honor the oath that you made to your family all those centuries ago. You slay those of our kind who would do harm to humanity, yet you make no effort to save these people from any of the countless other dangers that are out there. I find that most perplexing."

"I slay the guilty and protect the innocent who are unable to defend themselves. I make no allusions to being their savior in other regards—that is left in the hands of higher powers."

"Don't tell me that you believe God has anything to do with this?" She sounded scornful. "Griselda was right when she said that we are beyond God. The suffering of our prey is nothing more than the natural progression of things, the survival of the fittest if you like. There is no ultimate goodness or sense of justice in the world. If there were, then you and I would not be having this conversation. We would have long since gone to dust along with the rest of our family." Her eyes were hard around the edges as she said this, and her tone was laced with bitterness. "No, we must forge our own destinies. There is no one in the universe, no force out there that has the final say in how we choose to live our lives. Just as you chose to spend the rest of eternity avenging your family, I chose to rise up against my oppressor. *I* chose to give my sons and I a fighting chance in this world, and if human life must be continually sacrificed upon the altar of my will to ensure this, then so be it." Her eyes blazed with conviction.

"Griselda was a sadistic fiend who delighted in torture and bloodshed. She was evil in so many ways and had no conscience, no pity, no remorse..."

"And you killed her for that."

I nodded. "Yes, I killed her for that."

"The same way that you killed my children, the same way that you killed my sons Alec and Castillo?" Her voice trembled with emotion, and her anger was a palpable presence in the tiny room.

"I killed them for that—just as I killed Amaris and his other children, Dimitri and Kristoff."

"Ah, yes, Amaris—your Font. Tell me," she leaned forward and rested her chin on top of Andrew's head. He went very still but the look of revulsion and fear remained on his face. "What was it like to spill the blood that had given you immortality?"

There were so many words that could give voice to my emotions during this time, but I settled instead for simple and to the point. "I felt nothing. He and his children tortured and murdered my family—forced me to murder in return—and I merely repaid the favor. They thought that they could break my soul or my resolve by imprisoning me and forcing me to commit unspeakable acts of cruelty upon the innocent, but they were wrong. They underestimated me and died by my hand less than a month after they had forced the transference upon me."

One slender eyebrow arched in response. "Less than a month after your transference?" She toyed absently with a lock of Andrew's hair, seemingly deep in thought. "How interesting."

Something about her expression unnerved me, but I ignored it. Andrew's safety had to come before my own, and I reached for the last line in my defense. "They were guilty. All that I have slain were guilty, and I make no apologies for what I have done. If you want to punish me for killing your children, then do so, but leave him out of it."

"And who deemed them guilty? You? Did it ever occur to you that perhaps the individuals that you slew were dealing with their existence the only way that they knew how? That by taking life they were choosing to live? Hmm? Did it ever occur to you that you were both dealing with your existence the only way that you knew how? Their methods may have differed from yours, but they were all geared towards the same ends. The same applies to my children and me—every time that we take a life, we are choosing to live as well."

I didn't have an answer for that.

She nodded knowingly. "Of course you didn't. Because that would shatter the illusion wouldn't it? That would destroy the belief that you were not like the rest of your kind, would destroy the belief that you were somehow still human even after everything that you had done and been through." She shifted Andrew's weight in her arms and wrapped her denim-clad legs securely around his torso, hugging his sides with her knees. The gesture was all the more obscene given the look of terror on his face. "No, I cannot let either of you go for the same reason that you cannot let me or my children go: we would never stop hunting one another. We would never stop trying to balance the wrongs against the right, because neither of us could rest unless the other was dead."

One of my knives flashed into view as she retrieved it from where it lay on the floor. She held it up and it caught the light given off by the candelabra. "Both of us are unwilling to leave the past behind us. Even if I *were* willing, the deaths of Alec and Castillo are unforgivable. They were my sons and nothing can replace them. Daman is permanently scarred and must walk through eternity in shame—that too is unforgivable."

I knew that I was losing the battle and had to fumble for an adequate defense. I had to make her see that her quarrel had been with me all along. I had to make her see that her actions were as much responsible for how things had turned out as my own. "And what about the deaths of that couple you murdered? The ones you butchered and left to rot in an alleyway not far from here? What about them? Isn't what you did just as unforgivable? Who will speak for them if no one else will?"

I knew that she was behind the killings, knew it without a doubt. It made little difference that I was ignorant as to the how's and why's—all that mattered was that she pay for what she had done. It was indication enough that the bodies had been butchered in a way that no human could have done and were then disposed of in an alleyway less than three blocks from here. The fact that eight of her progeny had tried to accost me and the only witness to the crime, coupled with the eerie similarity of Andrew's injuries was even more compelling.

The look she gave me was one of cold indifference. "Unforgivable? I think not. Their deaths brought you out in the open exactly like I knew they would. Their deaths delivered you into my hands so that justice for the deaths of my children would at last be mine."

"But how could you know this? How could you know that their murder would get my attention and lead me to you?"

"I already told you: there are few places in this city where my influence is not felt. One of my children was fortunate enough to escape your blades nearly a month ago—unlike the one you killed and disposed of in the countryside. He simply followed you home afterwards, and the rest all fell into place. He watched you from a distance and when he was certain of your pattern, he was then able to enter your residence without you being the wiser. Darnell's intell helped me gain a sense of how to bring you to me on my own terms, though I very much doubt that he is of use to anyone right now—you made sure of that last night."

Darnell. Was this the man that I had slain last night in the alleyway? Was he the man with the weak aura who had begged me not to kill him? Was he the man who had been spying on me for days without my knowledge? I thought back to the night in question, a night nearly a month in the past. When the progeny had accosted me in the alleyway, I slew him and disposed of him on my country property like all the others. No one had seen me do this. Then suddenly I remembered: a lone car had passed me on the otherwise deserted road and had continued on into the darkness.

Or had they?

Now I wasn't so sure. As for when and how this person had managed to spy on me and then enter my apartment when I was gone, I had no idea. I patrolled the city every night, and it was very likely that they had seen me do this enough times to know when I would not be home. They would have seen the file folders and stacks of newspapers detailing violent and unsolved crimes that had taken place in the city. Was it so inconceivable that this knowledge could have been used against me? Looking at Aloysius' smug face, I knew the answer. Only one question remained unanswered.

"Why did you go to so much trouble to set up the murders the way that you did? Why butcher and mutilate the bodies in such a manner?"

Aloysius smiled at me and ran her fingertips along the edge of a puncture wound on Andrew's arm. "Why, to attract your attention of course. If I had simply murdered them like any common thug in this city would have with a knife or gun, the story would have been buried in the paper and that would have been the end of it. No, I had to make their deaths stand out in such a way that they could not be ignored, least of all by you. I do admit that the puncture wounds were a nice touch. 'Vampire' murders indeed. Who would have thought that that rag of a tabloid would have seen the truth when all the others were blind to it?"

"You staged the murders to get my attention." Even saying it out loud did little to quell my growing rage. I had been steadily picking off her children one by one for months waiting for her to make the first move to confront me, had spent nights contemplating her reluctance. Now I knew. She had been biding her time, had been scheming and plotting the murders to be as horrific as possible, all for the sake of drawing me out into the open. She had been aware of my presence the moment I had killed the first of her children and she had sought to level the playing field ever since. It had worked, but at the cost of two innocent lives.

It seemed I had underestimated Aloysius. I was so inured in my own self-assurance as a hunter that I was convinced that I had always had the upper hand. She had shown me otherwise.

"And what about Wendell and Andrew? Why was their suffering added to this if you knew that I would seek you out regardless? Why torment them?"

"Simple. You killed those closest to me, so I will kill those closest to you if only superficially. This is all about getting even isn't it? You kill one of mine so I kill one of yours, and the game goes on forever and ever without end until we are both left with nothing but our own bitterness. Nobody wins under those circumstances. Our desire for revenge will be a poison we give to ourselves and what then? No, only one of us must be allowed to walk out of here. Only then will the balance be restored. I may live forever without my sons beside me, but I *will* have the satisfaction of knowing that their deaths did not go un-avenged."

"You're insane."

She nuzzled Andrew's cheek and he tried to turn away from her. "You would know all about that, wouldn't you? I may kill with impunity as you believe, but I have never taken a souvenir of my kills much less put them to such garish use." She stroked the initials carved onto the bone handle of the knife. "Such ruthlessness to have severed the limb from Amaris while he was still alive; I dare say that you are even crueler than I am."

"I am nothing like you!" Indignation colored my voice as much as hopelessness. She was determined to drag Andrew down with me, and nothing I said or could say would deter her otherwise.

"In some respects that is true. Your aura blazes with an intensity that I have never seen before. It is like some great, crimson force that outshines all the other lives around it. Over three hundred years of feeding off of your own kind, of feeding off of progeny and Fonts...such power you must possess."

I stared across the seemingly unbridgeable chasm that lay between Andrew and me and knew in my heart what she had meant. Three-hundred-and-forty-seven years old—three-hundred-and-twenty-eight of those spent devouring the life force of Fonts and their progeny alike—over three centuries of unspoiled potential, of having never shared my blood with another. Was it so inconceivable that I had by my own unwitting actions attained the status of a Font as surely as Aloysius and the others had? Was it so inconceivable that my desire to not become the thing I hated most in the world actually resulted in such a thing? Was it possible that the truth had been staring me in the face all those years, and I, blind with rage and vengeance in equal amounts, had refused to see it for what it was? Did I dare believe that my desire to cling onto the last shreds of my humanity was actually my downfall?

I stared at her blankly.

The man in the policeman's uniform and a few others stood up suddenly and shoved the massive candelabra to the floor. The candles were knocked free from their moorings and began to set various parts of the room ablaze. The flames were sluggish at first but they soon began to catch and burn with a fierce heat.

I turned back to Aloysius who sat there staring at me with calm serenity. I was completely at her mercy just as she wanted me to be, and there was nothing that I could do about it.

The arms restraining me gripped me tightly in an unbreakable embrace, and Andrew was equally helpless. Soon the entire room would be engulfed with flames, and I had no doubt that he and I would be left to die here while the house succumbed to the inferno.

As I watched, Aloysius tossed one of my knives across the room and my captor caught it one handed. I knew what he meant to do with it and closed my eyes.

A bolt of white-hot agony shot through my back and rocketed pell-mell throughout my nerve endings, bowing my spine and forcing my head upwards. My eyes flew open and I cried out miserably as I felt the blood soaking through the lining of my coat. He let go of me and my hands clawed the air as the blade sank in once more. My body folded in at the waist and I began to sink to the floor, delirious with the pain and accompanying blood loss. With a savage growl, the man twisted the knife in deeper all the way to the hilt, and I felt the blood leave me in a torrent. I slipped silently to the floor and lay on my side with my eyes squeezed shut. I heard the unmistakable sound of my captor laughing at me underneath the roar of my heartbeat in my ears.

"Now *we* are even." He had stabbed me twice as payment for the two scars that I had marked him with the night before.

"Coward," I gasped. "Stabbing an unarmed woman in the back like this…if our positions were switched, I'd die of shame."

He kicked me savagely in the gut and I screamed. I tried to get to my knees to crawl away from him, but he kicked me again and I fell forward. He kept kicking me until my screams gave way to pathetic mewling, and then he left me lying there in a pool of my own blood.

From in front of me I could hear Andrew frantically calling my name, and then the sounds of agony as Aloysius and her son took turns slashing him with my knives. They were careful to avoid hitting any major veins or arteries, but they made sure that their blows would do the maximum amount of damage. Andrew cried out and thrashed helplessly in their arms, trying desperately to heave himself into a sitting position. Dark eyes stared impassively at him as the knives continued to slash at his body, cutting him to ribbons. I could only watch helplessly as he grew weaker and weaker while the blood began to pool around him on the dusty floor. His aura pulsed sporadically, flickering and fluttering like a dying flame. A fine sheen of sweat beaded his brow and his breath came in labored gasps as his struggles slowly began to cease. I knew that even if Aloysius and her son chose to cease tormenting him that he would not survive. The affliction—which had been slowly eating away at him for months—was about to triumph. His body simply couldn't defend itself against the relentless onslaught any longer.

His body twitched feebly and she allowed his weight to slip silently to the floor. His head lolled to the side and his eyes stared into mine as the light began to fade from them. I shut my own eyes and lay there on the dusty floor.

I had failed him, just as I had failed Wendell. I was so blinded by my own sense of superiority and skewed sense of righteousness that I had not only walked straight into the face of danger, but I had dragged two people—two innocent people—down with me.

Footsteps approached me and stood inches away from where I lay on the floor. I knew that it had to be Aloysius but I refused to look up, refused to gaze into that beautiful, haughty face and see my defeat mirrored in her eyes. She knelt beside me and the closeness of her presence threatened to choke me.

She spoke to me even as I refused to look at her. "He is too weak to walk himself out of here, but you have the power to make him strong again."

My mind was too clouded by pain and despair for me to comprehend what she was saying to me. Andrew was dead as

I would soon be. If the knives didn't finish us off the flames surely would.

My vision swam in a frightening collage of Aloysius and Andrew's faces, one mocking and filled with triumph, the other slack and filled with a terrible blankness that only the dying possess. Flames licked up the sides of the walls and the stench of burning timber filled my nostrils. As the blood loss began to ravage my body, I could feel myself becoming limp and weightless, free and without a care.

It was over.

Even as consciousness eluded me my memory was very much alive. I saw again the look of terror on Andrew's face as the knives slashed him over and over. I saw again Wendell's bloodied and bruised face, his eyes staring helplessly out at me as I knelt over him on the gurney. I saw once again the faces of my family as Amaris and his children tortured and killed them, saw the tiny earthen mound beneath the tree and heard my voice whisper the oath once more:

*"No peace for the wicked. For as long as there is breath and life in my body, I will spend my days dispatching those who threaten the innocent. For as long as there is breath and life in my body, I will have them fear me as their victims once feared them; for as long as there is breath and life in my body, I will never forget you and the oath that I have sworn upon your memory."*

I had failed Andrew and Wendell as surely as I had failed my family. Aloysius and her children would continue to stalk the city or elsewhere killing with savage abandon as they had always done, as others of my kind would continue to do around the world.

*No.*

I coughed weakly and blinked my eyes against the stinging smoke. No, I couldn't give up now—too much was at stake.

My vision righted itself and I stared into her eyes. I would *not* give up. Not now, not ever.

"I will see you dead—one way or the other."

She smiled. "Perhaps, perhaps not. I have found a punishment that is suitable for the transgressions you committed against my children. You swore that you would cling onto the last semblance of humanity left to you, swore that you would not become the thing you hate or force the transference upon another, but we shall see. Your power fades, but it is not gone—you may still succeed in changing him regardless of this. Save yourself, or turn him and save yourselves; the choice is yours. Just know that the choices I have left you with are impossible and will each have their own set of consequences, so it is up to you to decide which one of them you can live with."

And with that she was gone.

The overhead beams groaned and cracked as the flames raced up and over them. Bits of charred wood and embers whirled and danced in the air, but I wasn't seeing any of it.

*'Save yourself, or turn him and save yourselves; the choice is yours . . .'*

Did I really have the right to make such a choice? My life had always been my own and I was free to live it the way I wanted. By the same token I could also end it when I wanted, but Andrew's life? Did I have any right to choose whether he lived or died, whether he would join me in eternity without a say in the matter? He was already dying and if I did this then I would save him from certain death. I would take his life and give him another one, but it may not be one that he wanted. He would be forced to watch while the passing years claimed those he loved one by one, and with each loss he would gradually lose a piece of himself.

If I did this—if I chose to believe what Aloysius had said and attempt to bring him over—I would be no better than Amaris, perhaps worse. If I chose to save myself and leave him behind, then I would condemn him to a cruel and terrible death. If by some slim chance I could get us both out of here without the blood transference and get him to a hospital he might live, but only temporarily—the disease ravaging his body would eventually finish him off. If I chose to let the flames consume us both, then his blood would stain my hands either way. If I chose to do nothing, then the oath that I had sworn upon my family's memory would be broken and the bodies of innocent victims would continue to pile up, unchecked.

*If, if, if. . .*

"God help me, I don't know what to do!" I pounded the floor with my fist and it came away bloody. The blood glowed crimson in the firelight and seemed alive, a slithering wet thing.

Alive. Live. Life.

I made my decision. I knew that no matter what I decided that there would be consequences. The most I could hope for was that the choice I made would have the least.

I dragged my body across the floor one laborious inch at a time, the blood from my wounds leaving a dark and sticky trail behind me. My ribs and muscles shrieked in protest as my body demanded that I rest and feed to restore my strength, but I ignored it. Sheer tenacity and strength of will drove me forward and kept the weakness at bay long enough for me to close the distance between us. As I neared Andrew's seemingly lifeless body, I saw that his chest rose and fell the tiniest bit—the body's last attempt to sustain life before the darkness descended.

I drew him up into my arms and cradled his head in my lap. My knives lay scattered on the floor around us, and I reached out for the one nearest me. My fingers barely had any strength left to grasp the handle, but I managed to bring it up towards my left wrist. The metal was hot as I lay it against my skin.

"Forgive me," I whispered. It had the lilt of a benediction to it and it could have easily been intended for Andrew as it was for God.

I drew the blade across my wrist. The blood welled up dark and thick, almost black in the firelight. I dropped the blade and tilted Andrew's face toward my hand, gently pressing the wound against his slack mouth. For a breathless few seconds nothing happened, but then his lips began to work sluggishly against my flesh. A violent shudder went through his body as he drew my wrist against his mouth, and then his lips molded tightly around the wound.

I screamed—not in agony, but in ecstasy.

I sagged heavily against him and my right hand pressed his head against my arm with a fierce determination. The pleasure was so intense I never wanted it to end, never wanted to relinquish this sense of complete abandon ever again. Each swallow wrenched a desperate moan from me, and as his tongue probed the wound, delving deeper and deeper into the font of life flowing from me to him, I gasped his name and pulled him closer.

Never had I felt such pure, unadulterated pleasure, never have I felt such burning passion that threatened to consume me and everything that I touched. Even as I writhed on the floor, the flames lapping eagerly around me were a soothing, cooling comfort. Even as I knew that each swallow further solidified my own damnation, I urged him to go on, urged him to take me into himself and to make me a part of him forever.

My mind was a riot of emotions in those moments: love, tenderness, pleasure and pain, but underneath them all was bitterness and shame—bitterness over my lost humanity and the injustices of the options Aloysius had left me, and shame over the pleasure I felt in the arms of a man I barely knew. The pleasure I felt in those moments was greater than what my husband Nicholas and I had experienced in our bed during our short marriage, was greater even than the sweet evil of my first kill. The pleasure was all I was, was all I knew in those tenuous moments between life and death, became all that I despised.

I knew now what it was that compelled our kind to seek out eternal companions. The desire to share a part of ourselves with another on a level few could imagine made the desire to appease our loneliness pale in comparison, made all other desires seem trivial and inconsequential.

To feel our life flowing into the body of another, to know that *our* life gave *them* life in return—*this* was the essence of eternity.

He released me suddenly and I collapsed onto my side and lay staring up at the ceiling. Flames roared through the timbers and reworked the ancient wood down to its most basic elements. I was spiraling down into blessed oblivion with my heart pounding slowly and steadily in my ears, and everything I was boiled down to the blood flowing in my veins, boiled down to the blood flowing in the veins of the man lying beside me.

I closed my eyes and let the darkness come. I had made my choice but I still felt cheated, still felt as if I had been denied and lost what was most dear to me.

Strong arms picked me up and buoyed me through the air. My hands dangled limply at my sides and the wounds in my back and wrist continued to bleed sluggishly. I didn't have the strength to open my eyes, but I knew that when I did open them at last that I would see the world in a whole new light—for better or for worse.

# Chapter 35

We exploded out onto the lawn just as the roof caved in. I heard rather than saw the destruction as the walls folded in and the structure collapsed to the ground like a house of cards. The faint screech of sirens came from just up the road and the air was thick with smoke and dust. By the time that I was gently lowered to the ground we were both coughing and choking from the debris swirling in the air.

The pavement felt cool and wonderful against my skin after the heat of the passion that had boiled in my veins. A shower of glass rained down on me and I winced, turning my head to the side. Neither Andrew nor I had driven here so I could only surmise that he had to find us an alternate source of transportation. Strong arms once again picked me up and I was set down against soft, musty-smelling upholstery. The seat pressed into the wounds on my back and I cried out, flailing weakly in pain.

"I've got it. You're okay now."

Andrew's voice. I turned my face away from him because I didn't want him to see how much pain his being alive caused me. I also turned my face away from him because I didn't want him to see how much I needed him in those moments.

His hands gently readjusted me so that I was more comfortable, and then they secured the seatbelt around me. I wanted to say that it wasn't necessary, but didn't. I just let him feel like he had some semblance of control over what was happening—I would deal with the fallout later.

He got in the seat beside me and after a few tense moments of frustrated fumbling, the car roared to life. Andrew was silent beside me as the car rumbled away from the curb, and I didn't know if it was for my benefit or his. I couldn't seem to make myself care either way, and as the car turned towards the right, he suddenly cried out. The car jerked violently to the left and swerved dangerously from side to side as the pain of his transference finally set in. I had given him more blood than I could spare and it had bought us a small amount of time, because the more blood transferred, the longer it takes for the body to process it to begin the transformation. If I had given him any less, he would have been immobile and helpless as his body succumbed to the onslaught and he would have been unable to drag us both away from the burning house. Either way I risked one or both of us dying during the process.

Small, helpless sounds filled the cab as he flailed miserably against the seat, his feet kicking mindlessly against the floor. His fists smashed against the windows and steering wheel over and over again as his body writhed and contorted of its own volition, twisting and turning at grotesque and impossible angles. I didn't have to open my eyes to see the agony he was suffering from. My own transference had been equally painful, and despite what else I was feeling in those moments I felt genuine sympathy for him.

The violent spasms slowly began to cease and with a final convulsive yell, the car careened through a chain link fence and came to rest with an abrupt stop.

I opened my eyes. I had to see what consequences my actions had.

Andrew sat next to me in his torn and bloody shirt, his face pinched and twisted. His hands were knuckle-white against the steering wheel and he was doubled up with the pain. He threw his head back and screamed—his mouth yawning open until it seemed that his jaw would break—and then he sagged back against the seat.

His head slipped to the side and he saw me staring at him. I don't know what he saw reflected on my face, but whatever he saw there caused him to extend his hand towards me in desperation.

I took it.

He clasped my hand as the final wave of agony washed over him, and then he was still. I stared at his hand as if I wasn't sure what it was, and it was then that I saw the crimson film enveloping us. It swelled and expanded in sync with our breathing, swelled and filled our line of vision until it obscured everything else. Andrew saw it too and the look in his eyes was one of pure wonderment.

All of his wounds had either vanished or were fading away from his skin, leaving it smooth and flawless. The dark circles under his eyes and all of the tiny lines that time had given him during his short life smoothed out until he was left perfect and unblemished. The green in his eyes seemed more vibrant and the colors in his hair practically danced and whirled in the dim light of the streetlamps.

I felt my breath catch in my throat. The sight of him was beautiful and terrible all at once, but I could not tear my gaze away from him. The film gradually began to shrink and collapsed in on itself until it dwindled away to a single crimson strand. I found myself reaching out for it and when my fingers brushed it, a shiver ran down my spine. Andrew felt it too and he shut his eyes tightly. His expression was almost beatific in its sereneness, and for the briefest of moments, a dim memory of the passion that we had shared back at the house flickered forth. My own body responded to the memory and I felt my heart speed up. It was a dim memory, but a powerful one no less, one that we both felt down to the very core of our beings.

Andrew's aura shone forth in a brilliant array of reds and gold, the dark and disease-riddled miasma gone forever. I had made him strong with my blood, but only time would prove his resilience.

I knew now that we were completely and utterly bound to one another. My life was his and his was mine. He was my progeny, my child, my curse.

God help us both.

# Chapter 36

The lights of the Interstate seemed to flow by at disquieting speeds, and the once-familiar skyline of the city seemed alien and terrifying. My perception of things was compromised by the blood loss that I had suffered, but I knew that my own inner turmoil was as much to blame.

The car finally came to a stop at a seedy little motel on the wrong end of town—just the kind of place that wouldn't care how much blood the clientele showed up in so long as they paid with cash. My legs were rubbery and unsteady and I ended up leaning all of my weight against him when I got out of the car. He didn't protest and helped me to our ground-floor room at the end of the short row of units. He managed to get the door open with me clinging to him like a child, and after flicking on the lights he scooped me up and carried me over to the bed.

"Your wounds are still bleeding; I'll need to take care of them for you."

The significant turn of events wasn't lost on me as he drew my arm out from beneath the covers. Less than twenty-four hours before our positions had been reversed, and neither of us could have predicted how dramatically our lives would have changed during that short space of time.

He ran his finger lightly along the edge of my wrist, his eyes seemingly transfixed on the spot where he had drawn immortality from me. The memory of his mouth upon it only an hour before made me squirm and he hurriedly let go. It was difficult to tell in the dim light if he was just as uncomfortable as I was, because he was back at my side with a damp washcloth before I could make up my mind.

His hands were gentle as they methodically cleaned, bound, and then dressed the wound on my wrist with a torn up sheet. There was no sign of the heat that we had shared earlier, but I knew that it boiled just beneath the surface. The wounds on my back proved more difficult as I had to partially disrobe. He helped me to turn over on my stomach and he repeated the treatment on my back. These wounds were deeper, more severe, but I wouldn't let him take me to a hospital.

I knew that I had to feed in order to heal and restore my strength, but Aloysius and her children had to be long gone by now. Who would I feed from if not one of them? I didn't want to answer that question, so I lay there and suffered in silence.

The weakness from my blood loss and the pain of my beating began to take its toll on me, and I could barely keep my eyes open as he tended to me. He kept insisting that he take me to the hospital, but I kept insisting that I knew what I was doing. The police would undoubtedly be looking for me after the disappearing act that I had pulled back at the apartment complex, and the severity of my wounds would raise too many unanswerable questions. He finally relented, but he seemed reluctant to stray too far away from me. He sat at a respectful distance away from me in the only chair in the room, and when exhaustion finally pulled me down into a troubled and restless sleep, his face was the last thing I saw before I closed my eyes.

✞ ✞ ✞ ✞ ✞ ✞ ✞

I awoke some time later to the sound of low murmuring coming from my right. Andrew stood in profile by the phone talking in hushed whispers to someone on the other end. I was still slightly delirious from my injuries and only managed to hear snatches of conversation.

I shifted slightly and he hurriedly thanked the person that he was talking to and hung up.

"I found which hospital Wendell was taken too. The doctors say that he is fully conscious and appears to be doing well despite his injuries."

I nodded silently, thankful that Wendell would be fine.

Andrew stood there awkwardly as if unsure what to do or say. He straightened and reached for my coat which had been hastily thrown on the floor.

"I should probably go check on him. He has no one else, and we're his only…" He seemed unwilling or unable to finish the sentence. "If you're sure that you're all right, I'll go, but if not…"

"Go. I'm not fine but I will be."

He hovered near the edge of the bed and seemed reluctant to leave. He seemed to finally accept my silence as reassurance and headed towards the door.

"I'll be back soon." Then he was gone.

I didn't want to be left alone with my thoughts anymore than I wanted to be left alone with him, but it seemed I didn't have a choice either way. I slowly rolled onto my side and clutched the pillows tightly. The familiar and comforting weight of the sheath around my waist wasn't there for me when I needed it most, so I found comfort where I could.

I thought about what the next few hundred years would be like between Andrew and me. While he seemed reluctant to leave my side, I was eager to have him gone from my sight. Every time that I looked into his eyes I was reminded of what I had lost and what I had gained.

I had lost the last remaining shred of my humanity, but I had gained a companion for the coming years—a companion that I had never wanted in the first place, but which Fate had seemingly thrown my way.

I thought about how I would come to terms with what I had done and if Andrew would ever forgive me. His reluctance to leave me and his tenderness towards me was puzzling, but it had to be a side-effect of the transference. I had learned over the years that the transference was very similar to love or sex: it could be a mutual desire steeped in seduction, or it could be forced like rape. With the former, the resulting bond would be powerful and unshakable—the child would do anything and everything for their maker. With the latter, bitterness and resentment would prevail. With Amaris my transference had been a lot like rape, and he had paid the price for his indiscretion.

I wondered if there would be a price to pay for mine.

# Chapter 37

Wendell lay on the bed breathing slowly and rhythmically. The pain killers that the hospital had prescribed had kicked in some time ago and he was fast asleep.

I stood with my back to the room facing the open window, missing the ceaseless flow of the traffic outside. The motel was in an area of town where the traffic was the least congested, and where the presence of patrol cars was rare and infrequent.

Andrew sat in the lone chair by the air-conditioning unit staring at Wendell's sleeping form. While some of his more serious injuries were mainly broken ribs and a mild concussion, they would heal and there was no permanent damage that the doctors could see.

I was glad to hear this; it helped to ease some of the pain and disquiet that I felt about the day's events.

My own injuries had stopped bleeding, but they were healing with almost human-like slowness. They would undoubtedly leave scars behind, yet another reminder of my actions that I would carry with me throughout eternity.

I saw Andrew staring at me through the reflection in the window, and I found myself once again pondering my actions. Did I care for him, if only in the sense that I now felt responsible for his life, the same way that I felt about Wendell's? Did I keep him close to me because as his Font, his life was directly tied to mine and that if he should die, then so would I? Was it love that had ultimately driven me to change him, or was it merely the lesser of two evils given the circumstances of a few hours before? I barely knew him and he barely knew me. He did remind me of my late husband, but he would never be able to replace him. It had been wrong of me to even consider such a thing, and I prayed that wherever Nicholas was that he would forgive me. I still felt like I was married to him even after all these years, and the shame I felt over the pleasure that Andrew and I had shared back at Aloysius' lair stemmed from this.

I found myself turning these questions around and around in my mind, but I didn't have any answers.

Andrew's continued silence offered none in return. I knew better than to believe that just because he didn't tell me how he felt about all of this, that it meant he felt nothing.

I couldn't stand the silence any longer. With no answers being offered from either side, my conscience was being forced to make up for this discrepancy with guilt and self-loathing. I had to do something, anything to allay my own doubts and put my fears to rest.

"I need you to drive me back to Aloysius' lair."

The statement seemed to startle Andrew out of his silent musings, but after a brief moment his reflection nodded slowly.

I let the sheet fall to the floor and then I reached for my coat, ignoring the sudden wave of nausea that threatened to drive me to my knees. Even the act of getting dressed was nearly too much for my weakened and battered body, but I pushed the fatigue away and set my jaw in a hard line.

Striding swiftly and purposely to the door, I opened it and stepped out into the cool November morning. The air was redolent with the first promise of winter and I tilted my head back and let the wind blow softly across my face. The sun would be rising in less than two hours, but already the songbirds lent their voices to the air. I found myself reflecting that these were the mornings of my youth, when technology and progress had not yet left their indelible mark upon the world. These were the mornings of simpler times, of happier times.

This was the morning that marked a new beginning for Andrew and me.

# Chapter 38

We rode in silence through the streets that were gradually filling up with early morning traffic. Andrew needed no assistance finding his way back to the house, and I let him drive there at his own pace. It was a risky thing to do given that we were in a stolen car, but it was something that could not be put off any longer.

The barriers that the police had set up to deter curious onlookers began nearly three house-lengths before we reached our destination. The house—which had been a shadow of its former glory the day before—was now completely obliterated. Charred and blackened timbers jutted out at odd angles toward the steely sky, and the ground was still wet where the fire department had attempted to battle the blaze. Yellow police tape stretched around the perimeters of the house and surrounding trees, and the remains of the wrought iron fence lay twisted in the wreckage.

The sharp smell of burned wood filled my nostrils as I picked my way carefully and purposefully through the rubble. My boots crunched in the broken glass and sheetrock that pebbled the ground before me, and in the early morning light streaming through the clouds, I saw a flash of metal winking out of the debris. I dropped to my knees and began to carefully paw through the wreckage one handful at a time. It was a slow and arduous process, but I had a mission to complete. Before long I had managed to recover all four of my knives, though they were badly singed and stained with soot.

I made my way back to the car where Andrew waited patiently behind the wheel. He hadn't asked me my reasons for coming here and had opted to wait for me until I had finished what I came here to do. As I approached the car, I saw that he was staring at his hands rather than the remains of the house. It seemed logical that returning here so soon after the tragic events had unfolded was too painful for him. The ground was still warm where the fire had finally burnt itself out, and here I was demanding that he revisit the scene before his own wounds had had sufficient time to heal.

Selfish. Selfish but necessary.

I had accomplished what I set out to do and could now take the next step. I got in and sat down silently beside him, cradling the knives against my chest. I slowly unrolled the motel towel that they had been wrapped in and examined them more closely. The bone handles were little more than blackened stumps, and when I ran my finger over them they crumbled into ash. *This is the end of an era,* I thought as the ash gave way under my touch, *but it's also the start of another.*

I saw Andrew staring at me out of the corner of my eye.

"You're going after her aren't you?"

I ran the tip of my finger against the edge of the blade and felt the metal bite into my skin. Even without handles they were still sharp and fully functional.

"Yes." I rolled them back up in the cloth and set the bundle on my lap. "I am."

"You mean *we* are." He started the car and it rumbled forward.

I felt myself smile despite everything that had transpired. "Yes; *we* are."

Like Amaris and Griselda, Aloysius had placed me in a situation where everyone involved lost. She had given me a choice, but the options presented worked in no one's favor. That choice had served as punishment for the transgressions she felt I committed against her and her children, and she had used my own guilt and revulsion over what I was to her advantage.

She was all the more dangerous and evil because of this.

She had no need to get her own hands dirty. Why would she when she could use my own choices against me? Like Amaris and Griselda, Aloysius had to die.

I had my own reasons for going after Aloysius and her remaining children, as did Andrew. The choices that she had given me may have forced me to relinquish the last shred of my humanity, but I at least had the benefit of a choice. Andrew had had to relinquish his humanity on account of that choice and had no say in the matter, so he had every reason to desire revenge as well.

I sat there with my hand absently stroking the bundle on my lap. I may not know what the immediate future holds for us, but I do know that a world without Aloysius and her children is a better, safer place. She will undoubtedly be on the hunt by now seeking to replenish her strength and increase her ranks. The question is where. Neither one of us is in any condition to travel over long distances, but time is of the essence. The longer I wait, the quicker the trail will pile up with innocent dead.

Aloysius may have wounded me and forced me to make an impossible choice, but she did not kill me. She may have left me bloodied and beaten, left me weaker than I'd been in centuries past, but I was not dead. Not even close.

What doesn't kill me only makes me stronger. More importantly, what doesn't kill me should beware, for I will never stop hunting it to set wrongs to right.

✞ ✞ ✞ ✞ THE END ✞ ✞ ✞ ✞

C. L. Warrington has an M. A. in Anthropology from the University of Texas at San Antonio, and is currently teaching six grade Language Arts. She is actively working on the next three installments to her "Edge of the Blade" series in between work and the minutiae of daily life.